MW00893315

THE G.L.O.V.E.S SERIES: BOOK 1
(Gifts of Love of the Eternal Spirit)

THE HEALING TOUCH

By

Analiesa Adams

Loving yourself is most important!

Analiesa

The Healing Touch

Copyright © 2017 by Analiesa Adams

Cover by **http://thebookcoverdesigner.com/designers/betibup33/**

Dedication

In memory of Crystal Stone who devoted her life to enlightening those individuals lucky enough to cross her path. She soothed the soul, healing many with her touch. I will always remember her bright loving eyes, which confirmed for me her connection to a higher spirit. The smile she gave to all was contagious, as was her serene and loving countenance. May she find the heights of spiritual oneness sought after through the many lives she's achieved here on earth.

Her legend lives on in this lifetime in many ways, including the continuation of her dream of the Crystal Voyage under the new name of **Crystal Spirit Spiritual Center** in **Tacoma, WA**, where harmony and peace reside, and learning about one's spiritual self is of the utmost importance. If you are in the area, make it a point to visit a while, to renew your soul and refresh your spirit.

Definition of Terms Used:

Vaginismus – An involuntary contraction, or reflex muscle tightening of the pelvic floor muscles, which generally occurs when an attempt is made to insert an object (tampon, penis, speculum used for a Pap test) into the vagina. This muscle tightens and causes pain, which can range from mild discomfort to severe burning and aching. Vaginismus may be **primary** (i.e. lifelong), or **secondary** (occurring after a period of normal sexual function). It may also be **global** (occurs in all situations and with any object) or **situational** (may only occur in certain situations, such as one partner but not others, or with sexual intercourse but not from use of tampons or pelvic exams or vice versa). (http://sogc.org/publications/when-sex-hurts-vaginismus/)

Various treatments are available for women with this condition. Please contact your physician for further information.

The Healing Touch - *The G.L.O.V.E.S Series: Book 1*

Things always happen for a reason. That's what
SUZANNA HAWTHORNE had heard all of her life. But, she
couldn't understand why her life was turning out this way. She
didn't know which was worse, being labeled sexually
dysfunctional, or having this ever troublesome empathic ability.
She'd resolved to live a life without someone special to love,
which didn't settle very well. Especially when her youth filled
night terrors return. The relation between the nightmares to her
physical condition had never come up before. That is, until now.

Public misconception and emotional conflict, endured
by the virile and handsome NICHOLAUS BRACH, DVM,
causes him to hide his supernatural ability to heal others for
years. Yet, he can't seem to hide anything from his new
assistant, Suzanna. He finds her intuitive perception a priceless
quality for his professional practice, and is drawn quickly into
wanting to share more than just his love for animals. Confused
by her objections to acknowledge their intense physical and
spiritual connection, he finds himself intrigued by what she is
trying to hide.

When a long time friend suggests they find out how the
G.L.O.V.E.S. organization could help, they embark on a pursuit
to learn more about the paranormal gifts they've been given.
What begins as a journey into self-discovery for Suzanna turns
out to be a real life nightmare, when her dreams become reality.

Acknowledgement

My appreciation goes without saying, but in acknowledgement I
would like to thank Garland and Toby of Spiritual Eros (sex and
intimacy coaching) for their enlightening answers to all of my
questions. For information and guidance contact them at
www.spiritualeros.com.

Table of Contents

Chapter One

"Baby, you need to relax." Dean huffed. "Try and do what they talked about today. Close your eyes and think about your favorite place."

"Okay, I'll try," Suzanna whispered. She turned her head to the side, the soft feather pillow cushioning her head, the scent of freshly washed sun-dried linen reminding her of her most favorite place.

The beach always relaxed her. She let her thoughts drift to the shore side, walking along the waterline, the warm sun on her shoulders, water curling around her feet as the waves wash up onto the sand.

Why wasn't this relaxing her? This should be relaxing. No matter how hard she struggled to ignore the interference, the stirring need to escape continued to daunt her.

Dean's hands travelled all over her, pushing to far, too soon. She wasn't ready. A knot began to form in the pit of her stomach. Each touch of his fingers seemed like little knives piercing her skin.

The empathic senses she'd been born with switched into overdrive again. She couldn't displace her receptive response to the sexual urgency he exuded. The self control she'd sworn to hold onto immobilized, panic swirling around her as if the winds of a hurricane were about to sweep her away.

Sweat beaded against her top lip, and her heart pounded thunderously in her chest. His body pressed against hers, suffocating her ability to break free of the strangling sensation settling over her.

"No...no...don't," she began, pushing his hot palm away from her breast.

"Suz, you've got to let go. Try to think of how much you want me. You've waited a long time for this. Just let it happen."

Poised between her legs, Dean's desire bounced off the walls slamming against her in his expectation. His gaze, almost creepy, she tried to remind herself was meant to reassure her. Though he was following all the directions they'd been given earlier, his efforts did nothing but send a chill down her spine as if he were not supposed to be there. He continued to knead the tips of her extended breasts with his fingertips, and dipped his head down, using his tongue to caress her nipples.

Suzanna breathed in deep, willing her over active sensitivity to cease. She closed her eyes and tried to concentrate on what he was doing. A wedge of excitement rippled down her torso and inspired her to try again.

Oh, how she wanted this—she needed this to happen.

She nodded. "Okay, go slow please."

Her breath caught as he encompassed the sphere of her breast in the luscious heat of his mouth, his tongue's languid strokes around the heightened peak sending streaks of fire down through her core.

She forced herself to imagine the warmth of the sand between her toes, the sun heating the air around her, and slowly began to drift into an aroused state of excitement. A place void of caution and the anxiety she'd grown to expect.

It seemed like mere seconds before the sudden invasion of Dean's erection pierced the portal to her innermost being. Suzanna's eyes shot open and the rhythm of her heart tumbled over itself in double time.

Unable to overcome the onset of sudden panic, her lips trembled in uncontrollable quivers as the perspiration trickled down her forehead. An immediate pain shot through her abdomen with a ferocity rendering all other feelings nonexistent. Her vaginal muscles clamped down hard, all of a sudden forcing the intrusion out.

Suzanna screamed out, overwhelmed by her body's continued involuntary refusal to any male sexual contact. She grabbed the sheets into her fists in anger. Hot stabbing pains continued to pierce through her vagina in quick succession, as if she'd sat on a porcupine.

"Damn it!" Dean yelled out, the abrupt expulsion of his sensitized member a surprise. "What the hell."

He jumped back and slid out of bed to grab his jeans and head toward the couch. As he stuffed one foot into the pant leg, he swore, losing his balance.

Suzanna sat up with a slow effort exhausting what energy she hung onto. She listened in helpless silence as Dean zipped up his pants, swearing again when the zipper caught. He pulled his T-shirt over his head and sat down to tie his shoes. His face turned an unusual shade of red in exertion, and he sat back to stare into the darkness of night lurking outside the sliding glass doors.

"I'm sorry," she whispered, defeated by her own body. "Don't be mad with me. I promise to keep working on it."

Her movements were quick and somewhat shameful as she slid her arms into the flowered silk robe brought along in hopes to add to the anticipated excitement of the evening. Now, she felt dirty. How had she thought she could do this? She gathered the edges of the robe close to her throat and wrapped her other arm around her waist to cloak every inch of her body. She came forward to stand at his side, unsure of what to do next.

Dean's hands hung limp between his knees, his chin drooping down toward his chest. Exasperation floated from every angle of his body. She shivered suddenly as she sensed a shift in his thoughts. He took in a deep breath and exhaled a slow stream of decision, and she knew her dreams had slowly drifted from the room without a chance of redemption.

"I can't do this Suz. I thought I could, but I'm sorry I just can't deal anymore."

On the coffee table the handout from this morning's seminar flashed a blatant mistruth goading her to insist upon fulfillment of the title. *"Vaginismus–Be in Control: Don't Let the Pain Control You."*

Good Lord, how on earth could you control this thing?

"Please, give me another chance. I know I can do this. We haven't given it enough time," she pleaded.

He shook his head and as he rose up their eyes met. The pity written on Dean's face hit her hard.

"Honestly, I don't really care anymore."

She hadn't foreseen a response like this. Her body froze and she barely felt Dean pull her to him as he gave her a light kiss on the lips. His action, now permeated by the goodbye she had known would come for some time now, but wasn't ready to accept.

"I adore you Babe. This has been going on for close to a year now. There isn't a man alive who could take this kind of frustration."

The words hurt. She knew what came next, though she couldn't help but ask. "So I guess we're breaking up?"

He stared over her shoulder for the longest time, the affirmation evident when his eyes met hers again. He reached down and pulled the keys from his pocket, placing them and the room card into her hand.

"Here, take the Volvo. You can drive back when you're ready. I'll find a hotel tonight and take the bus in the morning."

Tears formed, though she refused to let them fall as she watched him pack his bag and head out the door. He'd been her last chance before giving up. Her lifelong dream to start a home of her own, children at her feet and a man to love was ending in disaster.

She understood now, her mistake had been to believe it even possible for someone like her.

Suzanna stood, a blank stare her only expression, blinded by the realization this must be her ultimate reality. Her desire to love, rejected by all, betrayed by her own body. No doubt existed. She was sentenced to a life of solitude and loneliness.

The delayed emotion began to crash around her like a freight train barreling through the mists of the tamped down fear she kept hidden away. Shudders ran rampant over the surface of her body, and the tears began to stream down her face. As she threw herself onto the disheveled bedcovers she shoved her face into the pillow, the sobs she'd held back for so long barely muffled.

Much later, she lay in the middle of the bed her bare legs pulled up under her chin, her arms wrapped around the tear drenched pillow.

What do I do now? She asked herself. She gave a half-hearted laugh and pulled the covers over her chilled body. There was only one thing she could do.

Head back home and pick up the shattered pieces of her dreams.

* * * *

The clink of the coffee pot against the sink caused Suzanna to wince. She hoped she hadn't disturbed her mother's sleep. Her mother deserved as much sleep as she could get. She worked hard and needed the rest.

Soon a delightful aroma of the dark roasted brew awakened Suzanna's senses as she took her first sip.

Thwack. The morning newspaper hit the front steps.

Suzanna grinned. *Perfect timing.*

A chill from the morning mist brushed against her face as she bent down to pick up the paper. She shivered turning toward the door as she began to unfold the headlines, but the neighbor's dog started barking from across the street, so she hurried to get back inside.

Opening the paper wide she began to search the classifieds for both a job and an apartment. Better to start as soon as possible, though she knew her mother would argue she was welcome to stay as long as she wanted.

"Can't wait around forever," she sighed as she rose to search for a pen. "Procrastination won't change a thing."

Suzanna believed with her whole heart the sage advice of a motivational speaker she'd once heard. Having memorized the wise words, she repeated them out loud to herself, as she had many times before.

"Embrace the probability for improvement. Advance beyond your unfortunate circumstances. Stagnate in your pain and you miss the opportunities that surround you."

She knew in order to survive in this world she had to rise above the negativity and focus on a positive future, no matter how distant it may seem.

The red pen in the junk drawer turned out to be the only one she could find, so she took it back to the breakfast nook and sat back down, coffee mug in hand. The dismal front page headlines read *'Depressing Unemployment Rates Skyrocket.'*

Figures.

Just her luck, job availability was almost imaginary these days. After a brief view of the employment section, it became apparent positions for childcare givers, with or without a degree, continued to be nonexistent. The end to her internship at the daycare center couldn't have come at a worse time.

Perhaps she could just take any job. But, no, taking orders at the local burger joint wasn't necessary—not yet. For kicks she opened to the real estate rental section knowing full well she needed to find a steady source of income first.

Her mind wandered as she browsed column after column of apartments and houses, ready to be rented or purchased. None of which she could afford, of course.

She caught sight of an article from another section of the paper she'd set aside. 'Missing child found chained in basement of 40-year old man' headed the first paragraph under a picture of a malnourished child, his sad sunken eyes staring straight into the camera's lens. A sudden wash of panic poured over Suzanna, a fear so great it brought tears to her eyes. She continued to stare into his eyes, as if unable to do otherwise. Heart pounding in her ears, she could almost visualize the terrible things this suffering soul had seen.

She forced herself to pull the grocery coupons over the picture and breathe in several deep breaths.

"This isn't your fear. Don't allow others pain to affect you like that. You can't control what goes on," she reminded herself. "Feel compassion, but do not take it on yourself."

Oh, how she wished she didn't get these feelings.

After a couple of sips of coffee, the sensation of fear subsided, and she was able to breathe normally. She closed her eyes and began the exercise she'd been taught to shield her being from further outside interference. She imagined herself covered in a bright white light, breathing in love and breathing out fear, breathing in peace and breathing out negativity, breathing in…

All of a sudden, a pain shot through her head like a spear. Not again. Taking a deep breath, she placed her head between her palms and pressed hard against her temples. This seemed to relieve some of the ache that had begun to nag her on a daily basis.

All I want is a boring, simple life. Like everyone else. What I wouldn't do to end this hell.

She shook her head, blew out the breath she'd been holding and picked up the paper again.

Time you realize your normal is abnormal—compared to everyone else. Suzanna laughed at herself for thinking she could ignore her reality. Her life obviously wouldn't be easy and comfortable. She'd better just accept it and move on.

The empathic senses thing she'd discovered when she was young caused more distress than she deemed worthwhile, and the sexually debilitating condition the fates had cursed her with, seemed to tip the scales toward total abnormality. Although her sensitivity to feelings and emotions of others was bothersome, she could at least handle them better than the physical problem. No matter how much she wished for it to be true, she would never be considered normal.

She had no doubt she was considered an empathic sensate. Not that she liked it. Her ability to sense the emotional and physical state of other beings haunted her daily. She'd learned early on she was considered strange, not like everyone else. Keeping quiet about her senses didn't feel good, but seemed to be the best way to hold onto what sanity she could. Unsure of the reasons for being saddled with this ability, she refused to allow it to become the focus of her life. After all, happiness was to be like everybody else.

Right?

A shift in atmospheric energy told her she'd made too much noise and awakened her mother. Though still very early, her mother tended to be a light sleeper. Suzanna noticed a pattern of her mother's increasing inability to sleep for long periods of time. She tended to rest for shorter naps when she was able. When she'd suggested to her mother to see a doctor, her mother had laughed and told her she was just feeling her age.

"Buenos Dias, Niña."

Suzanna lowered the paper as Carmen came into the kitchen from the outer hallway. Ever present Coco, her Shih Tzu, lay in her arms. His loving commitment shined bright in his eyes as he looked up at Carmen. The dog gave Suzanna a sagacious look and turned back to nuzzle his nose against Carmen's jaw.

"Morning, Mamma. How are you today?" Suzanna asked, already aware of Carmen's pat answer.

"*Bien, Niña.*"

Good, she is always good. Suzanna knew better.

Her mother's slight build seemed almost invisible under the heavy warm housecoat she wore this morning. Suzanna noted the fabric, now frayed at the elbows, had faded into an indescribable shade, somewhere between blue and purple. She frowned, unable to recall what color the garment had been brand new. Her mother's penchant to save on unnecessary expenses continued even now, past those hard years Suzanna remembered in her youth.

Carmen appeared frail in the morning light. Wispy strands of hair hung lifeless around her thin boned features. The gray abounded in her past crown of glorious brunette curls. To Suzanna, her mother would always be beautiful, though the vibrant Hispanic vitality she once enjoyed had diminished into a pale exhaustion.

So focused on her own troubles, Suzanna realized she'd become more oblivious to the needs of her loved ones than she cared to admit. Was her mother ill? Or had age really taken its toll on her?

Carmen strained to reach up for a mug from the hooks under the kitchen cabinet. Suzanna watched carefully. Her senses detecting the pain rippling across her mother's shoulders, intense enough to make her want to rub the spot beginning to pulsate on her own shoulder blade. Times like this she wished she didn't actually feel the physical sensations as well as the emotions of others. Being a sensate sometimes was a real pain—literally.

"Here let me get that for you." Suzanna rose and came around the end of the counter to help.

"*Gracias,*" Carmen said, as her weak smile spread slowly. "I'm fine, just a bit stiff this morning."

Suzanna surveyed her mother with a doubtful eye. She understood her mother's light response was intended to downplay the reality of her suffering.

"I've told you it doesn't do any good to lie to me. I know exactly how you're feeling."

"Your mind, it is full with many things, dear. No need to worry about this old woman's aches and pains."

Carmen sat carefully on the chair. As Suzanna poured her a cup of coffee, she saw her mother peer at the newspaper across the table in an attempt to discover what she'd been reading. 'Real Estate–Rental' must have caught her mother's attention as Carmen began to shake her head.

"No. I won't allow it. You stay here. No leave."

Suzanna sat down at the table. "Thank you, Mamma. But, if I sit around here much longer, I'll start to feel sorry for myself, and you know I won't do that."

Her mother's thoughtful study showed concern.

"No. You are right. This is not your way. Why you so upset? Dean. He makes you cry. You have much pain." Carmen placed her hand over her heart then reached out to pat her daughter's hand. "Why not try again? He a good boy, he cares much."

Suzanna breathed in deep to take quick control of the heightened emotions the statement caused. Several months had passed since the workshop in Lincoln City. She'd tried to talk to Dean, but he refused to discuss their relationship any further.

"Mamma, I did. Dean isn't interested anymore. He's had enough. Things didn't work out for us." She attempted to sound strong, yet she truly feared a lifelong sentence of loneliness was not far behind.

She rose to rinse her cup in the sink, when she turned back she saw the confusion in her mother's eyes.

"This problem you have. I not understand. Does this make him leave?"

"Yes mamma." She knew her mother didn't truly understand the severity of her condition. Of course she didn't.

Suzanna had never been able to explain the details, too embarrassed to admit to something sounding so insane in the first place. How could she explain her body reacted on its own without her control? That just didn't make sense. Not even to her, and she was the one it happened to—time after time.

Suzanna gave her mother a hug, one she hung onto longer than usual. Coco squirmed between the two of them, wanting in on some of the attention.

"I'm sorry."

Carmen's weak whisper stirred Suzanna's heart. This wasn't the first time she'd heard the despair in her mother's voice. Something in the past had happened. She had no idea what would make her mother feel so guilty. Her mother continued to refuse to reveal the source of her misery. The thing concerning Suzanna the most was she felt her mother hid a vital piece of information. But, what could it be?

At times she wished she could read minds, too.

The sadness surrounding the older woman changed to failure and extreme shame. Suzanna didn't know how to interpret this at all. So many times before, when this happened, she'd been unable to convince her mother to reveal what troubled her. Now the only thing she knew to do was to show her how much she loved her.

"I've told you before Mamma. It's nothing you've done or could do anything about. So stop worrying. There's no reason to be guilt ridden for something that isn't your fault."

Her mother's expression remained the same. "This doctor you see, he not know what to do?"

"Not really. His only other solution is iffy. Kind of a 50/50 deal I'm not too interested in. I think I need another opinion."

The doctor proposed a surgical treatment, but offered no guarantee of success. In fact, the possible side effects sounded worse than the condition itself. Something she wouldn't risk.

"Be strong. Don't give up. You ask me, I think you relax more, this fix the problem."

"Yes, well, I'll have to work on that." Suzanna held back the outright laugh bubbling up. "I'm going to take a shower and go down to the unemployment office to find out what they've got. Probably nothing though, it's like the lists never change down there."

"You find the right one soon enough," replied her mother.

"I hate my internship at the center ended so quickly. I'm going to miss those kids."

"Everything will be fine, *Novia,* you'll see. And no worry about moving, I won't hear of it."

"I suppose you're right. I was just dreaming."

The limited motion in Carmen's shoulders prompted Suzanna to watch more care as her mother pulled a skillet from the stove.

"You busy today. I fix my *Niña Chilequilas* to eat," she said, falling into her native Spanish.

The difficulty of Carmen's movements again radiated a pain through Suzanna's own shoulders. This time the sharpness caused her to reach back to soothe the sensation. She really needed to work on controlling her physical receptiveness more. To blind the emotional side was hard enough. She found it was getting harder to do either one.

"Mamma I need to get there early. I'll pick up something on the way." She bent to kiss her mother's cheek. "How about we make some *Enchiladas* for dinner? I love them so much."

"No, no, remember we have dinner with Roberto and Luis tonight. It's their birthday this week."

"Oh right, I forgot. I've got to stop and get a present for them."

"No, no. I pick up something for us both. Okay?" Carmen stated, her firm tone signifying no questions were to be asked.

"All right," Suzanna responded, more relieved than anything. She wasn't sure when she would get her next check. Birthday presents were definitely not in the budget. "What time are we supposed to be there?"

"Seven, Niña. I be ready at six. We get there early."

The glow brightening her mother's eyes was fierce. Suzanna still couldn't figure out why her mother loved her cousins as much as she did. She supposed because they were the only boys in the family.

"Okay, Mamma. We will get there early." Suzanna started toward her bedroom and turned back around. "I'm going to stop at Lucy's on my way back, but I promise to be back in time."

"You better. You two *Niña* talk and talk, and forget everything else. The *Niño* are in town together first time this year. I can't miss them. I be very mad," Carmen warned, brows furrowed together.

"Don't worry, mamma, I'll be back," Suzanna chuckled over her shoulder as she left to find out what the day had in store for her.

Carmen sat down and held her cooling coffee cup in her hands as she stared out the window to the vision of her beloved garden. The colorful petals of the late spring flowers fluttered in the gentle morning breeze. Thoughts of her delight in seeing the twins drifted to the conversation she'd just had with Suzanna.

My Niña is so stubborn.

Ever since childhood Carmen remembered her daughter's fierce resolve to never allow anything or anyone to stand in her way. Yet, she continued to have this problem with her male friends. None seemed to stay too long. Every one of them broke her little girl's heart. As a mother, she sensed the truth under the strong-willed defenses her daughter built around herself.

The truth could not be denied. Carmen knew who was to blame. She was.

Guilt welled up into tears and threatened to overflow.

Suzanna's problem might very well be something she had done, or rather left undone. Carmen didn't understand the exact difficulty, but was sure intimacy was involved. The horrid memory she kept tightly locked away surfaced momentarily, forceful tears streaming down her cheeks.

If only she'd opened her eyes sooner. Maybe then her daughter wouldn't suffer so much.

Her head shook with silent tears as the ache in her heart crept forward. Her children had suffered so much for her actions. She couldn't fathom what would happen if they ever found out the truth. Some may forgive, some may not.

So many things to regret—so many things she could never amend. So many people she'd hurt. None of them would know how sorrowful these things made her.

None of them could ever know.

Chapter Two

Suzanna sat on the couch, between her knees Kimi, her best-friend's daughter, sorted through the pieces to her favorite giant puppy puzzle.

"Here, this is the eye to the black one," Kimi began waving about the piece in her hand.

"Good job. I think it might go here." Suzanna pointed to the spot where the piece would fit snug above the snout of a black Labrador pup.

Lucy tossed the rest of the toys from the middle of the floor into a toy box at the corner of the family room. She sat down, and a heavy sigh escaped as she propped her feet up on the coffee table.

"So, how's it going?"

Suzanna knew what she wanted to know. They had always been able to read each other's mind.

"Oh, all right, I guess. It still hurts. But it's not as bad as I thought it would be." Suzanna had been somewhat surprised the breakup with Dean hadn't caused the heartbreak she'd imagined. Over the last couple of weeks she hadn't thought of him much at all.

"Well, if you ask me, Dean was never the right person for you anyway."

"Thanks for the support, but I'm not sure anyone will ever be right for me." Suzanna tried to keep a light heart in her answer. Truth of the matter was, this didn't feel light.

Ineffectual hindsight now confirmed her fears. She should have known better. A meaningful relationship, for her, carried the label of being unrealistic and almost stupid. Reality was she may never find someone to love. She wished she had paid attention to those internal warnings she'd had about Dean. She'd known he wouldn't be able to handle the time necessary to work through her problem. Her insightful instincts could be useful at times, no matter how disturbing they seemed.

"Nonsense, you just haven't looked hard enough. You're different. That's all there is to it. Someone out there is going to have the good sense to realize what a wonderful person you are, and look past all the unusual characteristics you have."

Suzanna gave a not very convinced smile. "I suppose."

Lucy had no idea how unusual she really was. As close as they were, Suzanna had never been able to open up and tell her about her physical condition. There would be way too many questions she couldn't answer.

The doctors, unable to tell her the reason why, gave her the technical terms of her condition, and the many things she may experience when it happened. Their educated guesses for the cause were no help. The question 'why' remained a mystery to them, as well as to her.

"You know, what you can do is really not all that unusual. My grandmother used to talk about seeing ghosts. Now that's weird."

Suzanna giggled. "No, I can't walk around saying I see dead people."

"Being able to tell what someone feels is just an enhanced sense we must all have. It's just not developed in most of us."

"I know. Your mom gave me a pamphlet the other day about this place for people like me. She said I should go talk with them and find out more about this ability I have."

"I don't know why you haven't done it before now. If it were me, I'd want to know everything there was to know about the why's and how's. I guess I'm just that way," Lucy said emphasizing her interest. "What we found on the internet is far from being the only thing to know about what you can do."

Suzanna held out a piece of the puzzle the little girl was searching for and delighted in her excitement as she fit it together against its matching piece.

"I know. I just never knew who to ask. I don't want to talk with just anybody. Your mom seems to trust this place. I'm going to find some time to check it out."

"Sounds like a good idea. You're finally going to do what I've been telling you to do for years," Lucy rolled her eyes at Suzanna and sat forward to stand back up again. "Hey Suz, you're still looking for a job, right?"

"Yeah, I haven't had much luck at the unemployment office or the want ads."

"Well, hold on to your socks! I have an outrageous opportunity for you. Remember the part time job my Mom picked up a couple years ago?"

"The one with Mr. Perfect, as you call him. She works for Brach's Veterinary Hospital, right?"

"Right," Lucy said and held her hand up to stop the conversation. "Hold on. Kimi, I need you to go brush your hair and put on some new socks. We've got to go meet Daddy for dinner," Lucy prompted her daughter. A small argument ensued about changing the socks, stifled quick by a mother's expertise. "Where'd we leave off?"

"You were telling me about the perfect job."

"Right, well, guess what? He needs someone full time. Now his operation is up to speed Mom's decided to retire."

"She's finally going to take the trip around the world with George?"

"No, I doubt they'll go that far. She can't stay away from the grandkids for long. She told me Brach needs a new assistant."

Suzanna raised her eyebrows. Now this might be a possibility. "I should probably go check it out."

Lucy nodded. "The great part of the job is it's not all about paperwork. You get to help with the animals and stuff. Mom says it's the best job she's ever had. And Brach's the dreamiest. If I were single I'd have to go after him myself."

"What is this? A job opportunity, or are you trying to fix me up with Mr. Right?" Suzanna grimaced. She didn't want a man in her life. Pain and humiliation would not exist in her vocabulary. Not anymore. No matter how much she wanted a relationship, without a miracle, it wouldn't happen any time soon.

"Job first, and then who knows. Leave your options open here, Sweetie."

Suzanna gave a sideways grin and nodded her head to make her friend happy.

"Don't mean to rush you out, but we're going to need to get out of here to go meet Danny at the restaurant."

"No problem. My mother and I are having dinner with my cousins tonight. I'd better get home before long, or she'll be having a fit."

Lucy followed Suzanna to the front door. "I told Mom you'd be by soon to submit an application. Better get there soon. A job like that won't last long. She said she'd look for you."

"I'll go out tomorrow morning."

The sound of happy skipping in the hallway could be heard from behind Lucy.

"Mommy, look. Is this what you wanted?" asked Kimi from behind her mother. When Lucy turned around Suzanna had to stifle the laugh as she caught sight of a pair of pink tights pulled up over the little girls jeans.

Lucy made a slight sound of frustration. "No, baby, let's go find something else to put on." She turned to Suzanna with a shrug. "I've gotta run. See you later."

Suzanna shook her head at her friend's obvious familial chaos and walked down the steps to her car. She started to envision the type of job her friend had described. It certainly had made Mona happy over the last few years.

She smiled. This would be perfect. Kids and animals she could handle. She'd made them her specialty, for a reason. None of them asked any question too hard and they weren't interested in her personal life, which was exactly what she needed. Perhaps this would be the answer to her prayers.

* * * *

Jose's Cocina couldn't be better if they tried. In the Alki Beach area of Seattle, Suzanna didn't care if it was a little out of the way for them to drive. The smile on her mother's face was worth the extra effort. Reviews, such as "the best authentic Mexican restaurant around," and "won't go anywhere else," were true to their word. Nothing much to look at from the outside, but the food was excellent. Everyone in the neighborhood and beyond knew it, evidenced by the amount of people inside every night of the week she'd been there.

Suzanna stood at the front entrance of the little cantina, waiting for the arrival of the two birthday boys. The unusual late evening heat for June, cooled by the salty breeze off the water, made her feel as if she were standing at her favorite bar at the ocean.

They were late again as usual. She shook her head. Those boys were always late. Suzanna smiled and glanced back. In the far corner, her mother looked to have started up a serious conversation with their favorite waiter. He listened, intent on what she was saying then burst into an abrupt laugh, which could be heard across the room. He bent over to say something only Carmen could hear, and her face lit up. She replied back, picking up the drink menu to fan her face.

Mamma, such a flirt!

Glancing at the art prints around the cash register, she spotted a few new ones she hadn't seen before. A print of one of Jose Guadalupe Posada's satirical works caught Suzanna's eye. The cartoonist's detailed depiction of animated skeletons was not her favorite, though could be a definite conversation starter. This time, she noticed an affluent woman drinking and dancing in the company of what appeared to be the devil. She tried to focus in on the title of the print.

"Hey, Suz, who's caught your eye?" A strong arm came around her waist, and she was swept up into a bear hug and a kiss on the cheek.

Luis. Always the kidder. Suzanna gave a quick hug back and stepped out of his arms. Roberto stood beside his brother, with a smile that would melt any woman's heart, gleaming down at her. He had always been the strong and gentle type. Not Luis. He was all action and heartache. It always surprised her how different they were from each other. The twins were identical in looks, not behavior.

"Well, it's about time you showed up." She gave Roberto a kiss on the cheek. "We were just about to give up on you two."

"You wouldn't do that. We're here now. Let's party." Luis swung her around in a pseudo dance move and nudged her toward her mother. "I'm starved."

As they greeted their aunt, Luis lifted his arm and motioned for the waiter to come.

"Carmen, how are you doing? We haven't seen you, for what, two years now?" Roberto took hold of Carmen's hands, and held them in a soft loving fashion. Her eyes shined bright with the tears he triggered.

"I know, el Nino are so busy. No time for mamma...ah and la tia. Marta, she tell me Roberto, you use your GI bill to learn to teach. Why, you not happy at your job now?"

Roberto let go of Carmen's hands and sat back. "It's not that I don't like the job at the center, I just know there is so much more I can do if I had a teacher's degree to back me up. So many of those kids need help, but they won't let me go beyond my training now to help. I'm just looking into it now."

"My do good brother here, always wanting to help. Me I'd rather be on my own, doing my own thing. My GI Bill can sit on a shelf for all I care. Can't hold me down to a regular job," Luis interjected.

"And you, I not know what you do. I hear you flying around, taking people all over the country, the next time you work in secret spy job. You worry me." Carmen shook her finger at Luis. "You need to settle down with a beautiful senorita, and give us grandchildren."

That brought a chortle out of Luis. Suzanna looked at her mother and raised her brow. Carmen flushed when their eyes met. Grandchildren? Mamma must be getting her words mixed up again.

"Oh, no. Not for me. Maybe Roberto here, but definitely not me," Luis refuted between mouthfuls of fresh crisp chips and homemade salsa.

"What can I get started for you?" the waiter asked as he came up to the table. "Does anyone want a drink?"

"Chiles Asados and Ceviche de Pescado to start with," Luis ordered the usual appetizers they got when they met on occasion. "Oh, and bring out a bottle of your best Patrón, glasses all around. We're celebrating."

Suzanna grimaced. She wasn't too keen on drinking Tequila straight up, but she would sip on a glass just to make her cousin happy.

"Luis, you are so pushy. Maybe the ladies would like to try something different today. By all means, let them choose first." Roberto shook his head and rolled his eyes at Suzanna.

Carmen was quick to jump in. "No, no, this is your night. We have anything you want. Mi Ninos, they deserve best."

Confusing her English and Spanish words again, Suzanna had noticed her mother's mixing words before, though not as much as tonight. Maybe because they'd spent a lot of time with the boys when they were younger, she probably felt like they were her children.

The spicy scent of hot grilled peppers wafted past her nose as the plates of food were set down in front of them. Her mouth watered as the chiles and queso fresco met tortilla chip and she lifted it to her lips.

Luis poured the first round of shots and lifted one in the air, waiting for the rest of the group to follow. "Salud!" He cheered and threw the liquor down his throat. "Ah, that is some good stuff."

Suzanna took a sip of the strong drink, its fiery tongue snaking its way down to her stomach. All of a sudden, she felt as if she were being watched. Little flutters of awareness waved over her, some as fiery as the fermented blue agave she'd just swallowed.

She lifted her eyes and scanned the crowd of people, all enjoying the night's festivities. Her senses directed her across the room where she saw a tall well built man, his dark hair curling to his collar. He stood in the entry, a woman hanging on his arm, as they waited to be seated.

Suzanna's eyes met with his, and he held her gaze. Goose bumps rose up on Suzanna's arms, tendrils of recognition squirreled down her body, as if she knew this man—in an intimate way.

Ridiculous, purely ludicrous. I've never seen this man in my life.

She watched as they came closer to where she sat. The whole time, as the man followed the woman, his eyes never left hers. His smile left her feeling a little giddy.

Oh, great. They're only a couple tables away. Now how am I supposed to concentrate?

If that wasn't bad enough, this man made sure to seat his date or wife, as she may be, first. Her back turned to them. He slid into the seat facing Suzanna.

Just as she tore her gaze away from him, she saw the corners of his mouth turn upward his dark eyed gaze boring a memory into her soul. She took another sip of Patrón and almost choked on the burning liquid.

Thank goodness. The waiter brought their entrees out and set them on the table. Luis threw back another shot and shouted, "Salud," before diving into his Carne Asada.

Conversation waned as they ate. Suzanna found it hard not to glance at the mystery man. Many times she found his gaze was returned. It was as if she was his date and they sat across from each other. She could feel the heat of a blush brush across her face every time their eyes met. She couldn't tell the exact color of his eyes, but the brightness of them sparkled at her as he smiled.

When the young woman across from him would reach out and touch his hand, Suzanna felt a twinge of something close to what she knew as jealousy. She gave in to her fantasy for a minute and imagined what it would be like to have someone like him by her side. Just for her.

She watched as he paid attention to the other woman, laughing and talking in an intimate low voice. He seemed so tuned into what the woman was saying, but then he would shoot a glance in Suzanna's direction again, and she could almost feel the sparks fly between them.

Quick to pull her gaze back down to her plate, she berated herself for her display. What on earth was she thinking? No way, no how, was she ever going to get a man like that to be hers.

Aggravated at her own thoughts, Suzanna turned her attention to the topic at her own table. Prickles of heat popped up on her neck and she knew he was looking at her. She had a hard time avoiding the attractive man's eyes.

"You still see the spirits, Roberto? Marta, she tell me you see them since you in Afghanistan. You still feel the deceased with you?" Carmen had no qualms in asking direct questions, it appeared.

"Mamma," Suzanna reprimanded.

"What?"

"No, that's ok. I'm alright. After all, you are almost like my mother." Roberto said, his soft smile glowing. "Yes, there are times I still feel they are with me. Not all the time. I think it must be I feel guilty I should have done more for them, that's all." He shot a quick smile at Suzanna. "Maybe I'm more like you than you think. Seeing and hearing things that aren't really there?"

Suzanna gave him a look, and scrunched her nose up at him. "Funny."

"When will I see you again, *Niños*?" Carmen pressed.

"I've got an appointment at the University of Washington. You might be seeing more of me, if I decide to start my courses there," Roberto offered. "Or, if they decide to take me."

"Well, I don't know about Roberto here, but I'm going to be basking on the beaches of Baja for a couple of months. A connection of mine has a resort down there. All Tequila and babes in bikini's for me." Luis set his glass down with a clink. "Hey, Suz, you want to go partying tonight? I've got a line on a really hot club downtown. Dance 'til you drop, I say."

"No, thanks for the offer, but I better not. I've got an appointment for a job first thing in the morning. Don't want to miss that."

For some reason Suzanna couldn't help herself from glancing over to the other table again, and found the handsome stranger staring back at her. He was sitting, one arm propped against the back of the chair, looking very relaxed and very sexy. His date must have gone to the restroom, because she was nowhere in sight. He picked up his glass and raised it in acknowledgement of her and nodded his head toward her to do the same. As if unable to stop, she also picked up her glass, her gaze locked in his, and they shared the last of their drinks together.

Luis turned around then turned back. "Hey, who's the Muchacho over there?"

Suzanna, a bit embarrassed she'd been caught ogling a man, cleared her throat and said, "I have no idea."

The man threw one more glance her way as he stood to meet the woman at his side. Suzanna sensed as if a single word came to her from him, floating in the air across the room to her.

Caliente.

Chapter Three

Suzanna shuddered as she stood in the confines of her bathroom at her mother's home. The beam of the nightlight cast eerie shadows around her, taunting the fear to resurface. She reached out to grab the water glass at the edge of the sink to soothe the dryness of her parched throat. Unaware of how shaken she'd become, the glass tumbled out of her hand and clattered against the cool hard surface of the marble.

The remnants of the dream began to fade as she placed her hands on either side of the basin in an attempt to steady her shattered nerves. Pulled out of a deep sleep, she'd awakened drenched in a cold sweat. The comforter lay crumpled on the floor, the sheets pushed to the end of the bed, as if she'd tried to escape from the invisible horror.

Well, that didn't last long. Must have been that darned Patrón.

The stint of several months since the torturous nightmare came to her had not been long enough. Though, this time around, the night terror was different—it seemed more real than ever before.

She viewed her disheveled image in the mirror. What she observed caused her to laugh.

"Suzanna Rae Hawthorne, get a grip. You are not a child. You can't let some stupid, faceless boogey man control your life. He isn't real. He never has been and you know it!"

Her gut feeling told her something altogether different, but she attributed that to her overactive imagination. She didn't appreciate the weird twisted game her mind played on her in the dead of night, and almost wished to never sleep again. Other than her disastrous experience with men, sleeping was the only other time her strong resolve to be in control stopped working.

The cool water on her face failed to wash the residue of the nightmare still lingering in her memory. Through some deep breaths and focusing on the nightlight shining in the mirror, her willful determination surfaced and she regained the hardened impenetrable self she depended on.

She walked back into the bedroom where the soft rays of early dawn filtered through the sheers to reveal the promise of a new day.

Her careful movement of the colorful flowers on her dresser released a pleasant burst of fragrance. She sighed at the simplistic wholesome beauty of the lilacs, precious white lilies, and royal dark purple irises from her mother's garden. Radiance played in fanciful colors around the reflective surfaces of the floral vase creating a visionary display of an artist's palette against the walls. The warmth it brought made her smile and inspired her to renew her spirit.

Sleep would not return to her at this hour and too early yet to get ready to go down and put in an application at the veterinary hospital, so Suzanna threw on a simple pair of black leggings and an oversized T-shirt. She smiled knowing few pulled off wearing a tie-died shirt in such bright jewel toned hues as well as she could. Her next movement brought her long hair away from her face into an efficient French braid trailing down the small of her back to her waist. A swift glance in the mirror reflected a slender young woman in her thirties, the coloring of a gypsy.

As always, she dismissed her appearance and slipped out of the room making sure her bare feet on the wood floors made as little noise as possible.

When she entered the kitchen she found her mother was already awake, sitting at the breakfast nook, a cup of tea in her hands. Coco lay dutifully at her feet, his nose on top of his paws. He didn't raise his head, but he looked up at Suzanna as she came closer, his lazy eyes showing he'd rather be asleep in his bed. Her mother brought the tissue she held in her hands up to wipe at her nose, and Suzanna could see she'd been crying.

"Mamma, what are you doing up so early?"

"No sleep for me."

"Is it your pain again?" Suzanna walked over and placed her hands on her mother's shoulders. A throbbing ache pulsated up her arms and landed in the middle of her back between her own shoulders. It wasn't the pain she sensed first, there was something more there. The same sadness she'd felt numerous times radiated from her mother, though this time a strong anger was present. Not like her mother at all. "What is it? Why are you angry?"

Suzanna stepped back to peer into Carmen's face. Carmen closed her eyes and shook her head, and Suzanna could feel her shutting the door on her emotions.

"Nada, niña. Too late to change anything," Carmen resolved.

"Change what, Mamma?"

Carmen blew her nose and rose up.

"Life, niña." The anger Suzanna felt changed to a strong sense of defeat and regret. Something she herself tried very hard to steer clear of at all times.

Carmen poured the rest of her tea down the drain and rinsed out her cup. Placing her hands on either side of Suzanna's face, she gave her a kiss on both cheeks. "You go. Go see what is out there for you. Make good choices. Yes?"

Suzanna nodded. "I will." Her mother refused to open up about what bothered her.

As she watched her mother and Coco go back to their room, the gnawing feeling something not right stuck to her like peanut butter. The sticky sensation to her emotions almost brought her to tears.

Why wouldn't her mother tell her what was wrong?

* * * *

Located on the northeast side of Lake Washington, Brach's stood proudly on 43rd Ave E., out of place on the outskirts of upper class newer homes, and houseboats. Because she believed in finding out the most about a business before accepting a job, Suzanna had done some research.

The beautiful majestic building the clinic was housed in had been built in the 1920's, and fortunately for its most recent owner had fallen into a rezoning area. Nicholaus Brach purchased the property to become his residence and due to the zoning changes had been able to include his business, as evidenced by the purchase documents and permits she'd run across. He'd done some remodeling and lived upstairs, while running the veterinary clinic out of the lower level.

There was quite a lot of information about the building, but Suzanna hadn't been able to pull up a thing about the owner. Other than his being the only vet at the clinic, there didn't seem to be much information on him. The sole owner of the business, and some very impressive credentials was all she could find.

Suzanna observed the new SUV in the driveway.

He must fare well for himself.

The clinic entrance marked an ambiance as if the building welcomed her visit like an old friend. No big commercial signs stuck out to announce the location. The weathered brick walls were in excellent condition having withstood time and the effects of the harsh Washington elements. A wisteria in full bloom draped in welcome over the archway leading to the front steps like a canopy of color inviting the passerby in for a cool drink. The sign on the door below the fanned glass panel inserts simply stated "Veterinary Medicine – Nicholas Brach, DVM".

All of a sudden the door was flung open. Suzanna had to do a quick side step, slamming up against the wall, so as not to be run over by the guilty party on the other side of the door.

A tall woman, wearing shorts and a halter top, came through the door. In her arms she held a small dog whose head was barely visible at the base of a huge cone collar. The angle in which she held the poor animal was such that it hid the woman's face from Suzanna's view, and appeared oddly like her head.

"Oh, watch where you're going," the woman said, irritation oozing from her words. She continued down the steps, never looking back.

Suzanna couldn't help but stare after her. From the backside, Suzanna only saw the offender was a shapely blonde, hair cut short and spiked, struggling to keep upright on the high wedge sandals she was wearing.

"No worries, I'm fine." Suzanna said more to herself than the woman, who didn't seem to have any concern whether she'd done any damage.

Suzanna straightened herself, and tried a second time to enter the establishment. Through the entrance she thought she'd entered into a time warp. A precursor to the beauty of what lay beyond, the heavy oak door groaned in the effort to open. Wood floors gleamed in the brightness of the sun as it shone through the slats on either side of the doorway.

At one point she'd thought antiques would be a good fit for a career. No feelings or emotions to deal with there. That's where she'd been wrong. Soon she found they held a residual energy from their past history that irritated more often than interested her, and the unsocial proclivity to the field bored her to death. She did learn enough to recognize the antique Bessarabian rug covering the entrance floor. The bold floral sprays and vines in pastel reds, blues and yellows displayed against the black background spoke of its Romanian culture.

Impressive.

To the left, a set of double French doors stood out. The rich imported rosewood there and in all of the woodwork in the front entry warmed her heart. Through the crack in the door she was delighted to see books lining shelves from ceiling to floor. The mass of knowledge within wafted out of the opening to entice her open senses. She hoped she would have a chance to discover the riches they held awaiting her eager eyes.

In front of her the grand staircase led to the upper living quarters. Although the temptation to venture forth pleased her, she ascertained from good sense the impropriety of such an act. Besides, she needed to find Mona and put in her application for work.

A dog's sharp bark brought her attention to the right. This was a waiting area unlike any she'd seen before. Similarly styled as the lobby, a deep blue almost black carpet ran throughout the room, cleverly covered in a thick clear overlay to protect it from unforeseen piddle and poo accidents. The rich furniture, also protected, came from the same time period as the rug in the entryway. Ornately carved chairs and lounges were spread around the area for visitors to relax—so unlike what one would expect. The elegance reminded her of an earlier, much more leisure lifestyle, compared to the current on-the-go mad rush of today's life spouting convenience over style.

A miniature poodle being handed to a woman behind the reception desk whined a little and brought Suzanna's attention to them. Instantly she recognized the woman she regarded as her second mother. She considered Mona the most loving and generous person she knew, next to her mother. Lucy was her best friend, but Mona had also become a close confidant. Her own mother wasn't even privy to some of the things she'd told her.

As a single parent and hard worker, Suzanna's mother did her best to raise her two teenage daughters alone. When the demands of more than one job and all the activities of her growing children became too much, Mona had been there at the rescue.

Mona now portrayed the prominent grandmother figure. Her gray hair was bunched up at the back of her head in a bun, little wisps of curls trying to escape and surround her plump round face. Mona's soft heart made it easy for her to give lots of love without hesitation. Suzanna had experienced plenty of love from her kind soul.

Suzanna smiled when she heard the kind words meant to comfort the tearful pet owner.

"It won't take but a minute really, Mrs. Owens. FooFoo won't even know what happened to him. Shots are so quick these days. You go have a nice cup of tea over on the lounge there and I'll bring him back out in a snap."

She waited patiently while Mona nestled the nervous dog under her arm, and reached down to grab the chart off the desk. Apparent she was still unaware of Suzanna's presence, she made a small sound causing the woman to glance up. The familiar smile Suzanna loved so much spread over the older woman's face.

"Suzie, my dear, how good to see you. Lucy said you'd come down today." She ruffled and stroked the puffed-up fur of the small creature in her arms to settle him down. "Have a seat. I'll be back in a flash and we can have a little chat."

Mona went through the connecting door toward the diagnostic rooms. It swung back and forth on its hinges a moment, and halfway down the hall Suzanna saw the figure of a man, his face turned away from her. Mona stepped back through the door, poodle in hand, and held it open for one of the assistants to bring a not too excited bull dog back to its owner. Neither dog seemed too bothered by the other.

The man Suzanna saw continued to stand, his torso twisted, as if he'd stopped to turn and converse with someone in the exam room behind him. He wore a simple white lab coat over jeans, a T-shirt, and a pair of Nikes. His hair was a bit long, cascading in luscious dark auburn waves—the kind she often dreamt of grabbing a handful of in the throws of passion. Prickles of energy ran down her neck. There was something so familiar about him. Without even seeing his face, she felt as if she already knew him.

The bull dog sniffed at him as he was encouraged past the man, then plopped right down in from him, refusing to go any further. The man swung around, facing the floor, laughing as he bent down to pet the back of the head of the fat grumpy dog.

"Come on Murphy, it's time to go. I'll see you next week."

Suzanna's eyes opened wide. She did know him. The sound of his voice brought her right back to the night before at the cantina.

Oh my God, this was her mystery man.

She hadn't heard his voice as clearly before, as it had been mixed in with the many tones at the restaurant. Now the rich deepness of his voice latched onto Suzanna's ability to look away and she watched in curiosity. All of a sudden he rose up to gaze straight into her eyes as the door closed behind Mona. Though filtered by the distance, his intensity took her breath and whisked her away into another world, where a uniquely profound bond between their souls culminated into a burst of quintessential fire and light. For a fraction of a second she imagined he'd searched deep within her soul bringing forth her innermost desires. She wasn't sure if she believed in reincarnation, but if it were true she swore she'd known this man in another lifetime.

Whoa, that one is dangerous, she thought, turning to sit in the comfortable wing chair adjacent to Mona's desk.

Through the small rectangular window in the door she saw Mona hand the poodle to him and laugh over something he'd said to her, and they continued to talk for a bit. His occasional glance in Suzanna's direction kept her attention. Too far away to sense his true curiosity, she was certain his interest in her wasn't altogether professional. Just like the night before, the look in his eyes held so much more.

She tried in an unsuccessful attempt to focus on the magazine in front of her and turn the pages, her nervous fingers trembling. Is their meeting again like this just chance? Or is it kismet?

Not sure, but maybe this job isn't such a good idea after all.

Chapter Four

Mona tapped her pencil on the desk in front of her in a contemplative rhythm. She wondered why such a hard working, self-accomplished young women who had achieved high grades in school, honor roll status, and top placement in all of her classes couldn't grasp the need to find her real purpose in life.

Higher education for the young woman had taken some curves. From psychology to early-childhood development, not many understood her need to change. Mona knew the real reason she couldn't seem to settle herself. The challenges facing her every day life was enough to stop anyone in their path.

Aware of how the unusual skill had deterred Suzanna from going forward in some of her past pursuits. It didn't make things any easier, Mona pondered, when you don't accept yourself. Suzanna hadn't come any closer to expanding her vision of the importance of her empathic sensate abilities than when she was younger begging her for something to make it stop.

Being gifted wasn't easy. She knew from personal experience. Her gifts had their own challenges.

Suzanna was like a daughter to her. She had no need for her application. She'd seen Suzanna through life's high points, as well as some of the lowest. The girl had so much potential, if only she would pursue her gifts. But then, perhaps this would be an opportunity for her to discover her true self. The older woman studied the form for a few moments longer. When she glanced up, the nervous expression on Suzanna's face made her smile.

Mona reached out to pat Suzanna's hand. "Don't worry, dear. I'm not the final decision maker on this, though I am wondering something. I haven't seen you for some time. Why don't you tell me what happened to employment under the degree you worked so hard to get."

"There aren't any openings. This recession dried up all possible state funds for childcare, so parent's portion of the fees have skyrocketed. Families are being forced to find other options for childcare. I'd hoped to get hired after my internship with the center, but a couple weeks ago they told me they had to let me go."

"The current economic environment is rough for everyone." Mona considered for a moment the many options the young woman could choose. "Have you thought about going back to complete the degree you started in psychology? If handled properly it would be a field you could excel in."

"Look, I know you're talking about the empathic thing again, aren't you?"

Mona nodded.

"You know the reason I can't continue in that direction. At first, I really thought if I became an expert in what makes people tick I would understand what happens to me. But the whole time all the emotion was too much. I felt as if I were the one with the problems. I just couldn't handle it." Suzanna looked away as if embarrassed by her uniqueness.

"So what happens when the job market starts to open up?"

"Childcare is a field I think I excel in. Really depends though, I can always use a fall back option." Suzanna shrugged. "If this works for me I'll stay as long as I'm needed."

Mona nodded and waited for her to continue.

"I'm sure you've got a ton of applicants for this job, and I'm unlikely the most qualified. Mona, you know I would work hard, learn fast, and try my best."

"Actually, you're in luck. We haven't advertised the opening yet. You're the first applicant." Mona leaned back in her chair. "I have no doubt you can handle the responsibilities. My question is do you want more than a job? This is like a second home."

"I know. You've told me how much you love this place. I imagine…I'd feel the same way." Suzanna nodded as she looked around the room again.

Mona noticed the hesitancy in Suzanna's words and an odd nervousness in her actions. Not at all like her.

"You can become very attached to the animals and their owners. I'm not saying this would be easy. I think though this would be a place you could delve more into who you truly are. I can't tell you how important that is to me."

Suzanna nodded and looked down to her clasped hands in her lap.

"You've always been so supportive Mona. I appreciate all you do for me. It's just so hard to deal with this empathic thing. I don't know what to do sometimes."

Remembering Suzanna's youth, Mona had witnessed her troubles in differentiating her emotions from those of the people around her. At one point Suzanna told Mona she felt as if she'd gone crazy.

"At least you've been able to control how your senses affect you. I understand the difficulty in dealing with something so unique."

No newcomer to the spiritual side of the human psyche, Mona herself struggled daily in her own type of 'abnormality', as most people referred to things unknown to them. After all, like her mother had, seeing spirits from the other side was not what you would call 'normal'.

"Yeah, that little trick you taught me works most of the time," Suzanna responded.

Able to understand the nature of Suzanna's difficulties, Mona had helped her to control the depth of their effect. The important piece had been to teach her to remain compassionate without allowing someone else's pain, emotional or physical, to become her own. Understanding and managing the complexities to her ability's real purpose, while grounding her spiritual empathic self, was necessary so she could maintain a somewhat normal life. Mona knew when Suzanna matured she would want to learn more about the gift.

Mona believed now was the time.

"This is similar to childcare, but there is a side that might be difficult for you. Physical pain is no easier to deal with than emotional."

"I think I've grown over the last couple of years. I know what you're asking. Can I control my response to the pain and discomfort of others? I'll tell you this, I'm not sure I could manage a hospital yet, but I think I can do this."

"Animals are no different than humans. They have the same emotions people do. The difference is they can't speak in a language we understand."

Suzanna smiled, "Who says? I understand them quite well. Remember Whiskers?"

Mona laughed. Suzanna did have a way of talking to animals far beyond the normal communication level between different species. Suzanna held what appeared to be a conversation with Lucy's Siamese cat on several occasions. The pet would seem to answer her questions then do exactly as Suzanna asked. Something the owner never mastered.

"I know you can. That's why I think you'd be perfect for the job. When can you start?"

"Wow! Talk about knowing the right person at the right time. Is this a job offer?" Suzanna asked, her eyes widening.

"We need to speak to Nicholaus first. At the very least, I'm sure he'll give you a try. It's up to you from there. I have no worries though, you'll do fine." Mona stood and looked around the empty waiting room. "Stay here, he's in with Mrs. Allen and her pregnant Burmese. The poor cat's way past the due date. When they're gone I'll see if he's got time to talk."

* * * *

Mona led her to the closed French doors. She gave a brief light knock she slid them open far enough to stick her head in.

"Nicholaus, I'd like you to meet Miss Suzanna Hawthorne. Do you have a moment?"

Suzanna took a deep breath. She thought she could handle the animals pretty well. Now she needed to find out if she could handle working so close to Dr. Brach. This wasn't going to be easy.

Through the cracked door she saw his handsome face, and her stomach began to flutter. He sat, a book open in his lap and his foot propped on the corner of his desk. A genuine smile came across his face as he looked upon the older woman.

"Certainly, bring her in." He lowered his feet to the floor and rose to greet the newcomer.

Suzanna walked in with as much confidence as possible. Close up, his aura was even more intense than before. Through his bright grayish blue eyes she felt depth and understanding, as well as compassion far greater than most people. His effect on her was unquestionable. She almost faltered as she approached him, her hand held out. She'd never experienced anything like this before.

He possessed a high level of deep concentrated energy enhanced by what she perceived as a unique green and bluish haze that surrounded him. This wasn't the first time she'd seen colors emanate from someone, though now the definition of hues appeared more powerful than before. An unexpected calm refreshing sensation washed over her. The colors stood for something, but she couldn't remember what blue or green meant. She reminded herself to find out for sure.

"It's a pleasure to meet you Dr. Brach."

Even though she'd put up a guard to her senses upon entering the room, the instant their hands met a tingling traveled in light speed up her arm and spread over the entire surface of her body. Almost knocking her off her feet, she pulled her hand away, needing to break contact.

He continued to gaze at her in a soul searching manner. This changed to a knowing of some kind. She was certain he'd encountered the same energy between them.

It's not you. This is no ordinary man.

"The pleasure is all mine," he said, his grin widening. His continued scrutiny sent little chills up and down her spine. "I didn't think I'd ever see you again."

"You two know each other?" Mona raised her eyebrows.

Suzanna didn't know how to answer. She shook her head at first then changed it to a nod.

"Not really," Nicholaus offered. "We saw each other at Jose's last night. I will say, it's not often I meet someone with such spirit."

"I see." Mona looked at the two of them and chuckled.

Oh good Lord, is nothing a secret? Suzanna knew what Mona was thinking.

Suzanna forced herself to break eye contact. His unusual curiosity unnerved her, and the odd sense of having known him before was downright weird. To avoid more scrutiny she let her gaze wander. She turned to view her surroundings and caught a glimpse of the treasure she'd seen earlier. In awe, a small sound of pleasure came forth as she rushed forward to investigate more closely the jewels she'd discovered.

The walls were lined in an array of books holding an almost audible plea to be read. Many of them were old and frayed, while others still new had yet to be opened. Arranged in no particular order or subject, off to one side a group of novels, fantasy, mythology, and Sci-Fi, were mixed with mysteries and to her surprise a couple of romances.

She pulled one from the shelf and raised an eyebrow. She held a first edition classic of the romance *Wuthering Heights,* very valuable indeed. This and *Jane Eyre* stood oddly out of place to her among the non-fiction self-help books on one side, sprinkled between biographies and instructional manuals.

They must be his wife's books.

Directly behind his desk she presumed was his own personal treasury. Veterinary medicine, anatomy and strangely enough psychology stood out as subject matters, which made sense in his field.

Embarrassed a bit by her actions, she turned. Mona and Nicholaus had remained silent, curiosity evident on their faces.

"Pardon me. I love books. This is quite the eclectic collection you have here." This time she was the one who viewed Nicholaus with inquisitive interest. "In fact your whole facility is quite beautiful, not at all what one would expect."

The pride in Nicholaus' face spoke more than any words could have. She was drawn in by the color of his eyes as he continued his scrutiny of her. Deep blue pools. Pools of mystery and intrigue—a mystery she felt drawn to, yet not sure if she should try to solve.

"Thank you. Since we spend two thirds of our lives at work I wanted to create something special." He waved his hand across the wall of books. "This is in memory of my grandmother. She always wanted me to be well versed in all things. Her quest for knowledge must have rubbed off on me."

Suzanna dipped her head down to break the connection. To her surprise, she noted no wedding ring on his hand. Not that she cared. Again she found it hard to ignore his gaze, and tried to pretend she had more interest in the books than in him.

"Nicholaus, this is the woman I spoke to you about earlier. I believe she's a prime candidate for the Assistant position." Mona handed him the application. "In fact, if you approve, we can have her start to train with me tomorrow."

"You still insist on leaving me then?" The mock pout he gave felt genuine to Suzanna. He bent forward to take the paper from Mona and placed a kiss on her forehead. He whispered something into her ear which made her smile.

"So, you think you can handle this?" he asked, turning to Suzanna. "Today is pretty quiet. It's not always this calm. Some days you can't tell the difference between the animal and the pet owner. They're all frantic and scared."

"I have a way with animals. I think we have a non-verbal understanding of each other. The owners and I should get along as well. I've been trained to work with children and worried mothers. It couldn't be too much different."

Suzanna, disconcerted by Nicholaus' silent stare, felt the heat rise to her cheeks. As mild as her reference was, maybe she shouldn't have referred to her abilities.

"A way with animals you say? Let's see about that. I want to introduce you to someone."

The phone began to ring and Nicholaus glanced down at the digital screen. He held his hand up to the two women and said, "Why don't you wait for me out front. I need to take this call."

As they exited his office Suzanna heard him say, "Hello Mrs. Olsen. Yes, this is Dr. Brach. How is Buster doing?"

* * * *

Nicholaus knew the phone call would take a while. The caller was one of his elderly customers, and sometimes needed someone to talk to. Her boxer was perfectly fine, getting older like his owner, and had no medical issues to worry about.

"Thanks for waiting. Mrs. Olsen can be rather long winded at times. Let's go back to the hospital area, shall we?"

Again, he surveyed the woman in front of him. Unsure of why she had such a profound appeal to him, he took everything into consideration. She sported an extreme feminine casual look. Her broomstick skirt and sweater in a burnt orange hue brought out her natural coloring. Her silken black hair had a touch of brown throughout emphasizing the dark, melted chocolate in her eyes. Her skin reminded him of pearls, with a glow of exotic sexuality. The bountiful loose tendrils flowing over her shoulders teased him to touch the softness he imagined.

She is a looker—in fact downright gorgeous. His stomach took an unexpected twist.

Reaching out, he directed Suzanna down the hall, curious about what had happened before. The light touch of his hand on her arm, skin against skin contact, confirmed the feeling. Although a gentleman, he'd wanted to touch her again to test his response. Once again, a quiver ran wild trails up his arm to spark all types of different sensations. His heart began to pound and he became mildly breathless. The soft perfume of gardenias drifting from her hair as they walked down the hall silently beckoned for him to get much closer.

Nicholaus brought his arm down to his side and rubbed his fingers against the palm of his hand. The simplest touch had sparked this unusual response in his system. One he couldn't interpret. He would need to study her effect on him. This had never happened before, not to this level.

She is no ordinary woman.

They came to a standstill in front of the cages where animals mended from their injuries and sickness. Some gave excited barks, but most waited silently to find out if they would be the object of the arrivals attention.

"I want you to pick out the one with nothing wrong, at least not physically."

Suzanna looked over the group of animals. Nicholaus watched as her eyes came to rest in the far corner where a calico cat lay calm enough. Curled up near the cage door, it studied them with beautiful green eyes. The vibrant contrasting colors of black, brown, orange and white didn't detract from a certain aspect that drew attention from the fairly calm demeanor. Suzanna walked over to the cat, and they all observed the tensing of expectation showing an unwarranted fear in the cat's eyes. The cat got up and backed away, a guttural growl followed by a hiss heard across the room.

"May I?" Suzanna glanced back at Nicholaus and Mona as she touched the latch on the cage door.

"Be my guest. Careful though, she doesn't seem to like people."

Nicholaus was impressed by her lack of fear as she unlatched the cage and began to talk in a soft low voice to the resident. Curiosity overruled the calico's fear as Suzanna held her hand out for inspection. After a minute there was a slow movement inside the cage. She let the cat sniff at length then to his amazement she was allowed to stroke its head, followed by a scratch behind the ears.

Suzanna continued to talk, and soon after the calico warmed up to her and started to caress its head against the offered hand. Drawing her hand slowly from the cage Suzanna told the cat she wanted to pick her up. She spoke as if to a child, and asked if she would be allowed to hold her. The feline sat back on its haunches, considering her request. Then as if in agreement, reached its paw outside of the cage and touched Suzanna's forearm.

After this show of acceptance Suzanna scooped the calico up and held it securely against her chest. She continued what seemed to be a conversation while rubbing the inside of the cat's ears with her thumb and forefinger. To the surprise of the two onlookers an unexpected purr came as the creature settled into Suzanna's arms.

Nicholaus scrutinized her behavior as she turned obviously unaware she'd accomplished an outrageous feat.

"I told you." Mona smiled in happy conviction.

"I wouldn't have believed it if I hadn't seen it." Nicholaus shook his head. He viewed Suzanna and her newfound friend and explained, "This calico was brought in here by her owner a couple days ago. She said she is a vicious animal and needed to be put to sleep. I agreed to take her to find out if something is wrong. I can't find anything. Mona will tell you, she's given us some trouble. Nobody can pick her up. In fact she barely let me examine her. We've all experienced the wrath of her claws at one point."

Suzanna continued to rub its ears. "She's been abused. She's high strung and a little depressed and scared, but she's aware you won't hurt her. All she needs is some consistent love. You just need to calm her down a bit. I read about this technique. The rubbing of the ears acts like a natural tranquilizer. It puts them to sleep, especially in traumatic situations."

"How do you know she's been abused?" Nicholaus asked.

Aware of her swift movement to avert her eyes, he made out her soft answer. "I can feel it." Her demeanor told him she was wary of sharing this ability he considered invaluable.

Nicholaus reached between the cat's ears and stroked the transformed feline. He fixed his gaze on the woman in front of him and gave a slow nod. She enticed him like no other. Her pure natural beauty, and the extraordinary reaction, which struck him every time he touched her, must be some sort of sign. The obvious strong sexual attraction, and an unusual urgency to find out more about her, pulled at him.

When their eyes met, her momentary fearful expression troubled him. Why was she so afraid of him?

"You're smart and quick, two very important attributes to this job."

He reviewed the application in his hand and realized Suzanna's experience had nothing remotely associated with veterinary medicine. Though, he didn't consider experience the best qualification for the position. He needed someone to be able to follow direction and take initiative to handle situations with independent ease. What he wanted was a motivated individual to do a good job. Her intuitive nature would definitely lend to her ability to deal with irritated and worried pet owners, as well as scared pets feeding off of their owner's emotions.

"You're hired," he stated.

The abrupt decision surprised him. He didn't usually make decisions without weighing all the possibilities, especially with something so important. It bothered him he was unsure if he offered because she would be best for the job, or if he wanted to find out more about her personally. The fact she made every nerve in his body scream for attention was a bit alarming.

She avoided making eye contact, and her hesitation implied she needed to consider the offer. No doubt she'd felt the same electricity between them.

As she raised her eyes her next purposeful expression intrigued him. She held his gaze for the longest moment, and he swore her eyes saw more than the obvious decision to take a new job. Something else troubled her. She squared her shoulders and tipped her nose upward. How odd.

"What time do you want me to be here?"

"Nine o'clock. The office opens up at nine thirty." As he turned to walk away, Nicholaus glanced back. "If you want her, the cat is yours. The owner gave up her rights and asked me to either put her to sleep or find someone to take her."

"Thank you. I'd like that. I'll need to keep her here for a little while until I can get an apartment. Would that be okay?"

"No problem. By the way, her name is Fluffy." The cat heard the inflection in his voice, and its ears flattened out in an angry motion. Nicholaus laughed. "Don't blame me. I didn't like the name either."

"No, that won't do. I think I'll call you Cali." Suzanna nuzzled the cat one more time and put her in the cage. "Don't worry. I'll be back later. You won't need to stay in there too much longer."

* * * *

As she drove away, Suzanna's stomach churned. She'd never been asked to show her abilities from a total stranger. She couldn't help but wonder if she'd made the right choice in accepting the job.

What am I getting myself into?

She found herself clenching the steering wheel with her hands. Irked by her inability to do otherwise, she had been forced to display she was different. She'd learned from experience not to open up too soon. Most people didn't understand, and it was much easier not to show them at all.

Although, Dr. Brach's reaction was unusual, it was as if he already knew.

Mona. She must have told him about her. That was the only explanation. Mona knew better. Suzanna needed to talk to her again about spreading any knowledge of her abilities.

But, Dr Brach seemed open to the small amount she did exhibit. At least he hadn't laughed at her when she claimed to talk to animals. She could tell his inquisitive side was going to be hard to maneuver around though. She imagined he wouldn't freak out, but it would be best not to test his acceptance too early.

She began to replay the events of the morning over in her head and realized there might be a real problem. She'd been unable to assess his awareness of how his touch affected her. Her unquestionable physical response to him was going to be difficult to ignore. She'd found she couldn't keep a steady breath. Rather than the usual butterflies of meeting someone of interest for the first time, the all too familiar knots of anxiety had formed immediately, reminding her of the improbability of starting a personal relationship. She might appear normal on the outside to most men, but underneath the layers of abnormality eventually won.

The thought of what would happen if he became more intimate than the touch of a hand made her pulse rise. To work so close on a day to day basis was going to be very troublesome.

Then the contented purr and warmth of the animal she'd held in her arms filled her heart with a purpose, and she realized what meant the most to her. The animals needed her. She would have to figure out how to deal with the man later.

For now, she had to focus on the next item on her to-do list. She grimaced as she pulled up to her destination. This was not an errand she looked forward to, but there was no getting around it. Confrontation was definitely not her choice, in any form. Emotions, good or bad, tended to make her want to run. She breathed in deep, and exhaled with a sense of determination, hoping the strong hold she forced around her sensate abilities would be enough to get her through this.

She swallowed hard and tried not to let her fears overwhelm her. Yet the memory of her final time with Dean began to replay, reminding her of why she couldn't allow another intimate relationship form with anyone.

The therapeutic retreat they attended a few months back might very well have fixed her sexual problem. Experts claimed most individuals who followed the steps in their programs showed tremendous results, though she and Dean hadn't gotten far enough to discover whether the treatments would work for her.

In her eyes the workshop had been her only chance to find out, but success depended on a willing partner. Ultimately devastated, her hopes of recovery had been thrown back in her face. The image of Dean's expression flashed before her, his obvious disgust and pity heartbreaking.

To swaddle the emotions stirring within, she closed her eyes, took another deep breath to cleanse her outlook, and blew out the muddied viewpoint. She could do this. Negativity served no purpose. She would complete what she had to do without more anguish, and then move forward. She tried to center her emotions, anchoring them to what she held close to her heart. Forgiveness.

She'd been meaning to stop by to pick up her belongings she'd left at his place, but it never seemed to be the right time. Even with his insensitivity, to drag this on further would be defeating, for both of them. She wouldn't have bothered except for the expensive library book she'd left behind, which was now seriously past due. She needed to either return it or end up buying it.

Her firm knock produced an unfamiliar female voice from inside. "I'll get it."

Suzanna stared, as the door opened to reveal a young woman in her twenties. She held a long hair Chihuahua, with a cone collar around his neck. Nervous excitement shook its little body all over. He began to bark short little bursts of noise, piercing to the ear, magnified by the collar.

The woman now wore white shorts and a halter-top barely covering her voluptuous curves. As before, her spiked bleached blonde hair looked a little like the cartoon caricature of the result of sticking a finger in an electrical outlet. No doubt about it, this was the same woman who'd almost run her over a few days back at Dr. Brach's.

"Hush, Bruno." The woman cooed at the dog and tried to pet its head.

The little dog stopped the incessant barking, only to show his teeth and growl at Suzanna. Both the dog and its owner glared at her in hostility. Even without using her empathic senses she felt a strong immediate dismissal coming from the greeter. As if she wasn't worth the time to answer the door.

"Yeah, what do you want?"

Suzanna tried not to gape at the woman's rudeness.

"Who is it Sweetie?" Dean asked as he came up behind the blonde and wrapped his arms around her waist. Suzanna's eyes met his over the young woman's shoulder. Surprise kicked in and he quickly cleared his throat and stepped back.

"Oh…Hi…I didn't expect to see you here. I was going to bring the stuff to your mom's place, just hadn't gotten around to it."

Unsuccessful as she was, Suzanna attempted not to acknowledge the blonde's presence and stared at the man she'd thought was more than a boyfriend. It hadn't taken him very long to become involved in another relationship. That hurt. Not willing to show him, Suzanna smiled instead.

"No need, I've come to get my things. There wasn't much, a backpack with a change of shoes and a few clothes when we went to the lake the last time. Oh, and do you still have the book I left on your couch?"

Dean reached down behind the door and brought out a cardboard box, her things thrown into it as if they were trash. Her shirt pulled halfway out of her backpack, showed someone had rifled through, in search of who knows what.

"I think it's all here." Looking a little guilty, he stepped out from behind the woman who continued to stare at her. "Let me walk you out to your car, Suzie."

Suzanna turned to go back down the steps toward her car. She could hear them whisper heatedly back-and-forth. Then the blonde gave a loud snicker.

"Oh, she's the one? She doesn't know what she's missing does she? The poor thing," the girl called out in triumph, loud enough for Suzanna to catch her exact meaning.

She glanced back to find Dean giving an arduous kiss to the blonde, which caused the bleached blond to giggle. Impatient to get this over with, Suzanna stood at her car, waiting for Dean to bring the box so she could just go.

"I'm sorry Suzie, you weren't meant to see that."

"It didn't take you long, did it?"

"What, Christina? Oh, we've been going out for a couple of months now."

"I see. So, you must have met her not long after we broke up." Now angered more than hurt, obvious sarcasm dripped from her words, as she grabbed the box and shoved it into the back seat. "Was it really necessary to tell her about my problem?"

Dean looked away and cleared his throat again. "Oh yeah, well I'm sorry about that. It came out one night when she was pushing me to tell her why we broke up. I didn't mean for you to find out."

Suzanna continued to stare at him, and tried to determine what she felt about him. Oddly enough, she felt nothing anymore, only a sadness he'd been so unwilling to try harder.

"Well, I hope you give this relationship more than you gave ours."

His momentary blank expression changed to defiance. "Wait. Hold on, I did try. But you've got some real issues. I couldn't hold off forever for you to come around. Christina is just…more willing." Oblivious to his wounding comment, he turned to wave at the young woman still standing at the door.

"Came around, from what?" Enraged at his reference the heat rose to her cheeks. "There's a name. It's called Vaginismus."

All of a sudden she sensed his male ego come to the forefront. Then he bolstered his attitude with the next baneful statement.

"You're pretty and all, but I've thought about it. I think maybe you're a lesbian or something. Whatever it is, you can deal with it yourself. Nobody's ever refused me before. Tried to help you, but there's only so much I can do with a frigid woman. I didn't think anyone could be that cold."

Suzanna's mouth dropped open.

"I should have listened to my Dad. He told me not to get involved with you. It would be a waste of time."

Now his words made sense. She knew exactly where this was coming from. The one time she'd met his father he'd come off as a total jerk. He'd treated her as if she were just a skirt to be chased, and all women were only good for one thing. Until now she'd believed Dean was different. Unfortunately, his upbringing seemed to be winning.

They stood in silence. Then Dean did the next worse thing. "You didn't really think I wanted anything long term did you?"

His words swept over her, wrenching another knot in her stomach. Heat painted her cheeks in red fury, and Suzanna hauled off and slapped him as hard as her strength allowed. The crack of her palm against his cheek startled the dog in the next yard into a frenzied bark.

"Bitch!" he screamed rubbing his face as she climbed into her car.

His words daunted her as she drove off. *Lesbian, frigid, bitch, something wrong with you!* How many times had those same words come to her in the past? Dean wasn't the first one to say them. But she would make sure he would be the last.

She tried to nullify Dean's affect by remembering the words of the experts at the conference. "It isn't your fault. Don't blame yourself for what your body is doing. Let it go. There are ways to come back to life again. You, and only you, have the control to make it happen. From this point forward, you and your partner must work together to relieve you of this pain. It can be done."

Tears of frustration filled her eyes as she drove. Until she found a cure for herself she'd come to the conclusion intimacy was pure insanity. In fact, she didn't dare share her secret with anyone. She'd received enough proof—no man would stand by her. Even though the treatment options suggested by the specialists might work, she'd yet to find someone committed enough to work through the treatment with any positive result. Apparently, the male inherent need for instant satisfaction outweighed the potential outcome of an expected recovery for her.

She couldn't, no wouldn't allow herself to go through this again. Humiliation was the least of it. She felt as if her heart would break into a million pieces. Not because she loved him so much, but because she feared this was how she would be labeled the rest of her life. Nothing was worth so much misery.

Until she could beat this thing, it was best left alone.

Chapter Five

A week passed and Mona noticed Suzanna quite comfortable in her surroundings. As expected, she seemed to catch on quick, though hadn't been given a chance to familiarize herself with her new employer yet. Right after she started he'd left for a veterinary seminar about the newest surgical techniques used on the critically injured animal.

Nicholaus' part-time technician, John, offered to come in full time for a couple of days to help in any minor emergencies like cleaning wounds, and vaccinations. Anything more urgent, the neighboring veterinarian, who volunteered to serve as the on-call doctor while Nicholaus was gone, would be called.

John, still in training for certification was markedly nervous about being left to fend for himself. He appeared to be a quiet man. His geek like demeanor was pronounced by his thin childlike face, and dark horn rimmed glasses that kept slipping down his nose. He spent an inordinate amount of time up front with Mona and Suzanna, his gaze drifting toward the new office assistant. On several occasions Mona caught him staring at Suzanna with enamored starlight in his eyes.

"Dr. Brach will be back tomorrow. Tomorrow's Friday and we need to be prepared for the weekend. John, don't you think you should make sure everything is tip-top in the exam rooms and surgical care area?" Although she didn't say it, Mona had grown tired of his constant attention to Suzanna.

John, who'd been peering at Suzanna over his glasses as he pretended to review a file, almost skittered out of the room at Mona's prompt. As he reached the connecting doors, a ferocious blush rose to his cheeks.

"Yes, Ma'am, I was about to do that. I need to go check on the beagle anyway. He's been trying to rip his bandage off all day." He dipped his head shyly, "I'll see you later Miss Hawthorne." His quick exit was not before the blush deepened to a fresh strawberry red.

"He's smitten with you. Poor boy, can't keep his eyes off of you."

Suzanna giggled and turned to face Mona. "I know. He's sweet, but he'll get over it. I won't be going down that road for a very long time."

The way the sparks had flown between Suzanna and Nicholaus, Mona highly doubted her words.

She shrugged and said quietly, "Maybe." Then concerned, she turned to Suzanna, placing her hand on her shoulder. "Are you still struggling with your condition?"

Mona was well aware of Suzanna's physical difficulty. With nowhere else to turn Suzanna had run to her after being diagnosed the first time. She'd explained why she hadn't told her mother. Her mother still carried the older ways of the Mexican culture and just wouldn't understand. Mona had been there for her, through the tears and the anger, never once condemning her or making fun of the seriousness of her condition.

The subject was a difficult one to talk about, and they hadn't discussed it for some time. She hoped the girl had found some resolution.

Suzanna reached up and patted the hand meant to comfort.

"Yes…But Mona, I'm not sure what else to do. I thought I might finally be able to get rid of this thing at the therapy conference. Nothing ever seems to come out right for me."

"Perhaps it wasn't meant to." The sadness in Suzanna's eyes touched Mona. "Good thing you didn't open up to him anyway."

Suzanna shook her head, and looked up at Mona. "Even so, he tried to do all the things the experts taught us. I just couldn't go all the way."

"You may not have known it, but you felt back then he was not the one for you. You said yourself he must not have been able to get rid of his father's influence just yet."

Suzanna grimaced. "That's for sure."

"I can't believe you didn't see that earlier. Your intuition must have been telling you something."

"I know. There were signs. I think maybe I didn't want to accept what I saw. Everything seemed so perfect. Too perfect, I guess. I should have known better. Nothing is ever easy for me," Suzanna gave a deep sigh.

"Don't start giving up now. Trust in yourself. You need to keep strong, and believe in yourself. Use your gift. Your spiritual guidance won't lead you in the wrong way."

Mona discerned Suzanna's dismissal of her encouraging words by the roll of her eyes.

"I don't think I'll ever find someone."

"Believe me, when you find the right one, you'll know for sure. Then everything will work out fine." Mona considered the emotional drain seeping into Suzanna's usual bright eyes. "I think it's time for you to learn more about who you are and not what is wrong with you."

Suzanna raised an eyebrow and tilted her head in consideration. "I'm not sure Mona. This empathic thing doesn't seem to work for me. Though, now I'm finding, when I try so hard to suppress my receptions I get this damned headache," she said pressing a thumb to her temple.

"You are what you are, dear. You can't hide from being a sensate forever. Sooner or later you'll need to give in and let go of the boundaries you've set up." Mona knew the day would come when this would happen. "You'll be glad you did."

"I suppose you're right. It doesn't do me any good to worry so much."

"I sincerely believe if you do you'll find what you need to put an end to this whole thing."

"Do you really think so?" Suzanna's voice quivered.

"I know for a fact." Mona reached out to brush a bit of hair from Suzanna's brow. She might try to help more, but knew the girl had to make her own decision to discover the potential within waiting to be released. "I've still got the pamphlets from the organization we talked about. Would you like me to bring them tomorrow?"

Suzanna stood, reaching for her purse. "If I'm going to do this I suppose I have to start someplace. I'll take a look at them."

"Good girl." Mona smiled and gave Suzanna a hug, remembering what she'd seen earlier with Nicholaus. "Don't worry about a thing. I have a feeling everything is going to be fine."

* * * *

Friday arrived and flew by in a flash. The Doctor was back. It seemed as if everyone and their dog, literally, came to see him. By the end of the day Suzanna imagined she should have been exhausted, instead she felt energized. The experience of being involved with helping someone in need excited her sense of purpose and touched her in a way she hadn't expected.

The pets waited in vivid helplessness in their owner's arms for their turn to be seen by Dr. Brach. And each time, they came back out looking happier and healthier. Curious—it was as if they'd been instantly cured by their visit to the vet.

Suzanna found herself elated to be a part of something so important. Healing of the sick and injured had always been a passion of hers, yet she'd never found the right fit. Pursuing any type of medical field hadn't felt right. Her endeavor into psychology hadn't turned out so well. Uncertainty of whether she'd be able to handle the outpour of emotion she might encounter from those afflicted with a medical condition caused her to stifle the desire to help others in a way that had purpose for her.

In learning about her own malady, she'd become entranced by the existence of the body's ability to regenerate cells, attack intruding sicknesses, and heal itself. This job might just be the answer to her search for purpose. Just because these were animals, healing couldn't be too different from humans, or any less important.

Fascinated by the idea of working with Nicholaus in the clinical area, she became excited to learn all she could to help. He'd told her he encouraged learning and expanding one's quest for knowledge, and welcomed her to read any of the books in his office.

During lunch she searched through the array of books behind Nicholaus' desk, hoping to find something to help her memorize the terminology and various procedures involved, to become a better assistant. He didn't own a "*Pet Medicine for Dummies*", so she settled on a veterinary dictionary and one of the simpler manuals on medical procedures.

Mona and John left for the day, leaving her to delve into her new treasures with an enthusiasm that surprised her. She spread the books out in front of her and attempted to match them together.

The pounding of her head reminded her of how hard she'd tried all day to protect her empathic senses from the incoming barrage of emotion and illness. Release of such a strong hold felt impossible as she stretched her neck struggling to relax. She wished she had a cup of steaming hot chamomile tea. That would relax her. Instead she took a swig of the bottled green tea open on her desk.

She heard the doors open behind her and sensed Nicholaus' presence. Even without visual confirmation she recognized his individual energy signature.

"I wasn't aware anyone else was here with me." His deep sexy voice made her quiver as she turned to find he'd stepped around the end of the desk. He swung his leg up and sat with ease on the corner in front of her.

"I'm sorry, should I leave? I was brushing up on some terminology. I hope you don't mind." A bit intimidated by his easy demeanor, much to her dismay she began to speak in an unusual hurried pattern. "I borrowed a couple of the books from your office."

Nicholaus reached out and flipped each book over to examine her choices. His every movement fascinated her for some reason. The handsome set of his jaw, the way he brushed his hand through the curls at the nape of his neck. She hated the fact his closeness took hold of her ability to look away.

"You may stay as long as you'd like. You're welcome here."

Her careful study of him must have caught his attention and he smiled a slow sexy smile. An odd sensation of warmth traveled through her whole body. The obvious increase of activity in her cells created a rush of blood to her heart. She wondered if he too experienced the energy sparring between the two of them, almost as if at war with each other.

"Impressive. I didn't believe anyone would be as committed to learning as I am," he commented.

"I love to learn new things. This is such a great opportunity for me. I'm not sure you realize how much I appreciate your taking me on. I'm sure someone more qualified would apply. So I'm trying to make up for my inexperience."

"It's not necessary to try so hard. As far as I can tell, you have more than I need." The slow sexy smile returned, followed by a bright twinkle in his eyes, the same way she'd seen the first night at the restaurant. She immediately became alert.

A flush rose to her cheeks as she realized the pass he'd made at her. The unmistakable glimmer in his eyes taunted her to respond. Her temporary innocence was quashed as she shut the door firmly on her emotions and tried to raise her guard again.

"Yes, well, I aim to please." Her sarcastic tone bled through the words without question to her meaning. She rose quickly, though his gaze caught her attention, as if he were trying to make a crucial decision.

She realized the continued battle of energies between them would be dangerous. She needed to leave. As she began to gather her belongings a sudden sharp pain shot through her temple. She dropped her bag abruptly to bring her hand up to her head.

"What's wrong?" Nicholaus jumped from the edge of the desk to ease her down into her chair.

"I've just got this headache. It'll go away soon." She could sense his concern for her had erased the previous male egotism.

"Let me see what I can do. I've learned some interesting acupressure methods which might help."

Nicholaus brushed her hand aside to place his cool soft fingers to her temples. Oddly, as he began to apply pressure, an almost sensual sensation spread through her head from the tips of his fingers. As she closed her eyes, she saw a curtain of gold light surround her, wrapping her in warmth. The pain floated away to nothing as if it had never existed.

"Wow, how did you do that?" She questioned amazed at the instant relief.

His fingers remained for a moment longer then trailed down to the slim line of her neck. All of a sudden, she sensed a change in his intent. Without question it felt very sexual. Maybe he hadn't meant it that way, but everything in her told her to beware.

She felt the need to get out of there as quick as possible, but his touch left her unable to move. The energy between his fingers and her skin increased to an incredible volume, as if a fire would ignite.

Gathering her wits she rose from her seat and reached out to grab her purse. "I…I need to leave," she stuttered.

"Are you sure?" he asked, reaching out to slide a seductive finger up her arm.

That stopped Suzanna short. She closed her eyes and paused to catch her breath. His touch activated an electric reaction in every molecule of her already motivated body. She hadn't been sure if he'd meant the touch to her neck to be sexual. Now the contact of skin to skin made an inferno sear through her in a very pleasing manner.

As she regained control, differentiating her own emotions from the pure male sexuality he emitted was difficult.

"Why did you do that?" she asked as she opened her eyes again and looked straight at him with solid confidence. His eyes had turned a dark steel gray, piercing her with an almost analytical stare. To defy his affect on her, she stared back at him intending to convey a hard as rock message, as if she could and would take him down without thinking twice.

"I find this very interesting. I wanted to see if you perceive the same thing I do."

"I don't know what you're talking about." Suzanna refused to let him know he'd sparked something with an exponential growth potential that scared her. She must not allow this to happen. This needed to stop before this went too far.

It would only end in devastation.

Without warning he leaned forward with the slightest of movement, and placed his lips on hers giving the gentlest kiss she'd ever received. Yet, his lips contained more blazing raw passion than any other man had ever shown her. Her hands automatically came up to rest on his chest, her body responding to his touch before she could withdraw.

Nicholaus' grin as he pulled back told her he was pleased with her reaction. She stepped away, almost toppling over the chair behind her.

"Then tell me you didn't feel that."

The kiss somehow scrambled her brains. Words refused to form. Her ability to shake free of the sensations he'd ignited impossible. Yet she forced herself to stand straight as a board, the brick façade coming forth again.

In an effort to appear uninterested, she brushed an imaginary speck from her skirt. "Look, I won't say you aren't attractive. To tell you the truth, I'm not interested."

"Are you married?" He questioned.

"No."

"Got a boyfriend?"

"No."

"I won't believe it if you tell me you're a lesbian."

This comment struck a raw sensitive cord. Anger rolled up in force and she slammed the table with the purse she'd picked up from the floor. Her eyes flew up to engage his. If looks could kill, she intended him to be flattened in a second.

"I am not now, nor have I ever been homosexual. I'm just not interested. I suggest you let it go. Nothing is going to happen between us. So don't push it."

She turned and walked out of the office with as much dignity as she could rally to her aid.

In the darkness, she sat in her car, unable to move any further. Her bones had melted to gelatin and her brain a sudden bowl of mush. Although tempered by anger, the effect of that one simple kiss stunned her.

For a brief moment, when their lips touched, she would have given anything to be next to him, to feel his skin against hers. The magnitude so powerful any comparison to a previous experience was inconceivable. Without checking her responses to him it surely would have gone much further.

She already knew, no matter how strong her desire, disaster was immanent if she contemplated his offer of intimacy. She'd been through this too many times, with enough proof, any type of intimate contact invariably ended in more heartache. It just wouldn't work. She needed to give up, in order to maintain what sanity she had left.

She needed to convince Nicholaus he didn't want her.

The question was, how?

* * * *

Back at the office, Nicholaus sat at his desk and blew out a whistling breath. He wasn't sure what pushed him to go so far. Curious if she would admit to feeling the same energy, he'd wanted to push her buttons. For some reason he'd acted without thinking. He'd been unable to help himself, his hormones leaping unchecked into action.

He could still feel and taste her lips on his. What was intended as a simple kiss had resulted in a physical response more astounding than he'd imagined possible. His preferred cool act shattered as her affect on him grew deeper and more intense.

The soft smoothness of her lips against his, her breath upon his skin triggered a need for him to take her right then and there. The hidden fire she exuded silently urged his masculinity to pillage and plunder. Her innocence pulled at him. The purity in her lips brought the knowledge of soft, sweet surrender and the discovery of things not yet seen. Alongside came an odd need for him to protect.

At first her passion matched the excitement in her face. Then he witnessed the slow progression of fear bring down the Berlin Wall, severing any possibility of further discovery. This emotional roller coaster she displayed intrigued him.

She claimed she didn't want to have anything to do with him. Her kiss told him something totally different. He felt the aroused energy almost leap from her skin, and yet she was frightened by his touch.

She needed space, he could do that. The next move would be hers. Though, not being one to leave an unsolved mystery, he had full intentions to find out more about her. Why was she so afraid?

* * * *

The next morning, Suzanna made her decision. If she kept up the cold front, sooner or later he'd loose interest. Though what she found throughout the day, every time they passed each other images of his kiss and the urgent need he'd stirred within her made it very hard to maintain her composure.

She wasn't quite sure what to make of Nicholaus' indifference. He treated her as if nothing at all unusual had happened between them. Perhaps what happened hadn't meant anything to him. She didn't dare try to read him. The results might be harder to handle than not knowing.

As she watched him take hold of a beautifully colored parrot, he spoke with ease and competence describing the treatment plan to the owner. He glanced back to meet her gaze, his eyes blank and unreadable. Too far away to do otherwise, she couldn't help but wonder what he was thinking, or more importantly—feeling.

Mona came up behind her, and startled her out of her thoughts.

"Suzanna, why don't you get us all some lunch? It looks like we'll have our hands full for a while."

"Oh, alright, I guess lunch would be nice, wouldn't it." She glanced toward Nicholaus and back to Mona. "What about Nicholaus? Doesn't he need some help?"

"Don't worry. I'll lend him a hand. This might be my last chance to do what I've grown to love."

Suzanna knew Mona would miss this place. Maybe she should give her a chance to say her goodbyes in private. She stood and grabbed her purse.

"I guess I can lock up for a bit. You go help with the bird. I'll get the usual at Millie's Café. Be back in a few."

Mona, amused all day by the interaction between these two, intended to find out what made them act so strangely. Something must have happened. She also knew the probability of grave results if Suzanna wasn't handled in the right way. She and Nicholaus needed to have a talk. He needed to understand a few things about the young woman.

She followed him back to attend the tropical bird brought in for oil dowsed feathers.

"How on earth did he get all that oil all over him?" she asked.

"The owner said he placed him by the kitchen sink and somehow it turned an open bottle of olive oil onto itself while stretching its wings." Nicholaus held the bird in one hand and prepared his worksite with the other. "I wish people would think before they do things. He should have patted the oil off with a paper towel, something that would soak it up quick. Instead he used a wet towel which only worsened the effect of the excess grease."

"This won't be easy, will it?"

"Not in the least," he said blowing a drifting feather from in front of his face.

Mona helped by getting out the cleaning agent reserved for this type of mishap. Nicholaus held the beautiful bird over the tub of soapy water with one secure hand. He began a gentle splashing with the other, working the soap into the feathers.

Looking up he smiled. "I still can't believe you're leaving today. It seems like only yesterday you came to save me from myself. You sure there isn't some way I might talk you into staying?" he said and winked.

Mona smiled. She knew his flattery was genuine.

"I can't believe it myself. This day arrived so fast. But we all need to retire sometime. Now George is retired, we want to go have some fun. This is going to be the first chance we've had to take time together alone for almost 20 years. It's time we relax and rediscover what we mean to each other."

The sudden wave of emotion caused a slight sniffle and she saw Nicholaus glance up at the sound. The small tear she brushed away was joy mixed with sadness. She folded her arms over her chest and watched Nicholaus' careful handling of the bird. She would definitely miss this young man.

"Mona, you deserve every bit of it. You know you've been my saving grace since you started, but most of all you've been a good friend. It's hard to let you go. I'm kind of jealous of George. He's a lucky man to have you."

With a hearty laugh, she put her hands on her hips and shook her head. "You're such a flirt!" Then she remembered why she'd come in to talk to him. "Seriously though, Suzanna will do a good job for you. She already has the office down pat. I don't believe you'll find anyone better."

"I can see that. Besides, how could I go against your express recommendation?"

She smiled, "I'm glad you recognize my expertise in choosing the best for you."

"So what do you want to tell me?"

Mona smiled. He'd seen right through her.

"She's a smart and enthusiastic girl. She's also beautiful and sexy." At Nicholaus' lifted brow she said, "You can't disguise the facts from me Nicholaus Brach, you're attracted to her."

Grinning, Nicholaus said, "You caught that did you?" He rubbed his nose with his shoulder and continued to carefully bathe the bird.

"Any blind person can see the sparks fly between the two of you. Suzanna isn't your regular girl. You need to watch how you go about any of your attentions."

"Not regular? What does that mean?"

"I'm not at liberty to go into detail, but you need to know, she's had a rough time of it. She struggles in many areas, one of which you can associate with." At the crease in his brow, Mona realized she would have to expound on her statement. Of anyone, Nicholaus was the one person who could understand some of what Suzanna fought with every day of her life.

"And that would be?"

"I told you before she's got a special intuitive nature. She can't know that I've told you this, but she's different, like you. Not in the same way though, hers has to do with feelings and emotions. She's a sensate with empathic abilities. It's hard for her to accept, but she's slowly coming to terms with her own gift."

"She's a sensate? Maybe that explains it. There's this immediate connection between us." He laughed. The slow nod of his head was followed by a mischievous grin. "Mixed with my abilities could result in a rather interesting combination."

Mona needed to clarify what she meant. "Nicholaus, all I can say is she's special. There are things about her I can't explain to you, and when the time comes, she will have to tell you yourself. She needs to be treated with care, and not to be played with. She's had a lot of hurt and doesn't need any more."

Nodding in agreement Nicholaus rotated his shoulders to relieve the tension building from his tedious job.

"I already knew that somehow. But, you know me Mona I'm not going to do anything to hurt someone. I can't say for sure what, if anything will happen. I can assure you, if something does you don't need to worry about me hurting her, at least not intentionally."

Mona's grandmother character came out. "See that you don't young man. I chose her for this job not only to keep you in line, but to give her a place to open her eyes and spread her wings. I think you understand what I'm telling you."

She and Nicholaus exchanged a long silent contemplative regard for each other. In acknowledgement he nodded his head and returned his attention to the bird beginning to flutter in his hands. He'd had enough of this treatment.

"Now, I've got to rinse this bird down and see where we are in getting this stuff out of his feathers."

Satisfied she'd done what she needed to do, she reached over to get a lab coat. "You want some help? I've got an extra pair of hands."

Chapter Six

The first week on her own after Mona's retirement flew by quicker than she'd imagined. Suzanna found she had no problem keeping up on the paperwork, happy to be asked to lend a hand in the back every once in a while.

Nothing more happened with Nicholaus, which surprised her. She'd expected at least some attempts to get next to her again. He acted as if the other night had never occurred. On the occasions she did find herself close to him she got weak in the knees. The incessant fluttering of her stomach and the pounding of her heart was uncontrollable in his presence.

Acting cold toward him wasn't as easy as she'd hoped. She found herself laughing at his refreshing sense of humor, impressed by his extensive knowledge of almost everything. Without further coercion on the physical level, she was beginning to relax around him.

Suzanna flipped through the pamphlet Mona had given her. She hadn't told Mona yet, but she'd already begun to open up to the idea. Being an Empath didn't seem to be such a bad thing after all.

"G.L.O.V.E.S. What an odd name."

The mystical picture of hazy images of planets and timepieces entwined with hues of blue and purple on the front intrigued her. She was drawn in as if she belonged there. Mesmerized, it all but jumped off the page and surrounded her in a warm gentle light.

What on earth does all this mean?

One thing she knew, she definitely needed to do a more in depth study of her sensate abilities. More apparent than ever, they were showing quite clearly to her now. Since the day she stepped into this office, whatever was going on with Nicholaus seemed to have kick started all sorts of sensations. The clarity of the moods and emotions of every person and animal coming through the door showed stronger to her than she ever remembered before.

Setting aside the pamphlet, with the morning being so slow, she warily browsed the internet for an official site to confirm her most recent search on psychic abilities. The website she found the night before had encouraged her, stating empathic individuals were not as obscure as they had been in previous years.

She'd read how experts now considered these weird feelings she experienced to be an inherent ability that all humans possess, more so in some than others. Reading the reviews, the general public's reaction of such an unusual gift of sensing the emotional and physical state of another being was mixed. Some wholeheartedly believed in it, others thought it was a bunch of hogwash.

Though based on thorough testing and testimonials the scientific community had begun to prove this ability to be, in fact, real. They now categorized it as an enhanced sensory perception that could be diagnosed by the intricate electrical firings of the brain during a psychic session.

Aware not all information on the web could be trusted, she browsed quickly through the most questionable one. Too many sites claimed the answers to all her questions, and the perfect way to use the gift—for a hefty fee. These were obviously deceptive spider webs cast from a bogus commiserate entity waiting to sucker her out of a quick buck.

"No, thank you, I'm too smart for that," Suzanna chuckled.

She clicked on a website revealing some with this ability perceived only thoughts and emotional connections, where others had a combined ability, much like her, to experience a physical sensation of other individuals. Not remembering which site she'd clicked on she glanced up at the web address— *Gloves.com.*

Wait a minute, I know this one. She reached down and grasped the pamphlet she'd laid aside earlier.

As she turned the brochure over in her hands, she glanced again at the information. It gave a brief description of an organization maintaining a true understanding of '*the gifted*' and expressed a desire to share their insights. Mona had circled the contact number for her, and wrote the name '*Marianne*' below the bold statement '*Service Fee–Donations Only*'.

"This must be where I should go." Tucking the pamphlet back in her purse, she decided to give them a call later to find out what they were all about. "I sure hope this Marianne knows what she's talking about." Suzanna knew if Mona had recommended them, she could trust them.

Motivated by a new confidence, she decided to test her reception to her environment. Slowly she released the impenetrable wall she forced around herself each morning. If she could learn to live without the constant tension she'd grown to depend on maybe these blasted headaches would go away.

From where she sat behind the desk she perceived the faded remnants of energy left behind by the people and animals passing through the office that morning. To bad, nobody was close enough for her to sense right now. She wanted to practice.

She remembered how often she'd wished she didn't possess the gift. During her youth the usual teen age emotional and hormonal changes mixing with her untrained capabilities had overwhelmed her sensitivities. Frequent hiding in her closet had been the only way to escape the confusion. She was lucky Mona had been able to teach her how to block the external energies around her.

But now she realized if she were to help others as much as she wanted to, she needed to be able to control the response she allowed within herself. To do that meant to let down her guard.

The front door swung open with a burst. A young woman flew through the opening, holding an animal carrier, and ran into the reception area. Inside the carrier, a small black and white cat crouched in fear as the owner thrust the cage onto the desk. A mournful cry radiated through the room when the jostling of the container stopped.

"Please, Boots has got something wrong with him. He doesn't move at all. I think he's in pain."

"Dr. Brach will take a look at him. Have you and Boots been in before?"

Suzanna took hold of the carrier handle. An immediate sharp jolt shot through her stomach and stopped midway down her intestines. The intensity of discomfort remained and didn't move any farther. She could discern the difference. This definitely was not her pain. The removal of her hand from the handle caused a fading sensation, yet she still felt the intuitive pain in her gut.

"Yes, yes. He's been in for his shots, maybe about a year ago. Please, you've got to help him."

"Don't worry. Dr. Brach will take care of him. I'm going to bring him back right now. You sit down and try to relax. I'll return in a minute to get your information."

Suzanna pushed the button on her desk to notify Nicholaus a case was being brought into the back. She took a deep breath before she grasped the handle again. The stabbing pain shot through her body before she had time to refocus her guard. She didn't have time. The poor kitty needed help now.

As she stepped into Exam Room Three, she gasped, the pain having increased with relentless force. She placed her hand on the wall and worked to control the need to sit down.

Nicholaus entered the room behind her. She tried to cover up the pain she'd encountered, but her facial expression gave her away.

"What's wrong? Are you alright?" He took her by the shoulders and led her to the chair by the door.

His immediate concern combined with the touch of his hand had the oddest effect. She felt an unfamiliar internal energy source run through her body as if in search of something. She would ask him about this later. For now the pain was too intense to ignore. She raised her hand to her stomach where the agony had settled.

"I'm fine. The cat's not. Don't ask me how I know. His intestines are blocked. They are about to explode." Seeing Nicholaus' inquisitive gaze, she gestured toward Boots. "Just check that first, please."

His hand remained on her arm, his eyes searching hers. Then he nodded his head briefly and turned to the cat.

"Well, Boots, let's see what you've gotten yourself into."

The cat hissed and made a pitiful low growl as Nicholaus took him from the carrier. The distress in the animal's eyes was more than Suzanna could handle. Until she learned to block out the pain and suffering of others and still be open on an intuitive level she needed to shut it down. This new use of her gift would take some serious practice.

Suzanna rose out of the chair anxious to leave the room. "Do you need me? I should go get some info from the owner."

"No, but send John back here, I might require an assist from him." The pain diminished and she took a slow deep breath, and caught Nicholaus taking a second glance at her. The intensity in his eyes relayed his concern. "Do me a favor. Ask Patricia if Boots has been eating anything unusual."

She smiled at his acceptance of her intuitive analysis, and started to walk out. "Thanks."

Taking his stethoscope out of his pocket he looked up, "For what?"

"For not laughing at my diagnosis," she explained.

"I don't see anything to laugh at, do you?"

Their eyes locked in a moment of scrutiny. His unspoken acceptance gave her spirit a lift. "No. I guess not. I'll go get John for you."

Back in the waiting room, Suzanna sat across from Patricia. The young woman appeared to be in her twenties, dressed in jeans and a faded Husky's T-shirt. Worry drained what was a very pretty face as she rubbed her hands together, turning toward the connecting door.

"Has Boots been eating anything strange? Cats tend to eat some bizarre things sometimes."

Patricia began to shake her head then hesitated. "Well, I did find him chewing on a plastic grocery bag the other day. He'd eaten the handles off, not like shredding them, but actually swallowing what came off. I thought that was kinda weird. I didn't think much about it. I found he'd done the same thing to the edge of the trash bag in the bathroom. So I took everything I could find out of his reach."

"Good idea, anything more?" Suzanna asked.

"Oh…and then he ate a rubber band I couldn't get him to spit back out." Tears popped into the young girl's frantic blue eyes. "Do you think that's the problem?"

Suzanna tried not to grimace. "I'm not sure, but I'd better go tell Dr. Brach. It might be important."

* * * *

This was the worst day yet since she'd started. Pets were being brought in left and right with one thing or another wrong. Some ended up being kept for treatment and monitoring, while others were sent home after a short visit with Dr. Brach. One Terrier puppy sat in his owners lap, his little front paw held up in the air as if any pressure would cause him pain. Soon after, he pranced in happy abandon out of the office, as if all his ailments were cured.

Suzanna wondered if Dr. Brach was a miracle vet. Perhaps that odd energy wave she'd sensed earlier was a sign of some sort.

A small Siamese kitten had met up with a mousetrap, its lower leg caught in the wire mechanism while trying to dislodge the tasty morsel of cheese. Suzanna picked up a sensation of bruises and possible crushed bones causing a pain unfamiliar to the mewing kitten. Within an hour Nicholaus called her back to bring the pet out to its owner.

Although the leg had been wrapped in hardened cast like bandages, Suzanna no longer sensed any discomfort whatsoever.

She stroked the kitten Nicholaus handed her and found the intense anguish she'd experienced earlier coming from the feline's little body had faded. Now nothing more than slight confusion existed.

"Did you give her some type of pain killer?"

"No. She's too small."

"What are you then, a miracle healer?"

Nicholaus raised his eyebrows with an almost guilt ridden expression. "Lucky, I guess."

The exhausted mass of fur in her arms curled into a natural ball shape and began to purr.

"Hmmm…." she murmured not believing a word. "Then why does it seem like you're hiding something?"

Nicholaus shrugged his shoulders and turned away from her to clean up the tray behind him. She didn't appreciate his non-responsive answer, but decided to leave the subject alone for now.

The last patient of the day lay next to his owner's feet. In silence, both Irish-Setter and the man next to him resembled an elderly couple, content with each others presence. Their slow stiff movements caused Suzanna to suppress a giggle when they stood up with a creak and moved toward her.

The old man's shoulders bowed forward, his steps no longer steady, mimicking those of a wind up doll. In opposite proportion, his bright charismatic smile would knock any woman off her feet.

It was true what they said about pets and their owners. The Irish-Setter looked very much like the rickety old man beside him. The once shiny color of his younger years had turned to a dull gray infused coat. The only difference was his long and sagging face showed eyes that appeared as if he couldn't care less. All he seemed to want to do was lie down to take a nap.

"You're new here. Where's that spirited young thing I normally see?" The old man leaned against her desk and narrowed his eyes as if to focus on her face through his faltering sight.

Tickled by his description of Mona, Suzanna remembered her friend's characterization of some of the regulars. This must be the infamous Patrick O'Brien, known for his gadding about town with his Setter, aptly named "Boyo". In his adventures the old man would hit on all available, and sometimes not so available, women. Supermarkets, banks, parks, made no difference to him.

"It's nice to meet you Mr. O'Brien. That's a mighty fine pup you've got there. Mrs. Freeman has retired. I'm Suzanna, and I'm sure we will get along splendidly."

The old man brightened at the reference to his dog and reached down to give his best friend a pat on the head. He pushed his glasses up and stepped forward to peer at Suzanna.

"Retired, you say? I told her that man of hers wasn't good enough for her. She should have run off with me years ago. Lord knows I offered enough times."

He came around the end of her desk and leaned in with shameless interest. If she hadn't been informed of his reputation she might have been embarrassed by his obvious effort to view every curve she possessed.

With a long sigh, he shook his head. "Alas, you're a bit young for me. I like them older, with a little more meat on their bones. But I could be talked into giving you a run for your money."

Grinning at his mischievousness, Suzanna now understood Mona's description of him.

"Well, I might have to consider that. But let me take Boyo back to visit Dr. Brach. B-12 shots, isn't it?"

"Yes, the old boy needs to get some kick in his step again. He seems to be wearing out these days. Unlike me, I'm up for just about anything," he said with a boyish wink.

Suzanna winked back. "I can tell I'm going to need to keep my eye on you, you tomcat." She took the dog's leash and led him away. In the background she heard the old man chuckling as he made his way back to the waiting room seats.

Boyo padded along at a slow pace. He glanced up long enough to find out who was with him. Not recognizing this new person, he sniffed her fingers with curiosity. At the slight touch, Suzanna recognized an immediate stiffness settling in her hips and an overwhelming tiredness loomed over her. She blocked her receptors and decided not to practice openness this late in the day. She was tired enough on her own.

She brought the Setter into the exam room stocked with various types of medications and vitamins, and waited for the doctor to arrive. A moment later, Nicholaus stepped in. He too exhibited a tired, worn down to the bone appearance and gave a weak smile as he approached them.

"Hey Boyo, come back to see me, did you?"

The dog perked up immensely upon seeing him. He moved next to Nicholaus and nuzzled his palm as if in search of something expected.

Suzanna raised an inquisitive eyebrow at Nicholaus.

"I normally offer him a snack. I forgot this time." Nicholaus picked the animal up and placed him on the exam table. "Why don't you go find me one of those bones he likes so much? I keep a stash in the cabinet in Exam Room One."

Nicholaus turned his attention back to the Setter. Guilt was not something he enjoyed. He'd known full well he kept the bones in another area, and wished he hadn't lied to her. But he had to get her out of the room. This should give him enough time to do what he needed before she came back.

Boyo's tail wagged a slow trail back and forth as he continued to nudge his nose into Nicholaus' palm. "Okay boy, just a minute. I've got to get the B-12 out. Stay there."

Nicholaus went to the small refrigerator where the pre-filled syringes were stored. Not finding any, he frowned when he realized John had forgotten to re-stock this room. Filling a syringe himself with the contents of the liquid vitamin vial took longer than he expected. Boyo gave a light whine, his impatience getting stronger.

"Ok, boy, here we go. I'll give you the shot first, and then we can take care of the rest."

His back to the door, Nicholaus gave the B-12 injection, knowing the vitamin with properties to increase energy and bone density was desperately needed by the aging canine. He placed the syringe on the counter and turned to run his hands over the dog's fur appearing as if he were petting him in friendship. He talked to Boyo in a soft tone, with a slight lift of his hand above each hip he paused. A bright white light shot through his fingers into the animal's stiffened joint. He did this for both the hip and shoulder joints, the dog licking him in love as he proceeded.

The noise behind Nicholaus alerted his guard and he found Suzanna, with dog bones in her hand, staring in confusion at the picture before her.

"That was strange. Did you see that? Or do I need to go visit my optometrist?" She handed him the snacks and peered at Boyo.

"See what?"

"All those bright lights and sparks," she made a face at Nicholaus as he pretended to be puzzled by her question. "Ok, that proves it. I'm making an appointment as soon as I can," Suzanna mumbled, barely audible, as she left the room.

This was a new development. Nobody ever claimed to see his healing ray of light before. To his knowledge the only ones who could witness the transfer of energy were other healers. He lifted Boyo back down to the floor and decided playing innocent was the best way to handle her curiosity. He needed to introduce Suzanna slowly into his world. She'd probably understand, but sometimes understanding only went so far.

Mona had accepted him with open arms, though he took over a year to build enough courage to tell her about his abilities. He'd found she had a deeper insight into spirituality, extraordinary senses, and things not yet understood by this world. This had prompted him to reveal his hidden secrets. Though, he may need to step up the pace with Suzanna. She appeared already aware of his differences. Perhaps because of her uniqueness his explanations wouldn't be as difficult.

Nicholaus walked Boyo out front. Suzanna's baffled expression, he imagined, was a result of Boyo's sudden youthful appearance. The dog pranced around him, obvious affection in every bounce and rub the dog gave to him. Nicholaus reached down to pat the dog's head as he talked with Mr. O'Brien.

"Are you behaving yourself Patrick?" Nicholaus asked with a laugh. "You know you're not as young as you used to be."

With a loud guffaw Patrick placed his hand on Nicholaus' shoulder. "When are you going to figure out Nicholaus, my boy, you're only as old as you want to be."

Nicholaus saw him peek at Suzanna, a lustful scrutiny in his eyes.

"And if your girls get to be any younger, I may break into my teens again. Old, my foot," he claimed stomping his foot in fun at Nicholaus.

The laughter sounded good after such a long day. Suzanna's nightmares had disturbed her sleep more lately, so by this time of day exhaustion would set in. The dull throb returned to her temples and she thought perhaps the lights she'd seen earlier were due to her fatigue.

As she prepared for the next morning, out of the corner of her eye she caught the slightest hint of increased brightness. Her head shot up and she focused on the stream of light. Nicholaus stood at the front door with the old man, patting him on the shoulder in a friendly goodbye. The small flash of violet light passed between the two again. She swore to herself. Obviously she needed to make an appointment for first thing the next morning. Something must be wrong with her vision. Either that or Nicholaus was some type of magician.

Nicholaus came back to sit on the edge of her desk, a weary sigh escaping his lips. "It's been a long day today. I think I'll go put my feet up and toss down a beer."

Suzanna nodded in agreement, "Sounds good."

"Been meaning to ask you about what happened earlier this morning with the cat. In fact, all day long, you pre-diagnosed half the animals before you brought them to me. What's up with that?" She determined by his demeanor he thought he knew the answer to the question.

She studied him for a moment and wondered if she should open up. On the off chance he was only guessing, she decided against telling him so soon. Not now, not yet.

"I learn quickly. I thought I was being helpful," she said hoping that would be enough for now. His eyes held hers.

"You were a tremendous help today." He reached out and took her hand in his. "But, please understand, if you ever need to talk, about anything, you can come to me." He squeezed gently emphasizing his offer.

Suzanna sensed the sincerity in his voice. He was open and willing. For some reason he made her want to crawl into his embrace and lay her head against his chest. She yearned to soak in the pure male strength he possessed. The desire overwhelmed her so much it required an extreme effort to pull away.

To sever the connection she pulled her hand from his and smiled. "Thank you, Nicholaus. That's very kind of you. I'll remember next time I need to talk."

All of a sudden the front door swung open, and a bundle of person and animal rushed through. In a brief second Suzanna recognized her mother, a coat thrown over her robe, house slippers still on her feet. Her beloved Coco lay almost lifeless in her arms.

"Help me, *por favor*. I know not what to do. He no eat. Just lies under chair and whimpers. No allow me hold him." Tears poured down Carmen's face, her voice high pitched and frantic.

More worried about her mother than the little dog, Suzanna rushed forward to support her mother's tiny frame. She glanced at Nicholaus and gestured for him to come take the animal.

"It's alright Mamma. We'll take care of Coco. Dr. Brach is a wonderful doctor."

Nicholaus tried to lift the dog from Carmen's arms. She wouldn't let go.

"Don't worry Mrs. Hawthorne. Let me take a look and see what's bothering the little guy."

Her hesitancy to release Coco from her grip, had Nicholaus placing his hand on her arm for reassurance.

"You need to let me bring him to the back for a bit. Why don't you stay here and talk to Suzanna? She can get you a cup of tea. You deserve some TLC, too."

Carmen stared, searching with tear laden eyes into his, and slowly let Coco go. "*Por favor*, can I see him soon? Him need to know, him be better. Him safe here," she implored.

"Of course you can. Sit down and relax, I'll send Suzanna out to get you."

When she handed the cup of tea to her mother, Suzanna kissed her on the cheek and said, "Mamma, I'm going to find out if Nicholaus needs anything. You sit here and I'll come get you."

Carmen glanced at the door Nicholaus went through, then at her daughter, and again at the door. She nodded in reluctance. Coco had achieved the title of best friend. Suzanna knew the dear pet was loved as dearly as one of her mother's own children. If anything happened to him, she wasn't sure how her fragile mother would manage.

Nicholaus had started his initial examination when she came into the room. Coco whimpered at the sight of her. She put her hand out to calm his fears. Her instincts led her to let down her guard and open her sensate self. At first, the strong male presence of Nicholaus flowed over her, confident and composed. Then she discerned a sharp pain in her lower back on the right side. The intensity surprised her. As bad as it was for her she couldn't imagine the debilitating effect on an animal as small as a Shitzu.

Remembering her studies earlier in the week, Suzanna touched the place where the discomfort projected from the little body. The immense pain increased so she knew she was right on.

"It's his kidney. I'm pretty sure," she said indicating the area under her palm.

Nicholaus shot a glance up from his patient, their eyes met and he paused and nodded his head impressing his acceptance of her insight without question.

"Then he's probably got a kidney stone. Those can be very painful."

He brought his stethoscope down to the dog's belly and listened.

"I think you may be right. I'm going to need an X-ray to make sure. Then, if that is the trouble, we can start him on a calcium channel-blocker to help dissolve the blockage. It will take a couple of days to work, so I may want to keep him here to monitor he passes the stones without further trouble."

He picked up the dog gently and turned to face Suzanna.

"Your 'feelings' have saved me a lot of guess work today. You've quite the 'intuition'. Perhaps sometime you'd like to tell me more about it?"

She had to divulge the truth soon. He wouldn't wait much longer. Nodding she followed him out to the X-ray machine.

"After we are finished here, you can bring your mother back. I'd like to discuss the treatment and reassure her Coco is going to be fine."

"Thank you, Nicholaus."

Nicholaus held her gaze. She didn't need to explain. He understood what she meant.

Relief filled her heart. Finally, her odd insights would not be questioned. Maybe now she could start to use her gift for something worthwhile.

He nodded and glanced down as the whimper from the small animal in his arms drew his attention away.

* * * *

Nicholaus wasn't surprised. Suzanna's initial diagnosis was correct. Her ability to identify the location of the problem helped to eliminate some of the tests he would have done otherwise. Coco definitely had kidney stones. The size of one of them concerned Nicholaus. Adjustment to the level of medication might be necessary if it didn't dissolve quickly enough. He'd continue to monitor the progression for a day or two.

Though, the older woman appeared to be in worse shape than her pet. Nicholaus couldn't help but notice Carmen's pained gait and careful movements as she walked toward him. Her shoulders slumped forward and she had difficulty in turning her head. Suzanna led her to the chair to sit, and he discerned her favoring her right leg. He may need to treat both pet and owner this time.

Carmen sat, stiff on the edge of her seat. Tears continued to trickle down her cheeks as she waited for Suzanna to return with some tissues. As she'd gone out the door the phone rang.

"Suzanna, would you get that last call for me, might be something important." He'd need some extra time with Carmen. "Then go ahead and lock up for the day," he called after her. That should give him just enough time.

He turned to Carmen. "Coco will be fine. He's got a large kidney stone causing the pain. Unfortunately, these take a couple days to pass through the body. With your permission I would like to keep him here to monitor while the medication helps to dissolve the stones."

"Will he have more pain?" Tears welled up into Carmen's eyes again.

"No. I'm going to give him some…treatments to alleviate the majority of his discomfort right now."

Carmen grabbed his arm. "You promise me he won't hurt. He's my little blessing. I can't stand he's in pain, too."

The tears spilled over again onto her cheeks, a slight sniffle followed. His heart went out to her. She obviously had her own personal experience with pain. He knew he couldn't let her leave without helping her, too. There was no way to treat her without her knowing what he was doing though. He had to take the risk.

"Carmen, I've observed you're in pain. What if I told you I might be able to help you?"

"I don't take pills. They make bad things happen. The doctor, he say no more they can do. This Osteo-arthritis is what *Ancianas* get. Pills they kill the liver and heart. Not good."

"This isn't medication."

"I take that…what is it called? Oh…chondroitin and glucosamine," she stumbled over the words. "It helps, but not so much. My shoulder it still hurts me." Carmen moved her arm around and scrunched up her face.

"There is a form of natural healing not many believe in. I could use it to help you. It deals with energy."

Carmen's eyes grew round with interest. "Ohhh…*si*…we have some like you where I come from. *Mi madre* she told me about them. But, I don't understand how."

"Let's just say God works through me to heal the sick and injured."

"*Si*…*si*…is like she told me."

"If you want my help you've got to promise me you won't tell anyone, not even Suzanna." Nicholaus said, starting to second guess his quick decision.

She seemed to consider for a moment then nodded her head. "*Si*, I want help, *muchas gracias*. I tell no one."

"Alright then, I'm going to touch your shoulder, where it hurts. If you like we can test this out, and if you feel better tomorrow, you let me know and we can do some more."

"*Si*, señor. Will it hurt?"

"Not at all, you might be a little tired afterward. That is a normal reaction to your body beginning to heal itself. Soon the pain you feel now will go away."

She nodded, a small smile reaching the corner of her mouth.

"I need you to close your eyes and concentrate on all the areas that hurt. I want you to imagine the pain flying away from you, and believe deep down in your heart this can really happen."

He placed his hands on both shoulders and closed his eyes. By envisioning the white light of healing power in his mind's eye, he directed the universal energies to flow through his arms and out to the palms. The sensation tickled a little bit as he focused on the powers from above to channel through his body. It entered the top of his head to come out through the fingertips. His full intention directed for less pain and easier movement. For some reason this time the universal spirit took longer than he expected. He withdrew only after he'd received the release from above.

"What the heck was that?" Suzanna questioned as she stood at the doorway, tissues in hand.

Continuing his innocent role, Nicholaus responded with a surprised, "What?"

"Wow, I've really got to get these eyes checked!" She rubbed her eyelids softly then opened them back up. Both Carmen and Nicholaus stared at her, and he hoped she would construe this as confusion and not guilt. "All those colors and sparks. Didn't you see that?"

Carmen gave a chuckle, "No, Suza." Nicholaus patted Carmen's shoulder to express his thanks. She held her hand out to grasp her daughter's arm. "Let's say *adiós* to *mi bebé*. Can you take me home, *novia*? I'm tired and need a *siesta*."

He saw Suzanna catch the wink her mother gave him. Suzanna squinted, and glared briefly at him. He knew even though she wasn't sure what was going on they hadn't fooled her for a minute.

"Of course, I'm sure Coco will be fine. You should get some rest while he's here."

"I come back and talk with Dr. Brach *mañana*." Carmen waved at Nicholaus as Suzanna led her out. "Take care of my Coco."

Chapter Seven

Suzanna walked through the empty apartment, not too thrilled with the choice. Definite low budget choice within her price range and close enough to walk to work if she wanted. But something about it didn't feel right. She paused and tried to come up with a reason she felt so uneasy about the space. There was plenty of room for a single person. Being in the middle of the building it didn't have much window access.

That must be it. I hate dark spaces. A chill suddenly ran down her back. *Maybe some sun lamps would help.*

The dark, closed in atmosphere, felt almost morbid to her. Like a tomb encasing what once was alive. Brightened only by the windows at opposite ends of the apartment, the dismal sunlight brought to life only the dust particles floating in the air. A light movement to her right made her jump. She thought for sure she'd seen something whoosh past her. Her stomach churned as her senses went on alert.

Oh Lord, this is not going to be easy to get used to.

This feeling was hard to describe, as if the remnants of a past energy cloaked her in its sticky residue. It made her cringe. But whatever this was, she really couldn't be picky. Tightening her jaw, she focused her attention on the facts.

Suzanna took a deep breath and turned to the apartment manager. Whatever this feeling was she would overcome it. She hadn't met anything yet she couldn't conquer.

"I'll take it."

"Wonderful. When is the soonest you can bring me the deposit and first month's rent?" The manager's eyes widened in surprise, as if she were about to shout for joy.

"Tomorrow, Friday is when I get paid. Can I pick up the keys at the same time?"

"Certainly, bring your check by the office and I'll have the paperwork and keys ready for you."

Suzanna thought the woman's reaction rather odd. She seemed ecstatic, and Suzanna could sense a form of elation from the woman she didn't quite understand. Renting an apartment couldn't be that much out of the ordinary for a landlord.

On her way out the door, the strange chill she'd gotten earlier settled over her again. The slightest whiff of rot crossed her path, this time mixed with a tacit emotion—a deep fearful emotion—left behind by who knows who. Whatever it was, it felt evil. Like before the feeling came and went too quick to give her time to figure out. So she forced herself to dismiss it as nothing but her own nerves.

Once back at work she rushed through the front door while glancing down at her watch.

Shoot, I'm late. By only a few minutes but it bothered her nonetheless.

Nicholaus sat at her desk the phone pressed to his ear against his shoulder, a file folder in his hands. She couldn't help notice how good he looked. It bothered her how quickly he could unnerve her.

Today he wore a long sleeve button down shirt, the sleeves rolled part way up showing his well-manicured hands and muscular forearms. His jeans fit him perfectly, his masculinity neatly outlined by their crisp lines. She tried not to be too obvious in her scrutiny.

"Mrs. Ryan, I'll be glad to see Petals this afternoon. I don't think this is anything serious. It's probably a superficial wound."

He acknowledged Suzanna's arrival with a nod of the head, and continued to listen to the person on the other end of the phone.

"That's fine. You can try to bind the wound up. Remember though, cats don't care for bandages, and she'll try to chew it off and might do more damage. She'll be fine. Bring her in as soon as you can and I'll take care of her." Nicholaus shook his head and placed the receiver back in the cradle. "Morning," the briskness in his voice told Suzanna he was a bit irritated.

"I am so sorry I'm late. I went to take a look at an apartment for rent. It took a little longer than I expected. I promise it won't happen again." She placed her things on the desk and hurried to the other side to prepare for the start of the day.

A brochure of the apartment building slid off her purse landing on the floor in front of Nicholaus. He bent down to pick it up for her.

"Is this the place?"

"Yes. It's only a couple of blocks away. The manager said the apartment hadn't been rented for some time. Could use some airing out, but I guess I'll go ahead and take it," she said shrugging her shoulders. It still didn't feel right.

"14B?"

Stunned she looked up and caught the slightest hint of humor in his eyes. "Right, how'd you know?"

"I'm surprised you even considered the place. There was a big write up about it in the local paper. I think it even reached the evening news."

The queasy feeling in her stomach jumped up a notch. She was afraid to ask. She felt as if the lump in her throat made her swallow audibly. "What about it?"

"They found a body in there about a year ago. Some said it had to be suicide. Others thought it may have been homicide. They've had a heck of a time trying to rent the apartment out again. As sensitive as you are I didn't think you'd consider it."

That was it!

The sickness in her stomach raged and the blood drained from her head. She needed to sit.

"Oh, my God," she whispered looking around for a chair. Nicholaus took hold of her arm and brought her down into the chair behind her.

"Whoa, didn't mean to freak you out. Sit for a minute. I'll get you some water."

When he returned he sat on the edge of the desk facing her.

"What was that all about?"

Suzanna brushed her hand across her face and tried to regain her composure. What she felt earlier hit her like a punch to the gut when Nicholaus told her the history of the apartment. It was death. Not a simple natural death. Someone had been killed there. The obvious face of evil had permeated the walls and tried to reveal itself to her.

"I really wish you hadn't told me."

"Better to find out now then to move in and find out later."

She took a deep breath and exhaled slowly. She knew he was right.

"Don't know what they think it was, but I can tell you it was homicide. I can't brush it off now. It would haunt me at night."

"Brush what off?"

"My intuition gave me a weird sensation. I couldn't quite place it so I thought my over active imagination was at work again. I guess I should trust my feelings more."

"Don't know why you don't trust yourself anyway. I can't see you've been wrong yet."

This made her smile. Up until now, most people thought she made really good guesses. But it was so much more. She'd stopped telling anyone about her empathic senses because nobody believed her. They didn't understand. They couldn't.

She took a long sip from the water. "Well, I guess I better look some more. Doubt I'll find anything more this week, there haven't been very many places to rent around here."

She noted a change in Nicholaus' disposition. His brows came together as if waging an internal battle. His long gaze made her uncomfortable.

"Tell you what, if you need a place to live, I've got this guesthouse out back. I've been thinking about renting the place out again anyway. Kind of small, but I think it should be big enough for you and Cali."

She wondered the other options he may have been considering. His quick decisive smile brought warmth to his eyes, making her feel safe, and somehow wanted.

Maybe this wouldn't be such a bad idea. You couldn't ask for anything more convenient.

"Are you sure?"

"Seems like the best option to me. You wouldn't have any reason to be late again." The glimmer of humor in his eyes softened his words.

"Can I take a look?"

"Sure. If you feel up to it, we can go now," he said glancing down at the scheduling book. "My first appointment isn't for another half-hour or so. Let's go see the place."

As soon as she walked through the front door of the little red house she knew she was home. Through the multitude of windows at the front, the sun poured in on the same beautiful wood floors as the main house. She gasped at the unforgettable view of the gardens through the back windows, only a glimpse of which could be seen from the outside walk. So many colors seemed to envelope her senses, and she rushed forward to open the windows. Tulips, irises, and lilacs she recognized, but on closer inspection, flowers she'd never seen before created a painter's heaven with their canvas of color. The fragrance of these precious jewels floated in, wrapping her in a blanket of warmth, soothing and filling her with a sense of comfort.

She turned to Nicholaus. "This is so wonderful. I can't believe how beautiful it is."

Nicholaus only nodded with a melancholy look in his eyes. He urged with a motion of his hand for Suzanna to continue through the house.

They walked from room to room without speaking. A few pieces of furniture, left by the previous resident, looked as if they belonged there. Suzanna peeked under the dust covers and found them to be of good quality, classic style pieces she would love to incorporate with her own. She could be quite comfortable here.

The bedroom at the far end of the house surprised her. It was huge, spreading the whole width of the house. The full walk-in closet at the one side of the room caught her eye. Then to the right, the sliding glass doors framing a small private garden captured her attention and took her breath away.

She rushed to open the doors and heard the trickle of a small stone waterscape leading to a pool beneath. A bench had been placed close by in partial sunlight surrounded by plants of all species. Flowers, now in full bloom, provided a pleasing array of color everywhere she looked. All of a sudden, a humming bird swooped down and began gathering nectar from a brightly colored orange Asian lily. If only she had a camera with her. She could only smile at this wonderful paradise.

The creation of something so beautiful could only have been designed by someone with a clean and loving spirit. She was about to ask who had lived here previously when she turned and saw the bed of her dreams.

In the middle of the room stood the frame of an antique king size sleigh bed, made from a gorgeous ebony-colored mahogany. It had no mattress in place, but she could imagine one there. She'd always wanted one of those big pillow top styles that felt as if you'd sunk into a cloud. She could sense a tremendous joy here in this room. The same she'd sensed from the moment she stepped through the front door. There had been love in this house, especially in this room. It made her want to wrap her arms around the feeling and never let go. Here was the perfect room to claim the longings and fantasies she'd had all her life. Suddenly she got a strong image of herself wrapped in Nicholaus' arms, deep in his embrace after making love. It shocked her so that she lost her breath for a moment.

Berating herself for letting these type of feelings for Nicholaus to exist, she could feel the blush brush her cheeks, and was glad to see he stood looking out at the garden. Embarrassed, she hoped to avoid his curiosity, so she moved forward out of view in case he should turn around.

"I meant to tell you I've got an appointment this afternoon with my optometrist. I want to make sure there isn't anything serious going on with my eyes."

Nicholaus had followed, closer than she imagined, his response so close it made her jump.

"No problem. Just let me know when you're leaving."

Suzanna's heart pounded, the tenor of his voice pleasing her ears, and a trail of excitement flew down her spine. She scolded herself for not having more control.

As they walked back to the front room a simple peace surrounded her. Peace wasn't something Suzanna could claim on a regular basis. She had to keep at bay the energies left behind by others, or worse yet, the current ones right beside her. But in both cases, what she felt here was wonderful, as if she were walking into freedom.

Each room had its own feeling of silent happiness. A refreshed positive foundation anchored by love—and lots of it. Most people had no idea about the energy signature left behind by others, too closed to their own perceptions to sense such things.

Suzanna could feel them all.

As they walked past the kitchen she swore she could smell freshly baked cookies, straight from the oven. So strong was the scent, she took a second look before moving on. The counter was empty, a stream of light from the back window it's only inhabitance.

"Who lived here before?"

"Mrs. Bluit lived here over 30 years. She and her husband were the grounds and housekeepers of the main house until the previous owners of the property passed on. The whole estate was left to them, but they couldn't see moving into the big house when they loved this place so much. When her husband passed away, taking care of the property was just too much for her to handle. That's why she put it up for sale, with the condition she could live here for the rest of her life."

A gentle smile came to his lips. "She started to paint later on in life." Walking to the far wall he touched a painting on the wall with affection.

Suzanna looked more closely and recognized the likeness of an earlier time of the gardens through the bedroom glass doors. So much care and love had been placed with each brush stroke.

"Edna was a beautiful woman, inside and out. She would bring flowers and bake me cookies every week. I was blessed to have known her as long as I did."

"Were they chocolate chip?" Suzanna asked with a smile. She knew she'd been right about the cookies.

Nicholaus nodded and looked at her, his head tilted to the side. "How did you know?"

Suzanna shrugged in silence, unsure of this new sense of past trace aromas. She needed to ask someone about this.

"Anyway, she told me she was waiting patiently to join her dearly departed husband in heaven. She passed away a little over a year ago. I haven't been able to bring anybody else in. It just didn't feel right." The deep soft memories of his dear friend showed in his eyes. He looked away. Then his intent gaze came back to her, the pause making his next statement more profound. "Until now," he said, softly.

Suzanna stood immobile. His eyes captivated her. The bond they held in that brief moment made her feel as if she were exactly where she needed to be. The break in eye contact was difficult, but she knew if she stood there much longer she would end up in his arms—the place she belonged—yet couldn't be.

She turned in a slow circle to absorb the ambiance of the room. "This is all so beautiful. I love it. I'm not sure I can afford the rent though."

The average rent on a house in the area would be way out of her league. A residence of this type would be thousands of dollars.

Nicholaus paused thoughtfully, "Tell you what, for the convenience of having you close I'll charge you the same as you would have paid for '14B'. There isn't an additional mortgage for the place so we'll keep it to a minimum."

"That is way too generous. You could get three times as much for this place. Are you sure you want to do this?"

He nodded, as if considering it again. "Yes. You're a good employee. I like to make you…umm my employees happy."

The slip in words troubled her, though she didn't sense any underlying ulterior motive. So overjoyed at the offer she forgot herself and instinctively gave him a hug. He stiffened then lightly wrapped an arm around her to return the hug. Suzanna felt an overwhelming amount of energy rush over her body in a flash as it passed from Nicholaus to her. The sensation of their intermingled energies grew instantly like fire feeding fire.

Time seemed to stop. Neither of them seemed to want to let go. As they stood in each others arms she had the strangest sensation this wasn't the first time. They had been here like this before, perhaps in another life.

Suzanna stepped back, but the energy continued to spark between them under the surface.

The power of the emerging heat couldn't be easy for him to handle either. She eyed him waiting for a belated reaction. His self control impressed her. She appreciated he didn't push her for anything more, though his eyes showed the forced restraint he now employed. That hug had not been the most sensible move on her part. It would be unwise to make the same mistake again.

"Thank you so much. You don't know how much this means to me." She paused and looked around at the glorious space. "I guess I better accept it before you change your mind."

His silence bothered her. Even without any visible evidence, she immediately sensed again a war being fought in his thoughts. His jaw tightened and eyes changed to a steely gray.

"You haven't. Have you?" she asked, afraid she may have pushed too far this time.

He smiled again, easing her anxiousness. "Not at all, when do you want to move in?"

"Is this weekend too soon?" She was surprised by her own excitement.

He shook his head.

"Oh, can I keep the furniture? It's perfect."

"No problem. I'd have to ship it off to the thrift store if you didn't need it anyway."

"Awesome."

"Do you need help moving your things?"

"I'm not sure, I don't have too much. I'll let you know. Thanks for offering though."

Suzanna followed Nicholaus out, pleased at the turn of events. She'd hoped for a new start and this was it. As they walked, she took another long look at the man beside her, careful not to let him know. She stifled the instantaneous grin.

Deep inside she longed for the touch of his hand again, and she yearned to take him up on the intimated offer he'd made days before. She knew not to get her hopes up for something as questionable as a relationship with him. It wasn't possible. Yet everything about him made her want it so much more.

* * * *

"Are you sure you don't see anything? It keeps happening. There has to be something wrong." Suzanna voiced her doubt again to the optometrist, her speech muffled as she spoke through her teeth with her chin shoved into the cup of the retinal digitizer.

"I honestly don't find anything, Suzanna. The optic nerve is undamaged. There aren't any retinal tears or detachment. You tell me there hasn't been any trauma. When is it you see these flashes again?"

Taking her chin out of the cup, Suzanna waited as her eyes adjusted to the light. The doctor, a petite, attractive, blonde woman, came slowly into clear view.

"I'm not sure. I think it's only at work…when Nicholaus is in the room." This thought just occurred to her. Was Nicholaus the key?

"Sounds to me like stress. It's a new job, isn't it?" When Suzanna nodded the optometrist put down her instruments. "Is he attractive?"

Somewhat distracted by her own thoughts about the flashes, Suzanna didn't quite understand what the optometrist said.

"What?"

"Is this Nicholaus attractive? You're still single, aren't you?"

Suzanna nodded, still not sure why this would have any bearing on her eyes.

"It could be a spasm of the blood vessels in the brain caused by increased blood pressure and decreased oxygen. Try making sure you are breathing properly around him, and I suggest you keep track of when these flashes occur. If possible, take your pulse soon after. This could be the culprit." Her optometrist stood up and gave her a card. "Give me a call if anything seems different or if the flashes worsen. At this point I don't see any reason to be concerned."

Maybe what the doctor said had merit. There was no question about the effect Nicholaus had on her body, definitely more than simple physical attraction.

Now she was determined to find out why his natural energy signature differed from any other person she'd encountered.

She picked up her purse and muttered to herself, "There's a culprit alright, but it's not my blood pressure."

* * * *

That night Suzanna sat in the living room, with Coco curled at her feet. She'd just discovered in the book from the library, entitled "You and Your Aura", what the blue and green colors she perceived around Nicholaus represented. Those surrounded by these colors were sensitive and compassionate, healthy in their love of people, animals and nature. Calm and cool in demeanor they tended to be teachers, therapists, and no surprise to her—healers.

The book lay open in her lap, as both she and Coco watched her mother flit around the house doing all sorts of unusual chores. Carmen began to clean the fan blades of the ceiling fan, looking as spry as a teenager.

"Mamma, what has gotten into you? I haven't seen you act like this in years. And what have you done with your hair?"

A little chuckle escaped as Carmen stepped down off the step stool and fluffed her new hairdo, now voluminous with curls and no longer gray.

"Oh, this, you like? Miranda, she give me perm, and added color."

"That's not it and you know it."

"I not know what you speak of," Carmen replied shrugging her shoulders.

"Ever since Coco got sick you've been acting younger every day. It's like watching you age backwards a year for every day. Are you taking some new vitamins or something?"

"No. Not vitamins. I will tell. I'm seeing someone. But, no, no more questions. That's all I say."

Suzanna sensed Carmen's excitement quickly turn to guilt as if she'd said too much. She turned away from her and began to dust the shelves with a vigorous hand.

"Seeing someone? What? Like a boyfriend?"

That was almost unbelievable, Suzanna hadn't seen her mother show any interest in the opposite sex since her father left them years before.

Carmen laughed outright. "Boyfriend? You make me laugh. No, no, just treatments, is all. I feel so good. Oh…but I tell you no more, I promise."

She rushed into the kitchen, and put on a pot of water for some tea. Suzanna, acutely aware Carmen had become very nervous, stood in the kitchen doorway hands on hips and watched her mother flutter around.

"What treatments, and promised who?"

"I no tell you, even if you mad at me."

"Mamma, I'm not mad." Annoyed, Suzanna blew hard to get the strands of hair which had come loose from her ponytail out of her eyes.

Worried her mother might have fallen into the trap of some unhealthy scam, she moved to sit at the kitchen table, and searched for the best way to express her concern.

"Don't you think I should know what you're doing so I'd know who to ask if something happened? I know I'd want someone to do this for me."

Carefully placing the teabags and sugar bowl on the table, Carmen sat down and gave a sigh of resignation.

"Some things, they are better you no understand." There was a sad intonation to her words.

Suzanna felt the shame she'd felt before, emit in strong currents from her mother again. She could tell this statement addressed more than the current subject. Frustrated by her mother's constant unexplained guilt she held back her reaction and reached across the table to touch her mother's hand.

"Mamma, you know you can tell me anything."

Carmen sighed in exasperation. *"Novia,* who do I fool? I not keep silent for this. Soon you know." She stood back up in nervous agitation to check the water on the stove. "You know now, I think. Can't be bad to tell you, but promise me *novia* you not say a word about Dr. Brach."

The hair stood up on the back of Suzanna's neck. Her thoughts jumped to the ways Nicholaus could contribute to her mother's youthful activity.

"What about Dr. Brach?"

"He fix me. Just like *mi madre* said about the magic ones, he touch you, and the pain, it go away. I see him with Coco. Since *la noche* when I first see him, he give me treatments, too."

"What kind of treatments?" Wary, Suzanna eyed her mother.

"I not know all he say. Something about *energia.* It get better and better. I no have pain now."

Suzanna realized she hadn't sensed her mother's intense pain in the shoulders for days. She responded slowly, "So you think he's healing you?"

"Si, si he do," her mother exclaimed. "No worry, *novia,* I no take pills to harm. He calls it…an *energia* boost." Carmen came forward and put her hand on her daughter's shoulder. "Do you no trust Dr. Brach?"

Finally Suzanna could put together all the disjointed puzzle pieces to this mystery called Nicholaus. There was the unusual healing of some of the animals, Boyo's metamorphosis from old and worn out to almost puppy like behavior, Mr. O'Brien's youthful character, and now her mother's transformation. And all of it was connected to the times she'd seen the strange flashes of light coming from Nicholaus' hands. She wondered why she'd missed what was now so obvious.

"Novia, you alright?"

Suzanna looked up into the loving eyes of her mother, more disappointed than angry. Not at her mother though—at

Nicholaus. He'd lied to her, and kept secret something she should have known. She couldn't understand how he felt right about this. If they were to work together like Mona had said, as a close knit family, she needed to know this type of thing. He'd formed a huge wedge in the trust they needed to have with each other.

She patted her mother's hand and stood to give her a hug. "I'm fine mom. A little tired. I think I'll go to bed if it's alright with you?"

Carmen gave her a kiss on the cheek. "Hope you no get sick. I hear people, they talk about bad thing. You go sleep. Maybe you get Dr. Brach give you a boost, too," she said giving an added chuckle. She turned back to the whistling teakettle.

As Suzanna padded back to her bedroom, she muttered to herself, "Yeah, he's going to give me something alright—an explanation."

* * * *

Next morning, Suzanna pondered how to broach the subject with Nicholaus. Still agitated, she needed to figure out the best way to handle the situation. To catch him in the act then force him to tell her would be preferable, but probably not the easiest way. Or maybe she should present him with the facts and see what he had to say for himself. Either way, she was going to get an answer.

The day was fairly slow, so Suzanna decided to go to the back to check in on Cali and give her some love. If things went as she'd planned she would move into the guesthouse the next day. But now she wasn't so sure she should go forward with the move. It all depended on what Nicholaus had to say for himself.

She'd heard of healers, but wasn't too sure how she felt about them. Most of the media coverage concentrated on the negative aspects, as with anything abnormal, including the abilities she possessed. She didn't consider her gift too spectacular. An overly sensitive intuition was all. Everyone had it, although not to the degree she experienced.

Healing wasn't normal. Very few ever claimed to be able to heal others, and most of them proved to be impostors. Though she didn't think this could be a deception. Her mother's ailments had improved. She couldn't ascertain whether Nicholaus could be the reason, or if it was a psychosomatic response to suggestion, and her mother's belief in the '*the magic ones*'.

She'd almost convinced herself it had to be the power of suggestion when she realized the other aspect to consider—the physical response from the animals. Animals aren't prone to suggestion. Their response could only be reality.

Suzanna stroked Cali's soft fur, her thoughts focused on how this new development affected her.

Shouldn't we have an open relationship if we work so close? Or am I expecting too much?

It upset her he hadn't revealed his actions when it came to her mother's health. More importantly, he'd lied to her. His evasive behavior showed a clear indication of guilt. Lying she wouldn't tolerate, in a professional or personal relationship.

Cali obviously sensed Suzanna's internal turmoil and instinctively began to rub her nose against her cheek in an attempt to disrupt her thoughts. Suzanna laughed down at her, and gave her a hug, returning the kisses.

"No, it has nothing to do with you. You're such a sweet kitty. There's something I need to work out with Nicholaus."

Suddenly she sensed the atmospheric change. Startled, she got up from her chair to find Nicholaus leaning against the doorframe with an inquisitive look on his face.

"Work what out?" His eyebrows came together as his forehead creased in a frown.

"You scared me! You shouldn't go sneaking around on people. It's impolite."

It surprised her more that she hadn't sensed his presence. Her thoughts of him had been so intent, his presence must have come naturally to her.

Not yet ready to approach the subject she turned to put Cali back in her cage. She kept her back to him for a minute and struggled to compose her thoughts. But, this was harder than she liked to admit. Every time he came close to her she lost all control of both mind and body. Tongue tied, words escaped her. She found herself melting at the mere thought of being close to him.

"I'm sorry, I didn't mean to. What's on your mind, Suzanna?"

She turned back to face him. It was time.

"You're a healer. And don't try to deny it. The cat's out of the bag, so to speak." She couldn't help but grin at her own pun then quickly became sober again. This wasn't something to laugh about. He needed to understand the seriousness of the matter.

"You're right, I am." His inquisitive expression changed. She saw his eyes held secrets he wasn't ready to divulge just yet.

"So, when were you going to tell me? Especially when my own mother is running around like she's twenty again? Didn't you think I would notice?"

"I would have told you sooner or later. It wasn't time yet."

"Don't you think it's something I should have known? You held back some very important information, and then you lied about it when I asked. How am I supposed to trust you?"

He looked surprised at her response. This was good. She'd caught him off guard. Now he would have to admit his guilt.

"Lying and trust? I think you should consider your own actions. You haven't come out to tell me you're an empathic sensate either. Am I supposed to guess?" he retorted.

At first she was angered by his accusation, until she realized he was right. The anger subsided. Her empathic self was not something she liked to admit to, let alone explain.

"Touché," she said acknowledging his point. "But we aren't talking about me here. Don't try to turn this around on me."

"Wouldn't think of it. But, don't you think you've got some things to explain, as well?"

It was clear she needed to come clean about her own abilities. Nodding, she turned to him.

"All right, you go first."

Chapter Eight

This wouldn't be a short conversation. Nicholaus knew he needed to tell her everything. He couldn't hold anything back because she'd be able to tell right away.

"Come on, we need to go sit down."

When he grasped her hand he almost wished he hadn't. The small electrical push was enough to send ignition sparks through his system. All of a sudden, every body part came to attention to take control of his original intent. He desperately wanted to lead her up the stairs to his bedroom, where he could rid her of the sexy short skirt and tank top. To feel her skin next to his own, and engage in some hot and steamy passionate sex. It seemed to be the only thing he could think about when he touched her.

Forcing the thought from his mind, he led her to the leather couch under the massive southwest windows in his office. The sun shone brightly through the shears and glinted off her dark hair to create a halo effect at the back of her head. As she sat down the short mid-thigh length skirt rode up, enticing and teasing him to reach out to touch.

He considered his options as he gazed at the woman before him. Beautiful to look at was obvious, though the inner beauty radiating from within was what captivated his interest. Past that, he respected her as a colleague, trusted in her spot-on instincts, and enjoyed her company.

But there was more to it than that.

He couldn't forget the way she'd tasted when their lips met. A yearning quickened his need to discover all the delectable places she would taste good. It pulled at him to find out everything about her.

Again, his mind wandered to the possibility of her naked in his bed, the sunlight streaming over her soft ivory skin and silken hair. With a forceful sweep he kept these thoughts at bay. Now was not the time to make any inopportune suggestions.

She'd asked him to step away, and that was exactly what he had done. It had taken much effort to not pursue any intimate possibilities. For some reason she didn't want to test the waters with him. He had to respect her request. But it wasn't easy.

There was no doubt what he needed to do now. "First I would like to apologize for not telling you sooner, especially about your mother. I should have confided in you, as a matter of respect."

She stared at him in a long moment of silence. He knew she must be assessing him, her senses fully open, looking for any conflicting emotions. Funny, he wasn't uncomfortable with it at all. Nodding slowly, she remained silent.

"Where would you like me to start?"

"There are a million questions, but I think you need to answer the most important one first. Why didn't you tell me?"

"Honestly, I was planning to, but the opportunity hadn't presented itself. It really isn't something you can say in passing, or talk about freely with everyone. Until I saw whether you would work out, I didn't want to take the chance. I've had troubles before speaking out too soon, so I've learned to keep my mouth shut."

He was glad when she seemed to relax.

"I have too. What kind of troubles have you had?"

"Same as you, I imagine. You know, people treat you different when there's something they consider abnormal about you." He grimaced in memory of past experiences. "I tried early on to talk about it with people. Guys sort of ignore it like they don't know you've said anything. Women are either unusually interested but freaked out about it, or I've had some who shy away and stay as far from me as possible. Even my own father thinks I'm involved in some evil magical wizardry."

"Is it evil? I don't know much about 'healing'. Most of what I've heard tends to be sort of negative. I can't see how it could be though. Such a positive thing couldn't come from something evil, could it?"

"Far from it," with a pause to collect his thoughts, he folded his hands over his knee in an open gesture. "What most people don't understand is it's not a power that comes from me. It comes through me. I am a vessel through which healing becomes possible. It's truly a gift from God, and I've been blessed with the ability to use it."

He looked straight into her eyes, hoping she would grasp the significance to what he said.

"So why don't you practice it openly? There'd be thousands to come see you. You could make millions."

He shook his head fervently. "This can't be taken lightly." He laid his hand on hers, knowing she'd sense his honesty. "For me it's not about money. I've been given this gift to help others, to offer them something they wouldn't be able to receive elsewhere. I will only heal where I'm led. To publicize it and bring glory to myself would dishonor God and my own beliefs. If I were to do that I wouldn't be who I am now."

Suzanna looked down at their joined hands then looked up again, her expression one of acceptance.

"You are very confident in what you say. You've thought about it for a long time, haven't you?"

Relieved she understood his personal decision to keep quiet, he smiled softly. "It hasn't been easy, but I feel very strong in what I've done."

"Why do you think you've been chosen?"

"That's a really good question. I've searched long and hard. The only plausible answer I've come up with comes from my background in the Romanian culture which is deeply rooted in the Christian belief."

He wasn't sure how far he should get into it, but decided it was all or nothing. If she didn't understand, then it would be up to her to decide what to do next.

"My Grandmother was very much a believer. She taught me all she knew and encouraged me to find the answers for myself. Of all the research I've done there is only one conclusion that made sense to me. Remember, the original and greatest healer of all was Jesus."

"True," Suzanna agreed thoughtfully.

"If you believe in God, or as some call it a 'higher being', then you know all things are possible. There are so many cultures that advocate natural healing, and a spiritual connection with this higher being. Many of them are much healthier than we are. Unfortunately, here in the States the most prominent focus is more on contemporary medical treatments. People, like you and I, are considered odd and out of place here. But, we wouldn't be elsewhere."

"That's for sure. I've often thought I was born in the wrong country. Maybe I wouldn't be considered such a freak if I were someplace else."

Nicholaus could see she connected to what he said on all levels. He felt as if he could tell her anything. Relief flooded over him in a wave when he realized he could finally open up. Normally his words were laced with reservation, depending on who he spoke to. Other than his grandmother, Mona had been the only one he'd been able to talk to, until now.

"You know, it doesn't really matter what you call Him. God, Allah, Buddha, it's all the same. In each culture, in their own way, the same cord of beliefs run through them. In Christianity it is believed that through a belief in Jesus our destiny has been saved. And through that belief we can perform the same types of miracles He did. In fact it speaks directly about it several places in the Bible."

"Do you really think so?" It was obvious she'd never considered this before.

"I know so. After all, I'm living proof, aren't I?"

"I guess so. Although I only know of a few things you've done here recently. I would love to hear about all the other things you've been able to do so far."

She was truly interested, not because it was strange, but because she wanted to know him better. Nicholaus was excited to have found someone to talk to about his life that wouldn't treat him like he was diseased or a specimen to be researched.

"What about you? Maybe we could swap stories sometime?"

She looked away, a slight blush tinting her cheeks. "There's not much to tell. I feel and sense things that don't belong to me. Kind of creepy really, I'm not sure what good it is."

"I can tell you it's an invaluable tool, especially to someone like me."

He watched the blush rise deeper into her cheeks.

She's never been praised for her abilities. She doesn't realize what a jewel she is.

She brushed it aside, as if untrue. "It's not anywhere close to being able to heal someone."

"Not true. I believe we've all been given something special with its own importance. In certain scriptures it talks about how all of us are blessed with different kinds of gifts, to be used in blessing others. Mine happens to be healing. I believe yours is empathy and true compassion."

"You think this is a gift? I'm not so sure. Most of my life I've felt it was a curse!" she laughed.

"I'm sure it felt that way sometimes," he said with a slight grimace. "There've been times in my life when I wished I could ignore it too." His thoughts turned briefly to his mother. Her choices in life had affected him and his father in so many ways. It still hurt to think about it. "But, I can't because it is who I am."

He saw Suzanna look at him as if waiting for him to say where his thoughts had turned, but he wasn't ready to go there yet. That part of his life would have to wait for another time.

After a few moments of silence she asked, "So you turned to healing animals, why is that?"

He wondered when that question would surface. "I suppose this might look selfish, but I've done it this way for some time because I haven't figured out a way to heal people without everything becoming a total disaster."

"You healed my mother."

"There's been a select few. Some are aware of what I am doing, others I've given some help as an added benefit of friendship."

"Like Mr. O'Brien?" Suzanna asked.

He confirmed with a brief nod.

"I suppose it would depend on who you think you can trust," she commented.

"I've felt the need to move further in my efforts. Haven't had time, until recently, to look into a way to do it."

They sat in silence, each in their own thoughts.

"What do you think this all means?"

Nicholaus hoped she would hear what he needed her to understand. "I believe we've been granted the ability to do all things. We have the ability, and everything we need to live peaceful, healthy and fruitful lives. Unfortunately, not everyone is capable of believing and achieving this. Our health is dependent on many things, and our thoughts contribute not only to our emotions, but to our physical health as well. Thoughts and emotions are choices that we have, and sometimes we allow our choices to lead us in the wrong way."

"So, because we choose not to believe we're unable to live the lives we are capable of?" Suzanna asked.

"Healing was, and still is, one of the great needs of Gods people. I truly believe He'd have me act in His name to heal the sick, and provide for the ones in need."

She looked away for a moment, when she looked back the slightest hint of moisture shone in her eyes. "So, do you think we are able to heal ourselves, too?"

"Yes, I do. So many are unable to believe in something they cannot see or feel, so they're unable to open themselves up to the possibilities." Her brief sadness prompted him, "Why do you ask?"

She shook her head, something akin to fear in her eyes. "No reason, I just wondered." She looked down at her clasped hands, "If all you say is true, this would change a lot of things in this world if everyone believed, wouldn't it?"

"Everything would change."

Nicholaus could see in her eyes a bevy of emotions pass through, each with its own affect. Her thoughts obviously had gone to a much different time and place. Then, returning to the present, she took his hand in hers and turned it over palm up.

"What are you looking for?" he asked softly.

She traced over his palm and fingers with her own then looked up to meet his eyes. "I wondered if there was anything to show me you are telling the truth."

"I think you can feel it. Can't you?"

Her gaze intoxicated him. He felt as if he'd been pulled into a pool of heat—a stormy pool of unanswered questions. Quietly she placed his palm back in his lap.

"You said it doesn't come from you. I see sparks of light that come from your fingers. What is that?"

Her touch had been like pouring brandy on the embers of a dying fire. He felt the flames, quick and ready, urgently waiting and hoping for more wood to burn. He had to back away from the fire or be burnt by his own actions. He nodded slowly to give himself a moment to settle.

"You probably remember in school they taught us all things are made up of atoms and neutrons. These particles of energy exist in all things. Sickness and ailments are a displacement of energy in its proper form. When I place a healing touch the healing energy coming to me from above and travels through me to the one in need. All I do is direct it toward a specific location, and ask for an intended outcome. That way the Higher Being knows exactly what we are asking to be healed."

"Funny, you really don't imagine it to be true when they say 'ask and you shall receive'. I guess what you're saying makes that true."

"Exactly, if you want something specific, you need to ask for it. If it agrees with what He has planned for you, then it will happen. That's why it doesn't work sometimes. What you've asked may not be in the overall plan for you here on earth. So, all we can do is believe it can be done and hope it's in His will."

Suzanna remained silent for a moment. "Wow, this is really deep. I'm going to have to think about this for a while. This opens up way too many possibilities," she said shaking her head.

"It took me a while to come to this point in my understanding, too. As for your being able to see the energy transfers from me, well, I'm not so sure. Most people can't see it. I think this might have to do with your sensate qualities."

"I suppose that makes sense," she agreed.

"I was researching the other day about your gift and found there are different types of empaths. You're obviously able to sense feelings of emotion as well as the physical sensory levels of other beings. You may be sensitive in other ways too. I'm not sure what it's called, but I remember reading something about it."

She shifted in her seat a bit. "I've looked into it some, though I haven't found anything I trust yet. It's hard enough trying to live with it. All those instructional books and websites are hard to follow, especially when you don't know what you are doing. I guess I need to look a little deeper. Mona gave me a name of a place she wants me to check out. She said she thinks it's time for me to find out what the possibilities are and realize I'm not the only one dealing with these types of abilities."

Nicholaus laughed. "She said the same to me. I only know what my grandmother taught me, what's available on the internet, and what I've discovered through my own practices. Where did she suggest you go?"

"It's got a strange name…something like 'Mittens'…No, wait, it's 'Gloves'. I've got the brochure in my purse if you want to see it."

"No need. It's the same one she wants me to see." From the couch he walked over to his desk and pulled a few loose pages he'd printed off the computer. Handing her the pages, he waited as she took a look at some of the services offered by the organization.

"Of course! The name is an acronym for 'Gifts of Love from the Eternal Spirit', or 'Gloves'. I hadn't put it together until now."

"I've made an appointment for Monday to speak to the founder. I'd like you to go with me." Nicholaus noted her look of surprise.

"Oh. Umm…well, I guess I could." Her brows knit with indecision.

Obviously she hadn't really thought about going yet. Nicholaus smiled. "Good. The appointment is early evening, after we close up here at the hospital."

Suzanna hesitated then nodded her head in agreement.

Nicholaus reached out and took Suzanna's hand in his. "Are we alright here?" He held her gaze for the longest time, her eyes searching for something he didn't know how to answer.

Lowering her gaze, she nodded and said in a small voice, "Yes."

"We won't keep anything from each other anymore. I promise."

The quick glance she returned in response bothered him. She was still keeping something from him. He wasn't sure what it was, but wouldn't let it drop for long without finding out what it was all about.

The bell on the front door sounded, and the yip of a small dog cued them it was time to get back to work.

* * * *

Suzanna started to bring the boxes in from her car when she heard the back door to the main house open. She stood up from her bent position to see Nicholaus come toward her. Brushing the moisture beads from her forehead, she smiled, delighted as he came closer. Even though she chose to have a positive outlook at all times, he always seemed to brighten her spirits when he was around.

"Need a hand?"

He smiled. His sparkling blue eyes lit up his whole face multiplying the positive energy she always felt surrounding him.

"That would be wonderful. I thought there'd only be a few boxes, but Mamma kept sneaking stuff in. I have no idea what's in them now. It'll be Christmas in July when I unpack."

When she reached into the car to pull out the next box it was larger than the rest and very awkward to handle. She struggled with it for a moment.

"Here, let me get that one."

Nicholaus had come up behind her, so as she straightened and turned around their bodies bumped lightly, his face mere inches from hers. He reached out to steady her, which brought her closer than she'd already been.

Suzanna gasped in surprise. Their closeness knocked the air out of her lungs. She couldn't breathe. She desperately wanted to reach up and drag his mouth down to hers, to press her body against his and feel the full impact of his muscular body next to hers. She knew a flush rose to her cheeks as she imagined what it would be like.

He looked deep into her eyes, as if searching for an answer then politely stepped away. He'd lingered long enough for Suzanna to sense he'd felt the same unsettling sensations.

"Pardon me. Let me get those big boxes. You can open up the trunk to see what's in there."

Unable to speak, she could only nod her head and slip past him toward the back of the car. From behind the trunk lid she took a deep breath to steady herself. Never before had she felt a physical attraction so strong. Even with her blocking techniques she couldn't ignore her response to him. They were like two magnets of opposite poles pulled together whether willing or not.

Not now. Not possible.

Suzanna squared her shoulders and put on a smile to cover the reality to her world. Grabbing a box to head inside, she turned and almost bumped into Nicholaus again.

Oh, God, this definitely won't be easy.

After a couple of trips, everything in the car was now sitting in an array of mishap all over the living room floor. Anxious to unpack, she surveyed where to start first. She'd looked forward to this all week long. It was as if the house had been waiting for her to come, and this move could only be described as the right thing to do.

"That's all of the boxes. My cousin, Roberto, will bring by the few pieces of furniture I have sometime this morning. Oh, and a mattress will be delivered this afternoon."

"Are you going to retrieve Cali today? She's beginning to display caged animal behavior."

"As soon as everyone stops with the foot traffic I'll get her. I know she must be going nuts."

"I'm sure she is." Nicholaus reached out and put his hand on her shoulder. "I hope this works out to be what you need."

The significance of his statement and his generosity hit her. Suzanna wasn't sure if he knew how much she'd needed this movement in her life.

"Thank you so much for everything Nicholaus. This is more than I could ever have expected to find. I can't tell you how much it means to me."

The job, the pet, the house, there was no doubt this was an unmistakable blessing. Without thinking, she went with her natural inclination to friendliness, and gave him a quick hug and a light kiss on the cheek. Or at least that was what she'd meant it to be.

The simplest of hugs turned out to be not so simple at all. His arms came up to give a returned light embrace, yet when she felt the pressure of his body against hers the rush of delightful sexuality was instantaneous. The impact so extreme, she felt her knees weaken.

Oh man, why do I keep doing this to myself?

She should have known better. The natural action she would have done with anyone differed with him. His arms, so strong yet gentle, and the brush of his cheek against her hair she knew were not intended to stoke the fires of passion, yet she could feel the increased energy as he continued to hold her.

And then he softly pressed his lips against her forehead in a way that made her heart flutter with a profuse undeniable response.

God, I wish I could show you what you do to me!

She needed to sever the connection, or give in to the urgency of her own feelings. Thinking him unaware of what she felt, she gave a quick squeeze and stepped away. Nicholaus' expression confused her. His lips were grim, but his eyes smiled which made them sparkle with laughter.

How does he know what I'm thinking?

The intense flush traveled from her sensitized breasts to her cheeks with light speed as she brushed past him in her effort to get as far away as possible. In the kitchen, she opened the refrigerator and pulled out a couple of bottles of iced tea she'd tucked away earlier.

"It turned out to be hot today. Would you like some iced tea? Sorry, I don't have any ice yet. I think they're cold enough." She spoke faster than she needed to in an unsuccessful attempt to dismiss the awkwardness of the situation.

When she turned around she found him leaning against the kitchen doorway. He blocked any type of quick escape, but she couldn't tell if it was intentional or not. The blue sleeveless T-shirt he wore showed his tanned sculpted arms and the firm outlines of an equally muscled chest. Luscious hair dampened by the heat curled haphazardly around his face. The smile he now wore showed his comfortable easy style. His head was tilted to the side as if he'd watched her reach into the refrigerator, appreciating the view from behind. This brought more heat to her already flushed face.

Suzanna handed him the bottle and watched as he drank a healthy portion of its contents. He set the emptied bottle back down on the counter then began to walk slowly toward her. His movement had purpose, the look on his face intense and without humor. Whatever this was, it was totally serious.

She tried not to participate in the role of a smitten woman overwhelmed by the charm and muscles of a good-looking man. Unfortunately, she'd not yet recovered from their last touch. His eyes, bright with object intent, captivated her ability to move. It felt impossible to act indifferent as she had before, so the next best thing would be to feign indignity and become defensive.

"You're in my way. Let me through."

"Is that what you really want?"

Not knowing what she'd do if he touched her again, she put her hands on her hips and tried to pull in as much power as she could muster.

"I told you before, I'm...I'm not interested," her voice broke as she started to panic, not in fear, but in total wanton submission to the man who came toward her.

"I hoped you might reconsider. You can't tell me you aren't interested. I find it curious, every time I get close to you there is nothing but interest, attraction, and a hell of a lot more." By this time, he'd inched her back against the wall, his body again only a breath away. "You can't deny you want this as much as I do."

The wall behind her stopped any type of escape as his body pressed against hers. He reached up to cup the back of her neck in his palm, his eyes never leaving hers. Slowly, he pulled her mouth to his.

There was no fighting it anymore—she gave in without pretense. Her continued resistance was futile. She could do nothing *but* respond, and closed her eyes to drink fully of the feeling he aroused.

In a fervent battle of urgent need they began to explore the passions their locked lips ignited. He tasted of sweet tea and heat, his essence enticing her to search for more. She nipped at his lower lip, then again came back to the lips that enthralled her. The contrast between salty and sweet pleased her immensely. She wrapped her arms around his body to pull him closer, desire overtaking her every move. He took and she gave. Two wills equally matched, both vying for position.

Suddenly the true knowledge of what she'd only imagined became reality, and to be touched by him with such passion, brought all of her fears forth. The sound that came from her throat now was not of passion but dismay, a whimper in the face of her own internal conflict. Unable to speak, she quickly dropped her arms and stiffened, attempting to ward off any further physical connection with him. She hoped he'd get the message.

Nicholaus pulled away, his eyes a dark steely gray. He reached up to wipe away the tear she'd tried to hold back as it slid down her cheek.

"Hey, hey…I'm sorry. I shouldn't have rushed you. You're killin' me here. I've never made a woman cry with a kiss."

Shaking her head in fierce denial, she pushed past him to find some space. What had happened was more than she'd ever imagined could be possible. His arduous attentions sparked an equally fervent passion inside of her. She felt as if she were about to combust. Every atom in her being raced around in a feverish rush, as if her body had taken over all sensible thought and now controlled her actions. Desperate to give in to the pure sexuality he'd forced her to see within herself.

She placed her hands on either side of the windowsill and stared out into the gardens, forcing her body to surrender back to reasonable functionality. The fear of reality was much stronger than her need for him. The pain of seeing him look at her in disgust when he found out what was wrong with her would devastate her. She couldn't face again another failed attempt at trying to be normal. Not with him.

"Are you all right?"

It was impossible to lie to him now, neither could she tell him the reason she'd pulled away. At some point she may have to. For right now all she could do was plead with his sense of right and wrong.

She forced up her wall of defense, the perpetuated strong front in the face of total internal disaster, and turned to face him. To her surprise her body shook, her fortitude not yet strengthened. She did her best to show a calm, strong outer demeanor.

Nicholaus came forward and took her hand in his. She couldn't stop the helpless tremble of her hand in his.

"Why are you afraid of me? What have I done to scare you?"

She found it hard to look him in the eyes, but took a deep breath and looked over his shoulder at the blank wall.

"It's not you. I'm not scared of you." She made herself look him in the eyes and went for the plea. "You're right. I am very attracted to you. I can't keep lying about it. Don't ask me to tell you why. Before when I told you not to approach me in that way I should have told you the truth. I just can't do this right now. Please, if you care, do what I ask."

She could sense frustration rush through him now. His frown confirmed he was trying to decide how to proceed with her request.

"It may be none of my business, but have you been abused?"

The question shocked her. She had to admit it was a valid question.

"No."

His expressive face told her of his disbelief. She pulled her hand away from him and crossed her arms over her chest.

"I can't get involved right now. It just wouldn't work out, anyway. It never has before. Please try to understand I can't allow there to be any intimate contact."

As she'd hoped, her defensive gesture made him take a step away from her.

"I can see you aren't going to tell me what this is all about yet, so I'll do as you ask. I can't promise not to be interested. You feel it the same as I do."

Nicholaus took a few steps toward the door then stopped. "There is something between us I think could be awesome. Don't put me in the same category as everyone else. I'm different, and you know it. I don't give up that easy, so when you're ready, I'll be waiting for you."

Chapter Nine

Nicholaus tried to do some research for a presentation he needed to prepare. A recent article he'd written on the increasingly popular non-invasive laser surgery prompted an invite from the Associated Veterinarian's Conference organizers. Yet every time he tried to focus on his speech, his thoughts would wander to Suzanna.

He'd heard Suzanna drive up earlier. Anxious for her to arrive, he knew she'd be bringing her belongings today. At the mere sight of her, his body went on alert. He had hoped by not forcing further contact he had worn down her resolve to not get involved. But his body took control of all logical thought and he'd pushed too far. Now it was abundantly clear, their connection was undeniable, though it produced a strange and unexpected reaction from her.

As he sat at his desk, he focused on what happened. Her clean female lines, accentuated by her exotic coloring, had been the precursor to what tempted him.

She affected him in so many ways. The mere thought of her created a physical response in him that was almost embarrassing. He uncrossed his legs in an attempt for more comfort.

Her hair, tied up in a knot at the top of her head, showed the slender line of her neck. It made him want to take a nibble just behind the ear where he imagined his touch would drive her crazy. He could still visualize her dressed in the tight tank top that molded to her noticeable curves, and the matching shorts showcasing her long, bare legs. This combination with an avid imagination made his mouth water, and his fantasies flourish.

He couldn't keep his hands off of her. When given the opportunity he'd acted on his hormonal urges, regretful as they were. When their lips met the kiss was meant to be light, but the small moan that rumbled deep within her was all it took to release his control. Almost as if the vibratory sound turned on a switch.

He wanted her. He wanted all of her.

As her lips parted for him, he'd held back his own moan when all of the wonderful tastes and textures he'd imagined materialized.

Then, in the middle of the most erotic moment of his life, in a flash the chain link fence went up between them. Through the fence he could still see her, the temptation remained, but the blazing physical connection was severed by an anxiety he'd not yet identified. Torn by the raging sensuality between them and the obvious pain it caused, the panicked look in her eyes distressed him.

She wouldn't come right out to tell him what distressed her, so he needed to figure out a way to get her to open up. Then they could move on to discover what possibilities lay ahead. For the time being, it seemed best to stay out of her way.

Nicholaus stayed in his office the rest of the afternoon. He could see the activity through her front door from his office window. He couldn't seem to concentrate on anything—anything but her, that is.

If she weren't interested in a relationship, she sure as hell wouldn't respond the way she did. He'd felt the urgent sexual need erupt as he held her. The further he delved, the more she seemed to want to give, bringing forth one of the most amazing feelings he'd ever experienced. This wasn't a simple physical attraction for him. If it were, he could satisfy his urges elsewhere. There was more to it than a simple match of gravitational chemistry. No way could he allow her to ignore something of such magnitude.

He closed the lid to his laptop and got up to pace the confines of his office floor. No doubt, her fears had chained themselves to her freedom with such weight she was unable to let go even in the face of her own extreme need. Fear, the most debilitating emotion known to mankind, had become Suzanna's stronghold.

He made the mistake of acting to quickly on his raging hormonal urges. She needed time to see he was different than anyone else, and could be trusted.

He paced back and forth pondering what he should do. Maybe she felt the physical relationship was all he wanted. That couldn't be farther from the truth. For the first time ever, he felt more than a passing urge to satisfy a need. Intelligent, gentle and sincere, being sexy beyond reason was only an added bonus. She inspired him to finally be his true self. The ability to talk freely with each other about their abilities without fear of judgment was freeing, and couldn't be overlooked.

He craved the snippets of time they shared, and wanted to find out more about her. He wanted to discover everything she struggled with, and how she grew to be such a beautiful woman. Understanding her was as important to him as exploring the need to know her in an intimate physical manner. He yearned to reveal all the things he instinctively knew to be true about their connection. To know her in a way he'd known no other. On all levels, emotionally, shared in the spirit, and unveiled by the physical union of two bodies.

Tapping his fingers on his thigh, Nicholaus shook his head slightly. Not many knew that he hadn't been involved with too many women. Even so, somehow what he experienced with Suzanna felt different. He needed to preserve what they had built so far, and see how this feeling could grow even deeper. Yet every time he got close to her his body took control of his ability to think. Just like Mona said, if he didn't proceed with care, he knew his actions would mean the end to a potentially strong relationship before it had been given a chance to start.

Taking things slow with her had to be the only answer. He needed to guide her to understand this was different, and help her want to explore what he envisioned between them. In the meantime, as tempted as he was, he'd have to put a kibosh on the hormones for a while.

He heard the back door open. She'd come in, no doubt to retrieve Cali and take the feline to her new home. He moved as swift as he could, wanting to catch Suzanna before she had a chance to leave.

As she pulled Cali from the cage, Suzanna's quiet laugh was muffled as the cat rubbed its nose against her face.

"Yes, Cali, this is the end to your stay here in your tiny cage. You're coming home to stay with me." Like the revving of an engine, the cat began to purr in enthusiastic spurts. Bringing the cat closer for a hug increased the volume. "You're welcome. Come on. Let's go explore the house together, shall we?"

When she turned to leave, again Nicholaus' close proximity surprised her. She hadn't felt him come into the room.

He's jumbled all of my abilities. Control is gone. I must have my guard up so thick up, Houdini couldn't get through.

Unable to handle any more of emotional upheaval she'd withdrawn and blocked all outer energies since that morning's catastrophe.

"Oh! You startled me."

"I'm sorry. I didn't want to disturb your conversation with Cali. She seems pretty happy to be leaving this place. Can't blame her there, I wouldn't want to be in a cage that long either." His smile was somehow different. It was soft, and inviting.

Suzanna looked away, knowing better than to fall back into his charms. She wasn't mad at him, but she knew it would be wise to be wary of any more close encounters.

"Well, I better get her home before she gets antsy. I'm sure she could use some exercise."

He reached up to touch her arm. Without hesitation she pulled away. She was glad to see her change in expression must have been enough to make him bring his hand back to his side.

"I would like to apologize for my actions earlier."

She'd been thinking about doing the same. It wasn't his fault she sent him mixed messages. She shook her head to emphasize her next words. "It's really not necessary. I'm sorry, too. I overreact to things sometimes."

"What happened was pretty intense, I don't blame you for reacting the way you did."

Blushing, she acknowledged his apology. "Thank you for understanding."

"Sometimes, against my better judgement, I lead with my hormones, instead of my head. Even then I can be kind of bull headed. I haven't been showing you my best side as of late.

How about if we forget what happened, and we start over again, as friends?"

Cautious, she looked at him, but couldn't sense any coercion for purposes other than what he stated. She did want to know him better. She liked what she saw in him, and appreciated who he was. Friends were hard to come by when you were created in a different mold than the norm. It would be nice to have someone to talk to when things got weird.

She replied with a shy nod, "I'd like that."

"I know you probably haven't had a chance to put your kitchen together yet. So, what would you say to us going to get a beer and a pizza at The Independent Pizzeria on 42nd? It's only a few blocks away through Madison Park. We could take a walk." When she didn't readily agree, as if reading her mind he went on to explain his intention. "I figure friends do that kind of thing for each other. As hard as you worked today, I'm sure you're starving. I know I am. Pizza sounds like the best solution to me."

Suzanna nodded. "I am hungry." It may not be the best decision she ever made, though his offer seemed simple enough. "No funny stuff, right?"

Holding his hands up in the air in an attempt to show innocence, he smiled. "None. Whatsoever!"

"Alright, I'll go show Cali around the house, and I'll be back over in a few."

* * * *

They took the walk in the beautiful evening air the short distance through the park to the local pizzeria. Once seated, Suzanna studied Nicholaus and discovered her surprise at how comfortable she'd been with him. They talked with ease as they walked, about the weather, and sights along the way. He made her laugh, and she began to relax her guard. He didn't push for romance, but she couldn't let herself forget what he said before. He wouldn't give up.

As impossible as it seemed, now she wondered if she really wanted him to.

Maybe there is a way, she thought as she glanced at his handsome face.

She felt herself blush when his eyes caught hers. She recognized he knew she had been gazing at him. The corner of his mouth turned upward in a slight grin as he looked back down to the menu.

As hungry as she was, she agreed without argument on a simple pepperoni pizza, extra sauce and cheese. Suzanna sat back and watched Nicholaus as the waiter served their beers. Her silence didn't seem to bother him. He appeared comfortable in the environment, listening to the 70's oldies playing on the jukebox.

She found she couldn't stop thinking about him. Beyond her reaction to his physical touch, there was something about him which left her wanting more.

"Tell me about your Grandmother. She sounds like a wonderful woman."

The smile in his eyes brought life to hidden memories. She'd picked the right subject to talk about.

"She was. *Bunica* was a definite godsend to me. She cared for me like a mother, and taught me all I know about healing. She'd say, '*You have the gift Nicholaus, use it wisely*'," he said mimicking his grandmother's voice.

"*Bunica* was her name?" Suzanna asked.

"No, sorry, that's Grandmother in Romanian. When she and I talked she would insist I speak the language. I forget sometimes."

"I can see you loved her very much."

His face softened as he spoke of her. The lines at the corners of his eyes would crinkle as he remembered some of the humorous ways of his *bunica*. Relaying the stories of his beloved grandmother, Suzanna could see him as a boy at the sleeves of his teacher and mentor. No doubt healing wasn't the most important thing his *bunica* shared with him. The development of the interpersonal relationship between them ran so deep, nothing else mattered.

"She loved me with no conditions. If I failed at what she expected of me, and believe me I did, she'd smile and bring me back to where I needed to be."

"No, you straying, I don't believe it." Suzanna surprised herself at the playful sarcasm which came so easily with him.

"You can believe it!" His returned playfulness made her smile. "I was no saint growing up, far from it. What I knew most of all was *Bunica* loved me, and I did my best, such as it was."

"I can imagine you were a handful." She picked her next topic with care. Not sure how to ask the next question, she did what she did best, and asked from an honest heart. "I haven't heard you talk much about your mother and father. Are they still around?"

As before, she saw a temporal shadow cover his expression, as he decided how to respond. Something in his parental relationship affected him deeply. Her sense of his deep sudden sadness overtook her curiosity.

"I'm sorry. I shouldn't have asked the question. This makes you sad. You don't have to tell me if you don't want to."

He shook his head. "I forget you can sense things. It's all right. I should be able to handle it by now."

"Things which affect us in an extreme way don't always go away completely," she said, thinking of her own family.

Nicholaus gave a half smile of acknowledgement. "My father lives a little way out of town, in the house I grew up in. I don't get to see him as often as I would like. Then as you know, he doesn't care for the direction I've taken with my life."

Suzanna stayed silent, knowing there was more to follow.

"My mother left us when I was fairly young, maybe seven or eight. Where she is right now, I couldn't tell you. We haven't talked since she called me on my fifteenth birthday."

Sorrow filled her heart. Now she understood.

"That is so sad! How could a woman leave her child like that?"

He shrugged his shoulders in feigned disinterest, and replied flatly, "Guess there were bigger and better things to explore. She had the gift too," he paused in personal thought. Then he looked up into Suzanna's face, with an anger not easily hidden. "From what I understand someone offered her a hell of a lot of cash to become their puppet."

"That's no excuse."

"*Bunica* tried to stay in touch with her, but after a while my mother stopped answering her calls. She didn't even come back for *Bunica's* funeral." He took a long drink from his beer then set the glass back down with a clink. "Enough about me. What about your parents? I know your mother a bit. Tell me more about her, and your father. I understand you aren't originally from here. Where did you grow up?"

"There isn't much to tell. My mother is originally from Michoacan, Mexico. She came up to Washington to live with family for a while then moved to California to start a new life. She met my father in Sacramento, and that is where my sister and I were born. We lived there until I was about eight. Dad left us the year before we came up here. We struggled for a while, but made out alright. I guess we have more in common than I thought. Dad still comes around on occasion, when he's feeling guilty or something. He's okay, just not what you'd call father material."

Nicholaus looked at her, his eyes soft with understanding. "It doesn't matter which parent leaves. It still hurts just as bad. I don't envy your having to deal with it over and over again every time he decides to come around."

"For some reason, I didn't notice too much."

That's an interesting revelation, she thought, her brows creasing. *Why was that?*

"Anyway, mom's sister offered us a place to live, so she moved back up to Sequim. Mom's family believes in taking care of each other."

"Where is Sequim anyway? I've heard it's a beautiful place."

"Oh, it is very beautiful. On the north end of the Washington Peninsula, there are trees and mountains on one side, and all the water and sea life you could want at your fingertips." Growing up there in her younger years had been her saving grace—always someplace to escape.

"Sounds awesome, I'll have to go sometime." Nicholaus took a long swallow of his beer. "Do you have other siblings?"

"No, there's just my sister, Rachel."

"Is your sister younger or older?"

"I'm the baby. She's six years older than I am. Rachel lives with her husband and two kids close to here. They found this awesome house out in the Capitol Hill area. She's so lucky."

"Are you still close to your sister?"

Smiling to herself, she thought of how she liked to remember their past relationship. "We used to be. I'm told, before we moved up here you couldn't tear us apart. I'm not too sure what happened. After Dad left, it seemed like she always hated me. She won't tell me why. She just says I was a pesky little sister. Maybe I really was, but I don't remember much detail up until we moved."

"I suppose families grow apart sometimes." His compassionate expression didn't hide the fact he was unsure of something.

Ignoring her senses, she responded to the statement. "I guess. I wish we could be close again. But, then I found Lucy, you know, Mona's daughter. She's just like a sister."

"Of course, she's a character," Nicholaus laughed.

"She and I have become best friends. After we moved over here for my mother's job, Junior High was really hard for me, until I got to know Lucy. Ever since then we've been buddies, causing Mona all kinds of trouble."

"I bet," Nicholaus said, with a chuckle.

Suzanna reminisced for a few minutes about some of the upheaval they had caused. "I still remember Mona coming home to find us with the biggest bowl of popcorn you've ever seen. We must have popped six or eight bags, we were so hungry." She giggled at the memory. "Though, she did give us the evil eye and some strong words about us possibly smoking some pot."

"I'm sure she took care of your munchies, and all your other ailments along the way. She's the mother of all mothers, and has blessed me with her presence every day for the last nine years." He obviously knew Mona well.

"I practically lived at their house until graduation. Lucy and I went everywhere together. Mona understood everything. She always knew the right thing to say and do." Her thoughts drifted to the times she'd needed her most. "She helped me through a lot of tough times. I don't know what I would have done without her."

Nicholaus nodded. "I don't know what I would have done either, which brings us to what she's asked us to do. How are you feeling about checking out Gloves?"

For some time now, Suzanna had reflected on this very question. "I know I need to find out more about being a sensate. Mona keeps telling me when it is time I will find out what I need to know. I think it's time now."

"You may be surprised. I'm sure you've only seen the tip of the iceberg of who you are. There's a lot more underneath, you haven't even discovered," Nicholaus encouraged.

"That's the scary part. What if I can't handle what's underneath?"

He reached out to take one of her hands in his and squeezed it gently. The simple gesture of support had tremendous meaning to Suzanna. "I know you can handle more than you think."

Through their connected hands, the warmth and the encouragement permeated through his palm.

"I hope so." She looked up and posed the same question. "What about you? How are you feeling about Monday?"

With the release of her hand, he sat back as he considered her question. "I'm ready for it. I've gone as far as I can by myself. What *Bunica* taught me were the things she knew from her own experiences, what had been passed down for generations."

"Was she a healer too?"

"Not in the same way as my mother and I. She learned the art of natural healing from her mother, using herbs and minerals. In their time they were considered witches. In reality they were only making use of the resources God gave us here on earth."

"But if your grandmother taught you about your ability are there others in your family she learned from."

"You're right. My great-great grandfather had the gift they say, but there aren't many records so long ago. There's no doubt I've got much more to master. If there's ever one thing *bunica* taught me, it's you can never stop learning. I just hope Gloves won't try to push me into something I don't feel is right. That's where the experience would end."

"For me too," Suzanna agreed. "I made up my mind a long time ago I would never let anyone push me into doing something I'm not ready for. My mother tells me I've always been that way, although…she calls it stubborn."

Nicholaus' gaze caught her eye. "Why do you think that is?" There was more depth to his question than she'd expected, which surprised her. The true meaning of his question lay somewhere under the surface, and she wasn't sure how to interpret it at this point.

She shrugged, nothing came to mind. "Part of my character I suppose."

Any further conversation stopped as the pizza was served. The heavenly aroma wafted through the air, tantalizing her taste buds. Suzanna dove for a piece, her hunger outweighing the need for communication.

They ate in silence until the initial hunger subsided. Looking satisfied, Nicholaus sat back on the seat and wiped his fingers on a napkin. As she no longer felt the need to fight for the next piece, Suzanna selected another slice with unnecessary care.

"I can't believe you're going for another piece. I'm stuffed!"

Suzanna smiled and looked up from her prize long enough to catch his eye before she bit into the delectable tidbit.

Oddly, as she chewed the morsel, she felt the need to make sure he watched her every move.

"I eat very slowly, and enjoy every bite. Unlike those of you, who bite and swallow, just to fill the void."

She licked the sauce from her lips, enjoying the various tastes and aromas, and placed each finger in her mouth to get every last drop of goodness. She realized her flirtatious actions had tantalized something more than his taste buds. She watched as his eyes became a darker shade of steel, his jaw tensing.

She couldn't deny her feelings any longer. The attraction would be there whether she wanted it to be or not. She couldn't help but want him to desire her, too. Without thought, she kept finding herself thinking, and acting in ways not conducive to being a forced celibate.

A blush heated her skin from the inside out. She lowered her eyes and finished the rest of her slice, a bit quicker than she would normally.

"Well, I think I'm finished for now. I better get back to Cali. This is her first night at the house, and I'd better be there."

She glanced back in time to catch Nicholaus' eyes as they changed back to their usual vibrant blue. Shaking his head, he laughed softly and slid out from the seat to offer her a hand.

Their walk home was quiet. Dusk had set. A deep glow of the evening sunset bowed out for the evening to the west, the view of Lake Washington majestic. The barest hint of color remained on the surface of the water, reminding Suzanna of a picture she once saw called '*Reflections*'. The colors of the landscape replicated a mirror like image on the glassy canvas of the lake. As they approached her front door, she wished the evening didn't have to end so soon. She'd enjoyed their time together, and found she craved more.

"Thank you so much for the dinner." Without thought she leaned forward and brushed a kiss across his cheek.

She realized her mistake when she felt the immediate increase of his blood flow. A bit disconcerted, she waited for his response, unsure if he would take action on her gesture. Instead he reached out and took her hand in his. Without saying a word he brought her hand up to his lips, this time it was he who made sure she watched his every move. In slow, seductive movements he turned her hand over and kept his eyes locked on hers as he pressed his lips to her palm. The heat from his lips sent tongues of fire up her arm. She feared he would feel the tremor his touch caused to run through her body leaving her breathless.

The slightest glimmer of a knowing smile came to his eyes as he whispered, "It was my pleasure. Sweet dreams." He turned and strode to his house, without as much as a glance back.

"Damn," Suzanna muttered, going in to search for Cali.

That night her nightmares attacked without mercy, drenching her in hidden fears and unexplained meanings. Suzanna sat, hugging her knees to her chest, exhausted to the bone. When Cali jumped to the bed she began incessantly rubbing her head against Suzanna's hand which lay limp against the covers. Soon, Suzanna realized she missed the comfort of another being and appreciated the feline's effort to calm her frazzled nerves.

Chapter Ten

Monday turned out to be slower than Suzanna expected. Two of the scheduled appointments cancelled and left her the barest amount of paperwork to occupy her time. Due to anticipation of the upcoming meeting at Gloves, a sickened knot in her stomach grew stronger as the day drew to an end. It was either that or the rough morning start had gotten to her. During her nights, sleep evaded her as the nightmare started to repeat itself, interrupting a peaceful nights rest with an almost expected appearance rather than an unusual inconvenience.

Not knowing what to expect from Gloves disturbed her. Did people walk around practicing their skills, or did they secret away in little rooms where nobody could see what they were doing? Healer, clairvoyant, sensate, astral projection, ghost reader were only a few she could remember reading about. The abilities they purported to support were endless—each with a different set of services available. Would the groups be kept separate, or would they mingle together as one collection of gifted individuals?

This is where she wished her overactive imagination would take a break.

"Are you ready to go?" Nicholaus asked from behind her.

Suzanna turned to see his change of clothes from every day casual jeans to a pair of black slacks and a gray sweater, the color of which made his eyes seem brighter and more vibrant. His sleeves were pushed up to show the sinewy shape of his forearm, and the form fitting nature of the sweater showed his muscular shoulders and slender waist. Unfortunately, her stare hadn't gone unnoticed, and Suzanna felt heat rise to the surface as the corner of his mouth turned up in a silent grin.

"I've been ready all day long." Unsure of what to expect, she'd changed her attire as well for the early evening meeting.

She'd put on a simple broomstick skirt in rich deep colors of purple and blue. The black gauze peasant blouse, worn over a fitted chemise, revealed her curves enough to entice the male eye. She'd left her long black hair loose pinned up on one side using an antique clip of European design.

"My *Bunica* would have been proud of you. You're a beauty," Nicholaus said in approval.

"Nonsense, I wear what looks good to me." Silently pleased by the compliment, she told herself she hadn't worn the clothing for his benefit. Or had she?

"If I didn't know any better, I'd say you were a gypsy come back from the past to claim my heart." She could feel the heat at her cheeks as he continued his gaze, smiling he brushed a gentle thumb along her jaw line. "Shall we see what this 'Gloves, Inc.' is all about?"

The phone rang making Suzanna jump, though she was thankful it distracted her from the persistent ache in her heart. This constant need to be wrapped in his arms again wouldn't go away.

"I…I better get that," she exclaimed with exuberance. Nicholaus' grin told her she hadn't fooled him. He seemed to know exactly how she felt about him. "Brach's Veterinary Hospital, how may I help you?" Suzanna paused for a second, surprised by the response, then handed the phone to Nicholaus.

"This is Nicholaus Brach," his professional air turned steely as he listened to the caller. Suzanna sensed him quickly force up the walls around his emotions and become void of all feeling, at least on the outside. "No, that won't be necessary. I don't care to meet with you." The thickness in his voice betrayed his outward appearance. He did care. "Do what you want. It makes no difference to me. Goodbye."

He hung up the phone and turned toward the door then stopped. Suzanna wasn't sure what to do. She knew how deeply the phone call had affected him. He turned back around, his eyes hardened by an emotion she could only describe as antipathetic.

"Before you ask, yes, that was my mother. She's back in town and wants to meet."

"Oh, Nicholaus, I know that can't be easy."

"To say the least," he grimaced. "And no, I'm not going to see her. There is no point."

"Give it some time, maybe you'll change your mind." Suzanna hoped he would rethink his immediate reaction. Contrary to what she'd expected, she'd sensed a genuine love from the woman's voice on the phone.

"Not likely." His terse response told her to drop it for now. Her heart went out to him. His lost relationship with his mother was tearing him apart. "Let's go."

The woman had sounded so hopeful. Suzanna saw this as a sign. It might be the chance needed to renew at least some connection between the two of them. Even if it was just a closure to the hurt he held so deep inside. Maybe there was some way she could help this to happen.

* * * *

The brick building appeared nondescript and rather plain on the outside, a small sign hanging over the door stated "Gloves, Inc." Except for the landscaped grounds surrounding the building, this looked similar to the other industrial warehouses in the area.

Suzanna paused to assess the environment before she followed Nicholaus inside. Upon entry, she almost turned around to leave as the immediate force of an active energy overwhelmed her. It wasn't a bad energy. It just surprised her with the immense power it held. Positive energies flowed in every direction, from every individual, from every object, each oddly enough connected as a whole. Nicholaus stood beside her just inside the door assessing the whole picture.

She saw the original three-story warehouse had been transformed into a beautiful open sanctuary, seeming as if they'd stepped into the Garden of Eden. On either side of the building stairways connected to the higher levels, which led to more open spaces and an occasional closed room along the outside walls. People mingled everywhere, some small groups engaged in collective conversations while individuals moved past on their way to achieve a goal of importance. She sensed an intense emotion of commitment and elation throughout the building. A strong dedication to a task at hand, intermixed with a joy of accomplishing the intended result, flowed from everyone. Stirring Suzanna's interest the most was the love and peace surrounding everyone in a very unusual way.

"Seems fairly normal," Suzanna came from behind Nicholaus as they moved further into the entryway.

"What did you expect to see, monsters and demons?" answered a voice from behind them.

Startled, Suzanna turned and saw a stunning woman. She appeared to be in her sixties, tall and slender from obvious discipline and hard work. She wore a tailored designer pantsuit in a rich plum color, her graying hair swept up in a classical coiffure. The attractive length curled and gathered at the back of her head to show a slender neckline.

The woman reached out and offered her hand. "Welcome, you must be Nicholaus and Suzanna. My name is Marianne Ross. I'm the founder of Gloves. Sarah told me you'd be coming by this evening."

After the exchange of polite introductions, Marianne led them to a charming seating area amongst the boughs of a Japanese red maple tree, and invited them to sit. From where she sat, Suzanna could see the roof had been constructed of some type of translucent material. The design allowed the stars to shine through at night and the sun to nourish the gorgeous array of plants and miniature trees during the day. She chose to stick close to Nicholaus, as her senses were picking up on a little more than she could handle all at once. She needed something familiar to anchor herself. They both sat still, gazing in awe at their surroundings.

"I've waited a long time to meet the both of you," Marianne started. Suzanna looked at her with inquisitive interest. "Mona has told me quite a bit about you over the years."

"I wondered how Mona knew about this place. How long have you known each other?" Suzanna asked.

Marianne smiled. "She and I have known each other since college, a little over forty years. She helped me in the formation stages of this organization. She'd have still been with me if we didn't have that falling out so long ago. A different time in our lives, and thank God we both came to our senses."

Suzanna felt the woman's openness. Evasion or mistruths did not seem to be one of her characteristics. "Is that why she never mentioned you before now?"

"That and Mona tends to keep to herself about things of this nature. It wasn't until recently she began to admit she has a rather unusual gift. That was one of our lines of contention, I knew she had it, but she wouldn't talk about it."

"Did you know she had a gift?" Nicholaus prompted Suzanna.

Shaking her head, Suzanna responded, "I had no idea."

Marianne shifted the subject with expertise. "Instead of me boring you talking about a long history of the organization, why don't you ask me some questions? Maybe then we can piece together what you need answered."

Suzanna felt Nicholaus was anxious to start, but he first looked to her to give her the chance to begin. She gave him a slight nod, and he turned to ask, "We've read your brochures. You provide quite a lot of support, without charging any kind of fees. What I'd like to know is how can this be possible? What is the goal of the organization? Why does it exist, and what do you get out of it?"

Marianne took a long look at Nicholaus.

"You are a very insightful young man. You will have to excuse me if I seem hesitant in answering sometimes, my clairvoyance gets in the way, especially with new acquaintances."

Suzanna wondered if Marianne could read their minds. She'd never met anyone who had the ability before, but she thought she would have felt it if she had.

"I will tell you up front I don't use my gift without anyone's acceptance. My senses tend to go on alert when I'm talking with someone new. Don't worry. I won't look unless you ask me to," Marianne said, looking directly at Suzanna.

"That's a relief," Suzanna said under her breath.

"In answer to your question, I began this organization as a tool for others who also have chosen to use their extended sensory perceptions and abilities to connect with the universe."

"How many people do you help?" Suzanna asked amazed at the number of people she saw milling about.

"We have over two hundred members at the moment," she responded, then continued her account. "These people have connections far beyond the average person, and are often misinterpreted or misused. Being gifted myself, I found it difficult at times to make close relationships with others who didn't understand how I felt, hence couldn't understand the differences in our experiences."

"So, you started this in the 1960's? It must have been an unusual time to be dealing with this type of thing," Nicholaus stated.

"Very true, there was not much support, at least from people not considered potheads or druggies. It was hard at first, though over the years acceptance has blossomed. But I felt strongly about the need I saw around me. Originally, I formed Gloves as a networking opportunity and an outlet for these individuals to meet others like them. In order to understand oneself it is necessary to discover the nuances of various gifts others have been endowed."

"This turned out to be much more than a 'club', or networking outlet," Nicholaus stated.

"You are right. I realized early on how unsure these gifted individuals are about themselves and what their real purpose is here on earth. Like a bunch of tadpoles swimming around in the same pond with no focus on where they are headed. To learn what the possibilities are in life is a big key to deciding where you're going and how to get there. So I began putting together programs to help in different areas of discovery."

Delighted, Suzanna responded with a laugh, "I'm one of those tadpoles. Haven't quite figured out where I'm headed or what I'll turn into when I get there."

Marianne gave her a knowing smile. "Feeling safe in your environment is first and foremost. Knowledge is next, then comes an understanding of purpose, and last the necessary practice, or development of the gift. These are the areas we concentrate on here. Most important for everyone here is to gain one's wholeness as an individual, as well as an understanding of their part of the overall oneness of the universe."

Suzanna sensed Marianne's pause was to observe the effect of her words before continuing.

"As for why we exist, it is solely for the purpose of helping others to understand themselves, and to improve their lives."

Suzanna watched as Marianne paused then looked directly at Nicholaus. "You asked what I get out of it. I can see my answer to this is very important to you. So, let me assure you the only thing I receive is the pure satisfaction of having helped someone in need. Unlike some of the other networks out there, we are not here with grand schemes to make money. The greatest payment is the success of an individual, where it would have been a struggle if they hadn't come here."

"It takes money for something of this magnitude," Nicholaus stated, indicating with the wave of his hand the grand structure around them. "Where do you get the money to run it?"

"We are a non-profit organization. We operate on donations only. You can see in all the public tax records there are no salaries paid out to officers or board members. The donated money we receive from a few investment sources goes for cost of materials, the purchase of this building, and the salaries of a few individuals who work full time here and have no other source of income." Marianne's confidence helped to strengthen Suzanna's outlook.

Suzanna felt Nicholaus fit the pieces together in his mind like a puzzle. Then she saw him take a second look at Marianne's designer apparel and shoes and knew what his next question would be.

"So either you have a very wealthy husband, or you have other means of income. I don't imagine you picked up that amazing outfit at the local thrift store."

"Aren't you the charmer? Thank you for noticing, but no I didn't. In fact these are Jimmy Choo shoes, and the suit is a Milano I picked up in New York last week."

Suzanna's jaw dropped. "Are you serious?" The shoes alone cost a fortune.

"I don't usually brag about my accomplishments, but I wanted to make a point. Although my husband is quiet wealthy on his own accord, I'm also the Chief Executive Officer of Carver and Ross Medical Professionals, the leading recruiter for medical personnel in the northwest."

Before anyone could ask the next question she answered as if she already knew.

"What you might wonder is, wouldn't that conflict with the intent of the organization here? Actually not, you'll find quite a number of the members here have also been placed in hospitals and medical clinics throughout the area through Carver and Ross. And what might seem as a difference in principles, is a simple and true understanding of how healing is meant to be."

Suzanna glanced over to find Nicholaus' full attention held by the words Marianne spoke.

"You see, we are capable of doing great things, through the universal being we call God. If we focused on replacing the bad energy of our own ailments with good energy, most of us could allow the healing of our own bodies. Herbs and other substances are the remedies of the earth and are very successful, when used properly. They are the medicines of the universal supply." Marianne paused.

Nicholaus replied with a nod of his head.

"When they don't work, the next step should be to look toward healers who can channel the energies of the universe through themselves to the ailments in need of healing. When other means are necessary we have been given the ability to learn and develop methods to cure and heal, that's where medicine and medical treatments come in. I'm sure you can understand, Nicholaus, because this is what you have been doing for many years now."

"Nice to know I've been heading in the right direction on my own," he acknowledged.

"What I do see however, is you are an infant in the development of your gift. There is so much more for you to learn. You've used your gift with a light touch. You have the ability to receive knowledge and in return give a great deal more than you have been doing."

He nodded in agreement. "So what would be expected of us if we should decide to come here?"

"That would be up to you. The services we provide are open to all who are interested and want to develop themselves further. You may use them as much or as little as you choose. The only thing we ask is you respect others for their needs and their own level of discovery. Help if you can, and conduct your behavior in a manner befitting your purpose in life." Almost as if she'd read his mind she added, "At no time would you be asked to do anything that makes you uncomfortable. You're free to come and go as you will."

Marianne looked from one to the other. Suzanna felt a strange intuitive question surface in her mind, and she realized Marianne had taken a quick peek into their comfort level to determine who to approach.

"Nicholaus, I understand you have a great beginning as a healer. Mona told me some of the amazing things she's observed and what you've told her."

The woman raised a hand to her shoulder and a man appeared seconds later at her side. He placed his hand over hers in a loving manner and Suzanna could tell these two people shared the type of love she envied. The look they exchanged made her wish for the day she could feel the same thing.

"Joe, why don't you take Nicholaus around and show him some of the benefits he can expect to receive by coming here. Suzanna, if you don't mind, I'd like to have a little chat with you myself."

Nicholaus' concerned look questioned if she would be comfortable if he left her. She nodded and gave him a smile. He followed Joe to a group of individuals who sat in another area, and she heard him being introduced as a possible member.

Suzanna looked back and found Marianne relaxed in her seat, legs crossed, looking at her with inquisitive eyes.

"Tell me a little bit about yourself Suzanna. Why are you here?"

Suzanna expected anxiety to overwhelm her. Instead she'd been put at ease by Marianne's genuine honesty and strength as an individual. She had closed herself off to the outpour of energy she felt when they first arrived. Now she found herself opening up, little by little. She trusted what she felt to be positive, and healing in its own way.

"Mona probably told you why I would be coming. I haven't looked much into this phenomenon much, but I know I'm different. I also realize these feelings are not going to go away, so maybe it's time I start learning more about my ability."

"Yes, it is time for you." Marianne paused, her intent gaze Suzanna felt was an analytical one. "Most empaths are ready to find out their higher purpose when they turn…what, I'd say about twenty eight?"

Suzanna nodded at her accurate guess. "I don't know about a higher purpose. I've only started thinking about how to use this in a way to benefit others. It's just so hard to deal with sometimes."

Marianne gave a soft smile reminding Suzanna of a parent's patient approval of a child's inner growth. "This can be a very difficult gift to handle, especially when you're young. I can see you learned the method of closing yourself off from Mona very well, though."

Knowing this unfamiliar woman could read her with such clarity was a bit unsettling.

"It comes in handy at times," Suzanna responded.

"I'm glad it works for you. When Mona came to me years ago, she begged me to give her an idea of how to help you. You struggled quite a bit as a teenager, so we decided it would be best to show you how to block your perceptions. In time you'd search for your own answers when you were ready to accept the gift you've been given."

She apparently knew more about her than she realized which comforted her in some ways, like she was talking to an old friend.

"Mona always told me, when I felt ready there was a whole new-world for me to discover." Marianne's gentle smile comforted her.

"Are you ready now?"

Before she'd arrived, Suzanna hadn't been sure what she wanted to do. Now she knew this was where she belonged. Finally, answers to all those questions. Why had she waited so long?

"I believe so." Taking in a deep breath, Suzanna made the decision she needed to find out everything she could. This would be a big change in her perception of who she'd thought herself to be—abnormal.

"What is important is for you to understand that there are others with the same and different gifts that you have. Everyone is unique. Everyone is special in their own way. Each one loved just the same by the Universal Spirit."

Wow, this is weird. It's as if she read my mind. Suzanna looked into Marianne's eyes for a moment. There she saw only the kind and peaceful caring she felt before. She felt as if this woman's aura she'd taped into was feeding and encouraging her own in a way that made her happy. In fact this was the first time she'd felt so at peace with herself in a long time.

Suzanna shrugged her shoulders. "I don't know where to start. I've read a little bit about what I might be. You can't trust everything on the internet. Some of the descriptions fit, and then others did too. I'm not even sure if any of this is true." She needed to know who she was, on the inside. She scrunched her brows together. "I can't deny the fact I'm different, but how do I know what I am?"

"The thing to remember about 'fact' is you don't have to physically see it, or believe in it, for it to be true. Same is true with 'truth'. There can be absolutely no fact to prove something. If you believe something can and will happen—it will become fact. It's a little thing we call '*manifesting destiny*'."

"I think I'd like to know more about that later. There are so many questions I have." Marianne's whole being exuded knowledge and information. Suzanna's inner fears were fading fast. She was finally in the right place at the right time.

"I'll be glad to tell you anything you want to know, dear. Tell me more about the types of things you've experienced."

Suzanna tried to sort out all the things she wanted to say, so many aspects she needed to understand about herself.

"I've come to realize that every emotion has its own physical sensation." Suzanna thought back to the conversation she'd had with Nicholaus. "Someone once told me our thoughts contribute a lot to our emotional and physical well being. I'm beginning to believe that's true. That's why there is so much sickness in this world. So much emotional pain can really do a number on your body."

"You are right," Marianne nodded. "Many illnesses come from the thoughts and emotions we allow ourselves to have."

Suzanna sat for a moment, her thoughts having travelled to her own problems. She tried to have positive thoughts all the time. Her emotions could be a little out of whack sometimes, but she was able to pull herself together fairly quick. Why couldn't she heal herself of this condition?

Maybe she could.

She pulled herself back into the present moment and pushed the thoughts from her mind. Marianne sat silent, a curious look in her eyes.

Lord, I hope she didn't see what I was thinking about.

Suzanna cleared her throat, and began again. "Most of the time, I immediately sense what someone else is feeling. The emotion and now even the physical sensations come to me very strong. Sometimes people will say one thing, but they are feeling another way. I can sense the difference. I don't hear words, like what they are thinking, I just feel their emotions as if they were my own."

She looked at Marianne to see her reaction and feel her acceptance of what she'd said. There was a true understanding of what she was saying. With this acceptance, Suzanna allowed herself to form a bond with Marianne. It happened so quickly, it surprised her, as if the other woman was waiting to accept her connection without question. Suzanna became very excited. Finally, she'd found someone to talk to who understood what she'd been hiding for so many years. Maybe now she could understand the why, and how, to it all.

Rushing forward, Suzanna almost stumbled over her words. "It happens with animals, too. They aren't much different than we are, although a bit simpler in their makeup. When I was about ten, I found I actually felt the pain and discomfort other people and animals experienced, but I really have to guard against that when it happens."

"As you should, you need to watch this with care. This ability can be dangerous for the untrained sentient."

"Sentient? That's a different term, I thought it was sensate. What does it mean?"

"In reality they are both the same thing. The sensate can perceive the physical sensation where the sentient is able to perceive both the emotional and physical nature of another being. What you've described is called clairsentience. Though if untrained this can be harmful. If you allow yourself to become one with an unhealthy being, in some cases it can shut down your effectiveness, and for others their own body begins to emulate the disease or pain and will suffer the same condition."

"Whoa, I'd never thought it could go so far. Now that I think about it, if I let the sensations in for too long I feel as if they become intensified, almost debilitating. I need help with it though. I still feel the effects, no matter what I do."

"One of the rules of allowance we teach here can help you to find ways to incorporate compassion without engaging in unhealthy involvement. The universal being, or eternal spirit, requires us to stay attuned to our individuality, and therefore separated from this occurrence."

"That makes sense. It's never good when you loose yourself to someone else, in any relationship, or with a person or other being you're able to read, right?" Suzanna questioned, knowing the answer.

"Very true, however the unification of two spirits is allowed to happen in cases where the formation of the bond between two entities is confirmed universally as being a whole. True love between two people is a very special occurrence. They are an integral piece to the universe as individuals, and a planned unified segment of the greater picture."

"Kind of like what people call your 'other half', or better yet a 'match made in heaven'?" With Marianne's nod of agreement, Suzanna asked, "Does that happen very often? Is there really a soul mate out there for everyone? Two beings getting together in this world, by the divine plan of the universal being, sounds like a chance in a lifetime to me."

Suzanna, although skeptical, was in awe of the true description of 'love' Marianne laid out for her.

"You will learn the many truths spiritualists have learned over the years soon enough. But in answer to your questions, this happens more than you might think. The key is listening to your inner guide. It will tell you if you've found the one meant for you. Otherwise, this becomes a battle between hormones and the need to control ones own outcome." Marianne smoothed a line in her slacks. Suzanna sensed the care in which she planned her next question. "How long have you and Nicholaus been together?"

Suzanna went blank, not understanding the question. Then it hit her and she could feel the furious blush rise to her cheeks.

"Oh, we aren't together, not in that way. I work with him and we both seem to have these abilities. We're just friends really. We thought it would be a good idea to come together to talk to you is all."

"Hmm…I see. Well, in either case, you seem to have a strong bond together. It isn't something to be taken lightly."

Suzanna found herself locked by Marianne's unique violet colored eyes. The wisdom this woman held she knew could be transferred through ethereal means, and there seemed to be something she wanted Suzanna to know. Unaccustomed to this way of listening, she didn't quite understand, and was about to ask when Marianne got up from her seat and looked to the returning men.

Placing her hand on Nicholaus' arm, Marianne drew him next to her. "Well gentlemen, I see you have finished with the tour. Nicholaus what do you think of our place?"

"You have done an amazing job here. You cover so much need, with so little exaggeration. I'm impressed by the simple, straightforwardness of all of your programs," Nicholaus responded.

"Yes, well, we all know why we're here. Most of our work is done beyond the physical senses. If anyone comes here expecting grandeur and satisfaction of the ego, they are in the wrong place." She patted his arm warmly then stepped away to face both of her guests. "So can I expect to see you again soon?"

Nicholaus and Suzanna glanced at each other and smiled. Suzanna tried to silently express her agreement before he responded. "I can't speak for Suzanna, but I know I would like to talk further with you about my own advancement. Suzanna?"

"Yes, I would too. I appreciate you taking the time to talk today. If possible I'd like to continue our conversation, and maybe we can see where it will go from here." Suzanna liked what she felt. Marianne was the kind of no nonsense person she respected. There were similarities between her and Mona. Though each had a much different approach, she could see herself becoming just as close to Marianne as she was with Mona.

"Excellent! I can be found most days here between two and six. If you'd like some specific time with me, I suggest you call and make an appointment with Sarah. She can make sure I am available for you. Otherwise I could be anywhere. I've been known to sit in on one-on-one classes, and participate in some of the group settings too." She turned to Suzanna. "Make sure you call Sarah, I would love to see you again, dear. We have some things to talk about. I have a feeling we will be working closely together." To Suzanna's surprise Marianne bent forward and planted a soft kiss on her cheek. The warm motherly gift was unexpected, but indeed welcomed.

All of a sudden, Suzanna got the feeling of someone watching her. She glanced to her left. Two young women in their late teen or early twenties, stood waiting for an end to their conversation. One appeared to be listening to what the other was saying, head bowed with an occasional nod. The other stood, arms folded at her chest, looking in their direction, impatience written all over her face.

Marianne motioned for the two to join them.

"Let me introduce you to my daughters, Kara and Josephine."

"Nice to meet you," Suzanna responded as she and Nicholaus acknowledged their presence.

Kara bowed her head in response. The difference in the two girls was unquestionable. Kara, had the beauty of her South Asian decent, perhaps India Suzanna considered. Apparently, she's an adopted daughter. As she watched the two, she felt patience, and an internal glow of peace and contentment surrounding this young girl.

The younger of the two, by maybe a year or two, was not so peaceful. She was tall, not yet grown into the expected stature of her birth mother. Suzanna could tell through her restlessness she didn't want to be there. Josephine's recognition of their presence was almost nonexistent.

"We saw that guy again. He keeps lurking around outside. Want us to call the cops on him." Marianne's quick glance toward Joe had him making his pardons to leave the group. He walked toward the door motioning for a couple other young men to join him.

"Josephine, be polite to our guests," Marianne prompted.

"Sorry. Hi, how are you?" Josephine asked, shifting from side to side, as if uncommitted to the manners she was forced to show. Suzanna felt an almost judgmental stance coming from the young woman.

"That's better. As for Mr. Starks, you don't need to do anything. I'll deal with him."

Suzanna glanced over to Nicholaus. His jaw clenched, his eyes a steely gray. After a moment, he stated the obvious question. "Is there something going on here we should be aware of?"

Marianne breathed out a heavy breath and shook her head. "As you would expect, we have our disturbances. This one happens to be coming from one of our competitors. A group called 'The Order'. What I can see, their only mission is to exploit the gifts of people like you as a way to make money. The leader seems to think if we join our efforts together he can steal away all of the members here. It's nothing to be concerned about. If they approach you just tell them what you think. They can't force you to do anything."

Nicholaus stood suddenly still, except for the obvious gritting of his teeth together. Suzanna could feel his previous concern turn to a rage of sorts. "Seems this wouldn't be what your members would want to deal with," Nicholaus said stating his own truth.

"Yes, well, it's time to file a restraining order. Perhaps that will handle what goes on here on my property. Unfortunately, I can't control what goes on outside of here." Suzanne became acutely aware Marianne's frown didn't display the extent of discord the event had spurred inside of her. "Nicholaus, be assured at no time will I allow these people to interfere with your desire to become what you are destined to be."

"I hope you're true to your word. I've heard of this group." Nicholaus narrowed his eyes, his brows coming together. "I'll have nothing to do with them. If you do partner with them, you can be sure I'm not the only one who won't come back."

Marianne stood silent a moment, her shoulders stiffening. She lifted her head high. "I have no intention of joining in on any of the games they play. We are what I told you before, a group designed for the explicit benefit of its members."

The noncommittal nod Nicholaus gave her made Suzanna wonder if he would ever come back.

Chapter Eleven

Neither Nicholaus nor Suzanna said a word on the way home. He pulled into the driveway and shut off the engine of his Mariner. His hands lay gently on the top of the steering wheel, as he looked off into the darkness of night. Suzanna took the opportunity to take a long studious look at him. He was so strong, yet at times like this he seemed almost lost in his deep surrounding sadness. She could sense his analytical mind hard at work as he sorted out the pros and cons of some secret internal battle. She longed to somehow take away the pain in his eyes. Before she realized her actions, she reached out to brush away a stray curl which had fallen against his forehead.

As her hand touched him he came out of his entranced state. The slow warmth in his eyes made her heart thump harder, and she berated herself for her inability to show more restraint.

"I just wondered what brought your thoughts so far away," she said in an attempt to brush off her mistake of showing even a fraction of intimacy.

Nicholaus looked deep into her eyes. Every time she gazed into those bright blue eyes, it was as if with every second she couldn't help but give him a little piece of her heart. Without a word, he got out and walked around the front of the vehicle to open her door.

She stepped out, her skirt billowing around her in the slight breeze. As close as he was, she could smell the scent of his aftershave, and was hit by a sudden need to be gathered into his arms. She moistened her lips with the tip of her tongue, longing to succumb to his fervent kisses. Slowly, as if reading her mind, his gaze travelled down to linger on her lips for a moment. A slight upward turn appeared on the corners of his mouth. She felt a tremble in her body in the anticipation of their lips meeting.

Would he kiss her again? He shouldn't. Oh, but she wanted him to kiss her again. Flurries of nerves tumbled in her stomach. She knew if he did she wouldn't be able to stop herself from kissing him back.

No. This wouldn't work. This couldn't work. She looked away, trying to collect her wits about her. They should talk. Talking was good. That way she wouldn't want so desperately to climb into his arms.

"You don't have to tell me what you were thinking about, but I've been told I have a good listening ear."

She was relieved when he nodded and took her arm lightly in his to lead her toward the back along the garden walkway to her front door.

"I was thinking about my parents, my mother in particular." They paused mid-path and he looked as if he were about to go on, then shook his head and said, "That story would take a very long time. Perhaps I'll tell you about it later."

Though she needed to be careful, Suzanna wasn't ready for the evening to end yet. She'd enjoyed their time together. There was no replacing the glorious feeling Nicholaus gave her as he stood next to her. She wanted to make it last as long as she could, so she ignored her internal warnings.

"Would you like to come in for a drink?"

As the words came out of her mouth, she knew she would suffer for her actions. This internal struggle between what she wanted and what she could allow to happen created quite a quandary. One she wasn't sure how to handle.

Hesitating a moment, he responded, "I think…I'd like that."

Suzanna opened the door and stepped through the threshold, revealing a very comfortable living space. She smiled with pride in what she'd done to fix up the place. Her few belongings were nestled perfectly with the furniture she'd asked to keep. The bright pastel pillows tossed on the muted plum couch brought life to the room, as did the potted plants placed in every possible space. Though, the center of attention hung from a stand in the corner near the window. The beautiful splendor of the pink Christmas-Cactus in full bloom seemed to welcome you into the house.

Cali slept curled in a tight ball on the ottoman, her head upside down, her paw covering her nose. At the disturbance, she lazily uncurled and sat up, watching the offending noisemakers with caution. Displeased by not receiving her usual greeting from Suzanna, she jumped down and walked out of the room, her head held high in indignation.

"I think someone is a little peeved." Nicholaus nodded his head in the direction of the departing cat.

"Probably, she's rather particular about her space," Suzanna chuckled.

She turned as Nicholaus began to take in the newly transformed living room, his view stopping at the impressive size of the cactus. Nervous, she walked over and plucked a wilted bloom from its frond. "Funny, it just keeps blooming. It's not supposed bloom until October."

"It must be happy. Have you had it long?" he asked, coming forward for a closer look.

"This is my mothers. She insisted I take it with me. Odd thing is the gardens outside are beautiful, but the houseplants inside would end up wilted and brown if I didn't take care of them. No matter how hard she tried."

Suzanna glanced up, and felt the blush rise to her cheeks. Nicholaus' attention was no longer centered on the plant. Instead his gaze settled on her face, an analytical look in his eyes, as if she was the subject to be studied.

"Hmmm, I see. She may have what's known as the 'black' thumb when it comes to her houseplants." He tilted his head and continued to gaze at her.

His eyes were so blue, so inquisitive it was hard not to gaze back at him. Suzanna forced herself to look at the pretty pink blossom in her hand.

"Mamma said she couldn't bear to see such a magnificent plant die before its time."

"I'm glad you saved it from an impending death." He smiled. "You have the same empathic touch for all living things."

"I suppose you're right." She gently reached out to touch the plant frond and felt as if she could recognize a response of appreciation. Then as Nicholaus moved to stand closer, her immediate reaction to him became undeniable. The light spicy cologne he wore made her want to bury her nose at his throat and gather him close.

No, no, no. Stop it, you can't feel like this.

As she turned away from him, she caught herself short of stumbling over the ottoman. Embarrassed, she walked toward the kitchen to escape the accumulating desire he'd prompted from her.

Lord I've got to make an excuse now. Drinks, maybe I should offer him a drink.

"Would you like a drink? I've got a tasty bottle of Merlot. It's a local brand from out on the Peninsula, and has a fruity, smoky taste. Picked it up on a road trip to one of the music festivals they have every year." She creased her eyebrows in thought, "Other than that, I've got some brandy, or if you'd prefer I could make some coffee."

Nicholaus followed her and stood silently at the doorway. The image of what happened the last time they'd met there hit her hard. She felt her heart pound a little harder as she remembered his effect on her.

Hoping Nicholaus hadn't been reminded of the same thing, she glanced up to see the twinkle in his eyes told her otherwise. He'd remembered.

Their eyes seemed locked. She couldn't look away. Then a slow grin appeared on his lips. He gave an almost silent laugh when he turned to pull a couple of her wine glasses down from the glass covered cupboard behind him.

"The wine sounds good. It's been a rather interesting day today. Maybe we could discuss what we thought about the organization."

Oh good, he's not going to talk about what happened.

Suzanna gave an inner sigh of relief and popped the cork on the wine, pouring a healthy portion in both of the glasses. She took a large sip of the mellow tasting wine to calm her nerves, and a deep breath to get her mind headed in the right direction.

"Yes, well, I didn't really know what to expect. Marianne seems very respectable. I liked her. She reminded me of Mona in a lot of ways." At Nicholaus' raised eyebrow, she continued. "Kind of that all knowing, all seeing type you can't question because it's obvious they know what they're talking about. She has a more polished exterior, but they both shoot from the hip and mark their target."

"You're right. I saw the same thing," Nicholaus agreed.

As they moved to the couch Suzanna sat on the end as far away from Nicholaus as possible, ignoring her underlying reaction to his being anywhere close. She was content in her own home, so she kicked off her shoes and brought her legs up onto the couch, one leg under the other.

"What did you see on your tour?" she asked.

"You know the general introductory walk-through. We talked to a few people. Joe showed me the classroom areas and reviewed the different types of services. There's a library filled with books about the extended senses, both herbal and holistic medicines, and healing too." Nicholaus turned his glass slowly around, the light reflecting off the sides. "I think that's where I would spend a lot of my time."

Suzanna felt there was something more. A sense of restriction came over her, as if being held back from growth. It was rather uncomfortable.

"What about meeting with Marianne? She said she would be glad to help us find what we need to learn and advance our skills if we want." She needed to get him to talk. It wasn't healthy to restrict oneself the way she felt he was doing.

"I'll be interested to find out what Marianne thinks would be most beneficial for me."

Little prickles of his resistance ran down her arm.

But that doesn't mean you will do it, does it?

Maybe she should try a different tactic.

"Don't you think the one-on-one or group training would be helpful?"

Nicholaus stroked the side of his wine glass. "I do, but I need to make sure there are no hidden agendas first."

"What do you mean? Do you think they're after something they're not telling us about?"

"I'm not sure. I've had some experiences with places who claim to be the real thing. So far they've all ended up requiring more from me than expected. I'm just wondering if the little incident at the end was a ploy to get us to come back."

"I don't think so." Suzanna shook her head. "I mean I didn't feel any type of deception going on."

"Maybe," he said with a shrug. The look he gave her wasn't convincing he believed her.

"Wait, I thought this was the first time you've approached anyone about your gift," she asked recalling a previous conversation.

"This is the first time I've gotten this far. There've been a few others I've contacted, but it never went beyond the first phone call."

With another sip of wine, he turned to face her and brought one knee up on the couch. He stared into his glass, as if it had the answers to all questions.

Silent, Suzanna already knew there was more to his story. She sensed his presence with her fade as his thoughts must have wandered off as they had earlier in the car.

"That's not all there is to it," she said softly as she viewed the lines of sadness in his face. This melancholy formed every time his thoughts changed to the same unsettling event or subject he had yet to reveal. All she knew was she wished she could take the pain away.

"I guess there's no covering up ghosts from the past. You'd be able to sense it like nobody's business." His response came out with a soft chortle.

She watched him rub his palms on his knees, as he tried to form the words to say. He took a deep breath before continuing, "I know about this group called 'The Order' that showed up today. It's an offshoot of the one my mother joined. She left us when I was about ten years old, to follow her 'calling' as she referred to it, enticed into joining this group who claimed to be the righteous order of the universal spirit. She wanted Dad to join her. He told me later he wouldn't leave a perfectly good job and his family to go traipsing around the countryside with a bunch of kooks in search of their purpose in life. Said he knew what his purpose was, and didn't need some dress wearing high priest to tell him where to find his soul."

Suzanna raised her eyebrows at him. The description of his father tickled her, though the serious subject didn't warrant laughter.

Nicholaus continued, "So, she left us to follow this dream of hers. I heard she's living in some commune outside of Houston now."

Suzanna saw the hurt in his eyes. His voice tightened and he needed to clear his throat to go on. The ache she felt was seated deep down, covered up by his refusal to show the evidence of its effects.

"She had the healing gift, too." His smile was not a kind one. "It seems to be in the blood."

He paused and took the last sip of wine from his glass. She'd never heard sarcasm from him before, and Suzanna began to get an intense confusion as if he were questioning his own gift. She realized the bitterness toward his mother's choices had caused his restraint to commit further on his own behalf. No wonder he'd responded to his mother the way he did.

"She chose to use her healing in a more oppressive manner by performing it as a snare for the high priest to entice members to join with him."

The puzzle pieces snapped together. Now she understood his hesitance to share his abilities with others.

"When she called me on my 15th birthday she asked if I would like to come live at the commune. Said I could straighten out my life and become one with the universe. I'd be working along side her to bring healing to the righteous."

"If you don't mind me saying, sounds like a rather pompous viewpoint. I take it the answer was 'no'."

"You think?" With eyes widened, his exaggerated facial expression emphasized his agreement. "I really struggled for a while, whether or not I even wanted to use the gift. I couldn't see how anything causing so much pain could be any good." He laughed. "*Bunica* straightened me out on that real quick."

"I'm so sorry Nicholaus." Suzanna reached out to touch his hand. His eyes shot up and connected with hers. She immediately was covered in the variety of emotions swimming around inside of him. Self doubt and guilt were combined with disgust and a faint repressed hostility. "But you must realize you are nothing like your mother."

He shook his head and looked away. "I know. But at times I wonder if I could be tempted into doing things I know aren't right. That's why I stay away from places like Gloves."

Suzanna struggled for a moment with the self doubt exuding from Nicholaus. She had enough of her own to deal with, she didn't need to take on anyone else's.

"I don't believe you could be. That would be against everything you stand for. It's not who you are. Besides, you're so aware of the possibility, you're more apt to stay away from that than to go seeking it out."

Nicholaus raised his eyes and gave her a soft smile. "You're right. Thank you. That's what my Bunica used to tell me." He shook his head and looked away, as if gathering his composure. "When my mother called today, all of those old feelings came rushing out. I had a real hard time not opening up and telling her where she could go."

"I can't imagine what you've gone through. It must be so hard knowing she chose this commune over you and your father." His pain was real. A deep seated pain, down in his soul. Suzanna began to experience what this must have done to him, and had to stop herself from accepting his pain as hers.

"No more than for you. What is your father's excuse?"

Wow. Nobody had ever asked her that question.

"Umm…You know, I've never did understand it. I used to ask all the time. But nobody had a very clear answer for me." She tried to recall how not knowing had affected her. "I guess, over time I stopped asking. I figured his absence was normal, and nothing I could do would change it anyway."

Nicholaus reached for the half empty wine bottle, his eyebrows raised in question for approval. With her nod, he split the rest between their glasses.

"So what did you think of Gloves? Are you ready to jump in and start learning about your extra sensory possibilities?" He chuckled a bit at the play on words.

"I actually thought I'd feel differently than I do now. I'm not sure how to explain it. The energies there are so intense, yet at the same time calmed my fears. Like everyone worked toward the same 'good'. It was kind of uplifting." She shifted bring her other foot out from underneath her.

"I felt the same thing," he acknowledged.

"I found out Marianne gave Mona the methods to help me survive my teen years. As horrible as they were, I don't know if I would have made it through them without those treasures." The finger she rubbed around the rim of her glass made a beautiful musical tone.

"Having something different about you is very difficult to handle sometimes. Believe me, I know." He took another sip from his glass. "At least I had someone to teach me about what to expect."

"If Marianne could help me then, I think she can help me now. In order to work with this ability, I really need to understand it better. Most times I end up feeling useless when things get too intense and I have to shut my perceptions down. Like restricting who I really am inside. At least when I'm working with you I feel like I can help by giving those poor animals a voice."

"Believe me you help more than you know."

A tiny yawn escaped from Suzanna's mouth, she raised her hand up in politeness. "Oh my, I'm sorry. I'm not tired. It must be this wine getting to me."

Nicholaus set his wine glass down and reached out to take one of Suzanna's slender feet in his hands. The well manicured toes painted a vivid red curled instinctively at his touch. He massaged the arch with his thumb and the unexpected touch of his hand had her choking on her wine. She began to protest, but the pressure he applied sent any negative words out of her mind. It felt so delicious she closed her eyes, and thought she may have purred at one point.

"You really shouldn't...hmmm, that feels so good..." She tried to focus on the conversation and not the gentle touch of his fingers and failed.

Overwhelmed by her response to him she was almost unaware of the movement. Yet her heightened sense of his energy signature told her he'd changed positions. She opened her eyes to find him next to her, mere inches away. He made no movement to close the gap, but his eyes told her what he wanted. She became entranced by the intensity of need shining through his bright blue eyes, the power so strong it became her own. All other thoughts swept away, she experienced only the urgency to connect need to need.

She leaned forward, her slow movement intensifying the moment. With her eyes locked on his, she fed from the energy course through her. At first, their lips met in a light touch. His kiss was gentle in response, yet he still did not come forward.

The kiss sent a tingle rushing forth in unyielding force through her system. She wanted more, craved more, and finally took more.

Her fingers sunk deep into his abounding curls as she pulled him closer to crush his mouth to her fevered lips. In return, his kisses roamed across her face, coming back time and again to feed on the source of her passions. She explored his face and neck with her fingers, following by hot wet kisses, and returning to gather the strength of the rising need as their tongues met in rhythmic motion.

Still he made no moves to take, he responded only to her urgency, though the fire pouring from him was contagious. He brought one arm up to rest lightly on her thigh and the heat from his palm sent shivers through her core.

This single act brought her back to reality in a snap. The lights went out as her immediate reaction mimicked a disconnection of power at the source. She jerked back, her eyes widened in shock as she realized what she'd done. Her hand came up to her lips in shame and she burst into gasping sobs. Jutting off the couch, she ran from the living room toward the back of the house.

Nicholaus sat still for a moment, stunned at her reaction, but could hear her heart wrenching sobs pour out as she went. Confused and concerned, he followed the direction he thought she'd gone and found her face first on her bed, her lamentations muffled by the comforter.

He sat next to her with care and gathered her stiff body into his arms. At first she tried to push away, but he didn't let go, not this time. Her forceful tears lessened after a few minutes into continuous heavy sighs. They sat, her body pressed against his, in silence for what seemed like a lifetime.

She began to sniffle, and he knew the waterworks had worked their way down through her nose. "Would you like me to get you some tissues?"

She nodded and pointed behind him on the nightstand where he found an open box ready to be used. Delighted he wouldn't have to move away, he retrieved the box for her.

"I'm alright now, you can put me down," she said, another sniffle necessitated.

"Not until you tell me why you broke down like that." At the insistent shake of the head he knew he had more work ahead to get her to open up. "You've got to help me out here Suzanna. I'm trying hard to understand what is going on, but you aren't giving me much to go off of here." He took her chin in his fingers and raised her eyes up to meet his. "I think I deserve an answer. At least so I know what I'm truly dealing with here. Right now I'm not sure if you're crazy or just a tease."

He could tell his references incensed her, but perhaps anger would work. She tried to push away. He continued to hold on tight and allowed only enough room for her to lean her forehead against his shoulder.

"I'm neither. I might as well be crazy, that's the way you make me feel."

"Why?"

The tears hadn't yet stopped, and the question seemed to prompt even more to run down her cheeks. She dabbed at them, the soaked tissue doing little to stop the flow.

"You're right. You deserve the truth. I'm just not sure how to tell you." She looked into his face then looked away again. "I'm sorry. I lost my head for a little while out in the living room. It must have been the wine. I normally have more control of myself."

"Believe me, I'm not complaining. You drove me a little crazy, too. You should let go more often. I don't understand what happened. Why the tears?"

Suzanna gave a long sigh. "It's not good to let go. It can't go anywhere. Because of this condition I have it will end up with us both being hot and bothered, then you'll end up hating me."

All kinds of thoughts flew through his mind. "Ok, that is just confusing. You're going to have to do better."

She took in a deep breath and moved far enough away to look into his face.

"Talk about embarrassing, okay, here goes. I have a condition called Vaginismus. Before you start to think it's some kind of venereal disease, it's not. The doctors describe it as an involuntary constriction of the vaginal muscles, a spasm of sorts. It happens to me when I get…excited."

She moved again as if to escape the confines of his arms. He still wouldn't let go.

"There's no way a physical relationship is possible, so it's better not to start one. Now you know. There's no need to say anything, I know you won't want to continue this. Just let me go."

He ignored what she said, and began to search his memory for some medical research he'd heard or read about in his recent journals. He skimmed his memory and nodded to himself as he rubbed her arm in an unconscious attempt to sooth her wounded feelings.

"Yes, I read about this in one of my medical journals a couple of weeks ago. The muscle becomes so tight it causes massive pain and prevents any type of penetration during intercourse."

"That about sums it up," she said in disgust.

"They indicated there are different types, though. If memory serves me right I believe 'acquired' is where the person was able to have intercourse in the past, but can't now. 'Lifelong' is where no type of sexual intercourse has ever been experienced. 'Situational' is where some penetration by some objects or partners but not others is experienced, and then there is 'general' where no penetration at all is allowed."

"Geez, it sounds like I'm talking to a textbook here."

"Sorry, I tend to be very focused on facts," Nicholaus apologized.

She rolled her eyes, and took a deep breath. "Hey, wait a minute. How do you know? I doubt animals have this problem. That's kind of creepy. Why would you follow female sexual disorders?"

Nicholaus kept his arm tight, not allowing her to move away. "I don't tell many people about this, because they end up getting the wrong impression. Not only do I have a doctorate in veterinary medicine, I also received a doctorate in medicine not too long ago. I felt I needed to widen my horizons with various options. My choice at this point is to continue my work with animals, though I keep abreast of medical treatments and therapies through continuing education and journals."

He was glad to see she seemed to relax a bit. "Oh, that makes sense. Do you think you might go into medical practice…for humans?"

"Maybe sometime in the future, but lets not loose sight of the subject we were talking about. Which type of Vaginismus do you have?"

Suzanna shifted a bit, uncomfortable with the subject. "I think mine is the 'lifelong', or at least it has been so far. The last time I went in to see the doctor he talked about some type of new surgery that only works half the time. I wasn't too interested in the odds, so I'm stuck with this condition for the rest of my life."

"If I remember correctly, there are several different types of non-surgical treatment plans."

"There are. Problem is you have to have a partner who is willing to go along with the treatment. Otherwise, it doesn't do any good," she said, oblivious to the present opportunity.

She tried again to move away from him. This time he let her go only to scoot back to settle himself against her pillows and cross his legs in front of him. He had no intention of going anywhere.

Suzanna, in an immediate defensive movement, sat on the edge of the bed to show she was ready to end the humiliation that went along with the subject being discussed. She looked back and gave a desperate sigh.

"Look, I know you want to discuss this. But, I'm sorry there really isn't much to talk about."

She took another deep breath and he could tell she had to force herself to say the next few words since they came out quick and breathless.

"We can't go any further with this thing between us, so let's drop it and forget it ever happened. I hope we can still be friends." She began to rub her hands together as if to get rid of an unusual feeling.

"Is that what you want? Just to be friends?"

Suzanna jumped up off the bed and threw her hands up in the air.

"Don't you get it?" she yelled furiously. "I can't have sex with you. Can't, not won't, I can't!" The tears began to escape again. "This is not what I want. I hate it. It is the most humiliating thing in the world to have to tell every man I've ever cared for that I'm no good, deformed. I'm incapable of carrying on any type of normal relationship!"

Nicholaus got up and reached out to take her by the arms, frustrated by her refusal to see the obvious.

"That's not what I asked you. Forget about what you can and can't do. Tell me what you want. Tell me what you really, deep down, truly want."

"You don't want to know the answer to that," she exclaimed, with pleading eyes.

"Try me."

Chapter Twelve

Good lord, why doesn't he get it?

Still hyped from her previous outburst, Suzanna screamed, "Damn it, I want you!" Everything came rushing forward in a crashing wave, her frustration unbearable.

"I want to experience every possible physical sensation you can get from me. I want to have my body so wrapped up in yours there's no way to tell where we begin or where we end." The heat of anger changed into the soft flow of tears which began to roll down her face. "I want to feel your strength. I want to experience all those things I've read about for so long."

She had never told another living soul about her dreams. Not these dreams.

"It's different with you. It's possible with you." She looked away and whispered softly, "Nobody has ever made me feel the way you do. This could be the most powerful thing I've ever felt. What I've dreamt of my whole life."

She had opened her heart and soul to him, and in their own way, admitting her feelings out loud freed her to speak the words she'd never said to anyone. She looked into his face and sadness overtook her when she realized her next words might never come true.

"I want your arms wrapped around me in the middle of the night, your kisses lifting me up throughout the day. I need your passion to encompass my whole world. You have no idea what it's like to never be able to be loved."

His hold on her tightened and she could feel the intense effect of her words, but not in the way she expected. She'd thought he'd resign to acknowledge and accept her lot in life, and perhaps resent her earlier actions like the others. Instead, he gave her a little shake, and she sensed the roll of anger beneath the surface.

"Why are you so willing to give up on yourself? If you won't make the effort to find out if I'm different, then I guess I'll never know what it's like to experience all those things with you either."

She never believed a man could want the same things. His revelation astonished her. She'd been so wrapped up in her own despair. Could someone else be hurt by the reality of her devastation as much as she?

"For reasons we won't get into now, most of my relationships haven't lasted very long. I'm not so normal either. I don't usually say this to a woman. It's not easy for me. But, I feel the same way about you." Nicholaus looked away from her then turned back, his gaze searching hers. "I want the same things you want. It seems to me we need to try harder to find out if it could happen. I'm more than willing to do whatever it takes to get past this roadblock you've let control your life for so long. I want to find out what is between us that makes us feel this way about each other."

Suzanna looked hard at him, not sure if she heard him right.

"Are you offering what I think?" Incredulous as it was, she believed he meant it. "You have no idea what you're getting yourself into."

"Perhaps, however, I think you forget who you're talking to here."

His arms came around her and he pulled her body up against his. She felt a sudden energy rush through her from fingers to her toes. Excitement coursed through her in passionate fiery tongues, racing along her skin in every direction. Suddenly changing to a soft seductive lathing, it felt as if she'd just dipped down into a silky smooth milk bath. Then she was back to the outright fervor encompassing her entire being.

"Oh!" She exclaimed in surprise. "How did you do that?"

"I've got control of my energies, the same as you do your receptors."

He ran a hand down her back and up again, leaving a tingling trail of need. Then with a gentle movement he bent down to leave soft kisses from the base of her neck to a spot just behind her ear. Suzanna moaned softly.

A smile warmed his face. "I'll warn you, I can unleash my powers of seduction at any time."

Suzanna's breath caught in her throat as sensual images ran rampant through her brain. His offer sounded like a dream come true, though she needed him to understand no promises could be made.

"But what if none of this works? I understand the therapies I've seen don't work for everyone." Her eyes glazed over as he continued to nibble on her neck.

"Let's not worry about that right now. Besides, I think the two of us have an advantage." His slow lick down the side of her neck tantalized a sexual response within to vibrate at full force. The tremor he caused settled somewhere deep inside and unleashed an urgency she wasn't sure could be fulfilled.

"Advantage?" Breathless, she held his arm to steady herself.

"I can't make any promises either, but if you allow it, I might be able to bring some healing from above." He continued to trace kisses down along the neckline of her blouse, just above the crest of her breasts.

The deliciousness of his actions caused her thoughts to cease. She fisted her fingers through his hair to pull him closer. Then all of a sudden, her eyes popped open with the realization of what he meant.

She scooted away to see his face. "Do you really think so? You said your healing had to be something you're led to do. Do you think it might work?"

Nicholaus smiled and brought her back against him. "I'm surprised you didn't think of this before. There is a good chance. All I can do is request for healing. Then we'll have to see what happens."

He couldn't know the considerable light his proposal brought into her heart. She found it hard not to jump around in a joyous outburst. Instead, she poured herself into a wholehearted kiss filled with passion and the bloom of possibilities.

The kiss sent a million pinwheels to spin loose through her head. As she pulled away again, eyes closed, Nicholaus leaned forward to rest his forehead on hers.

"If you keep doing that, you may have to brush up on your CPR," he claimed.

She giggled at the unbelievable wave of arousal washing over her. So desperate to satisfy the urgent need he'd awakened concerned her. She had no idea if she could satisfy a man. Sure, she'd read about the experience between two people, but she'd never gone past the initial foreplay steps. No doubt about it though, she knew if she were to ever learn how, she'd want it to be with him.

Her hand brushed through his thick hair, and she let down her guard to draw on her empathic self. She needed to know just how he felt. The vigorous movement of cells running throughout his body shocked her. In counter balance she sensed the voracious restraint he employed to keep them from transforming into action.

What would it truly be like to connect with him? Marianne's description of two joined souls intrigued her. Suzanna's intuition told her it would be astronomical.

She felt doubt form in his mind. Uncertainty in others was not a hard emotion to pick up.

"What is it?" she asked.

At first, he seemed not to comprehend her question, but understanding soon followed.

"I forget you can sense how I feel. That will take some getting used to. Then again, it could open up some very interesting possibilities on the physical side of things. I can see we'll have to experiment."

His hearty grin was contagious. She began to grin at her own thoughts on the subject then remembered he hadn't answered her.

"What were you concerned about a little while ago?"

"Thought maybe, I could brush past it for now." He nuzzled the side of her neck, then looked back to see she still waited for an answer. "No? Ok so, 'lifelong' means you've never had any sexual relations at all. You've never had any boyfriends?"

She moved out of his arms to sit on the edge of the bed, and struggled not to allow the worthlessness loom again.

"I've had boyfriends. They just don't hang around very long. If any physical relationship goes beyond the initial stages, and I try again to go all the way, they end up heading for the hills when I can't perform. Nobody has ever stayed long enough to help me find out if I could work through it."

"That doesn't say much for my fellow male human beings," he said, shaking his head.

"My last boyfriend stuck with me a little longer than most. We actually went to a therapy conference to find out what we could do to get past the problem. But he couldn't take the frustration I put him through."

Nicholaus sat down next to her and trailed a finger down the side of her neck, followed by a sweet kiss on the end of her nose.

"Looks to me like he didn't see all the possibilities," his soft breath caressed her ear with enticement. Then sitting upright again, he said, "Wait, so that means you're technically still a virgin."

She made a face of contempt and looked away. "Yes, technically, but it's not without my trying to negate the fact."

"Well then, you can be sure I will do my very best to help you attain your wishes."

Suzanna looked him in the eyes. There was truth and honesty. She'd never felt any reason not to believe what he said. She didn't know why he would want to put forth so much effort, but it didn't matter. His offer to help meant more than she could ever express.

"I would love to stay and try to work on it now, but I think maybe we shouldn't rush into this too quick. We're going to start out slow. Although, you do make a man want to rush to get to the finish line."

This was almost too much for her to comprehend. Most of the men she'd been involved with had pushed her too soon. Here this man wanted to help her to attain her wildest dreams, as difficult as it would be, but he also understood the need to not rush.

Could any man really be so sensitive?

He planted a kiss on her cheek and began to stand. Suzanna reached out to hold onto him. She didn't want to let him go.

"Don't go," she pleaded. "Could you stay with me for a while? I need to talk." His raised eyebrow caused a heated blush to shoot up into her cheeks. "Oh, who am I kidding? I need you here next to me tonight."

A little grin creased the corners of his lips. "Are you sure? I sleep in the buff you know." His eyes twinkled at her.

"Umm...oh...ok." The image of his naked body made her stutter, and her heart gave a confused beat of its own. "I do sometimes, too. I think we will wait a while for that. I do want to get more comfortable though. Do you mind?"

"Be my guest. I'm not going anywhere."

Suzanna walked to her dresser and pulled out a nightshirt and rushed into the bathroom. When she returned she found he'd turned off the overhead light, the softness of the bedside lamp glowed behind him as he propped himself against the massive pillows at the head of the bed.

She tried to be discreet, but realized the simple oversized gray cotton nightshirt barely reached the tops of her thighs. It had risen far enough to show the low-cut black bikini underwear she still wore as she hung her skirt in the closet.

Nicholaus groaned, "You have no idea how unbelievably sexy you are, do you?"

In an unsuccessful attempt at modesty, she pulled at the hem of the shirt then turned around to catch sight of his bare chest. The tanned, well-toned muscles displayed over his magnificent shoulders made her feel soft and feminine.

"I'm not sure what you mean," she replied with true innocence.

"Then it seems I'll have to show you...soon."

Suzanna scrambled into bed, averting her eyes from his nakedness. She lay down next to him not sure what she should do next. Nicholaus give a soft laugh and scooted down as he reached his arm out over her head.

"Why don't you try coming over here. You can't very well stay all the way over there."

Shy, she wriggled next to him, and switched to her side to place her head on his chest. She told herself to be bold, and decided to take total advantage of the situation. She reached up to place her hand on the back of his neck, and threw her leg over the top of his, pulling him as close as she could. His instinctive response brought his arm down around her waist to rest his hand on her hip. Without a need to open her senses she could tell the movement of his cells increase tenfold, then with his extreme control she felt them level off to a more comfortable speed.

"Is this…Are you going to be ok?"

"More than," he replied. He gave her a reassuring squeeze.

She could hear the thunderous beat of his heart under her ear, the warmth of his skin against hers caused on odd sensation to rise within her. She wanted to soak up every last bit of the wonderful comfort and secure strength in his arms. Yet an indescribable deeper need churned inside, to explore every inch of this magnificent man beneath her. With desperation she wanted to embrace all the potential physical and emotional connections between man and woman. She yearned for the love she knew could be achieved, but fear prevailed.

Her fingers itched to be able to touch his entire body. She knew though anything more would lead to the one thing frightening her the most, so she resigned herself to a light touch of the skin beneath her fingers. Soon comfortable security ruled over the need, and with the sound of his steady heartbeat she drifted off into a light sleep, thoughts of a tight and endless hold on this awesome fulfilling connection floating through her mind.

Nicholaus didn't lull to sleep with such ease. The touch of her body next to his brought forth an unusual need to protect her, at the same time her sexuality overwhelmed him. He reminded himself of the reason for being there. This was *just* a sleep over. There would be no physical action, only comfort for the both of them.

He wondered what could have caused this affliction to befall her. His mind worked to remember the articles he'd read about her condition, and concentrated on what methods he could use to help her. He hoped his knowledge and skill would be enough to help free her from the accursed life she'd been living. If not, he would continue his search until they could conquer this thing together.

He'd just drifted off to sleep when he felt her stir. He woke quickly as she began to murmur words of refusal in her sleep. Her disturbance was light at first, her movements increasing in some form of fear, as if being threatened or tortured in some manner. Suddenly, she screamed out in terror while uncontrollably thrashing the bedcovers.

Nicholaus sat up and tried to calm her down.

"Sweetie, it's all right. I'm here. You've had a bad dream. I'm not going to let anything hurt you. Wake up now honey."

He tried to caress her arms to relax her. She'd broken out in a sweat. Her breaths came quick, as she surfaced out of the dreaded nightmare. He felt her body shake, as the tentacles of her dream-like state haunted her final waking moments.

He held her against him, in hopes to stabilize her nerves with his forced molecular modulation. As she became more cognizant of her surroundings, she stiffened in his arms. Her eyes widened in confusion when she looked up into his face, clearly unsure of the reason for his presence in bed with her. He continued to whisper words to comfort her and hoped his strength in the moment would be enough to reassure her of her safety.

He saw the change in her expression when the haze of her nightmare cleared and she connected with the here and now.

"Are you alright?" he asked, continuing to stroke her back.

"Yeah, just a nasty dream I keep having. This time it was a little different though," she said shuddering, "I could actually feel it happening."

"Want to tell me about it?" He prompted, curious what had caused the intensity of her reaction.

"I've never told anyone. I don't know what good it would do."

"Maybe if you voiced your fears you would release some of the control it has on you." He saw the question in her eyes and clarified. "It's a form of therapy I read about in one of my psychology manuals."

She nodded and moved away from him, wrapping her arms around herself as if to protect against further intrusion. "This is really hard to describe." She wiped her sleeve against her sweaty brow. "I really don't like to think about my dream. I mean, it's hard enough having it plague me in my sleep."

Nicholaus sat in silence and waited for her to open up to him.

"I'm not sure if I can explain it. There's more of a feeling than a visual picture." She took another deep breath and went on. "It's dark, and I think I can see stuff I used to have in my old room back in California. There's this huge Raggedy Ann doll I used to have, about four feet tall. She sat in the corner with my other stuffed animals. Then I see this figure come toward me. I feel I should know him, but I don't want him there. I say I feel him because I don't actually see his face. I know it's a man because of his size and the shape of his shoulders."

There was another hitch in her breath. He could tell she forced herself to say the next part.

"I tell him to go away, but he just keeps coming. He gets me pinned up against the wall. That's when he starts touching me…in places he shouldn't. I don't want him to touch me in that way. I plead with him to stop. He keeps touching me, now on my bare skin."

Nicholaus saw the tremor of fear surface as if she'd begun to relive her nightmare on the conscious realm.

"That's when all the toys in the corner start to move, hopping and jumping around like they're all alive. Their faces change into these horrible evil creatures, and they come toward me, too."

He could see her internal fear escalating to the same frenzied state as when she first awakened. Her erratic breathing concerned him, but he knew she needed to tell him everything. He took her hand in his. The lower level energy he transferred seemed to help relax her again.

"Then what happens?" He kept his voice calm and gentle.

"This faceless man gets on top of me. He covers my whole body with his, and then…and then everything goes black."

"Has it ever gone any further?"

She gave a vehement shake of her head. "No, it's never gone beyond that point."

They sat in silence. Nicholaus didn't know where to go with her newest revelation. He'd never dealt with dream interpretation for animals. Body language was a different thing though. Suzanna was scared. She looked around her as if she were afraid of what might jump out of her dreams into the room behind her.

"The strangest thing…now I think about it, when everything goes black, I can still feel the terror, and a horrible sensation of invasion for what seems to keep going for a lifetime. Then I wake up screaming, crunched up at the head of the bed with the covers all knocked off onto the floor."

Her breaths continued to be quick, her gaze somewhere off in the distance. Nicholaus could tell she hadn't told all. There was more to it.

He continued to stroke her arm, although at this point his efforts to calm her seemed useless.

"What else?"

"Tonight was different. I've never experienced this before." She moved a little further away from him he noted, far enough where he could no longer touch her.

"I could actually feel his hands on me, as if he were in bed with me. It was awful, so real."

His instinct told him what she felt was probably the connection of his arm around her in the night. And the newness of his presence in bed with her may have instigated the transference of sensation into her dreams. He also saw this no longer remained a horrid little dream for her. It had become a reality.

"I...I could feel every place he touched me. I didn't want it. I felt dirty."

He saw her shiver and looked around for something to cover her.

Her voice caught in her throat, "I imagine this must be what rape feels like, only it didn't go as far as penetration, thank God. I don't even want to imagine if it went all the way to the end."

"Let's not start to put more worry to what's already there," he said as he reached to the floor and pulled the blanket back up to cover her shoulders.

"It's strange though, I think this is someone I should care about. I have no idea who he could be."

Nicholaus already had his own thoughts on whom, but why this person kept showing up in her dreams was the question.

"Suzanna, I need to ask you, have you ever been raped or molested?"

"No," she paused, "I don't remember anything happening."

"Are you sure?"

"I think I'd remember that, don't you?"

Nicholaus answered with a raised eyebrow.

He saw her glance at the clock then down to his lap. In her unconscious dream activity, Nicholaus' manhood had been uncovered. His nakedness hadn't been his first concern. Although unashamed, he reached for a corner of the comforter to pull over himself. But, her immediate uncomfortable reaction hadn't gone unnoticed.

She cleared her throat and looked away.

"I'm going to get some water. Would you like some?"

He shook his head. "No, I'm fine."

As she left the room for the kitchen, he thought it would be best if he left. The dream had obviously disconnected any need for closeness. He stood and reached for his pants, zipping them up as Suzanna came back into the room.

"What do you think you're doing? You're not leaving."

He looked back up and saw a firm decisiveness in her eyes. A look he didn't want to aggravate.

"I thought my leaving would be for the best."

"Well, it's not. I'll be damned if I let some stupid dream control my life." She sat down on the bed next to him. "I found out a long time ago just because I feel things with more depth than others, I can't let it rule how I interpret life. I know you're not the one in my dreams, I also know you helped me more tonight than you realize."

He admired her strength. A few minutes prior she'd been scared to death. Now she had total control, and a precise knowledge of what she wanted.

"I've been alone in my own mind too long with my weird perceptions and fears. I'd forgotten what it's like to share with someone. It feels good. If you're still willing, I'd like you to stay."

Without question, he nodded his head. "I'd like to. I just didn't want you to be uncomfortable."

In her eyes he saw her acknowledgment. She bent forward to kiss his cheek.

"Good. I'm not going to be able to sleep for a while yet. How about we watch a movie? Sometimes the distraction helps me to relax."

She took him by the hand to lead him to the living room. As she settled against him on the couch, she pulled an afghan up over her legs. Nicholaus thought she'd have an aversion to being touched, but she shocked him by actually wanting to be held.

He didn't expect the low sexy laugh she made.

"It's as if you make all the bad things go away," she said as she kissed his ear.

She brought his arm from the back of the couch and wrapped it around her middle, like a seat belt. Cali jumped up onto the couch and gave Nicholaus a suspicious glare. Then, without invitation, plopped herself down at the largest unoccupied space and began to lick herself. Suzanna reached out and stroked her head.

It didn't take long before the exhaustion of the night and the tragedy of the Titanic had her drifting off to sleep again.

He put all he could into the transfer of energies to calm and relax her. It worked.

His main concern now was her well being. He'd begun to put the pieces together to bring some rhyme and reason to the bundle of surprises he held in his arms. He had his own suspicions about what happened to her. How to prove them would be the hard part.

All too obvious, the combination of the dream she described and the condition she'd lived with all of her life were no coincidence. Though, she seemed to be unaware of any incident that could have started this snowball into motion.

The light from the TV flickered over her face, a face soft with innocence. He bent to kiss her cheek and realized his need to protect her stood foremost in his mind. Now she'd allowed him into her life, he swore he would be there to protect her from whatever could harm her again. If he ever found out who did this to her, he couldn't be sure he'd be able to limit his actions to make it right. He also knew in order for her to move on, she needed to acknowledge the possibility someone abused her as a child. To come face to face with the cause could force her to relive it all over again. And that disturbed him.

Soon the exhaustion of the evening made him drowsy and drew him into a light sleep.

* * * *

From his office, Nicholaus couldn't hear any music, though on occasion he would hear sudden outbursts of lyrics and humming from the front room. Curious, he stepped out of his office and walked toward the front reception area. What he saw was too entertaining to interrupt.

Suzanna had dressed in a pair of black leggings, with a long tunic of vibrant multi jewel toned colors. She'd slipped her sandals off under her desk, and now stood barefoot at the file cabinet, her toes tapping to the lively classic oldie he could make out blaring through her I-Pod.

He leaned up against the doorframe to watch Suzanna's animated dance, the papers in her hand stuffed into files as she went. Her hips swayed and head bobbed while she moved across the floor to what appeared to be her own beat.

She blurted out, "One way or another…" and hummed the rest of the phrase, then burst out again, "I'm gonna getcha, getcha, getcha, getcha," with enthusiasm she pointed at an unseen character in front of her.

Nicholaus couldn't help laughing. The sudden noise must have been heard, as Suzanna's attention came around to him. Though, instead of embarrassment, she reacted in a total opposite manner than expected. She smiled and danced toward him, singing the remaining words along with her I-Pod. He knew the rhythm to the Blondie song she sung, and laughed when she encouraged him to join in. Mimicking her foot and arm movements he started toward her.

They met in the middle and both broke out in laughter when Nicholaus scooped her into his arms to make an overly enthusiastic dip, which caused her to grab hold or lose her balance. Her natural beauty, high spirited character, and the unusual emotions she created every time he touched her, mesmerized him. His jovial behavior became zealous as they rose from the dip, and he brought his mouth down to claim hers.

She clung to his neck and returned every ounce of passion. The kiss lasted forever. Yet not long enough for either of them. As he lifted his head, her lips trembled from the ardor he'd aroused in her. He held her against him and whispered in her ear, "One way or another…."

In parting, a soft blush rose to her cheeks, her stunning beauty breathtaking. They stood still a moment then he brushed a hand across her cheek, gazing into her eyes, wondering how this woman could touch him in this way.

"Well, that was fun." Suzanna's breathless words revealed his affect on her, which made him grin.

He nodded, unsure of what to say. Needing to temper the fires she'd stoked within him, he followed her to her desk and asked the only thing that came to mind. "Are you going to be ready to visit Gloves tonight?"

Suzanna picked up the pile of papers on her desk, and turned to him with a smile. "Oh, yes. I can't wait to talk to Marianne again. I'll just finish up this filing then we can go."

"Sounds like a plan. Let me know when you're ready."

Back in Nicholaus' office, the lack of sleep settled back over him as he stared at his desktop. Finished for the day for his practice, Suzanna came to mind, the events of the night before replaying through his memory. He knew what he needed to do next. His laptop lay open waiting for his instruction. As he brought up a favorite medical site on the Internet, he typed in 'Vaginismus' to see what more he could learn about the subject.

A sudden thought occurred to him. This could be the most important research he would ever do.

Chapter Thirteen

Marianne stepped in with Joe, hand in hand. He whispered a private remark in her ear, and she chuckled at his unmistakable grin. She was about to give him an answer to his suggestive comment when she realized they had company.

"Joe, you're such a tease." Marianne planted a respectable kiss on his cheek, and turned to her visitors. "Welcome. Hope you haven't been waiting long."

Nicholaus stood and offered his hand to them. "Not long. We were just talking about the awesome design of this office," he said looking around their surroundings.

Marianne loved her office. The corner office exhibited two glass exterior walls facing a view of the Puget Sound. High ceilings and mirrored interior walls gave an illusion of wide open space, as if sitting outside amongst the reflective vision. She kept vases of flowers arranged in an array of colors throughout, adding to the overall splendor. Nicholaus sat back down beside Suzanna on the overstuffed black leather couch by the windows.

"I just can't believe how you literally feel as if you're out in the universe, with access to everything imaginable. I think if you focused hard you could actually connect with God," Suzanna acknowledged.

"Yes, I had this specifically designed for that purpose," Marianne smiled and held out her hand to Suzanna. "I'm so sorry we are late. Joe insisted on taking me for a quick drink before we got here. It's our 30th anniversary."

"Today is your anniversary? We didn't know. We could have made the appointment for another day," Suzanna was quick to say.

"Nonsense, my dear, I've always got time for my friends. We have plans to go out later and paint the town. I've even got my dancing shoes on."

She stretched her foot out to display perfectly manicured toes in a classic open toed pump. She'd dressed to match the intended affair, a low cut, black number intended to stun the onlookers, especially her precious Joe. He smiled proudly at her, and she came forward to straighten his favorite bright red bow tie adorning his well-cut black tux. This would be a night to remember.

Marianne sat down across from the pair, in a chair shaped more for the purpose of meditation than to conduct business. Joe stood behind her and placed both hands on her shoulders, a sincere gesture of his affection.

"Sarah tells me you have both decided to come join our group of friends here. I'm so glad to hear this. I can feel great things for both of you, and can't wait for them to happen."

Marianne looked from one to the other, and noticed a difference about their aura. The energy present now hadn't shown up before. She would never use her visionary eye to look too deep without an invite, so she left her curiosity alone momentarily.

"Nicholaus, I'm sure you are aware of the multitude of healing techniques we've begun to discover, some of which I know you already use. The most familiar are known as Reiki, chakra motivation, meditation, and visualization using the 'chi' or universal energies and circular vortexes available to all of us. These life influencing energies are what I understand you've been able to capture."

Nicholaus nodded his acceptance of her knowledge. "Pretty much covers it, though I know there is a lot more to learn."

"I would like to have you assessed first, so we know what level you're skill sets are at right now. That way, we will be able to tell where to start you out so you'll get the maximum benefit out of your time here."

She waited for his response before continuing.

"I agree."

She was glad to see he was open tonight, not as guarded as he'd been before.

"Then with your permission, I would like you to attend one of our introductory classes into healing. This will give you an overview of the different types possible, and will help you to measure your interest and abilities in each one."

"I think that would be a good place to start." Nicholaus nodded in agreement.

"Joe tells me you're an avid reader, and said you were quite impressed by our library. Reading is one form of learning, and it can be quite helpful to motivate one's desire to try new experiences. Me, I'm a hands on kind of girl. I'm most happy when I can get right in and try things myself. You are the only one to determine the pace and style most comfortable for you."

"I appreciate it. In the past I have tended toward learning by myself, but then I'm sure you can understand why. Viable groups in this area are hard to find."

Marianne smiled, she did understand.

"I did enjoy my grandmother's help in learning new things, so this might be a good opportunity for me to widen my experiences."

"Good for you. I'm glad to see you're open to new things. Although my library is extensive, it would be such a waste for you to restrict yourself. You'll find I am big on sharing with everyone who comes here the many possibilities available in life. So many of us have capabilities beyond our wildest dreams, but we confine ourselves to our own limited experience."

She looked to Suzanna, and paused.

"Suzanna, I would like conduct your initial training. You and I have some very similar gifts. I think we should explore your experiences here on a one-to-one basis, at least to start. Perhaps we can make this not so overwhelming."

In response to the question she sensed forming within the other woman Marianne leaned forward and patted Suzanna's hand.

"I may be busy dear, but I have a special connection with you. We need to discuss some issues before we can get started on what lies ahead."

She glanced back at Joe and he came forward. "Joe, why don't you and Nicholaus do some initial work with Andrew? Then when we are finished up here I'll bring Suzanna out to see what you're up to."

In her own smooth way, she directed people where they needed to go. She'd been told by others her energies made them feel as if the ideas came from within. Nicholaus stood and reached down to squeeze Suzanna's hand briefly showing his support. Marianne noted Suzanna hung on for a brief second longer before dropping her hand back to her lap.

As they walked out, Nicholaus could be heard asking, "So Joe, do you have some type of ability? I haven't been able to figure it out."

Joe responded with a robust laugh, and ushered him through the door. "No son, I'm just your average Joe. No special gifts for me. I'll leave that up to you and my Marianne."

Marianne waited until the door closed, then moved over to sit on the couch next to Suzanna.

"Suzanna dear, I don't mean to scare you, but I feel there are some things we need to discuss."

Suzanna nodded her head skeptically, "Alright, what do you want to know?"

"Mona and I have talked some. She didn't give any details, but I see there is more than just your ability to block your senses that holds you back from a full realization of your gifts. There's more than just being unsure of your own abilities. I can feel whatever this is hinders you in other ways, too. Do you know what this might be?"

"I'm not sure what you mean." Suzanna shook her head slowly.

"I have the ability to look into one's makeup, their past, their future, and their current state of being. Tell me if I can take a quick 'look'? I won't unless you approve."

Curiosity bloomed into Suzanna's eyes. "You said we were alike. Is this something I might be able to do, too?"

"Sometimes with the maturity of our known abilities, others may surface we don't know about. These and other gifts may be possible. This gift is one which needs to be handled with much care. First, you need to understand, in seeing the future I won't tell you what I see. If I did, it would affect the choices you make. What I see isn't set in stone, as it has not yet happened. My sight shows the outcome to the current situation as it occurs right now. The choices you make will determine the final reality."

"What about things that aren't currently happening?"

"They are what exist in your life blueprint, as planned by the universal being. However, this can change too, depending on the choices you make."

Suzanna laughed, "Sounds like a never ending story revolving around the choices we make. Seems like a battle between the universal plan for our lives, and our own bungling behaviors."

Marianne gave a gentle smile. "That is very true. If only we would all stop and listen to the Almighty Source for the answers to our questions."

She patted Suzanna's knee for comfort and tried to bring the conversation back around to her original direction.

"As for your special gifts, we have yet to discover what they could be."

Suzanna's eyes lit up as she exclaimed, "Oh, I meant to tell you about what else has happened. Whenever Nicholaus sends a healing touch out, I see sparks, or sometimes colors coming from his fingers. He says nobody has ever seen it before. Is that normal for people like me?"

Marianne's own excitement grew. She was more psychic than she'd realized. "Actually no, most sentient abilities focus solely on the sense of emotion. It seems you might have a gift of sight as well. We will have to look into this in more depth."

"Okay, I'm so glad I'm finally going to figure out what all of this means." The smile on Suzanna's face was priceless.

Marianne took Suzanna's hand in hers and asked again, "Before we can move on I need to look a little deeper, would that be okay?"

The hesitant nod Suzanna gave was what she needed. Marianne drew Suzanna's attention, sending forth a silent message for acceptance. "Begin to open yourself up to me. Don't put up your usual guards. Try to focus on an external object, such as my eyes."

This tactic had worked in the past. The unusual color of her vivid, dark violet eyes mesmerized the ones being analyzed.

What seemed like a second, was a full ten minutes in reality. Marianne's ability to suspend time while she explored Suzanna's mind went undetected by her subject. When she finished she gave Suzanna's hand a squeeze and laid it back in the other woman's lap.

Marianne sat back against the cushions, the heat of the exerted effort flushing across her cheeks. Lately, in such a thorough search, she found her temperature rose and she would become tired for a short time afterwards.

Must be old age, she thought woefully.

"Was I supposed to feel something?" Suzanna asked.

"Not usually. Some describe an odd flighty sensation," Marianne explained.

"My thoughts did seem to skip around a bit."

Nodding, Marianne remained silent. She needed to gather her thoughts while deciding how to describe what she'd seen.

"Was it that bad? Did you find anything?" Suzanna asked, giving a somewhat uncomfortable laugh.

"You have much pain, my dear. There are many things haunting your daily life. I sense you've held these inside for a very long time. I also felt there's been some release lately. Why don't you tell me about it?"

Suzanna blushed. "I suppose you know I've got a physical condition limiting my ability to become intimate with a man. I've struggled for as long as I can remember. I hadn't told anyone except Mona…until recently."

Marianne waited for Suzanna to continue, she needed the young woman to willingly trust her and to start verbalizing some of the pain she held so close.

"Who am I kidding? You already know everything about me now. In fact, you probably know some things I don't even know myself." Suzanna looked away, her eyes misting. "I hadn't told anyone else, until last night."

Suzanna paused at length, as if struggling for the right words. When she turned back, Marianne sensed the hurt and fear of rejection Suzanna had been holding onto. Still very prominent in her beliefs, they'd begun to lighten with the sprinkling of hope.

"Go on."

Suzanna cleared her throat. "Before, I led you to believe Nicholaus and I are just friends. I didn't realize we could be more. But, I finally had to tell him about this condition I have."

Uncertainty sprang into Suzanna's eyes, and Marianne saw she was not yet able to accept what had happened.

"I don't know why he wants to get involved. He is so willing to help me see if there is any way to work through this thing. I'm still amazed he would even want to try. But then, I guess you already knew that."

Careful not to affect Suzanna's choices with a reference to an expected outcome, Marianne was watchful not to let on about what she saw in her future.

"I am so glad to hear you and Nicholaus are connecting. It must be such a relief to be able to speak out. I will say this though. Remember the physical side of this is only a part of the healing which needs to happen. I saw an indescribable fear, a recurring fear much more important at this point." Concerned by the visions she'd experienced during the reading, Marianne waited patiently for Suzanna to open her own awareness.

"Oh, you must be talking about the nightmares. I've had those all my life. Can't seem to figure them out, or get rid of them," Suzanna revealed. "There's this sense of invasion, coming across in a physical form. Not sure why my mind wants to keep taking me there. But it seems to be trying to tell me something."

Cognizant of the underlying fears and messages the young woman's mind may be trying to surface, Marianne listened as Suzanna began to describe the events of her recurring night terrors.

"Have they gotten stronger?"

Furrowing her brow, Suzanna answered, "Well, yes. Last night the dream seemed different. I felt the touch of this man's hands on my bare skin. It was horrible. I don't know what I would do if the dream went any further. I'm really not sure how much more of this I can stand."

Marianne understood. She'd experienced part of the sensations Suzanna felt during the thorough reading. The memories of the dream were so fresh in Suzanna's mind they had distressed her as well. She imagined the fears would be tenfold in Suzanna's experience night after night.

"Suzanna, I see there is something, an event perhaps, causing those dreams."

Suzanna raised her eyebrows, eyes widening. "You mean this isn't just my mind playing some kind of weird trick on me?"

Marianne shook her head.

"What is it?" Suzanna asked.

"I'm afraid I can't tell. There is a part of you so tightly bound I couldn't get through. Your mind has built such a dense wall around whatever this is I can't access the memories. I can tell, however, this is a memory of an evil nature."

When a look of anxiety popped into Suzanna's eyes Marianne knew she needed to clarify what she meant.

"Don't worry, this is something you have experienced, not what you have done. I believe because of your sensitivity you've been unable to deal with this memory. So your mind has taken care of it in the only manner it knew how."

Suzanna jumped up and began to pace back and forth.

"So you're telling me something happened to me that was really bad. And instead of dealing with it, my mind just tucked it away behind locked doors. Now this thing is finding a way to sneak out at night in my nightmares?"

Suzanna's anguish washed over Marianne in a hot wave of fear. The need to reveal knowledge of this kind was never easy. She nodded, and watched as this new awareness settled over Suzanna.

"And you can't tell me what happened. Obviously I don't know either. Don't dreams all have some kind of weird coded message? It's all some kind of symbolism for what's on your mind when you go to bed, right?"

Marianne stayed silent, watching Suzanna's ability to walk through the steps to discovery.

"It couldn't be as simple as the dream is showing me what happened to me, could it?" Suzanna asked. First was denial, as Marianne would have expected.

"Only you will be able to answer that question, dear."

"I have no knowledge of being attacked. Don't you think I would have remembered something like that?" Suzanna asked sitting back down in the chair.

She breathed deeply several times with purpose taking control of her emotions. Marianne had been unsure if Suzanna's sensitivity would take the lead, creating a high level of distress. Not so, now. The young woman had more control than she'd thought.

"Okay, you said you can't get beyond the locked door. Not knowing, I'll drive myself crazy with all the unanswered questions. You're the experienced one here. Tell me what I should do," Suzanna pleaded.

Marianne tilted her head, focusing on Suzanna's inner strength. She had to give her credit, the girl had guts. Unfortunately, at the moment she couldn't do much to help.

"I've dealt with this type of situation on a few other occasions. The problem is you are the one to discover the truth for yourself. I may be able to help, but you've blinded me with your walls, so it will be up to you to break them down. Until you can do this I won't be able to do much more."

Brows furrowed, Suzanna sat for a moment. "Ok, so, I'm flying blind here, too. I have no idea what to do. Is there some type of methods you can teach me to start to work on breaking down these walls right away?"

"I think for a little while you should just give it a rest. Practice some meditation. Become more aware of who you are."

"Meditation doesn't seem like much of an effort."

"Not so. There is great healing in meditation. Here is one I would like you to practice." Marianne reached out and held one of Suzanna's hands in hers. "I want you to begin by doing your grounding exercises Mona taught you, then close your eyes and see yourself in a beautiful garden flowing with bountiful, colorful plants and flowers of all types."

"Okay, then what?"

"Picture yourself sitting in the middle of this wonderful place, and there is an emerald green light emanating from your heart. Green is the color of healing, and will renew your soul. Imagine it begins to surround you, and moves outward to envelope the entire atmosphere."

"Green is good, I like green," Suzanna offered.

"Mother Earth is a magnet and will pull the inharmonic energies from your soul, replacing them with only love, healing, and light. All energies that don't serve you will be washed away back into the earth to be transformed into positive energy."

"Wow. That's so cool."

"Be willing to release what doesn't serve you, and replace the space it took with the bright white light of our Almighty source. Become one with this light, and stay there until you feel you are done."

"Sounds like a wonderfully relaxing thing to do. I'm going to try that tonight." Suzanna stood, and gave a heavy sigh. "Though I'm just not so sure it will help me figure out what's going on."

"Don't worry. You've made your mind aware you want to break down those walls. Unconsciously you will be working on that very thing. Kind of preparation of the grounds for battle, shall we say, softening it up for the attack."

"Good. I like that approach. Head on. I'm not just going to sit back and let this rule my life anymore. Whatever it is needs to be gone." Suzanna picked up her things and started to walk toward the door. "When can I see you again? We need to keep working on this."

"Come back in a couple of days. Next time you visit we'll go over some methods to help bring this blockage down. There is a very interesting book in the library here about meditation and opening up your chakras. I think this would be very beneficial for you to study."

Suzanna turned and gave Marianne a hug.

"I feel better already. I wish I'd come to talk with you a lot sooner."

Marianne heard the feigned lightheartedness in Suzanna's voice. This discovery process would not be an easy one. She placed her hand on Suzanna's arm, "Me too, my dear," she said softly.

Suzanna let out a slow deep breath. "Well then, shall we go find out what our boys are up to?"

* * * *

As she walked out of the office door, Suzanna decided not to worry about what Marianne said. Even though she thought she could trust her, she still needed solid proof. Marianne's reading might be an educated guess based on the nightmares she described. If it were true, then like Marianne said, she would let her mind work on the problem by itself. Then when she came back on the next visit, she'd be ready. Ready to find out all she needed to know.

They passed several open areas where everyone was hard at work on one thing or another. Some were one-on-one with an instructor, others in collective groups. All seemed to be in a meditative state at some level, practicing what they were instructed to do.

"Most of these individuals you will not be able to visually see their field of practice because it deals with the mind. As you know, the empathic skills, clairvoyance, as well as all of the 'clair' senses, along with telepathy, psychometry, and synesthesia, are all experienced within the gifted individual."

"Psychometry? Isn't that where a person can hold an object and tell facts about an event or a person?"

Marianne nodded.

"This must be really hard to teach. How can you tell anything is happening?"

"Detailed communication to others is a very important part of their training. Otherwise, nobody would understand what they experience. There are a select few skills where someone on the outside can visually see proof of their abilities."

Suzanna tried to soak in all the information as best she could. Amazed, she now found she wanted to know all there was to know about the spiritual gifts.

"Like my ability to see energy movement?"

"Yes. The group up here is practicing what is called astral projection. They are a new group, so they may not be able to present themselves totally yet."

As they came upon the group Suzanna individuals sitting around the room in whatever form was most comfortable to them. Most had their arms outstretched as they rested on their knees, palms upward with thumb and forefinger touching.

She sensed the intense concentration in their effort to project their life force energy outside of their bodies in some form. One person in the corner seemed almost asleep, yet she could see the slight outline of a figure standing in front of him.

"There, the one in the corner. Is that his projection in front of him?" Suzanna whispered.

"Very impressive, you have more sight capabilities than I expected. Not many could see such a faint image," Marianne answered.

Walking forward, they passed a young woman who sat at a table across from another individual. They both looked down at a mug in the middle of the table. Suzanna stopped, curious as to what they were doing.

With a sudden jerk the mug began to lift off the table for a matter of seconds. Luckily it was empty, as the mug shook and bounced precariously about. She watched, as it plopped back down on the table with a loud 'thwack'. The young girl was ecstatic and began to laugh and clap her hands in excitement. The older woman reached across and patted the young woman's hands in congratulations.

"Did you see that? That cup was in the air. It was actually in the air!" Suzanna exclaimed, almost as excited as the young woman.

"I'm not surprised. Alisha is psychokenetic. She's been working on levitation for weeks now. I knew she could do it.

Now she'll have to practice hard to keep things steady." Marianne replied, as if floating cups were a normal day to day occurrence.

Suzanna moved on in awe of the unusual activity around her. The possibilities were endless.

Joe rushed toward them as Marianne and Suzanna approached. "Marianne, you've got to see this. Old Jake hasn't moved like this in years."

Suzanna hurried forward to see what Joe referred to. An old man, obviously 'Old Jake', was doing the soft-shoe in the middle of the room. He looked old enough to either have a heart attack from the movement, or his bones would start to rattle loud enough to be heard.

His cane was no longer necessary to keep him upright, so he used it as a prop in the little performance he put on. At the end of the musical number, which only he could hear in his head, everyone who gathered to watch began to clap and cheer.

"What got into him all of a sudden?" Marianne gasped.

"Nicholaus and I were in here talking with Andrew, like you asked. He was telling Andrew about one of his abilities. You know, Jake is always here in the healing room and he caught what Nicholaus said about the transference of energy from one being to another. Jake called out that 'he'd have to see it to believe it'. That's when we got a show of what this young man is capable of. Honey, we haven't seen this ability in years, not since…not since Jake!"

Marianne stood silent as Nicholaus made his way back to where they stood.

"He asked for it," he said with a smile.

"Impressive, not many can do that."

"All I did was motivate his cells to act more lively. It wasn't much."

"You have no idea do you? Reiki healing is one thing, fairly simple. The focus of energies to motivate the body's own ability to begin to heal itself is pretty standard. But transference of energy to encourage an immediate reaction of the metabolism is another, a much higher level."

Suzanna saw Nicholaus shrug as if it was nothing. Marianne watched the old man's movement.

"If you're not very careful, and this gets out, you will be mobbed by every elderly, tired, and overweight person out there. Especially, women, even the fit ones are in constant search of better and easier ways to increase their metabolism."

"I know. That's why I work with animals. They don't talk."

"Good idea, otherwise you're going to have a real mess on your hands."

Suzanna felt Marianne's intent change to analysis as she looked around, as if assessing the trustworthiness of the people near enough to hear. Now Suzanna wondered if there should be concern about the people here as well.

"One should always be careful," Marianne glanced her way, answering her unspoken question quietly enough so that only she could hear.

Nicholaus was too caught up in the activity around him to pay attention.

Old Jake came up and slapped a hand across Nicholaus' shoulder.

"My God, I haven't felt this good in years. I'm healthy for my eighty-five years, my body just wears out. Can't do it myself anymore. Problem is you can't motivate energy by yourself if you haven't got any to begin with." His old face crinkled into a grin, a sparkle in his eyes. "Seems these days it's all I can do to get my bones out of bed."

"I'm glad I could help you out. I'll be around, let me know if you need another little boost."

Nicholaus held out his hand to the old man and they shook as if they'd been buddies for years.

"I'll take you up on that son. Don't be a stranger. You'll find me somewhere here most days. Not much else to do anymore."

As the old man moved away from them, he did a couple more steps in time to his silent music. He shook his head and disappeared around the corner.

"He used to perform onstage with his wife Judith, who passed away some time ago. There's not much call for an eighty-some year old Fred Astaire these days," Joe said to explain the old man's last comment.

"You've done more good for him then you know. It's rough getting old."

Suzanna felt Marianne's comment came from personal experience. Joe threw an arm around her waist in an obvious effort to comfort her frustration with the inevitable stages of life. She brightened and turned to give him a squeeze.

"What about it? Are you ready to go dancing, my love?" Joe asked.

"Let's go. I'm ready to have fun," Marianne responded as she turned to face Suzanna and Nicholaus. "I forgot to tell you. We will be gone for a week. After tonight's festivities we will fly out to the Caribbean for a long awaited vacation. Suzanna, we'll get together after I get back. Set up some time with Sarah. I'm thinking every other day for at least two weeks."

Reminded of the reason for the frequent visits, Suzanna made a small sound, disappointed she would have to wait so long.

"Oh, alright, I'll do that. I hope you have a wonderful time."

She reached out to shake both Marianne and Joe's hand. At the touch of Joe's hand, a sudden sharp pain shot through her palm to settle in her left hip. She recognized immediately it wasn't her own. It had to be coming from Joe. Concerned, she didn't know if she should say anything. The choice to speak up was interrupted as Marianne and Joe began to walk arm in arm down the hallway toward the stairs.

"Nicholaus, Joe is feeling enormous pain in his left hip. He must be trying to tough it out because of their anniversary. Can you see if you can do anything for him?"

Without question, Nicholaus walked down the hallway and called after them. He asked if he could talk to Joe alone and led him to an empty room. Marianne raised her shoulders up in an unknowing gesture to Suzanna, and waited patiently for the men to return.

Suzanna didn't want to catch up with her mentor too quick, so she took her time as she walked toward the waiting woman. She watched some of the activity around her, hoping to delay any need to explain what Nicholaus was doing, in case Joe hadn't wanted her to know about his aches and pains.

In the other room, Nicholaus put his hand out to touch Joe on the arm. "Pardon my being so forward, but Suzanna feels you're experiencing some pain in your left hip. She asked if I could see if you'd allow me to try to help."

"Very perceptive girl you've got there. The bursitis has started to act up again. It's gotten beyond little Katie's capabilities. She keeps trying and what she does dulls the pain, then it comes back after a short time. I've been thinking, might be time to go see a regular doctor."

"If you don't mind, I'd like to see what I could do for you." Nicholaus gestured to the man's hip.

"Be my guest. Anything to keep me away from those wretched doctors would be appreciated. What do you need me to do?"

"I'm going to ask for the okay from above, I just need you to focus on the area needing to be healed. When I touch you in the general area, stand still until I remove my hand. Oh, and I know you already know this, but it helps if you truly believe this will work."

"You got it."

When Nicholaus removed his hand, Joe took a step forward and back again. Then he wiggled his hips back and forth a few times.

"By golly, I think you've done it! Old Jake wasn't kidding. You've got some powerful hands there. How'd you stop the pain so quick? Katie's never been able to do that."

"It's a little thing I do as an added bonus. The pain would still be there for a time as the bursa is healing, so I sent the pain receptors a little confusion so they wouldn't feel the continued pressure. It's not harmful, and will wear off after a while, by that time you should be on your way to a better you."

"Amazing! Down right amazing. I've got to tell Marianne about this. She's going to be so excited."

The two men came out of the room as Suzanna reached Marianne.

"If you're done with your little *tête-à-tête*...I'm starving. We are going to miss our reservations if we don't hurry." Marianne shot a smile to Suzanna and Nicholaus as she led Joe down the stairs.

"You'll never believe what else he can do. My bursitis, it's gone!"

They could both here him excitedly tell his wife the amazing thing he'd experienced.

"Another good deed is done for the day. I'm pretty hungry myself. How about we go to dinner?" Nicholaus asked as he took Suzanna's hand in his.

"Sounds fabulous, where to this time?"

Suzanna reveled in the awesome comfort of togetherness. She would have gone with him anywhere.

Chapter Fourteen

As Nicholaus sat and watched ten cute six-year old girls play princess with their dolls, he wondered why he'd agreed to come. Although, he was quite amused as they all giggled and talked, pretending in their proper tea party.

One quiet little girl, who had given him the eye ever since he'd sat down on the couch, got up and came over to him. She stood at his knee and just looked at him as if trying to figure out who he might be, not at all intimidated. He gave her a crooked smile to hide the discomfort caused by her intent gaze.

She ran off and came back with two play teacups in her hands. She handed him one of the teacups after she'd climbed up on the couch next to him. It became clear by the expectant look she gave him that she wanted him to be the first to enjoy his tea.

He'd been brought up in an environment where having afternoon tea with his grandmother had been a normal thing to do, so he knew his part explicitly. He raised the tiny cup up to his lips and made a tiny slurp of a sound, then dabbed at the corner of his mouth with an invisible napkin. This made the little girl burst out in laughter. The joyful sound filling the room attracted the attention of the rest of the little girls.

He enjoyed the appreciation of his antics, so he went on to pretend to munch on some invisible cookies with his tea, involved in a lighthearted but silent conversation with his cohort. This raised the laughter of everyone else in the room, including the three women in conversation near the dining room entrance.

The other little girls must have thought he and his newfound friend were having too much fun without them, so they began to scramble to get the best seat at his feet and around the furniture. Kimi came to sit on the arm of the couch beside him. She knew her duties as the proper hostess, and brought the plate of real cookies her mother gave them to enjoy with their tea. This brought on a whole slew of silly actions from the focus of the little girls attention. They began to mimic his actions, all in silent conversations in their own groups, interspersed with bursts of mirthful laughter.

He glanced up to catch Suzanna's gaze. Mona and Lucy stood on either side of her, as entranced by his performance as his small audience. The tender smile on Suzanna's face delighted him as she watched his interaction amongst the girls. He could tell she hadn't expected his ability to meld so quickly with the little ones, unlike most men who thought it beyond their male stance in life. Pleased in her positive response, he gave her a wink before he turned his attention back to the little girl who had climbed up into his lap.

"So are you and Mr. Right having a fling or what?" Lucy's boldly brazen question stopped any possibility of light conversation and produced a giggle from Suzanna.

"Lucy!" her mother admonished.

"It's alright Mona. I suppose it's pretty obvious."

"Do 'ya think? You two have been looking at each other like you've got some big secret. C'mon Suz, spill the beans. Tell us everything!"

"There's really not much to tell. Without question, we're attracted to each other. We've just been talking and getting to know each other. That's all there is to it," she said, unable to hide the slight blush rising to her cheeks.

"Ooh…Okay, so how about it? Is he a good kisser? He looks like he'd be awesome!"

"Lucille May!" Mona admonished again.

All objections were dismissed as Lucy began to whittle the answers out of Suzanna, who was relieved when Kimi started to tug on her mother's shirt tail.

"Mommy, Nicholaus says he's hungry. We want pizza. Can we have pizza now?"

"Nicholaus says does he? Well, I guess it's about time for lunch. Where's the phone? I need to order it." She followed her daughter to where the handset lay on the table and looked back at Suzanna. "We're not finished yet. I want to know details, every last one of them."

Mona patted her on the arm. "Suzie, don't let her bother you. You tell us when you're ready."

Suzanna knew Mona was just as interested to know the answer as her daughter, but in respect she pretended it didn't matter to lessen the appearance of nosiness.

"Where is Carmen? Wasn't she supposed to come too?"

"She'll be a little late. She said something about needing to stop at the store on her way here."

Suzanna reached down to dunk a chip into the delicious dip Mona made for the party when the doorbell rang.

"And there she is," she announced.

Nicholaus got up from his seat to answer the door. Upon seeing Carmen, he bent down and gave her a giant hug.

"How's my girl doing? I haven't seen you around the office much lately."

The color rose to Carmen's cheeks, in the same manner as her daughter. Suzanna was amazed to see her mother had begun to look like her old self again. Whatever Nicholaus did certainly had worked in her mother's case.

Distracted by the voices of the children, Carmen got pulled into the front room, packages in tow. She said in a loud voice, "I brought gifts for everyone." The little girls perked up and swarmed around her.

Suzanna watched as Nicholaus took the opportunity to evade the young charmers and slip past them into the kitchen from the opposite side. She could feel him sneak up behind her, surprised when he bent down to place a peck on her cheek.

He must have been amused by the noise she made, because he lowered even further to place a quick kiss on her neck.

He whispered quietly, "Please get me out of here! They're distracted right now. We can make a run for it."

Suzanna gave a soft giggle and placed her hand over his where he'd laid it on her arm. She saw Mona glance over, and gave a secretive grin, inching nearer to place her hand on Nicholaus' other arm. She gave Suzanna a wink.

"Suzanna, may I have a word with this charmer?"

"Of course," Suzanna nodded giving a slow rise to her eyebrow. What on earth spurred this conversation?

"Nicholaus, dear, why don't you take a walk with me in the gardens? I need some fresh air."

"Certainly, Madame, that sounds perfectly grand," he replied in mock propriety as he gave Suzanna a grin. He placed his hand over Mona's and led her to the door.

Once outside, they began to walk through the grass toward the rose garden, where bright shades of yellow, pink and white fluttered in the afternoon sun.

"I can't imagine Lucy has time to do much gardening." Nicholaus threw a glance at Mona, who gave a nod with her smile. "Might you be lending a hand? I've seen your gardens. This is pretty impressive, too."

"There might be a time or two I gave some needed guidance, and a hand here and there." They came to stop beside a magnificent white climbing rose bush, making its way up one side of an arched trellis. "I'm surprised you accepted an invite to a little girl's birthday party. Lucy was kind enough to ask, but we didn't imagine you'd risk a house full of female hormones," she joked.

"Women aren't so bad. I'm not intimidated by you. You're right though, I didn't know what to expect from a room full of six year olds. I don't think I've ever been charmed by so many of you at one time."

"We start early. It's an inbred characteristic to charm any male within reaching distance."

"Thanks for the warning, only it's a little late. Now I'll have to make a run for it the first chance I get," Nicholaus chuckled.

"So I hear from Marianne you have made quite the big splash over at 'Gloves'. She called me when they got back from their trip and told me all about the show you gave the other night."

"I don't know if I would call it that. It wasn't a show. I just answered a challenge, and healed someone in pain, nothing very splashy."

"Old man Jake has moped around there for years. He almost began to look like part of the furniture. He took a long time to come out of his depression after poor Judith passed. After he did, he no longer had the motivation to heal others. He's just been hanging around as a sort of consultant to the healers. Marianne says now he's been dancing around the place all week. He even got in on some hands-on training with one of the students. He says he's not ready to give up yet."

Humility overrode any other reaction he might have had in response.

"That's not because of me. His metabolism was shut down, I only directed a boost to jump start it again."

"Whatever you did, you've no doubt added more years to his life."

They stopped at the bench, next to a trickling water fountain. Mona sat and patted the seat next to her.

"So, I see you and Suzanna have gotten close." She gave him the motherly eye, and he knew she would come right out and ask. "You remember what I said. How close is close?"

"Let's just say I understand now what you meant when you said she was fragile. She told me about her condition."

"And?" Clearly she wanted a full explanation.

"And…we are taking things slow. I told her I thought I might be able to help her move past her problem. I won't hold anything back from you Mona. There really isn't much to tell, but what I can tell you is we haven't gotten there yet."

Her nod was slow and accepting. "And once you do?"

"Honestly, I don't know. I know I like her very much. I'm attracted to her for sure. I can't answer your question yet. We haven't even started to talk about an 'us', so how can I start to think along those lines?"

He knew Mona's real question hadn't been answered so he went on. "I know you want to protect her from any kind of hurt. Believe me, after I saw what she went through in her nightmares I'll do whatever I can to protect her, even if it means protection from me. I'm not going to hurt her Mona. I'd rather die than hurt her any further."

At first she seemed to accede, but then a new question popped into her eyes. "So, you saw her go through one of her nightmares? That would mean you were there while she slept."

"When she told me about her condition, she needed comfort. She asked me to stay and she fell asleep on my chest then woke up screaming like a banshee." He blew a labored breath through his pressed lips. "Mona, it was awful to see so much fear in her eyes. I didn't know if she would come out of it. When she did, she described the dream to me."

"The poor girl has been through so much. I thought the nightmares had gone away." Mona shook her head sorrowfully, looking toward the house.

"She said they've been back for a while, though they're worse than before. Marianne told her she had some ideas about them, but Suzanna wouldn't go into any detail about what she said. I have my own ideas where they're coming from."

Mona nodded as they watched Suzanna's mother come through the back door and start toward them. "Yes, Marianne told me Suzanna's nightmares and condition might get worse before they get better."

"What do you mean?" Nicholaus asked.

"Not now," Mona said quickly, as she indicated Carmen's approach with her eyes.

He was bothered by her statement, and realized he'd have to ask what she meant later as Carmen promptly planted herself beside him on the other side.

"Well, you have room for two women, no?" Carmen smiled placing her hand on his arm.

Mona stood. "I don't mean to run off, but I know Lucy might need some help with the pizza. Those children can be sweet as pie one minute then turn into the most demanding bunch I've seen in a long time." She bent and gave Nicholaus a kiss on the forehead. "We'll talk later." Turning, she sauntered off toward the back door.

"I'm sorry. I not mean to…how you say…interrupt."

"You didn't. Mona and I are long time friends. We can talk anytime. You on the other hand are pretty scarce these days. What have you been up to?"

"Busy busy. Since you laid hands on me, I feel like new. My granddaughter's first dance recital, so mia niña, Rachel, she ask me to help. Guess who makes costume?"

"Grandma, of course," Nicholaus grinned.

"They say it be easy. Ha! More pain than anything." She turned and gave him the mother's knowing look, and he knew he was in trouble. "And you? You busy, too. Don't think I miss little kiss you give my Suzanna." She raised her eyebrow at him.

"Hmm…you caught that did you? I tried to be discreet. Guess it didn't work."

"No. In room full of women, someone see you, always. Tell me, what you have for my niña?"

If he'd known he'd be drilled like this, he may not have come. Then again, he wouldn't have missed the opportunity to see this group together for anything.

"My intentions, is what I think you are asking," Nicholaus waited for her to agree. "My intentions are to get to know your daughter better. She's an amazing woman. I'd like to find out more. And before you ask, we haven't become intimate. If we do, I believe that is between us, and I'll let Suzanna be the one to break the news to you."

He'd covered everything in one breath. Carmen only raised her eyebrow again.

Good Lord, what else does she want to know?

Suzanna came out of the back door and started to walk toward them. The small knot forming in the pit of his stomach relaxed.

"Well, aren't you the charmer." Suzanna walked up to where he and Carmen sat. "I think you've impressed every woman in the house, including the birthday girl. They can't stop talking about you in there."

"I can't help it. Women flock over me." Nicholaus gazed up at her, the bright sun behind her head creating a halo effect.

Beautiful. Just plain beautiful.

Grasping her hand, he pulled her down beside him on the bench.

"Nicholaus and I just talk about when we make your wedding day," Carmen chimed in.

"Mother," Suzanna gasped. Nicholaus made a choking sound himself.

"Well, you two are perfect for each other, no? I think we not wait. You not get younger."

Nicholaus saw the mortification in Suzanna's eyes. He couldn't believe Carmen's indiscreet prompting for marriage vows either.

"You have to forgive my mother," Suzanna addressed him. "She's always been a little pushy about what she wants to happen." She glared at Carmen for a moment, only to receive a satisfied smile in return.

The exchange between the two was more amusing than anything. Funny, the interrogations hadn't bothered him at all. He wasn't scared off at all. Most guys would probably run away after being hit with such a forceful message. Instead he held back his laughter, though he couldn't stop the twinge of a smile rising at the corners of his lips. This wouldn't be the best time to make fun of the situation.

Suzanna's brows came together as she studied him for a moment. He knew she was assessing how he felt about her mother's questions, and hoped he gave her the right answer. Punching him softly on the arm, she made a face at him then turned her attention back to her mother.

"Mamma, Mona said she needed help with the cake. Could you go see what you can do?"

"Of course," Carmen stood and turned toward Nicholaus. "We not finished here Nicholaus. Talk again, no?"

"Yes, Ma'am," he replied.

Suzanna rolled her eyes as her mother trotted off toward the back door. "Looks like I saved you just in time. I am so sorry. I don't know how you've held up so long. You've been questioned by everyone but the Pope so far."

"It's well worth it," he said pulling her close. "I've wanted to do this all afternoon."

As he brought one hand up behind her neck, he brought his lips down to meet hers, and he felt the immediate connection between them. Warmth spread through his body, a comfort he'd never felt before with any other woman. He only knew, in his arms was where he wanted her to stay.

Inside, all three women gathered around the kitchen window, and simultaneously let out a sigh.

"She doesn't even need to tell me, I can tell he kisses like a dream," Lucy said in awe of her friend's newfound love.

* * * *

"Are you sure you don't need me to go in with you?" Nicholaus asked Suzanna as they stood outside Marianne Ross' door.

"Boy, I must look bad if you don't think I can stand up to Marianne," she chortled. "I know, I know…" she said at the look on his face. "The only thing worse she could do would be to tell me she can't help me."

The grim outlook hit a little harder than she liked. The nightmares were more frequent, their intensity even more difficult to handle. They wore on her. Her physical and emotional health was suffering. She hadn't told Nicholaus yet what she'd learned from Marianne. Though, she was pretty sure he had already come to the same conclusion.

"No, I need to do this myself. Thank you."

"Come to the library if you need me. Let me know when you are ready to go." He leaned forward and gave her a quick kiss.

"I'll try not to be too long," she said as she feigned a faint smile. She didn't feel like smiling at all.

"No worries. Once I get into a subject I can be lost for hours."

She'd hoped to displace the anxiousness settling over her, but it didn't work. She couldn't keep brushing this under the rug. Sooner or later the rug wouldn't be able to cover up the fact she had a major problem on her hands.

Marianne's intent gaze bothered her as she came through the office door.

"Good afternoon dear. How are you today?"

"Honestly not too good. If these nightmares don't go away I don't think I'll ever get any sleep. Seems like the only time I can sleep is when Nicholaus is there and he uses his energies to relax me. A lot of good that does, though, I still wake up screaming in the middle of the night."

"That's good."

"Good? What do you mean good?" Suzanna asked, the thought being incredulous.

"This means your mind has been wearing down those walls. It's only a matter of time before we can knock them down and get to the core of the problem."

"You better show me how to get rid of it soon or I'll end up in the nut house." Suzanna sat down, the plush softness of the chair enticing her to nod off. Sleep had been sporadic at best since the last time they'd met. She no longer felt like the person she once used to be.

"I believe you're ready for the next step. Are you ready?"

"Anything, I'll do anything to get rid of these nightmares." She sat up on the edge of the chair, her eyes opened wide in an effort to become more awake. "What do you want me to do?"

Marianne came around the desk and sat across from her in the opposite chair.

"First, with your permission, I am going to do an energy clearing of any negative attachments, things that do not serve you in any positive way. Memories, experiences, traumas all leave behind an imprint in your body of their effect. For instance, grief settles in your lungs, and anger settles in your liver."

"Really? Wow, so you mean emotions are what cause our bodies to not function right?" Suzanna had never heard this. But, somehow it seemed true to her.

Marianne nodded. "Especially, when a strong emotion is not expressed in the right way, or is repressed from being expressed at all. That's when you start seeing symptoms of physical issues."

"Ok, seems like that would be a really good thing to do then."

"There is only one drawback. My ability to clear these things is limited to what your spirit allows me to clear. There are some I've had to approach the clearing in different ways over a period of time."

Suzanna sat for a minute, trying to digest this new information. "So, you're telling me this might not work."

"I won't know until I start the process to see how you accept my help." Marianne reached out and took Suzanna's hands. "This is the initial stage of where I'd like to start. Don't worry, dear. We will find out how to make things better for you."

"What else do you want to try?"

"I would like you to begin using some meditative states to open up your mind before sleep. You may take a while to achieve these meditations. They can take some practice to get right."

"Open up my mind to the nightmares? Seems to me like that would be the worst thing to do."

"You need to train yourself to become open yet restrictive of what enters through your veil. You need to do this within the dream itself. Like astral projection, you would learn to move your conscious mind outside of your body and watch what is happening, without actually experiencing it."

Suzanna grimaced at the thought. "I'm not sure I could do that."

"I know you are frightened to think of watching something like this, but the whole time you will be consciously telling yourself you are only there to collect information. You will become more informed and less frightened. This should help to open up the doors to what your mind has hidden for so long. From there you should begin to see memories, and hopefully all will be revealed."

"What if it doesn't work?"

"Then there are a few ways I may be able to help you to release those memories. I don't use these techniques often because I feel it is always better for people to experience their own self-discovery."

"Does it involve voodoo dolls? I'm not sure I'd be ready for that yet," Suzanna laughed, trying to lighten the sudden dark cloud settling over her.

"No, but we could try hypnosis. It has been effective for some people. However, I will only use this method as a last resort."

Suzanna took a deep breath, feeling unsure how any of what Marianne described would be possible. At this point though, she would try anything.

"Ok, let's get started. Show me what I need to do next."

* * * *

The drive home was quiet. Nicholaus came around to open her door. More fatigued than when she'd gone into Marianne's office, Suzanna contemplated asking him to lift her up and take her inside. She gathered enough energy to get out of the car by herself, and held his arm as they walked to her front doorstep. Leaving the door open for him, she almost collapsed on the couch as she closed her eyes.

Nicholaus sat next to her, gathering her into his arms. "You must be exhausted. Want to tell me what happened?"

The tenderness in her heart grew for him even more. He could be so compassionate. She wanted to crawl into his arms and let him take away her troubles. But, they would disappear for a short time, only to appear once more with a vengeance. She'd wake in terror and the nightmare of her life would start all over again.

"I didn't tell you before because I needed to get comfortable with the idea on my own first."

She sat up straighter and brought her leg up under her while turning to face him.

"Last time I met Marianne, she told me some things I didn't like. I didn't want to accept them at first. Now I think she must be right." She saw the question in his eyes and continued. "She used her senses to look into my past, present and future.

Apparently, something holds me back from progressing in life and using my own gift fully. She found in my past I had blocked off access so tight she couldn't get past it. Something happened to me. She said whatever happened was bad, really, really bad."

"I could have told you that."

"Exactly. So I thought maybe she was just taking a stab in the dark. No offense meant," she said when she saw the hurt look on his face. "You know, I thought maybe from the description of the dreams she guessed something had happened. So she asked me to make up my mind whether I wanted to reveal this mystery or not. Then she told me to just let my mind work subconsciously for a while, and it would begin to prepare me for the unveiling of this deep dark secret."

"Seems to have worked."

"Yeah, I guess. You know the dreams have gotten more frequent and defined. They're terrifying. I can actually feel what he is doing to me." She cringed, a chill running down her back.

His next question sounded very technical, but she sensed a great deal of concern behind his words.

"Has the vision or physical memory progressed any further? Does he go through with the act itself?"

"No," she answered as she coiled into the arm he wound around her waist. "Nicholaus, I can't take this anymore. I've got to do something about this or go crazy."

"What does Marianne think you should do next?"

"Tonight she gave me something called a clearing. It is supposed to release any pent up emotions storing themselves in my body. She said there are areas so matted with what's been going on she couldn't get through them all. My chakras are all blocked and messed up. The crown chakra and the third eye chakra are so bad she said it was like cleaning out a closet stuffed full of everything imaginable. That took her quite some time."

"So there's progress?"

"Not as much as I'd like. She told me this clearing would have a healing effect over the next couple of days. That's why I'm so tired right now. I need to drink lots of water to flush out what she released, and rest as much as I can."

"Whatever you need just let me know," Nicholaus murmured, reaching up to brush away a sprig of hair from her face. Suzanna pushed her cheek into the palm of his hand, and he stroked her cheekbone with his thumb.

"There's also meditation exercises she wants me to practice. Says they will help me to open up my mind and be more cognitive of what goes on, rather than being so bloody terrified. She thinks this will help trigger my mind's ability to release some previews of what's been hidden away for so long." She gave a shudder anticipating what that might be.

As he held close, in the safety of his arms, she could have stayed forever, if he let her. All of a sudden her stomach gave a loud rumble disturbing the moment.

"Are you hungry? I am, too. How about Chinese? I've been thinking about the Moo Shu pork at this place called the Shanghai all day long."

She hadn't eaten all day, unable to eat waiting to hear what Marianne would say. "That sounds wonderful."

Nicholaus stood up to call in the order. "Chinese it is then." He placed a long sweet kiss on her cheek. "Don't worry sweetie. We'll get through this. Believe in that. I'm here for you no matter what."

Touched by his words, she leaned forward and took his face in her hands. "What have I done to deserve you?" she said placing a longer and sweeter kiss on his lips.

"I don't know. Whatever it is, I'm gonna keep doing it to deserve some more of those." He snuck another kiss from her before grabbing the phone on the kitchen wall.

Later, full of Chinese food, stretched out on the couch they watched Mel Gibson's 'What Women Want'. Suzanna didn't believe she'd ever been happier. There's nothing better in life than to be in the arms of the man you love, she decided.

The man she loved? *Do I love Nicholaus?*

Everything inside of her confirmed this to be true. This overwhelming closeness hadn't happened with anyone before. She'd experienced excitement and sexual tension, never had she been so secure and sure of the things she felt for him. She did love him. Now she was sure.

She murmured a sound of contentment, and snuggled up against him even harder.

"Whoa! Unless you plan on climbing into my skin with me, I don't think you can get any closer."

Lifting her face up for his kiss, she reveled in the knowledge she did love him. She poured herself into the kiss in an attempt to express her love through the touch of their lips, hoping somehow he felt the same way.

She made clear her intentions with the passion she showed, and Nicholaus seemed to follow her cue to the next level. He scooted into a different position and brought her around to where he could kiss her as she lay comfortably in his arms, her body pressed up against his.

As he looked deep into her eyes, he parted her lips to explore with his tongue. She accepted willingly, enjoying the sensation of his tongue against hers. He brought his hand up to fist in her hair behind her neck, pulling her head back lightly he began a trail of kisses down her neck. She moaned, and he nipped the vibration of her throat with his teeth.

Suzanna sensed his internal fight to keep himself from tearing the clothes away from her skin. She shared his urgent need for skin to skin contact, almost overwhelming her. She took his hand and placed it on her breast, her breath quickening under his touch. He continued to lick and nip at her neck as he brought his hand up under her shirt. Wanting to feel him closer, she reached up to unbutton her blouse. He moaned as she revealed a sexy black bra full of lace and bows and a clasp at the front.

"You're the sexiest woman alive. You're driving me crazy." His lips followed the curve of her breast to where lace met skin.

Suzanna wanted more. She wanted his hands on her skin. She brought his hand down to her stomach and relished the intensity of the sexual contact. The need became stronger than ever before. She wanted him. She needed him. She loved him.

"Stay with me tonight." She caught his lips with hers, and said it again. "Stay with me tonight, Nicholaus."

She knew he didn't catch her meaning.

"I don't think I can stay on the couch tonight. If I stay, I don't know if I could hold back again."

"That's not what I asked you to do." Her eyes smiled up into his, adrift in the glorious sensations he brought to her. She knew it would be different with him. She felt like everything would be all right.

"Are you saying what I think you're saying?"

"I want you to make love to me."

He needed no further prompting. Scooping her up in his arms, he lifted her with him as he stood. She wrapped her arms around him as she pulled his head down to hers. Hearts entwined, beating swift and sure, he brought her to the bedroom. Their lips locked in the kiss of new beginnings.

Chapter Fifteen

Nicholaus and Suzanna released their kiss long enough for him to fumble for the switch to the bed lamp. Suzanna shook her head and pointed to the far wall and he realized she wanted the light from the gas fireplace.

After another passionate kiss, he brought the fire to life and understood why. In the darkness the flames cast a low light as they flickered, creating a warm and romantic ambiance. When he turned back he stopped short. Suzanna hadn't moved. She stood still, the light shimmering over her skin. Enveloped in a heavenly glow, he was struck by the pureness of her inner beauty.

Slowly he moved toward her, wanting to preserve this vision in his mind. His lips met hers in a soft kiss and her breath quickened as he lingered in its simplicity, savoring the moment. He continued to lay light kisses against the softness of her skin, exploring the contours of her face. When he returned to her lips, he felt them tremble beneath his in a silent encouragement to take more.

He held back, knowing she couldn't be rushed. He needed to show her she could trust him. He wanted her to know this held more than a simple physical act, because it was more, so much more.

"I…I'm not sure if…" She stumbled with the words, and he knew she'd started to second-guess herself.

He placed his finger on her lips. "Hush…we said we wouldn't go there. No more can't, just want. Relax and run with the feeling honey."

She looked somewhat perplexed, then nodded her head slowly and began to grin. To his surprise she began to loosen the shirt from his pants and proceeded to daftly unbutton his shirt with an ease he never could quite accomplish. The shirt fell away to reveal his well-toned chest.

She touched the contours of his muscles as if she'd never touched a naked man before. Although her movements were tentative, to his surprise she followed her fingers with light kisses from his shoulders down to where the V formed at his navel.

Overwhelmed by the immediate response to her innocent touches, he sucked in a breath.

The button to his jeans fell open just as easily as she helped them fall down around his feet, her sultry giggle almost more than he could handle. He kicked his shoes off and stepped free of the pants to stand naked in front of her.

Her cheeks bloomed to a rosy blush and he saw her look away as if afraid of her next move.

"Touch me." Nicholaus reached out to take her hand and looked deep into her eyes. "I want you to touch me."

He kept her eyes caught in his gaze as he brought her hand down to the erection she'd caused. Her eyes widened with surprise, but he kept his hand over hers to keep her from pulling away. As she began to relax, her shyness turned into curiosity.

"Go ahead, do whatever you want to do."

"Anything?" she asked.

Her inexperience intrigued him, "Absolutely anything."

He thought he could handle her touch, but he hadn't counted on his extreme reaction. She moved her hand up and down, and around, as if to test its size. She let out a gleeful sound when she realized he responded to her touch. Reigning in ten angry horses may have been easier than restraining his urgency in his need for her at that moment.

Her next movement caught him totally off guard. She kept her hand on his erection and bent forward to kiss his lower belly along his hip line. This just about did him in. The bursts of heat he experienced from her touch a phenomenal sensation. The mere touch of her hand sent volts of energy straight to his groin, in immediate preparation for what he expected would be a volcanic explosion.

To steady his heart rate he lifted her up against his body. Her eyes questioned why he'd stopped her, and he grinned at her pure innocence.

"We'll have to stop that for a while, unless you want this to be over before it even gets started."

The shy smile told him she'd yet to understand her full effect on him.

"You're so beautiful. I want to touch you too. Before I do I need to know it's alright with you."

She nodded and looked up, her eyes bright and glowing in the fire, offering herself to him in full trust.

Her already loosened blouse fell from her shoulders as he brushed it to the floor. She seemed comfortable with the action, so he loosened her skirt and let it drop to pool around her feet. She stood in the most exotic underwear he'd ever seen. The black material barely covering the areas intended, and revealing all the places he desperately wanted to touch.

He placed a hand behind her head, and with his other hand to the small of her back he brought her forward to feel her body against his. The coolness of her skin contrasted with his already heated temperature and refreshed his need to feel more of her.

As sexy as they were, the little underwear needed to go.

He placed his finger under the waist of her panties while looking to her for acceptance. She nodded, with only a hint of hesitation. As he helped to guide them down her legs she wiggled to hasten the movement. He opened the clasp of her bra with one hand and let it drift to the floor. Now free of the unwanted item, he brought his hand up to fondle her rounded breast. His desires were expressed in the kisses down the side of her neck to meet his fingers on her nipple. Her moan told him she enjoyed this as much as he.

He found the taut, sensitive tip of her breast with his tongue and began to nuzzle and suckle. He heard her gasp. Her hands came up to his face to pull him away, but as if the sensation overtook her, she pressed him more fully against her bosom.

Slowly, he nudged her against the bed then picked her up to place her in the middle. He stood still, gazing at the exquisiteness before him. Her ebony hair spread out behind her on the pillows, gleaming in the firelight. Any fantasy he may have had etched in his mind dissolved as he gazed upon her body in full view before him. She was perfect in every way imaginable. The breasts he'd caressed were round and firm, her slender waist led down to hips begging to be touched. The softness of her skin, which had amazed him from the start, now glowed in pink perfection.

He lay next to her, gazing down at her radiance. Filled by an ultimate desire, he reached out to touch the softness of her skin. Her breath became quicker with every touch. Moving in slow determination, he brought his fingers down the length of her torso, to the little patch previously covered by her underwear. The dark color intrigued him. Further exploration brought him to where he found her moist and heated. Her moans prompted him to rub her most sensitive spot, at first in a slow circular motion, then with intense pressure and rhythm. Before long the culmination of sexual need she'd built up without release came forth.

"Nicholaus…ooh…Nicholaus!" she exclaimed.

He bent forward and quickly replaced his fingers with the motion of his tongue, which prompted another exclamation. He could feel her body tensing into an orgasm. Her frantic breaths told him she was close to climax, so he began to suck and titillate the rigid spot even more. Within seconds, she shouted out his name and collapsed into a series of spasms.

He was lost, intoxicated by her sweet innocence. Excited beyond control, he was unable to hold back any longer. He rose above her and placed himself between her legs, the tip of his penis just above the desired entry point.

Suddenly her eyes flew open and the look of terror stopped him dead. Her body became rigid and her legs tensed around him in an expulsive motion. The brakes had been slammed on. He should have thought first. She needed to be reassured, so he lowered himself to whisper in her ear.

"It's alright sweetheart. It's me, Nicholaus. I want you so much sweetheart. I want to make love to you. Don't you want me too?" Her hesitant nod encouraged him. "Let me make love to you. Let me show you how much you mean to me. I'll be gentle. Just close your eyes, and let go. Feel me next to you. Concentrate only on the sensations right now."

She closed her eyes and nodded. He could feel her relax as he rubbed her thigh with his palm. He started to build her excitement again by bringing her attention to his tongue on her breast. The tip of his manhood teased her, as he touched lightly at the entrance to her core.

He continued to distract her in other erogenous zones then began to add pressure with his erection. He thought perhaps he'd gotten past her objections, so he pressed further, the heated wetness allowing him to push past the entrance. Then it happened, almost as if a door slammed shut. He was shot out like a cannon ball, her vaginal spasm closed out all possibility of entry. She started to crawl backwards away from him.

"I'm sorry. I'm so sorry." She began to cry over and over again.

Nicholaus realized his approach had been all wrong. He pulled her into his arms.

"It's okay sweetheart. It's all right. Don't worry. Everything is going to be fine." He rocked her back and forth, extending his calming energies to encompass them both.

Only when she calmed did he try something different. He wouldn't let this opportunity pass her by again. He couldn't let her close him out.

"I'm sorry, I went to fast. I understand. Let me try a different way. We need to work through this, right?"

He knew what he'd done wrong and wouldn't make the same mistake twice. He decided he might as well put the brakes on his own needs for the time being.

"You felt how good the first orgasm was, right? This time I want you to keep looking into my eyes. I want you to focus only on what feels good. All I'm going to do is touch you with my fingers, nothing else. If it's alright with you I'm going to use some relaxation energies."

At first she didn't know if she could do it. But he made her feel so safe in his arms, and she didn't want to let go. He couldn't be faulted for the way she reacted. She'd hoped because of the newly discovered feelings for him it would be different. Even with the involuntary reaction of her body, she still craved all those marvelous sensations he was giving her, so she nodded her head in agreement.

Nicholaus broke visual connection momentarily to kiss her neck and concentrate on the spot below her ear. The sensation sent her into another state of excitement. He brought his head back up and regained her attention using his enticing eyes, darkened by sexual need. His touch to her sensitive breasts, taut with anticipation, sent a tickle of desire through her belly as he caressed and pulled at the tips with his fingers. The energy from his fingers shot ripples of need through her system. He began to stroke her body in other areas, stimulating an intense sexual message through his touch as he traced the outlines of her form, gravitating toward her center. Her heart beat harder as he stopped to stroke and explore as he went. Surprised, without any direct sexual contact, the increased energies traveled to her core, prompting her to moan as her orgasmic muscles tensed in preparation.

It became difficult to keep visually anchored with him. She wanted to close her eyes, to enjoy each touch, every kiss, but he'd requested her to stay focused for a reason. His eyes mesmerized her into an unusual level of comfort, different from before. His hands moved downward and evoked an odd feeling of relaxation mixed with an inner excitement unmatched by anything she'd experienced.

When he touched the spot where he'd induced such fevered arousal before, the same urgency began to build. She felt the need to move with his hand in search of the zealous release she'd achieved before. This time though, he backed off and didn't bring her to orgasm so quickly.

"Concentrate on me baby," he whispered. "It feels so good, doesn't it? You need to cum for me, don't you? Keep looking at me. God, you're so beautiful, you drive me crazy sweetheart. Concentrate sweetie."

Before she realized, he'd inserted his fingers inside of her and began to caress the g-spot. Confused, she didn't know what to do. The wild sensations were awesome. She'd never dreamt of feeling this way.

Then it happened again. She cried out in frustration when she felt the uncontrollable constriction show its unwanted presence. The same excruciating pain began to build, her reaction to flee kicking in. All of a sudden she felt an immediate rush, like a flow of water, spread over the spasm and it dissipated, leaving her free to feel the sensation of his fingers.

"There you go. You feel good, sweetheart. This feels so good." He added another movement. His fingers moved in, then almost all the way out, only to go back in to concentrate on further stimulation. "Cum for me honey, I want to feel you explode for me." His fingers became more insistent, claiming more from her response. "Cum for me, baby."

He broke the visual contact and quickly moved down to grasp her swollen clitoris in his lips. The warm friction of his tongue and the continued stimulation of her g-spot threw her over the edge.

She gasped in air as if she couldn't breathe. The pressure building inside so extreme, her body shook with what seemed to be an unending release of satisfaction.

Not even feeling him remove his fingers, it was as if she'd breathed her final breath, before lying quiet and unresponsive in his arms.

Sure, it was easy for her to relax. Nicholaus lay next to her, hormones racing, and a raging need for release of his own. He reminded himself to be satisfied she'd gone so far. She'd made definite progress. He would have to place his own needs on the back burner for a while longer.

Knowing this did nothing for how he felt at that moment. He knew she didn't mean to put him through hell. If what he was feeling wasn't hell, though, he didn't know what would be. She unconsciously snuggled up against him when he wrapped his arm around her to draw her close, making his unreleased desires worse. The need for her grew so great he didn't know if he'd survive the night.

If he smoked, this would be the perfect time to take a puff or two. Only he didn't, so maybe he could get up to have a drink without her knowing he'd gone. That probably wouldn't work. He really needed to figure out some way to get rid of his massive hard on.

Not wanting to wake her from her sleep, he did his best to stay calm. He had to think of something other than his frustration. So he found the least sexually charged subject he could think of, his work. He'd read about a new procedure in the latest medical journal, and he forced himself to find ways to incorporate this new method of care into his own practice. Maybe the change in thought would change his mood.

When he caught a whiff of her perfume wafting from her heated body, and felt her soft hair draped across his shoulder, he knew he'd go crazy before the end of the night.

* * * *

Suzanna woke much later. Nicholaus lay beside her, his protective arm wrapped around her. His breath came soft and constant and his eyes closed. She shifted to place her head on his shoulder and look up into his face. The warm contentment she felt inside was an unusual one. She'd slept so soundly. Then she remembered.

Nicholaus was the first to bring her to orgasm, the first to even approach real intercourse. He'd brought the most unbelievable sensations to life for her. A part of life she thought would never be found.

He was her first real love.

She knew he felt the same sexual desire as she, but she'd done nothing to relieve his tension. At first, she'd been curious to know what he experienced, so she unlocked her guard long enough to find the intensity of his physical reaction overwhelmed her. She'd needed to close down her empathic perceptions to direct her focus on her own sensations. Opening her senses during sexual intercourse would be incredible, if she were ever able to get to that point.

No question, he'd desperately wanted to make love to her with an urgency that scared her a bit. Again, the spasms had overruled, and she *unwillingly* hadn't allowed him to do so.

Ashamed of her inability to satisfy him, she didn't know how she would face him. How would he react? Everyone else dropped her without taking a second look back. Her issues were too much to ask of him. How could he want to stay with her now, knowing she couldn't meet his needs? Maybe she should end it before he left her truly brokenhearted. Because this time, she'd fallen in love.

Damn it! There has to be a way to keep him.

She knew sex could be different with him, he'd proven it tonight. She needed to figure out a way to keep him. She couldn't let him walk away. Somehow she would make it up to him.

She watched his peaceful sleep and reached up to touch the face she loved. He stirred and opened his sleepy eyes.

"Hi."

"I'm so sorry Nicholaus. Please don't hate me," she said the softness of her tone almost undetectable.

At first his expression was blank and briefly uncomprehending. Then he wearily shook his head and closed his eyes, drawing her close to him.

"Never, sweetheart, don't worry about it. I'll catch you next time," he said, his voice thick and drowsy. Before long his breathing became deep and steady again.

Amazed by the reaction, she'd expected anger, or at the very least sarcasm. Was it as easy as this? '*I'll catch you next time*'? Could he be any more easygoing? Her heart did another leap in her chest. She didn't believe it possible to love him any more than she did in that moment.

* * * *

When the sun filtered in through the curtains, it caressed her with its gentle push to wake up. Stretching like a well loved pussycat, her arms high above her head, Suzanna slowly came to the surface from her deep, deep sleep. She could smell the light scent of Nicholaus' cologne lingering on the pillow next to her. Filled by an unaccustomed happiness, she shyly opened her eyes to gaze at the love of her life.

What she found was the indentation of his head in the pillow and the rumpled sheets he left behind. Reaching out, she could tell he'd been gone for some time. He must have left her in the middle of the night without saying anything. She sat up in anger, the fierce pounding of her heart rushed forward.

How could he leave? She'd believed him to be more sensitive. Didn't he know she'd be devastated to find him gone?

Then realization dawned on her. Maybe he couldn't stand to be next to her any longer. He must have thought things over and decided she wasn't worth the trouble. Maybe she wasn't, but that didn't make it okay to leave without a word.

She admonished herself for being angry with him because she couldn't really blame him. She understood the real reason he'd gone. No need to make a big deal over it. Everything would be a lot easier to pretend last night never happened. What she needed to do now was prepare herself to make the change in her thoughts…and her heart. For now she'd let the anger burn its course.

How dare he leave like that?

She got out of bed to realize she was still naked. Intending to take a shower before heading into work, she headed toward the bathroom. A crash from the direction of the kitchen made her jump. Cali must be prowling again. Suzanna grabbed her bathrobe and threw it over her shoulders.

"Cali, what on earth are you doing?" she said as she came around the entrance to the kitchen and stopped short.

Nicholaus, his jeans still half open, shirt nowhere to be seen, cracked an egg over a bowl and looked up. A smile leapt into his eyes before it hit his lips. She saw his gaze travel downward to where her robe, not yet tied, fully exposed her nakedness. She grabbed the lapels and pulled it tightly around her.

"Morning," he said with a smile. "Sorry, I didn't mean to wake you yet. Pan slipped out of my hands."

Flabbergasted, she watched as he began to grate some cheese into the mixture.

"What are you doing here?" she asked pointedly, a frown creasing her forehead.

He looked at her in surprise. "I thought I'd make you a good breakfast this morning. You slept like a rock all night long. First time in a long time," he said, then added with a little chuckle, "I think *that* would be thanks to me, if I may say so myself."

Although angered by his nonchalant attitude, it was displaced by the smell of freshly brewed coffee. So she pulled out a cup and slammed it on the counter.

"Why are you still here is what I meant?"

"A little grumpy this morning, are we? Why don't you get yourself a cup there and have a seat. These eggs will be ready in a minute." He turned the eggs in the pan, and swiftly buttered the toast with a deft hand. As he passed her a steaming plate of heaven, he gave her a quick kiss.

"Not until you tell me why you're still here. I thought you were gone, but now I think you feel sorry for me. Is that what it is? Do you feel sorry for me? Well, don't. I don't want your pity."

Nicholaus came to a complete stop. He turned to face her, a look of confusion crept into his eyes.

"Look, I'm not sure what happened to make you wake up like this, but let me make one thing perfectly clear." He walked over and placed both hands on her shoulders to look deep into her angry glare. He verbalized his words explicitly, "I do not now, nor have I ever pitied you. Pity is the last thing I would ever feel for you."

She gave a *harrumph* sound of disbelief.

"I do think what happened was a step in the right direction. You can't tell me you've ever gone that far before, because I know you haven't."

His intensity scared her a little bit. She shook her head in acknowledgement. She felt his anger now. His calmness did not soften any bit of his scorn.

"You expected me to be gone, didn't you? Just like all the rest of the jerks you've been with." He nodded at her confirming facial expression. "I told you before, I'm not going anywhere. We will do whatever it takes to get you through this. I won't leave you in the middle of the night. I wouldn't do that."

There was nothing but anger coming from him now, so she had to interpret his words by themselves. Peppered by her own anger and negative self-worth, she heard him say he was there to help her overcome an obstacle. That he'd become involved solely for the purpose of healing another poor soul in pain.

Only this time he would rip her heart out at the same time.

She began to tell him what he could do with his 'help' then realized he couldn't be more right. She had never gotten so far before. Maybe she could block her own emotions for him and continue to find out if it were even possible to go all the way. But if she wanted to go for full recovery, she'd have to take what he was willing to give and not expect or hope for more.

Ignoring his intent wouldn't be easy. She didn't know for sure how far she could take this. Knowing he would leave either because he'd had enough of his goodwill giving, or because he'd found someone else who could totally satisfy his needs could stop any further progress. Unfortunately, it was worth the heartache to find out.

"I suppose you're right. Sorry." She knew her defensive attitude didn't match the words, but damn it, she was mad, too.

He took a long hard look at her, and said, "Finish your breakfast. I seem to have lost my appetite. I'm going to the office. I'll see you when you get there."

He grabbed his shirt from the back of a chair and left without another word.

He left in such anger she felt like she should apologize, but decided against it. She wouldn't make a fool of herself.

Not once did he say he cared about her. She was a research project to him. So be it, she'd reap the benefit then let him go. Maybe then she could find someone to love, who would love her back.

Chapter Sixteen

Why did I even bother? She treated me like some kind of unwanted appendage. I made her some breakfast for God's sake. You'd think she would appreciate the effort.

With that attitude, no wonder her other boyfriends gave up.

Nicholaus sat at his desk and drummed the end of a pencil impatiently on the calendar in front of him. He would help her with her problem, and stick it out until she could overcome this burden she carried around with her. Doing what he could to send healing to any affected area would be the right thing to do.

Everything else would be up to her.

He got up to pace the floor a couple of times, muttering to himself.

Damn it, that isn't all there is to it.

His only obligation was to fulfill the promise he'd made. The difficulty occurred as his good deed was combined with a definite need to explore his personal satisfaction. This whole thing started with his intense attraction to her, and a curiosity of the condition she described. Now he found he needed to reckon with something much deeper. Though, at the moment, he couldn't figure out what that was.

Over the last couple of days everything about her seemed to magnify every emotion he possessed. Their shared sexual attraction compounded the fact that he wanted her for more than sex, something he'd never experienced before. It confused him.

The night before, when he realized she feared his touch, he'd have done anything to make it all better. Her innocent sweet touches had pulled at his heart in every way possible. He'd felt on top of the world, knowing he'd be her first, that she had known no other. The desire to be her one and only remained even now. Her inability to satisfy his needs had nothing to do with how he felt about her. If anything, it gave him an intense need to keep her safe from anyone or anything that could ever hurt her again.

Whoa! Where'd that come from? He shook his head in silence. He wasn't accustomed to protective possessiveness, at least not for another human being.

The back door opened and closed. Nicholaus waited to greet her good morning, the second time around. Then in silence he watched as she quietly padded past his door, not bothering to even look to see if he was there.

All right, so she would make him speak first. He was man enough to do it. He got up from his chair and sauntered into the front room where Suzanna prepared for the day to start.

She glanced up briefly then went back to start the computer. Trying not to be angry with her, Nicholaus sat on the edge of the desk, to make his point he thought they should talk. Without a word, she gave him a dismissive glare.

He took a deep breath and tried his best to feel sorry for something he thought he hadn't even done. "I'm sorry for what happened this morning."

She looked hard at him, then replied, "Don't worry about it. It's over with. Next time don't bother staying, you're not obligated."

"Obligated?" *Is that what she feels from me?*

"Soon you can forget it ever happened. You can mark it up as a good deed done and we can move on with our lives."

The pens and pencils she straightened rattled in an unnecessary manner and the paperclips dumped out of their container.

"Forget it? You want me to forget what happened between us?" *What? Did I imagine the connection I felt?* Her rejection hurt.

Incensed by her passive attitude, Nicholaus knew he needed to get his mind around the whole thing. Having been up most of the night he didn't know what to think, let alone say. And he knew he needed to step back before he said something he'd regret.

"Fine, if that's what you want."

Her scowl became indignant. "Fine," she exclaimed slapping the container back on the desk, the paper clips flew everywhere.

The phone rang and Nicholaus reached down to grab it without losing Suzanna's staring glare.

"Brach's," he almost shouted into the receiver.

"Nicholaus, it's your mother. We really need to talk. Would you please meet me for drinks, or something? It won't take long, I promise."

His heart rose to his throat. He blew out a hard breath through pursed lips. *Why the hell did you have to call right now?*

"I said no. Now don't bother calling me again." He slammed the phone back down again.

He strode toward the door, then came back to open his mouth, desperately wanting to say words he knew would hurt Suzanna as deep she'd hurt him. For the briefest second he caught a flash in her eyes of hurt, anger, and something he couldn't quite put his finger on. He slammed his words back, turned and walked to the door again.

The heavy door swung open and he muttered on his way out. "I'm going for a walk. I need some coffee."

* * * *

Suzanna tried to be interested in the veterinary journal that came in the mail, but no matter how hard she tried she couldn't stop thinking about Nicholaus. He came back and disappeared into his office. His evasive maneuvers disheartened her, contradicting her need for acceptance.

Could she really be so wrong in what she felt for him from the start? If he were so cold hearted, wouldn't she have sensed he was all about the research, only wanting to prove he could heal her?

Though, she'd found an inability to read him correctly. Since they'd become intimate, her own emotions were flying so high, she felt as if she mixed her own along with his most of the time. There didn't seem to be a clear distinction between what they felt individually, which surprised her. She'd learned to control that a long time ago.

Over and over she went through the time they'd spent together in hopes to see something she missed. Each time she ended up with the same conclusion. He was caring, kind, and compassionate. He made her laugh one minute, and provided the security she craved the next. She'd always thought he cared for her, more than just friends, and she'd begun to think he might be able to love her the same way she loved him.

She reminded herself he never once said anything about caring for her, and became saddened again by the possibility her determination that morning had been right. The one thing she could pinpoint was how much he wanted her. But, she knew his physical needs couldn't match what she felt for him. Lust was no comparison for love.

The front door opened. Believing an unexpected patient was arriving she put her woes aside and raised her eyes to greet the visitor. To her surprise, the young woman, with the blond spiked hair came in with a soured look on her face.

"Where's Dr. Brach? He needs to see Bruno again."

"Do you have an appointment?" Suzanna tried to sound as professional as possible, though she really wanted to tell her to go find another veterinarian.

The woman shook her head, brows furrowed. "No. Just tell him Christina is here to see him. He'll have time for me."

Is that so? Suzanna quieted her immediate response to a mere, "I'm sorry, but you will need to make an appointment."

Christina glared at her. A hint of recognition lighted in her eyes. "Hey, you're that girl Dean was seeing. Boy did you make him mad." A grin appeared on her lips. "But, I made him forget all about you."

Suzanna cringed at what that meant, obviously, another jab at her problem. She really wished Dean had kept that to himself. She didn't need everybody to know, especially this woman.

"Dr. Brach is very busy. You will need to make an appointment." Even though it wasn't the truth it sure felt good to reject this woman's request.

"Look here, I want to see him now. Do you understand? Now," she emphasized by placing her hands on both hips, glaring at her.

Against every inner warning, Suzanna stood. "Wait here, I will see if he has time to speak with you."

Good Lord, the woman had no manners at all. Why on earth does she keep showing up to irritate me?

As Suzanna approached Nicholaus' closed door, she calmed her nerves by breathing deep. Rapping on his door she waited for an answer.

"Come in." Nicholaus stood at his bookshelves, an open book in his hands. He looked tired, his hair rumpled on one side and a reddish mark on his temple, as if he'd been resting his head on his palm.

"I'm sorry to disturb you. There is a woman here to see you. She said her name is Christina and she wants to talk to you about seeing a pet named Bruno. Should I show her in?"

Nicholaus sighed and moved his head from side to side as if to relieve some stress. "No. I'll be out in a minute."

Suzanna quietly closed his door and went back out front to find this Christina had helped herself to the water at the back of the waiting room, and was rifling through the snacks.

"Dr. Brach will be out in a moment."

Christina nodded and reached into her purse for her lipstick. "Of course he will."

As Nicholaus came out, Christina quickly put the tube back into her purse. She stood, beautifully manicured hands extended, reaching to grasp his in an intimate manner when he approached.

Suzanna couldn't quite hear everything that was said because Nicholaus had his back toward her, and they were far enough away the words were muffled. The woman placed a possessive hand on his bicep and glanced over his shoulder at Suzanna, as if to say he's mine.

Suzanna heard snippets of 'please' and 'I need you' from Christina, and 'I can't' and 'not now' from Nicholaus.

This is very confusing.

She couldn't help but watch the two, trying to figure out their relationship, if they had one. Christina gave an obvious pout when Nicholaus led her back to the front desk.

"Please make an appointment for Christina and Bruno for next week sometime," he said with a tired smile. Turning to Christina he almost bumped into her as she was following so close. "Take care, I will see you later."

As Nicholaus headed toward his office, Christina shot back, "You sure will, sweetie." She watched him as he disappeared around the corner. "That is one sweet hunk of a man, don't you think?"

Suzanna could only raise her eyebrows at the whole scene.

Christina turned, their eyes met, and she shook her head and burst out in laughter. "Why am I asking you? You have no idea."

Hoping her heart would pound harder in her ears so she wouldn't have to hear the blithering idiot. Suzanna quickly made the appointment for her and sent her on her way.

As Christina sauntered away she called out, "Bye, Dr. Brach, see you soon." She pulled the heavy front door and stepped outside, but before the door could close another person pulled it open to come in.

A bit rattled, Suzanna wished she had a few minutes to gather her nerves. The smile she intended to present to the newcomer was replaced by the widening eyes of surprise.

Great! What else can happen today?

Not the person Suzanna would ever expect to come in, her sister Rachel approached perfectly adorned. As usual, her high-priced designer slacks and silk blouse opposed her job as the mother of two. But being married to a high profile real estate mogul, she insisted she had to look the part at all times.

"Rachel!" Suzanna exclaimed as she came around the end of the desk to give her sister a hug.

Rachel gave her the high society kiss on the cheek without allowing her to get closer than a foot from her perfectly pressed clothes.

"Suzanna," she said in acknowledgement.

Well, things hadn't changed. Her sister remained just as standoffish as she'd always been.

Yet there had been a time…

"What gives me the pleasure of a visit from you today?" Suzanna said, acting brighter than she felt. She turned to one of the wing backed chairs, and indicated the opposite for her sister to be seated.

Rachel sat gingerly on the edge of the seat and looked around the place as if she expected hair and vermin to jump on her at any moment. She put her hand up to assure her salon styled hair stayed in place.

Her hair was similar in color to Suzanna's, yet not quite so striking. She hadn't been so lucky. The dark hair, cut just above the shoulder, was unruly and needed constant attention to look halfway decent. If she wasn't out buying clothes, she could be found at the hair salon getting another taming treatment to keep her appearances presentable. Her almost too light skin, prone to heavy circles at her eyes, required the use of heavy make-up to cover up the obvious imperfections.

"So, this is where you've ended up, at a veterinarian hospital? Really Suzanna, don't you think you could have found anything better than this?" Rachel said with obvious disdain.

So you've come in prime form today, sister dear.

Suzanna was in no mood for this today. She felt the blood rush to her cheeks accompanying her anger about her sister's insinuation of inferiority.

Just leave it alone, it doesn't do any good. She'll never see you for who you are, Suzanna reminded herself.

This time it was different though. She felt strong enough to at least make her position known.

"Not that you would understand, but this isn't just another lowly job. This is a choice to do something good in this world. It is a career I am going to enjoy. This business has been in good standing with the community for years, and the owner is a kind and caring man. I couldn't care less whether you perceive this to be on the lower scale of your spectrum. It happens to be on the higher end of mine."

"Well, I guess you've told me." The sarcastic smile she gave irritated Suzanna even more. Rachel leaned back slightly in her chair. "Isn't this cute? Little sister has her sights set on a doctor. Thing is, he isn't a real doctor. He just has a thing for horrible little creatures, like cats and dogs. I suppose you two would fit perfectly together."

The words brought the hackles up on the back of Suzanna's neck. She made sure her voice stood out loud and clear.

"Unlike you, these beautiful creatures have more heart than you ever will. As for Dr. Brach, he is highly respected in his field and has received many awards for his accomplishments. Veterinary medicine requires the same technical knowledge in anatomy, pharmaceuticals, and surgery as any other medical field. In fact it's more complicated because he has to deal with a variety of species, rather than just one human form."

Rachel rolled her eyes at Suzanna, blowing out a breath of impatience, which riled Suzanna even further.

"For your information, he also has a doctorate in medicine. If he wanted to, he could easily become qualified to practice as a medical doctor. But he's chosen a field to support beings unable to get quality care as easily as people. So, unless you have something more important to say I suggest you leave." As she spoke Suzanna rose from her seat, ready to show Rachel to the door.

"Easy Suz, I didn't realize how strongly you felt for him, or his creatures. Settle down, I'll try to be good," Rachel said with a smirk.

"Why are you here?" Suzanna waited for the next bombshell. Rachel never came to see her without needing a favor or when bearing bad news.

"Frank is in town and says he wants to see us both for dinner," Rachel said, referring to their father.

"Oh," Suzanna finally said. A sudden foreboding began to settle over her.

"If you don't want to come, I'll be glad to tell him you aren't able to make it," Rachel responded with an obvious excitement.

Confused by her sister's sudden change in emotion, Suzanna remained quiet. Then she said, "No, I'll be there. When and where?"

"Figures," Rachel said as she stood to brush off the invisible hair from her pants. "We'll meet at Ivar's on the Waterfront, tomorrow night at seven o'clock. Six thirty if you want to have a drink with us before dinner," she said in forced politeness as if having to include her in their plans.

The strong negativity in her tone was a silent message Rachel didn't want her there. Suzanna nodded. "I'll meet you there at seven o'clock."

Without another word Rachel turned and left, nose held high as she slammed the door behind her.

Nicholaus heard enough to be incensed. He'd come out of his office to see if he would be needed and realized the woman was no ordinary visitor. Close enough to hear, he'd stayed far enough behind the door to not be seen.

He waited before entering the room after Rachel left. With the obvious added stress of the conversation between the two sisters, he wasn't surprised to find Suzanna a bit pale.

"Who was that?" he asked, not letting on he'd already determined the answer by his eavesdropping.

"That is my sister Rachel. She came to tell me our father is in town. He wants to see us for dinner tomorrow night."

Nicholaus saw the wash of resignation cross over her face. "How do you feel about that?"

She didn't readily answer his question, only shrugged her shoulders without comment.

"When was the last time you saw him?" he asked more for the piece of information to fit into the puzzle than actual interest.

"He hasn't been up for close to ten years. I saw him when I'd just graduated out of high school and he hasn't been up since. Rachel's family goes down to see him all the time, but nobody ever asks me if I want to join them."

"Why do you think that is?"

She again shrugged her shoulders. He wasn't sure if she was lost in her own thoughts, or perhaps she still hadn't forgiven him for the morning. It appeared now was not the time to talk.

"I'm going to Gloves later on today. Would you like to join me?"

"Hmm…oh…sure,"

He wondered if she heard a thing he said.

"It looks like it's going to be a light day. Maybe we can head out earlier in the afternoon."

"Whatever you want," her vacant answer came with a half-hearted nod of her head then her attention appeared to be turned back to the magazine on her desk.

He interpreted her disinterest as an extended reaction from the morning's events, so he left her to her own thoughts. He still didn't fully understand what had happened.

* * * *

Things still hadn't picked up by afternoon, so with no scheduled appointments keeping him there Nicholaus decided to close up and head out to Gloves to do more research. During his previous visit he discovered some very interesting information one couldn't find so easily on the Internet. The books in Glove's library on healing were proven techniques, including the technical methodology he needed to make his own judgment as to the uses and quality of information. Most of the text he found on the internet, spawned from marketing spin-offs leading to the sale of some product. He'd found some information to be worthwhile, but it took time and was frustrating to weed through all the results from his searches on the Web.

He found Suzanna in the back room stocking the cabinets with a shipment of supplies received that afternoon. He wanted desperately to crack the ice which had formed between them. Quietly he approached her and wrapped his arms around her waist. He wanted to show her he still felt the same way about her, no matter what she thought, and gave her a sweet soft kiss on the back of the neck.

She stiffened at his touch. The cold front still in place, she continued to place the items on the inner shelves.

Her dismissal didn't surprise him and he stepped away, saddened by her continued rebuke.

"I'm going to close up now, are you about ready to shut down and come with me?"

She turned and stared at him blankly.

"Gloves. We were going to go to Gloves this afternoon," he said, concerned now about her forgetfulness. "Are you all right?" Her earlier paleness had not yet gone away.

She nodded absently and began to break down the unpacked cardboard box. In the process a hidden staple in the bottom of the box grabbed hold of her finger and tore through the skin.

"Ouch…!" she exclaimed, pulling her hand out of the box. The wound was deep enough it caused dark red blood to run down her hand.

Nicholaus immediately went into doctor mode. "Come with me." Flipping the water on in the sink, he tested its temperature with his own hand, pulled her fingers under the faucet, and reached into the cabinet over the sink to grab the First Aid box.

He wrapped her finger with the loosened sterilized gauze. "Here hold this for a minute. Put pressure on the wound to stop the bleeding and hold it up as high as you can."

Quick to prepare the rest of what he needed and he took her hand gently in his. When he took off the gauze, the bleeding had subsided enough to apply his bandage. First he needed to make sure there were no germs lingering about.

"This will sting a little bit." With a cotton swab, he soaked it in iodine and began to dab her finger.

"Ow. That hurts," she complained, scrunching up her face in protest.

"I know. I'm sorry."

He applied some antibiotic ointment to the wound, and topped it with a well fitted bandage for her fingertip.

He kept her hand in his as he looked up into her dark, expressive eyes. She didn't seem to be angry any longer. The need to bring the same closeness back swarmed through him. Her soft lips begged to be kissed, her soft curves pleaded for him to hold her in his arms. She would have to make the first move in that direction. He wouldn't push.

With a simple raise of her hand to his lips, he kissed the injured finger gently, his eyes never leaving hers. Instinctive to his healing character, he sent positive energies through her hand for a quicker and pain free healing. Her eyebrows creased, lips tightened, as if she were about to say something. He saw the change in her eyes from expression of a thought to a closure of the subject. She'd decided against opening up to him, and ended up giving a light squeeze of his hand with hers.

"Thank you Nicholaus. You're a fine doctor."

He stepped away from her. She wasn't ready. He might not understand, but he could give her the space she needed.

"Are you ready to go?"

Suzanna shook her head, and finished placing the bottles into the cupboard.

"I don't think I will today. I need to go do something. You go on without me. Tell Marianne I said 'hi' if you see her."

Awkward, they stood in silence, until she made the first to move out front to gather up her things.

Disheartened, he followed her. "So, I guess I'll see you later?" He hoped there would be a slight chance she'd want him to stop by when he got back.

"Yes, I'll see you tomorrow."

As quiet in her arrival that morning, she left him to stand there to wonder if she would ever look at him in the same way she had when she'd brought him to his knees the night before.

* * * *

Marianne found Nicholaus in the library immersed in a pile of books. He furiously took notes on a notepad in what appeared to be some kind of shorthand.

He lifted his head as she approached, lay his pencil down in respect, and gave her his full attention.

"Good evening, Nicholaus. You seem to be hard at work there. What have you found so interesting?"

"Gems and stones have always interested me in their uses in the art of healing. I've never found any material quite as extensive as what you have here though."

"Oh, yes, stones can be very useful when used properly. As you are aware, all things are a compilation of energy. They've been used for centuries in healing, especially in Asia."

He nodded thoughtfully. "The ancient eastern culture seemed to be much more intuitive in the use of natural healing. I've been studying various ways to bring them into my own practice."

"Stones come from the heart of creation and help to modulate and eradicate abnormal energies that cause physical and emotional illnesses. Everything we need to live healthy and productive lives has been produced by the universal oneness for our use. It's up to us to figure out how to use them for the right purposes."

Nicholaus nodded his agreement and sat back in his chair. "You're right of course. I'm thinking with the use of herbs, minerals, and various stones, one could almost eliminate the need for chemicals. There are so many people out there, like me, who haven't come to their full potential because they are so unaware of the possibilities."

"True. You also need to remember you've been given the greatest gift to help others, through the spirit to produce an even greater healing." She could tell he still felt uncomfortable about being labeled a healer. "You know, Nicholaus, you're nothing like your mother."

Nicholaus looked sharply at her. "What do you mean?"

"Your mother came to me many years ago when we first started this organization. Just like you, she had great potential.

She wanted to learn all she could about her gift, and was destined to do great things."

"Yeah, great things in the interest of 'The Universal Order'," he said with scorn.

"Unfortunately, people sometimes fall into the hands of greed and power, even when they may think it's for the greater good. The evil one has many faces, and loves to pull us away from what is right in the pretext of doing good deeds." Marianne softened realizing how badly his mother's actions had affected his life. "Nicholaus, I truly believe your mother felt she was doing the right thing. She became blind sighted by evil, and may not have had the maturity to realize what she'd been pulled into was wrong."

Nicholaus stared past her for a moment, lost in his own thoughts. "She's called me again."

"I know dear. She's called me as well."

"What does she think is going to happen? Am I just supposed to forgive her because she's decided to come back into my life?"

"Honestly, I don't think she expects that. There are things she needs to reveal to you I believe you need to hear." Marianne could read him well enough to know he still wasn't receptive to the idea.

"Like what? That she's sorry and I should forgive what she did?"

Marianne understood his pain, but what she'd learned may change his mind. "She asked me to tell you something if you refused to see her."

Nicholaus glared at her for a moment. "What?"

"She did leave for all the wrong reasons. When she realized what she had done she tried to leave and come back to you and your father. But I understand for reasons beyond her control she wasn't able to leave."

"So what changed?"

"I can't answer that dear. At some point you'll have to get the full story from her." Marianne could see the battle of right and wrong being fought in his mind, and wasn't sure which one was winning.

He shook his head. "What she did hurt us. I don't care what her reasons are, it wasn't right. I'm not sure I can forgive that." The cold tone in his voice wavered a bit as he spoke.

Marianne knew the battle had been lost, but the war had not been won yet. She covered his hand with hers.

"Only you will be able to tell when the time is right. Until you do, you may not be able to realize your own potential. Forgiveness is the key to true freedom. And it is in understanding the ways of the universal being that will direct you in the right way. Listen to the Spirit, and don't be afraid to let go." Marianne was saddened by he level of barriers still obstructing his spiritual growth. There was nothing more she could do than to suggest the right direction for him to travel.

He looked away. "I know," he said simply. "Doing it is something different."

They sat for a minute in silence. She wanted to let her words settle in.

"I haven't seen Suzanna for a while. How are you two getting along?" Marianne asked only to broach the subject, for she'd sensed the answer when she came into the room.

"I can't lie to you, you'd know it if I did."

Marianne gave him a calm smile.

"I'm not sure where Suzanna and I stand right now. I'm trying hard to understand, and I want to help her through this thing, but she won't let me in."

"Is that all you want from the relationship, just to help her through it?"

"Well, yeah...I mean, no," he answered, as if confused by his own feelings.

"Remember she can sense your confusion. She may be reacting to your own unclear thoughts."

"Probably," he said with hesitance at the new insight. "I've tried to be as positive as I can. Sometimes I think she feels totally different than I do though."

"Do you know what you feel?"

With a laugh he shook his head. "Not exactly, but I know she is the most important thing that's ever happened to me. She isn't like anyone I've ever met. There is something different about what we share. I haven't figured them out yet, but my feelings for her go deeper than I've ever felt before." He hesitated then looked up into Marianne's eyes. "I know it sounds stupid, but I don't want it to ever stop."

"Sounds like love to me."

Nicholaus stopped short to look long and hard at Marianne. She could see the play of emotion running across his face. His eyes brightened and he nodded as if to accept the realization.

"Have you told her how you feel?"

"I'm not sure I really knew until just now. In some ways, I guess I thought she'd be able to know without my saying."

"She may be confused with her own thoughts. Suzanna is a very special woman. Even though she is capable of sensing your emotions, you need to tell her outright the way you feel so she can sort things out in her own mind. She's had some very traumatic things happen in her life. Trust in many of her relationships has been her enemy. Don't discount the potential of your relationship with her by the confusion of the moment."

He understood what she meant. He was quick to process, Marianne noted. Almost like a computer, she could see his mind fitting the pieces together, filing away information for later use.

"She's told me about the Vaginismus, and the nightmares. You've directed her through some meditative ways to help her open up to her dreams. Do you think it will work?"

"I think this is the best way to start," Marianne acknowledged.

"The nightmares, and the physical condition, are connected in some way. If you could be there when she first wakes from those nightmares, she's horrified. I've read where some suggest what appears in the dream state may only be a symbol of what the mind is working on. It's obvious she relives whatever this is over and over again in her dreams."

"I agree."

"Consciously though, she doesn't seem to remember anything traumatic in her past."

"Her sensitivity has blocked her memory. I'm hoping to work with her until she can come to a realization by herself. She's built a very strong wall around whatever traumatized her. This technique may not work."

"Nobody should have to go through life in such turmoil. It's gotten worse. Did she tell you she's having sensory memories of her dreams?" Nicholaus frowned.

"Yes. That's also why I think she isn't just dreaming. Without previous knowledge, a sensory memory is impossible. Sensory memories can only come from a similar past experience."

"I wish there was more I could do to help her."

"Being there for her when she needs you is the most important thing right now. When you decide what you feel for her, don't hold back. She needs to know."

Nicholaus nodded. Marianne hoped her words had truly gotten through to him. Now she had more important information to relay, and hoped he would be open to receive it.

"Andrew tells me you have some very advanced skills. I would like to suggest you practice those skills and use some of the new ones you've learned on a select group of people who are in need of your gift."

"People?" he asked, his voice straining into wariness. "Isn't that a little risky? I've told you I don't want to be dragged into any type of massive media situation. I only heal where I am led." His eyes narrowed enough to tell her she'd stepped onto thin ground.

"Neither do we, dear, these are people who have come to us with a need. They don't want to spread any hype about what happens here. I've hand selected a few I believe you may be able to help, if you're interested. It's your decision who you attend to, just let me know." She handed him a couple of cards. Each had a name, address and physical condition written on them. "The one on top is the one I thought you'd be most interested in."

Nicholaus stared at the card. He looked up, a slight tear in his eyes. "This is my father."

"I know dear. I didn't think you knew. I think if anyone is able to heal him, it'll be you. You'll have the closest connection with him."

He continued to stare at the words on the card. Lymphoma–Stage II.

"He came to you? He doesn't believe in healing. Why did he come to you?"

"Sometimes when confronted with a life threatening disease, people will try anything. When medical treatments aren't working, or cause more pain than the original ailment, they look for other possible treatments, no matter what they are."

She took hold of his hand, and felt the furious upheaval of emotions inside of him.

"I've known him as long as I've known your mother. He does believe. He just doesn't want to acknowledge his belief." She saw Nicholaus' uncertainty and patted his hand. "Pray about it. Listen to your heart, it won't direct you wrong. Let me know what you decide to do."

In silence he nodded and began to collect his things to leave.

"Why didn't he come to me?" he asked finally.

"I can't answer that Nicholaus. All I know is he needs you now more than he ever has."

Nicholaus looked into her eyes, as if in search of something more. Marianne could see the bottled up pain through his eyes.

"Thank you Marianne. I appreciate your trust in me. There's something I need to do first. I'm going to think about this for a while. I'll let you know what I decide."

* * * *

Suzanna went to her mother's house that evening for dinner. Coco met her with enthusiasm at the door, ready for his dose of attention. She brought him up into her arms, and snuggled him with love. The heavenly smell of fresh baked berry empanadas wafted through the house, causing her mouth to water in anticipation of the wonderful tastes her mother had prepared.

Carmen brought out the Ceviche from the refrigerator when Suzanna came through the kitchen door. Coco jumped to the floor, disgruntled when Suzanna went to give her mother a kiss on the cheek. Carmen pushed away to pull the sweets out of the oven.

"I not let this burn. No want to throw them out."

"Don't say such things," Suzanna scoffed as she bent over the pan and drew in a deep breath. "Oh, I love you Mamma."

Carmen turned for a much longer hug and smiled. "I love you too, *novia*."

Flushed from the heat of the oven, her mother's face almost glowed in comparison to a few weeks before. Suzanna noticed her mother's new haircut, it suited her well. The slacks and sweater she wore were new too, an oddity for a woman who bought clothes next to never. Her mother's new attitude amused Suzanna. In thirty two years she'd never known Carmen to make such drastic changes.

"Go sit. Dinner, she *esta listo*."

"Don't you look mighty spiffy tonight? If I didn't know better, I'd wonder where my mother was hiding," Suzanna kidded.

"I know. This Dr. Brach, he make me a new woman," Carmen said as she placed the large crystal bowl on the table. She brought two smaller ones to serve the Ceviche. "Suzie, take *la Ceviche. You* too thin, you take *mucho grande*. I get the iced tea."

The Ceviche, a very time consuming dish with finely chopped vegetables and fish, must have taken her mother a good part of the day to prepare. Added to a batch of freshly made salsa and homemade tortilla chips, Suzanna couldn't imagine anything better. She began to wonder why her mother made the effort for such an extravagant meal.

Suspicious, she asked, "What is all this about? These are all my favorites. Either you have something good to tell me, or there is something really bad you don't know how to tell me. Which is it?"

"Oh, this?" Carmen asked humbly. "Can't I do good for my sweet *Niña*? I miss you. I thought you like the *Ceviche*," Carmen said with an exaggerated pout.

Suzanna gave her mother a smile then dug a chip into the Ceviche. "Of course you can. Anytime. If I'd known you'd cook my favorites for me, I would've moved out a lot sooner."

Conversation swayed over different subjects during dinner. Suzanna told her mother a little about her experience at Gloves. She didn't go into much detail, even though Carmen appeared interested. Carmen expressed her support, and told Suzanna she knew she had much to offer with her 'special' hidden talents.

Although conversation usually turned to the subject of boyfriends, Suzanna knew her mother had other things on her mind. She could feel her mother's mind working on the pros and cons of something, not sure yet how to tell Suzanna the problem.

Perhaps she would help her. Dinner wasn't the reason Suzanna asked to see her mother. She had a more pressing matter to discuss.

"Rachel came by to see me today."

Her mother's immediate reaction was masked by averted eyes and fumbling fingers. It was apparent to Suzanna she already knew.

"Oh? She come see you? I tell her where you work. This alright, no?"

"Yes, Mamma, it's alright. She told me Frank is in town." Her mother's quick frown told Suzanna she already knew that, too. "He wants to meet for dinner tomorrow night."

"Oh, he be nice. You go, no?" Suzanna studied her mother. It seemed as if her mother didn't want her to go, but she never expressed any negativity toward Frank. Suzanna frowned sensing a hidden emotion behind her mother's words. Fear? Or was that anger? Or, maybe both?

"I don't have any reason not to. Do I?"

Her mother shook her head a little to quickly with a sudden interest in wiping invisible dust off the end table with her desert napkin.

"Rachel and I got into it again."

"Oh, you two fight always. What she about this time?" the elder woman asked.

"Nothing really, Rachel just thinks she's so much better than me. It gets on my nerves," Suzanna said, her stomach tensing again by the memory of her sister's visit to the office.

Her sister's attitude toward her had driven a wedge forcing them apart. The insecure need to prove her superiority drove away any possible relationship.

Suzanna took a deep breath. "Then she acts like she hates me. Why Mom? What have I ever done to make her hate me?" The memory of her sister's words taunted her.

"Rachel, she no hate you, *novia*. She just…she change when her Poppa left."

"Why does she hold that against me? I didn't cause him to leave, did I?" Suzanna asked feebly, knowing the answer she'd received before.

"No, no, *mia novia*." Carmen got up and held her hands out to Suzanna. She drew her up into a hug. "No worry about her. You two make friends soon. She come in time."

Suzanna gave a deep sigh and pressed her cheek on her mother's shoulder.

"I wish someone could explain it to me. I'm getting pretty tired of being blamed for something that wasn't my fault."

Chapter Seventeen

The next day went smooth enough. No major emergencies, a few scheduled visits for shots, and a follow-up appointment was all Suzanna had to take her mind away from the upcoming evening. For some reason she couldn't help but feel an impending disaster waited in the shadows.

She replayed Rachel's dismissive attitude in her mind, and how her sister had in not so many words opposed her attendance to dinner with their father. Rachel really didn't want her there. She'd only asked out of obligation.

She didn't know why she kept trying to find the answers. She'd never understand her sister.

Suzanna pressed her fingers to her temples.

Damn headache.

Intense pain seemed too bound back and forth, between her temples, like a basketball game being played by opposing forces. The noticeable pounding in her ears was almost unbearable.

Unsure of what caused the pain she'd determined she could associate it with every time she felt the necessity to strengthen her guard against outside forces. Suzanna made a note in her Day-Timer to ask Marianne about this the next time she saw her.

She'd begun early that day to prepare for the event that evening, not wanting to be any more open to her sister's hateful influences, nor her father's egotistical viewpoints. She didn't enjoy spending time with either one of them.

Now as the time got closer she knew she needed to strengthen her guard.

"Shields up," she commanded, using the methods she'd been taught. She envisioned a bright light of gold starting at the top, surrounding her with protection. "Good and strong tonight. Double if you can."

The phone rang, almost causing her to jump out of her chair. Oh, this was not good.

"Brach's Veterinary Hospital, how may I help you?" she tried to sound as welcoming as possible.

"Hi Suzanna, this is Roberto," said the familiar voice on the other end.

"Roberto! How are you?"

"Bien, bien. Say, Suz, I don't mean to bother you at work, but I need you to look into something for me."

"No problem. Anything. You know that."

"I've been working on the classes I need, and the work necessary to complete my teacher's degree at the UW. The counselors are saying I would need to do an internship in my specific field I'm going to write my thesis on."

"Wow. So, how would I be able to help?" Suzanna frowned, not knowing anything she could do.

"Remember, we were talking about that place you've been going to, the one dealing with the enhanced perceptions? Well, I was taking a look at their website, and I saw they have a division for youth and teen programs. Wouldn't it be a great theme to show the correlation between troubled teens and the data supporting these types of abilities?" The excitement in Roberto's voice made Suzanna smile. If anyone would be able to do this, Roberto would be the best choice.

"I think you've got something there. You might even win an award for that study."

"I don't know about that, but as you know this has been a particular interest of mine."

"Yes, but I still don't understand. How can I help?"

"Would you put in a good word for me at the board? In an unpaid internship basis of course, working with teens at the center. I'll be submitting my request formally of course, but I thought it wouldn't hurt to have an insider recommend me."

Suzanna laughed. *An insider*?

"Certainly, I'd love to do that for you. I'll ask Marianne next time I see her."

"Marianne? Marianne Ross? Oh, you're on a first name basis with the big boss. Awesome!" Roberto's excitement spilled into Suzanna through the phone as he connected her with Marianne. She smiled. Good for him.

"No promises, but I'll see what I can do. You better write up your proposal and send it in to back up the good things

I'm going to say about you." She knew already he'd be welcomed with open arms to Gloves.

After hanging up the phone she made another note to talk to Marianne about Roberto's plan. This would be good. Seeing more of Roberto made her feel family had begun to accept her for who she really was.

At least some of my family.

A huge sigh escaped as she began to pack up her desk. She really didn't want to do this tonight.

Nicholaus flew around the corner. "You're not leaving yet are you?" An unusual anxiousness surrounded him.

Suzanna's stomach began to flutter, as it did without fail when he was in the room. The feeling made her want to giggle. Throughout the day he'd made her laugh again, and a glimmer of hope was surfacing. Maybe she'd been wrong. But she held back, still unsure of their relationship status. He still hadn't said anything to make her feel otherwise, and she didn't want to look foolish by assuming they had a real bond between them.

"It is the end of the day boss. I thought I could loosen the ball and chain for a couple of hours."

The comment seemed to make him smile, though the unexpected mirth changed quickly to concern. "Wait, you can't leave for dinner until I get back. Don't go anywhere. I've got to go pick up something."

"The office closes in five minutes. I'll lock up for you," Suzanna replied confused.

"Just wait for me to come back before you leave."

Watching him fly out the front door, she heard him jump into his SUV and skid out of the parking lot. Amused, she wondered what had spurred his unusual actions.

"You're a strange one, Dr. Brach. I can't wait to see what you've come up with this time."

After she changed her clothes, she started to put on a dab of perfume when she heard the knock at the door. She glanced at the clock and realized she needed to leave.

When she opened the door, Nicholaus didn't wait for an invite. He gave her a quick kiss and stepped into the front room.

As if to survey the space for a proper setting, he briefly looked around the room, then took hold of her hand and brought her toward the couch. The setting sunlight came through the curtains to enhance every color in the room, including the bright and excited blueness of Nicholaus' eyes.

He brought her hand up to his chest. She sensed the strong pounding of his heart and wondered what caused the reaction. As they sat on the couch he gazed at her in a different way. An emotion emanated from him she'd never felt before. This couldn't be possible. Her own energy must be bouncing off of him. Confused, she decided that must be what it was, her own emotions.

From his pocket he brought out an odd rectangular shaped jewelers box. She searched him for signs of emotion, and felt a jumbled mess of excited anticipation, mixed with extreme joy.

"I want you to have this. It's not much, but I hope you like it." He opened the box and she saw a glorious combination of tiny stones of different shapes and colors. They'd been arranged in a swirling fashion along a tiny rope of gold twisted around a deep green core of jade. Strong, yet feminine, she could see the precious craft used in the making of the breathtaking pendant.

"Nicholaus, it's beautiful," she said in awe as he took it from the jeweler's box to fasten around her neck. "I can't possibly accept this."

The soft smile on his lips moved her as he lightly touched the pendant where it hung above her breasts. "But you must. It was made specifically for you. There is no other to wear this."

Tears welled in Suzanna's eyes. She could feel his frazzled nerves matched her own. The hand he brought forward to touch the jewels shook.

"The Jade is for protection and relaxation. It should have a calming affect for you. The Opals will help to awaken your psychic intuition. Here the Sapphires and Emeralds will bring clarity to your insight and clairvoyance, while bringing physical and emotional healing. The Snowflake Obsidian helps to protect against nightmares," he paused to catch his breath, and pointed to the last stone. "And, the White Moonstone helps to augment all of the other stones effects." He'd touched each stone as he spoke of their metaphysical properties. "So, as you can see, this is meant for you and only you."

She brought her hand up to touch the precious treasure. He'd thought of her, with each stone he'd picked. She loved him without a doubt.

His efforts counted for something–didn't they?

"I almost forgot. Here," he said touching the stones again. "This is the Garnet, which is highly protective and increases confidence and security. It has an added bonus though. It also enhances sensuality and sexuality. I couldn't resist adding that one to the mix." The smile on his face was just boyish enough to make her laugh.

"Nicholaus, what am I going to do with you?" She hugged him, the tug at her heart a constant reminder of her love for him.

"I don't know, but I hope it's soon." She saw the humor in his eyes invite her to forgive and forget. Unfortunately, the brief hug was too short for her to put a definite label on the odd emotions she sensed from him.

She couldn't trust the myriad of messages she was receiving. Her emotions were running so high, certainly his must have mixed with hers to create this indistinguishable mass of reactions. Pulling herself together, she broke his grasp and took his face in her hands. The gentle kiss she gave would have to be enough for now. She didn't want to leave, but she didn't have a choice.

"You're way too sweet Nicholaus. I don't know what to say. Thank you, from the bottom of my heart." His original brightness changed to a softness she yearned to hold onto. She placed a kiss on the tips of her fingers, and laid them on his lips. "We should talk. Not now, I need to leave. If I'm back early enough, I'll stop by."

He grasped her fingers to lift them to his lips, his eyes fastened on hers. Then he traced a light line of kisses up the back of her hand before flipping it over to kiss her palm.

"I'll be waiting."

* * * *

Suzanna walked the short distance under the Alaskan Way viaduct to the crosswalk. The wind blew lightly across the water, bringing with it the scent of salt water and sea life. The crispness refreshed her, but the difference in temperature made her shiver as she walked through the restaurant door. Her nerves moved around like little Mexican jumping beans in the pit of her stomach as she walked into the bar area. The weight of the gemstones around her neck gave her added confidence. Approaching the party of two, she took in a deep breath to bolster her self assurance.

She decided to go casual in her usual sandals and broomstick skirt. The vibrant colors were enhanced by the richness of her new necklace against the black lacy chemise she'd chosen. As usual, in the eyes of her sister, she would be under dressed for the occasion.

From her seat by the window, she saw Rachel watch her approach with an undeniably contemptuous expression. She of course was dressed to the nines in a powerful red tailored suit set off by hints of lace and pearls from some high priced designer. No doubt she'd done this to intimidate and dominate the evening.

Her father had his back to Suzanna then turned as Rachel announced the arrival of his other guest. He smiled, and as Suzanna came closer she saw the man she recognized as her father. A little older, a little larger in stature, but the same man she remembered. He stood to greet her, and she immediately got a flash of a faint image from her dreams. A figure loomed over her for a split second, the same size and shape of the man standing beside her.

Not now!

He'd changed since she last saw him. His dark hair now peppered gray, skin wrinkled with age. She'd received her mother's color and petite size. Though, side by side she knew she favored her father's facial features.

"Hi Dad, how are you doing?" she asked offering a slight hug, while denying the immediate need to flee away.

His hearty hug was a bit more possessive than she thought necessary. His hand casually landed close to her breast, and stayed there much too long to be considered appropriate.

This must be all in my mind, she thought frantically, still fighting the need to escape.

"Here is my little girl. What a beauty you've turned out to be," he said while looking her over once or twice, the fixed gaze at her figure unsettling her.

"No more than your other daughter, she's got more going for her than I could ever hope for," she said in an attempt to move his attention away from her.

"Well, that's for sure, but there's no reason to get into all of that just yet," Rachel said, in a rather feline manner as she ran a finger around the rim of her martini glass.

Suzanna could tell Rachel would be in prime form tonight, and reminded herself to watch her reaction to her sister's competitive nature. In no way did she want to start acting like her, as she'd found herself doing in the past. Damn, it was hard being an Empath.

"Let's move on into the dining area. I think it's about time for our reservations," her father said, totally unaware of any discord between the two of them.

Rachel came forward to walk with their father to the dining table. Instead, Frank placed his hand below the waistline on Suzanna's back in a very intimate manner, to direct her toward the front desk. She could feel Rachel's disapproval without needing to see her face. She desperately wanted to push his hand away, but didn't know how. She'd either offend him or bring more attention to what might not be so obvious to others around them.

While being seated at their table, Frank insisted Suzanna sit next to him. She knew she wouldn't feel comfortable. The options were to sit next to someone who made her uncomfortable, or next to her sister who didn't want her there in the first place. Either way the choice was not good.

"What have you girls been up to? I haven't seen you Suzanna in what, eight or nine years? Why haven't you come out to see me when Rachel comes out?"

Disturbed by the question, she searched for a way to tell him she'd never been asked. "I think it's been more like twelve. I guess the opportunity hadn't presented itself to me," Suzanna replied softly.

Rachel took the opportunity to jump in and take control of the conversation. She began to tell them about her children's accomplishments, and stories relating to her husband's business dealings since their latest visit to see Frank. This brought a light into their father's eyes.

"You know, Dad, I think you and he should form a partnership up here. We would be closer together." Rachel paused long enough Suzanna started to wonder what she was trying to say. "You know he loves real estate like you, and of course you could be closer to your grandchildren."

Frank reached out and covered his daughter's hand with his.

"Rachel sweetie, that's tempting, but I'm not ready to give up on Hawthorne and Lowell yet. Commercial real estate in Sacramento is still bringing in the big bucks. As much as I love you and the kids, I'm not so sure there's a market up here. When it starts to dry up down there I'll look your husband up to see what he can bring to the table."

In short, money before family, Suzanna thought.

His success was a mystery to her. Why they'd struggled with finances as they grew up she could never understand. Surely there would've been child support offered, but then she remembered her mother's adamant refusal. She'd wanted nothing from him.

He continued to listen with great interest while Rachel's gleeful approach to telling some of her stories became almost childlike. Suzanna couldn't help notice the drinks kept appearing in front of her father, one after another, without ceasing.

Her mind began to drift and the pendent moved gently against her. She reached up to fondle it with love. As she watched the ferries come in and out of port, she tried to remember more about this man sitting beside her. She felt she should respect him, but couldn't seem to bring up any feelings or emotions for him. Known by the locals as a straight shooter, he apparently was a good businessman. She couldn't remember any reason to distrust him, and her mother had never said anything against his character.

So why does he make my skin crawl?

During their conversation, she realized Frank and Rachel had formed a bond she and her father never achieved. She thought she should feel a love for him like her sister did, though couldn't see a reason. She didn't know enough about him.

Her memories only went back to the time when he'd left them, nothing before. It was the same time she realized she was different from everyone else. She'd felt the family's pain through the whole horrible scene. His departure, without explanation, had been sudden. Her mother had been filled with guilt and hatred, but her sister took his leaving the hardest. Rachel had been traumatized by his leaving. Adjustment for her took a long time, and Suzanna wasn't sure if she'd ever gotten over it.

All of a sudden segments of her nightmare began to flash through her head. Inhaling quickly, she reached out to grasp her water glass with the hand that she'd used to rub the stones at her neck. The flashes diminished as she took a couple of large gulps of her water.

This was a first. She'd never experienced this during the day. Historically, once the nightmare occurred it would vanish until the next time it popped its ugly head into her dreams at night. She could feel the sickly trickle of sweat run down her back. Not a good sign. It took some time to gather her composure without showing the others something was wrong.

Bringing her back into the conversation, Frank turned to her, "What have you been doing Suzanna? Rachel tells me you're working at a Vet's office?"

She imagined she knew exactly how Rachel told him by the way he asked the question. He seemed as doubtful of her success in this career choice as her 'sweet' sister had.

"Yes, I am." She didn't feel the need to justify her choices, so she tried to find something else that might be of interest. "I've been working with someone who believes I have a special gift."

Why the hell did you bring that up? The last thing you want to do is give them more ammunition to think you're crazy.

Unfortunately, it was too late now. She had to clarify what she meant.

"It's believed, I am what is known as an empath. I have an ability to feel others emotions and sometimes see things others cannot."

Her sister made a sound of disbelief. Clearing her throat, Rachel made an obvious sign to their father, indicating Suzanna's obvious nonsensical imagination was at work.

"Really, *that* sounds interesting. I remember your mother told me once she felt you were more sensitive than other little girls." He made a knowing grin to Rachel across the table. "And what do you think? Do you think you have this 'gift'?" He sounded as if he were talking to a small child with little understanding of the real world.

She knew when she'd been made fun of, so she backed away from the subject. This was not the time, place or people she wanted to explain her feelings about the wonderful things she'd discovered. Neither of them would be receptive to the truth. They would only try to make her feel inept and silly.

"I'm not sure. I'll let you know what happens," she said not meaning a word of it.

"So, are you involved with anyone? Rachel tells me it seems like you can't keep anyone around for very long."

Why am I even here? Rachel seemed to have told him everything he needed to hear.

Suzanna hesitated to answer the question.

"Nobody at the moment," she answered. The truth would only open up an area of discussion she wasn't ready to get into just yet.

Frank reached out and put his hand on her upper thigh to give her a little squeeze. This time Suzanna could not ignore his inappropriate action. In fact his touch made her quite sick to her stomach. She quietly picked up his hand and placed it back in his own lap.

"That's too bad. A pretty thing like you shouldn't be without a man." The grin in his eyes was enough to make her bolt. She tried to keep her cool. Either her father was a lecherous old man, or he simply did not understand the boundaries between family members. Or, maybe it was both.

"Just haven't found the right one yet." Thank God, the waiter came with the check. Not soon enough. Suzanna was ready to go. "I'm not going to waste any more of your time here. I've got to get up early for work tomorrow, so I think I should be headed out. It was very nice to see you again. Maybe we can catch up together later," she muttered with no sincerity at all.

She couldn't get out of there quick enough. The multitude of emotions flying around in her head couldn't be deciphered. The disconnected thoughts and unexpected fears made no sense to her at all. Mixed with the contempt flowing from her sister and the odd sexuality from her father, the emotions of the night were too much to handle.

Frank stood to give her a final hug. In her ear he whispered, "I'm staying at the Hilton for another week to clear up this real estate deal. If you'd like to come see me, I'd welcome the company." His heavy breath thick with Gin reminded her of something she couldn't quite place. Again, he squeezed her just a little too intimately.

Not knowing how to interpret his comment, her heightened heart rate made the blood rush to her cheeks. She muttered more to herself than for anyone else to hear, "I don't think that's going to happen."

Rachel stood with them, condescension bright in her eyes. "Order us another round of drinks Dad. I'll walk Suzanna to the door. Then you and I can catch up some more. I can't wait to tell you about our trip to Havana. It was awesome. I'll be right back."

Silent, they walked toward the door. Suzanna felt lightheaded. She didn't know if the one glass of wine she had with dinner affected her this way, or if something else was wrong.

"Well, aren't you the sly one. He always did like you better." Her sister's accusation made no sense to Suzanna at all. She stared at Rachel in disbelief.

"What are you talking about?"

"He's always had more interest in you. I should have known better. The only time I can get his attention is when I visit on my own." Rachel sounded like a jealous teenager, pouting by the end of her words.

Suzanna was really confused. "I'm not sure what you see. You have and always will have the upper hand here. I'm just here as a bit of entertainment for the both of you."

"If you even think about seeing him by yourself, I'll know exactly what is going on."

Suddenly too tired to even try to make sense of her sister's statement, she wanted only to get out of there as quick as she could. She opened the door to the street and stepped out into the cool breeze.

"Goodnight, Rachel. I'm sure I'll see you sometime soon. Until then give your kids a hug for me."

It took a few moments after she reached her car to get her thoughts focused on the drive home. That's what she needed to do, just focus on home, and not think about anything else. If she concentrated on anything that just happened at the restaurant, she would surely go mad.

The music on full blast, she tried to force all other thoughts from her mind. She drove home in personal silence, fiercely concentrating on the lyrics coming from the radio.

She felt numb. Even by blocking out all the emotions she could, she became so confused she didn't know what to think. One minute she wanted to cry, the next minute a hysterical laugh would come bursting out. By the time she walked through her front door she was totally drained.

Cali had curled up at the end of her bed. Suzanna threw her things down and crawled in with her, in hopes to find some solace in the comfort of her newfound friend. She wanted to be in the arms of Nicholaus, but didn't feel she could move any further. Lulled by the warmth and purring from Cali, she forced herself to attempt one of the meditative states Marianne taught her.

She closed her eyes, focusing on her inner self, imagining herself as a tree, roots extending from her root chakra located at the base of her spine through the bottom of her feet. She forced the roots to feed into the earth travelling to the depths of the center of the earth. Negativity, fear, confusion all running down out from her core to disperse into the hot molten lava to be returned back up as new growth under the sun.

The image calmed her soul a bit, but she could feel of all nights, the nightmares would come tonight. She held on tight to the necklace while telling herself to be open to her dreams, to act only as an observer. The repeated mantra Marianne taught her helped her mind to shut down and she fell into a light sleep.

Nicholaus stood at his window, unsure whether he should find out how the dinner had gone for Suzanna. He wanted to hold onto her, to comfort her after what she must have experienced. He knew her sister wasn't easy to handle. He'd all but convinced himself her father had something to do with both, the physical confinement she'd wrapped around herself, and the reoccurring nightmares she endured.

If only he could help Marianne to tap into the depths of her mind and unleash the memories Suzanna held at bay. He hoped the pendant he'd given her would speed up the process.

But is it enough? He thought, wracking his brain for anything more he could do. Then he remembered Marianne's wise words.

Marianne's right. All I can do now is wait, and be there when she need's me.

He had talked himself into at least going down to check on her and say goodnight when he saw the light go out in her bedroom. Maybe she didn't need him as much as he thought.

Ignoring his inner guide, he sighed and settled himself into bed with a medical journal.

* * * *

Hours later, Suzanna began to toss under the covers. Cali took off at the first sign of unsettled movement, having already experienced what would come next.

The nightmare returned. This time it had a different twist. Suzanna felt as if she stood outside of her body, watching the scene progress. The labored breathing of the man who came into the room put a fear into the image of her as the child who hid under the covers on the bed. Again, the toy animals danced around the room in a hysterical manner, as if on orders to attack.

She could smell the horrible scent of alcohol mixed with heavy cologne, a sickening smell she remembered from her distant past. She heard herself plead with the big dark figure to leave her alone, but her pleas fell on deaf ears. Suddenly, she found herself unable to maintain the position of an outsider and she jerked back into the frightened child cowering on the bed and crying out for help.

This time she heard the dark figure's slurred speech say, "Hush baby girl, we're going to have some fun now."

He began to fondle her privates, cooing and hushing her cries of fear. Normally, she'd wake at this point screaming in terror. Instead, the horrid scene continued. She felt him cover her with his body, his weight suffocating her every breath. She tried to scream again but his shoulder had covered her face and muffled the sound.

An intense pain shot through her hard enough to wake her from her disturbed sleep. This time her Vaginismus had set in. Grabbing her stomach, she continued to feel the spasms tear through her stomach and radiate down her legs.

She'd just been raped. She knew it now. She didn't know when, and she didn't know who, but she knew she'd been raped. Incoherent, and unable to take control of herself, she stumbled from her bed to search for the one person she knew could help her.

Through her front door she ran, ignoring the pain from the rocks in the driveway tearing into her bare feet. The back door opened easily, as if being left open for her. Tears ran down her cheeks as she called out his name. A horrendous ache hovered over her eyes making it almost impossible to see. Suzanna stumbled through the house to the grand staircase and tripped up the stairs, frantic to find Nicholaus.

Nicholaus instantly awakened at the sound of the back door opening. He jumped from his bed and by the time he made it to his bedroom door, Suzanna fell against him, gasping and trembling like he'd never seen before.

Scooping her up in his arms, he sat back down on the bed and held her there in silence as she cried and whimpered still under the nightmare's embrace. He poured all of his energy through his unique way of calming her fears, and held on strong while waiting for the terrors to subside.

It tore him to pieces when the first thing she said was, "It hurt so bad. I couldn't take any more. The pain was unbearable."

He knew the dreams had taken a step forward.

"Shhh…it's alright, I'm here now. Nothing will hurt you like that again, ever." He began to soothe her with gentle caresses down her arms. The slow rhythmic manner would lead the negative flow of energies from her body out through her fingers as he introduced newer positive energies to replace them. "It'll be alright sweetheart. I'm here. I'm here for you."

The shudders and tears continued longer this time. Unsure if his efforts were working, he continued to force his healing positivity into her trembling body. Yet, in his mind he fumed, enraged by this unseen intruder.

At the first sign of her quieting down, he reached back to grab some tissues he placed earlier at his bedside, specifically for this reason. In silence he offered them to her. After an attempt to clean up her face, she buried her face in his shoulder again and sat for a bit of forced tranquility.

"I'm sorry, I didn't know where else to go. I needed you."

"I've told you. I'm here for you any time you need me." He took her chin in his fingers to make her look into his eyes. "Understand?"

She nodded and looked away as if uncomfortable with the visual contact. He released her chin to let her dab at her nose again.

"Thank you. I guess I must have woken you up."

He saw her take stock of her surroundings. Overhead the light was on and his medical journals lay haphazardly across the bed.

"Or were you studying?"

"I think I'd dozed off. I'm still dressed, so I hadn't gotten into bed for good just yet." He took a second look at her attire and realized she still had on what she'd worn earlier that evening as well. "Looks like you weren't ready just yet either."

On closer inspection, he saw her torn skirt and bare feet. She winced as he took a foot into his hand and a small rock fell to the floor from an open wound.

"Whoa, what have we got here? Looks like you need some medical attention." He placed her on the bed and kissed her red nose. "Stay right there, I need to get something to clean you up."

From the bathroom he returned with his first aid box and some cool wash cloths.

"This is getting to be a ritual. One I don't want you to get used to," he said in reference to her injured finger, which had healed incredibly fast as expected.

He could feel her watch him as he cleaned the dirt and gravel from her foot, and glanced up to confirm the fact as her eyes met his.

"Nicholaus, I want to apologize to you for the way I've acted. You don't deserve it, and I feel horrible."

Although relieved to hear she realized he didn't deserve the bad treatment, he needed to find the right words to say in response. He'd been thinking about it and understood Marianne's words of wisdom.

He took her hands in his and kissed them both. "Sweetie, I don't know where all of this is headed. I'm not sure either one of us knows. You have to believe me when I tell you I feel there is something different between us. Something I can't ignore."

Suzanna nodded, and a shy blush crept onto her cheeks.

"I miss you when you aren't with me and I can't seem to concentrate when there is tension between us. There is this incredible energy I feel between us when we are together. Let's see what happens. I want to learn more about you…about us."

He could see the uncertainty and a brief flash of self doubt cross her face.

"I know, I feel it too…" she hesitated.

"But, what?"

"Sometimes I can't understand why anybody would want to be with me. It's hard for me to understand why you'd want to stick around. Nobody's ever done that for me before, not by choice anyway."

He saw her attitude change as she looked to the past for answers. He needed to return her to the present.

"I don't care what happened in the past. What matters now, is that you and I are here, together. If you ever start to question what I'm doing, or I'm not clear in what I've said to you, stop and ask me to clarify. You might be sensing something I haven't even recognized for myself. Don't react before I can even figure out what I've done. Agreed?"

"Agreed," Suzanna smiled and gave him a gentle kiss.

"Should I assume you'd like to stay with me tonight?"

"Can I?"

"I wouldn't have it any other way. Let me find something more suitable for you to sleep in. I think that skirt might get uncomfortable." He rose to retrieve a T-shirt out of his dresser. "This one should work. I'll go wash up, and be back in a jiffy."

He returned to find her nestled under his covers, eyes closed. Her head rested lightly on his side of the bed, her nose close to the pillow where his head lay in slumber. She jumped when she caught sight of him and moved her head to the other pillow with a look of guilt.

He removed his clothes, smiling at her awkward glances, and got into bed next to her. He pulled her next to him and waited until she'd settled herself against his body. Her silken hair brushed against his skin and reminded him of his need for her. He wouldn't suggest any sexual contact, but wasn't sure how much longer he'd be able to keep this up.

Thinking again of the reason she'd come to him in the first place, he softly asked the question he already knew the answer to.

"Want to tell me about it?"

With a very long pause her breath hitched, and very quietly, she stated the simple words, "He raped me."

Even though he'd known the answer, hearing her say those words made him crumble. Then the anger charged in and overtook all other thought.

"You're mad," she said stiffening.

"Not at you honey. Not at you." He brought her closer to him and waited until the anger passed through him. "Suzanna, nobody will ever do that to you again. I promise."

He felt her nod her head in silence against his shoulder before pressing herself closer to claim the security he offered. The exhaustion of the day took its toll and she drifted off to sleep.

Chapter Eighteen

Suzanna woke from her slumber and realized she wasn't home in her own bed. The quilt, pulled up to her nose, was a very cozy feeling indeed. Nicholaus' manly scent reminded her of whose bed she snuggled in. A slow smile came to her face when she heard the shower water in the bathroom. Imagining him naked under running water made her tingle all over. The events of the night before forgotten, she could only think of the way he'd comforted her. When she lay next to him he made her feel alive.

As always, his kindness and compassion outweighed any expectation she could have imagined, though it was her physical reaction to him that astounded her the most. Every time he came near, the cells in her body jumped with a will to satisfy some hidden agenda she didn't know needed to be addressed.

She needed to make more of an effort. That was all there was to it. She couldn't expect someone else to fix her problems. All she knew was she wanted him near her, with her, always.

Maybe that grounding exercise would help in this case too. She went through the same exercise she'd done before, willing all negativity to pass through and out of her. Replacing any fear with only love and contentment. Hopefully, it will work this time.

She slipped from under the sheets, pulled the T-shirt she wore over her head and snuck into the steamy bathroom. Nicholaus, unaware of her entry, stood with his back turned toward her. The hot water pounded over him and brought a healthy glow to his skin.

At the sound of the shower door opening, Nicholaus spun around. The water dripped down his face as he blinked furiously. She stepped in, water splashing over his shoulders to sprinkle her skin to a glistening dew. She'd pulled her hair into a knot at the top of her head, exposing her slim neck and shoulders, completely bare except for the necklace she refused to remove. As she came toward him with deliberation, she gave him a mischievous smile.

No words were exchanged, but the energy exchanged was charged to explode at any moment. With his own intentional movement Nicholaus reached out to take her face in his hands. The soft and gentle kiss he gave seemed simple enough, though something far more complex was going on. Suzanna's immediate response to his touch ignited the flames continuing to burn deep within her. The kiss became more insistent. His lips seemed to search for an unspoken answer. She gave without hesitation. He sucked and teased, as if devouring the tastes she brought to him. Both desiring to fulfill each other's needs, yet truly were in search of their own satisfaction.

Nicholaus pulled back. His breaths came in short bursts. She sensed his restraint being fully employed. He placed his hands on either side of her on the shower wall and brought his forehead down to rest on hers.

"Oh God, I want you. You can't keep doing this to me. I'm only so strong. I don't know how much longer I can hold out."

"Doing what?" she asked coyly.

His eyes slid down to his hardened erection and back up again.

"Oh!" she said innocently. "Well, I thought maybe I could help you with that."

She kept her gaze engaging his, seeing his surprise as she bent down to one knee, and took him tenderly into her hands to caress the object of attention. She began to wrap her lips around the tip, to tease him with her tongue. Sensing his every nerve escalating to a breaking point enticed her to give even more. She wanted to bring him close to what she imagined would be meltdown.

Pulling her up, he appeared to need a moment to bring his mental faculties back into order.

"Honey, honey…you can't do that. I can't control my response with you right now."

"I want to please you," she pleaded, hurt by his rejection.

"I know you do. But I don't want my first time with you to be so one sided."

"Maybe it doesn't have to be," she implored.

It took a half-second for him to interpret what she meant. He scooped her up into his arms and stepped out of the shower, grabbing a towel on his way out of the bathroom.

The minute it took to dry the wettest part of them seemed like a lifetime. He threw the towel to the floor and lowered her onto the bed.

By this time, need overruled any rational thought, for the both of them, though after a moment she felt him putting on the brakes.

"What is wrong? Why did you stop?" she asked as he pulled away from her.

"You give me all the reasons to take you and satisfy all of my own penned up passions. But I have to remind myself you don't need to be manhandled. I won't do that to you. Lord knows how much I want to," he said bending down to caress her neck with his warm soft lips. "I want you to trust me. Open up and experience everything you are feeling."

He looked deep into her eyes, asking for her acceptance. She would have given him anything at this point. No request was too big. She was his.

Nodding, she closed her eyes to focus on the feeling of his lips and warm breath landing in all the right places, her body responding to every light touch of his fingers. The glorious sensation of excitement he induced, every minute they were together, was enough to bring her closer to the one outcome she'd begun to desire.

The level of urgency rose with her need to explore those things yet to be discovered. Knowing it was possible with him, wanting them both to feel the same.

Somewhere in the background the same anxiousness lumbered around, hanging on and waiting to show its ugly face. She knew she needed to concentrate on Nicholaus, but the expectation of disaster wouldn't leave her. She knew she wanted him, and he would be the only one she'd ever want.

Keeping a strong focus, she parted her legs and encouraged him to slip between them. Not yet penetrating, he came close enough to where the tip of his erection teased the point of entry. Her first immediate reaction impelled her to close up and reject him. This time she fought back. She wanted desperately for the focal point to be the way he made her feel. Surprised, she realized she wasn't as terrified as before.

She nodded as he looked into her eyes and waited for acceptance. Nicholaus made no sudden movements. He eased himself into her with a slow sliding sensation. The same odd sensation of a relaxing energy she'd felt before came over her, this time though it emanated from his body. To her surprise, the impending tightness loosened and began to drift.

His first entry was very hard for her to handle. Panic remained just under the surface, but she held on, not allowing it to take over. Though anxiety had her every movement tightly bound, like a bundle of firewood strung together with rope, waiting off to the side to be burned.

"Sweetheart, concentrate on me, only me."

His soft, caring gaze lifted the terror and it began to subside, replacing it with a greater need for love. She continued to focus on his eyes, to open her empathic ability to sense outside of her own self. This seemed to help.

She sensed his anticipation, and a built up excitement waiting to be unleashed. His reserved passion overwhelmed her, the strength of his need overpowering her instinctual demand to escape. Instead she grasped hold and allowed herself to meld with the sensations he experienced.

Lord, this is awesome.

She knew the intentional slow movement to push forward was meant to calm her fears. Now able to focus on the sensation of his body next to hers, she began to fully experience him inside of her. With his extreme control, she felt him rein in his own powerful need. She used his strong energies to feed the sensual ones building in her own body.

Carefully, he moved in and out mere centimeters at a time. She sighed softly, her breath cooling their wet skin.

"You have no idea what you're doing to me," he whispered in her ear.

Her only answer was the tightened grasp she held at the back of his neck. New sensations erupted throughout her body.

The slight coarseness of his belly rubbing against hers, the unusual pressure against her hips and thighs as his movements became more fervent, and the heat pouring from both of them were all new. She felt the urge to open wider, to welcome him in to fill her every need.

Suzanna began to move to him as he drove into her, further intensifying the whole experience. As he made longer, harder thrusts, she could feel a fever grow deep in her belly, followed by a desire to achieve the unknown. A throaty moan came from within as his forward thrusts caused her eyes to glaze over, the culmination of her physical response to his touch growing higher.

"Go with it, honey. Let it go." His breath tickled the water drops in her ear.

All she could do was go with it. His arduous rhythmic motions stirred the burning fires deep inside and a different type of centered tension began to build. This one tugged at every inch of her being, encompassing her, as it pulled and gathered the nerves in her body together in an unbearable accumulation of need—a need begging to be released. She called out his name, overcome by her body's fevered rush to claim its victory.

As she convulsed around him she held on long enough to revel in the experience of Nicholaus' own release. His vigorous hold also let go and she joined him as their spirits flew together into oblivion.

A bit later, Suzanna surfaced from the aftermath of the most joyous experience of her life. In the warmth of Nicholaus' body next to her, she snuggled closer to bask in the awesome love surrounding her. She blinked to adjust to the light and saw he'd pulled the blankets up over her to keep her protected from a chill.

She glanced into the face she loved, and found he watched her with a look she couldn't quite interpret. His expression, sweet and gentle, had what she thought at first to be adoration, though she didn't think that could be true. She found it difficult to read his emotions. The only thing she could ascertain was a sort of contented happiness emanating from him. The other emotions she felt must be her own overpowering love and affection for him.

Unsure of what to say, she grinned at him and pulled him closer for a soft kiss on the lips, and suddenly her stomach gave a loud rumble. The smidgen of dinner she'd been able to get down the night before hadn't stayed with her very long.

"I don't know about you, but I think I'm hungry," she chuckled.

She scrambled out of bed to reach for her camisole and torn skirt on the floor. This awkwardness wasn't familiar. But really, what did you say to the man who broke through an impenetrable wall in your life, to bring forth an unimaginable physical feeling that left you craving more?

"What do you say I go down and make us some breakfast?" she asked as she pulled the camisole over her head.

"Sounds like a good plan," he responded, a curious grin on his face.

He held out his hand to her. She came to him and he wrapped his arms around her, the side of his face pressed against her stomach. She reached up to run her fingers through his sleep mussed hair. An unusual emotion skittered over her senses, settling over her heart. Confused, she pulled away to look down into the gorgeous blues she loved so much. What she saw there flustered her even more.

She wasn't confident in her sense of what he was feeling. So with a quick peck on the cheek, she spun out of the room as if the hounds of hell were chasing after her.

The heavenly aroma of fresh brewed coffee wafted through the house and drew Nicholaus to the kitchen where Suzanna busily prepared breakfast. Scrambled eggs mixed with the glorious scent of freshly crisped bacon made his mouth water. Silent, he sat at the breakfast bar as she poured him a cup of coffee.

"What are your plans for the day?" he asked.

"I promised Marianne I would drop by this morning to talk. Otherwise, I don't really have anything official planned," she replied with a cheerfulness he did not share. "Why? What did you have in mind?"

"If you don't mind I think I'll go with you to see Marianne. She and I have something to discuss."

He knew his statement left something to be desired, especially to someone like Suzanna.

Suzanna gave him a curious look. "Is there a problem?"

"No problem. I need to let her know my decision on something she asked me to be involved in."

She raised her eyebrow in silent question and waited for him to continue.

"Last time we met she asked me if I would become more involved in the practice of healing people. She said I should consider extending the use of my healing to benefit certain people," his voice was laced with a hint of trepidation.

"Oh, that's wonderful. I think that would be so good for you. So, why the face?" she asked, her brow furrowing as she must have picked up on his hesitance.

The steaming plate of food in front of him should have been enticing, but suddenly he'd lost his appetite.

To make her feel appreciated, he picked up one of the pieces of toast and took a big bite out of the slice. The crisp bread stuck in his throat with his next statement.

"One of the clients is my father."

Suzanna's eyes widened in surprise, "Oh, no! What's wrong?"

Torn after hearing the news, he'd only been able to forget when Suzanna was in his arms. For a time her needs were greater, but now he again faced the reality of his father's condition. His stomach began to churn.

"He has an advanced stage of lymphatic cancer." Nicholaus dropped the toast back to his plate and picked his coffee mug up instead. "The mortality rate at this point is almost nonexistent."

She narrowed her eyes at him. "And you didn't know about it, did you?"

With a shake of his head he took a long sip from his cooling coffee. "Nope. He hasn't said anything at all. He chose Gloves over me."

"Wait, didn't you say he doesn't believe in the healing gifts? Why would he go to Gloves?"

"I guess he does believe. Maybe he just doesn't believe in me." The seething anger began to surface again.

This frame of mind won't get me anywhere, he thought. So he forced it away and grabbed the fork before digging into his breakfast.

"Either way…" he said, chewing on his first bite, "I'd like you to go out there with me to talk to him."

"Of course, you don't even need to ask." She reached out to squeeze his hand, and he didn't let go. He needed to pull from her some strength to get through the pain.

They sat for a while and ate in silence.

"I'm going to tell Marianne I want to go through with the hypnosis," Suzanna gave a deep sigh.

Nicholaus turned so he could see her face.

"You think that's the best thing to do?"

"I think so. I can't take this anymore. You saw how bad it was last night. What if you hadn't been there to help calm me down?"

"You're right. I've been thinking the same thing."

"I need to know who this person is, one way or another. I think if I knew, all these nightmares would end. Obviously, they're just going to keep happening until my mind decides to clue me in on what it's been hiding all of these years."

He could tell she retraced the steps of the night before, as she shuddered and wrapped her arms around herself in a protective manner.

"I don't think I could go through that night after night. I can't take it anymore Nicholaus. I can't even explain what it was like."

"You don't have to," he agreed. The sooner they uncovered the truth the better it would be for her. Then maybe she could live her life in the present. "I think you're right. Let's both talk to Marianne."

* * * *

Nicholaus and Suzanna walked up the pathway to Gloves and from the corner of his eye he caught the movement of a man at the side of the building taking a drag off his cigarette. He felt Suzanna tense up as the man began walking toward them.

"I don't trust him," she said quietly.

"I don't either. Don't worry. I'll protect you." Nicholaus didn't figure the man would try anything stupid out in broad daylight.

"Hi, how are 'ya?" The man asked as he centered himself right in front of their passage. "I'm Chris Stark, and you must be Nicholaus Brach. I've been hearing a lot about you."

Nicholaus stiffened and looked over the smaller man dressed in a suit, his tie loosened at the collar. He seemed harmless enough.

"How do you know my name?"

"Let's just say, I've got my ways."

"What do you want?" Nicholaus asked. Something told him he didn't really want to know.

"You can do some pretty amazing stuff. That energizing thing you do is awesome. My boss wants to have a chat with you."

Nicholaus knew immediately where this was going.

"I don't think so. Now, please let us pass," he responded holding out his arm to brush past, allowing Suzanna to pass without coming too close to the small-minded man.

"Hey, you should hear what he wants to say. He's got money, lots of money. I'm sure you two could work out a deal to make you a very rich man," he said jingling the change in his pocket. "Leave the little lady here and we can go see what he has to offer."

Nicholaus was repulsed by the idea they thought he would even consider something like this. He reached out and grabbed the man by the collar.

"Tell your boss I am not now, nor will I ever be interested in any type of scheme to make money." He pushed the man aside and joined Suzanna at the steps. "I suggest you leave now, and if you know what's good for you, never come back. Next time, you may not like what you get."

"Oh, I know. That hot-headed Irishman has made all kinds of threats too," Nicholaus knew Stark was referring to Joe. He straightened his tie and laughed. "You have no idea what you're giving up. Better watch your back. I don't think Mr. Haughton is going to like this."

* * * *

As Marianne sat across from Suzanna and Nicholaus, she felt the escalation in the physical and emotional closeness they shared. The two in front of her had bonded, solidifying the intimacy she'd foreseen the last time she saw them together. As for Suzanna, she sensed the hidden secrets she held so tightly were coming to the surface. This was a good sign.

"Are you sure this is what you want to do? I think with time you will open up enough to discover for yourself what happened," Marianne asked Suzanna.

"I can't wait that long. I can't keep going through this night after night. It's tearing me apart," Suzanna pleaded. "And these blasted headaches have got to go." She rubbed at her temple.

Nicholaus gently reached up and replaced her ineffectual fingers with a healing touch of his own. "Thank you," Suzanna said appreciatively.

"I have to agree. I may only be a bystander, but if something doesn't surface soon, Suzanna may endanger herself." Nicholaus stated. "If she hadn't come to me last night, she could've been hurt much worse than she was." Nicholaus said as he grasped onto Suzanna's hand and began to stroke her knuckles with his thumb.

Marianne watched them in silence, and agreed with their reasoning.

"I'll be out of town tomorrow, but we can start on Tuesday," she said. "I can't give any promise it will work. I can do no more than try to lead you through the maze of your own mind. Hopefully we will hit on the right pathway and find what you seek."

Suzanna let out a loud sigh and started to rise.

"Anything would be better than this infernal waiting. Thank you so much for listening, and understanding."

"My pleasure," Marianne's focus turned to Nicholaus. "I think Nicholaus needs to tell me something as well. Don't you?"

As Suzanna sat back down Nicholaus took hold of her hand again and stared down at their connection. Marianne watched him bring his thoughts back to his own problem. She already knew his answer, but needed him to confirm it to himself by verbalizing his thoughts.

"I've decided to go forward to visit the people you've selected for me to see. I asked Sarah to set up some appointments for me tomorrow afternoon."

"Is your father one of them?" Marianne asked.

"He is," he answered shortly.

"When you go, Nicholaus, follow your heart. Don't let your head and the past events rule over what could be a long awaited outcome," she said concerned by his inability to understand his father's decision to keep his disease quiet.

She knew the heart, filled by the everlasting spirit, ruled in this situation. Otherwise, failure was a certainty.

"I just hope he can see it the same way," Nicholaus replied.

Marianne stood and came around the end of the desk to take hold of his hands, passing to him a grain of positive thinking she felt he might need. "He will. You need to let him know there is no other way."

Nicholaus stood, his brow furrowed. "There is one other thing I thought you should know. When we came in today I was approached by that man you've been having trouble with lately."

Marianne's stomach dropped. It was getting worse. A day didn't go by now where she didn't have to deal with his harassment. She'd known they would approach Nicholaus. They would be foolish if they didn't try. He would be a real money maker for them.

"What did he say?"

"I think someone here has leaked information. Stark said his boss, a Mr. Haughton, wants to offer me big cash for using what I can do."

"I was afraid of that." She grimaced. "Yes, I know Mr. Haughton well. Richard has been a thorn in my side for a very long time."

Good lord, how long am I going to have to deal with this man. Why can't he just be satisfied with his millions and give it a rest.

"I told him not to come back. I think you'd better get that restraining order in place though. That way you won't have to deal with him directly. If you see him you can call and have him picked up."

Marianne shook her head. "I've thought about that. Unfortunately, the problem is if it's not Stark it will be someone else. Throughout the years we've had several of his kind lurking about. And if it's not on my property it could happen to any one of us anywhere. The restraining order can't protect us from the world."

Marianne had known he wouldn't succumb to their offers, but was concerned about the rest of her members. Some of them may not have such a strong constitution.

"You don't have to worry about us," he said glancing toward Suzanna who nodded her agreement. "Is there anything you'd like me to do?"

"Thank you, but no. There's not much that can be done at this point." She moved to Suzanna, and gave her a hug. "Come Tuesday, afternoon. I'll have Sarah call you with a specific time."

"Thank you. I can't tell you how much this means to me." Suzanna's heartfelt response touched her.

"No need dear. I know."

As they began to leave, Suzanna suddenly turned back toward Marianne. "I totally forgot. My cousin, Roberto asked me to find out if you would consider taking him on as an intern in your youth program. He's really very smart, has a degree in psychology and is working toward a master's in education. He'd be a great help to you. He has awesome insights when it comes to dealing with troubled youth."

Marianne already knew he would be a great asset and hoped he would find Gloves to be a place he could expand his knowledge and, find the truth, to become the man he was intended to be by the universal oneness.

"Yes, he actually contacted me the other day and we had a delightful talk. He's going to come speak with me next week."

"Oh, good, I told him he didn't need me to help him. He stands out on his own. Listen to what he has to say. It's very interesting."

"I agree," Marianne smiled. This connection with her new friends here was turning out to be very interesting indeed.

* * * *

As Suzanna and Nicholaus left the building, deep in thought over the most recent events, Suzanna reached up to rub the stones on the pendant. An attachment not yet removed since being placed around her neck. They barely reached the car when she thought about the confusion and disgust she'd had about her father's attentions the night before.

Within seconds, she felt as if the air had been knocked out of her lungs and she doubled over in pain, gasping for air.

"What the…" Nicholaus wrapped his arms around her and she sensed his calming force spread over her like a thick cascade of honey being poured from a jar. "Easy sweetheart…take it easy."

He opened the car door and eased her into the seat, keeping skin to skin contact with his hand on her arms at all times. He knelt in front of her while he continued to push the calm protective energy around her.

"What's going on, sweetheart? Tell me what's wrong."

She took a couple of shaky breaths and regained control of her focus.

"I'm not exactly sure. It's starting to happen to me while I'm awake now."

"This happened before?" he asked anxiously.

"Last night, at dinner, the strangest thing happened. I was minding my own business, just listening to the conversation, and wham! It was like I'd jumped into my nightmare again." She trembled, grateful Nicholaus was there.

"We were right to come to Marianne today. This has got to stop," he said.

She couldn't argue. Weariness had overtaken her and she was beginning to fold.

"Not soon enough for me. That's for sure." She sighed.

"I was going to take you for a drive out to Whidbey Island to a little café on the water, but maybe I should take you home. You should rest."

"Absolutely not," Suzanna was quick to reject his offer. "I'm not going to sit around feeling sorry for myself. Besides, it'll take my mind off my own problems for a while."

Nicholaus studied her face then nodded, and they proceeded to go forth with his original plans. Truthfully, she didn't want to be alone. She was beginning to feel like a total nutcase.

Chapter Nineteen

Nicholaus watched Suzanna as she helped to pack some items for their patient visits. She hadn't slept much the night before, and he could see the fatigue in her eyes.

"Are you sure you don't want me to cancel this afternoon? You're exhausted. We could just kick back and relax," he said in hopes she might agree. It might be a good excuse. He wasn't sure he was ready to do this yet either.

"No way," she exclaimed putting both hands on her hips. "You are not going to get out of this. Those people need your help and you know it."

"I won't leave you here by yourself. I can't chance something happening to you again." He wrapped his arms tight around her waist.

"I'm going with you, but don't worry about me I'll be fine." She reached up to pull his face down to hers. Her soft and supple lips met his, her gentle scent of gardenias drifting up to sensitize his awareness. Mesmerized by her dark sultry eyes, he swore his heart skipped a beat. Caught by the moment, he knew it was time to tell her how he felt.

"Suzanna, I…" The knock at the front door disrupted his admission of love. Swearing under his breath, he dropped another quick kiss on her lips and went to answer it.

The woman standing before him was in her early fifties, dressed simply in worn but clean clothes, her hands gripped together in front of her.

"Can I help you?" Nicholaus questioned.

She stood silent and appeared to be studying him. It made him oddly uncomfortable.

"Nicholaus?" she asked, her voice trembling.

Something about her inflection of his name reminded him of his grandmother. That made him stop short and look more closely at the woman. Recognition set in and he suddenly tensed and brought his stature straight.

"Mother," he acknowledged. Manners overruled his immediate reaction to close the door in her face, so he gestured her in with his hand.

"Oh, Nicholaus, you've grown to be such a handsome young man," she said staring at him, for the lost son that he was.

He wasn't sure what to do. He hadn't decided if he wanted to talk to her yet. She glanced past him at Suzanna and gave her a teary eyed smile.

Suzanna came forward and held out her hand. "Hello, you must be Nicholaus' mother. My name is Suzanna. Won't you come have a seat?" She gestured toward the clinic's seating area.

The woman moved timidly in and sat, her purse held tight in her lap. "I really can't stay long. I see you are headed out. I hoped I could talk with you for just a minute, Nicholaus."

Nicholaus stood frozen in the same spot. Turmoil fought its way to the surface and he spouted out, "I told you I didn't want to see you." He never intentionally hurt anyone and he wanted to kick himself when the pain jumped into her eyes.

"I know. But you have to know I wouldn't bother you unless it was important. I'm begging you, just hear me out."

He paced back and forth and could hear Marianne's words in his head. *Lead with your heart. The Spirit will always lead you in the right way.* "Alright," he consented, and forced himself to sit across from her.

"Nicholaus, I know nothing I could ever say would make up for what I did to you and your father. There isn't a day goes by I don't hate myself for my stupidity. I realize now if I don't try my best to make amends I will never have peace in my soul."

The sound of her voice brought out memories of his childhood, sitting on her lap as she told him the ancient story of Romulus and Remus abandoned on the banks of a river, left to be raised by a she-wolf. He'd always loved that story. For months after she'd left them, he'd sit and wait for her return, reciting the story to himself. Until it began to fade and all he had left was the longing to be loved again. Over time that disappeared too.

"Go on."

Carlotta began to wring her hands, obviously torn by her next words. "I know what I'm going to tell you, is a little hard to believe, but you deserve the truth."

"What? That you left us for some outlandish idea a group of idiots can take the place of your own son and the man who loved you?"

"Oh…I'm so sorry," she said digging into her purse to pull out a tissue. "You have to believe me when I realized my mistake I wanted to come back to you. But they wouldn't let me. This group I got involved with turned out to be no more than a cult led by an insane egotistical religious fanatic."

"This Universal Order, I've done some research on it. There was nothing showing anything illegal going on, or any questionable activity. Seems to me to be a simple commune of hippy type brush offs from the 70's. If it was so bad why didn't you leave?" Nicholaus stated the facts as he knew them.

"The only reason nothing unusual is known about them is because they weren't doing anything considered illegal, at first. We were all duped by the promise of a higher calling, to live the life God intended us to have. And most of the inhabitants lived simple beautiful lives, as long as they paid homage to the 'Almighty One', as he liked to call himself." She dabbed her eyes and looked toward Suzanna then back to Nicholaus. "But for some of us it was more like a stockade. We were expected to do our job, and…to…service the leader, when summoned. He took a special liking to me and kept me close to his side. I was used to lure people in, claiming our commune had superiority over all other living situations." She looked away in an attempt to gather herself.

"Oh, my God, that's horrible." Suzanna exclaimed reaching out to grasp her hand in support.

"So you're saying you weren't paid for your services?"

"At first, but later on I was lucky to get my meals and a place to sleep every night. I was put on what they called a faith lock down. No phone calls and I couldn't leave the compound. They had this hold over everything I did and said. When I called you on your 15th birthday it was allowed only because they had heard you had the power too, and wanted me to convince you to come join with me."

"You're here now, what changed?" Nicholaus asked, skeptical of the whole story.

"About 10 years ago Howard, the 'Almighty One" was found dead in his cabin. He died of a heart attack. I'm not sure, but I think it was drug related. His group leaders tried to keep the whole thing together, but soon after everything fell apart."

"10 years is a long time." He narrowed his eyes at her, wondering if he could believe a word of it.

Carlotta dipped her head down. When she raised her gaze up again he could see the torment on her face. "Yes it is. I didn't dare try to come back then. I was so ashamed of what I'd done." She stopped, her eyes imploring him to believe her.

Either she is telling the truth or she's one hell of an actress.

Nicholaus thought for sure he'd stepped into the twilight zone. This was a little too much for him to handle. He stood up again and paced back and forth. He stopped in front of her and tried to get a feel for her honesty and couldn't.

Suzanna came to his side. He raised an eyebrow at her.

"She's telling you the truth," she whispered.

He paused for a minute to assess the upheaval this caused. "Okay, so assuming I believe you. What are you asking me to do?"

Tears began to stream down her face. "I don't expect you to forgive me. Please, all I ask is for you to give me the chance to get to know you. I can't stand to live another day not knowing who my child has turned out to be."

The stinging at the back of his own eyes couldn't be ignored, and Suzanna gave him a look he couldn't deny. He reached down and lifted his mother to her feet. She clung to him as if her life depended on it.

"Alright now, we don't have much time at the moment. I'm not really sure what to make of all this. You'll need to give me a chance to think this through. I can't tell you what my decision will be, but I can promise I'll think about it." He'd never been one to make a snap decision. This warranted some real thought.

The sniffle was to be expected, and she stepped back to view her son. She seemed to pull herself together. "Bless you." From her pocket she pulled a slip of paper. "I'm staying with a friend. Here's her number. I'll wait to hear from you."

* * * *

The afternoon flew by. He'd scheduled to visit four elderly people, in hopes of possibly healing their ailment. Nicholaus watched in amazement as Suzanna's penchant to help others grew stronger and began to outweigh her inexperience in the medical field. As with the animals, she could guess the problem with each patient, which helped tremendously in his next case.

Mrs. Kozlov, a Russian immigrant, was not able to speak English and depended on her young granddaughter's interpretation of her native tongue. She eyed Nicholaus warily as they came into her small living room, scented with the fragrance of spiced orange potpourri.

There was little need for introduction because Suzanna quickly earned the older woman's trust. The assignment card simply stated 'head'—the only word they could decipher from the request for help. The granddaughter was unable to find the right words to explain. Through some animated hand gestures from the woman, and Suzanna's own techniques, Nicholaus determined the woman suffered from headaches known as an ocular migraine.

"What I can tell is she has this sharp pain in her forehead and then everything goes black for a bit. The sight comes back, but the pain stays for hours. She had one earlier today and the pain is still there." Suzanna gathered from the woman's gestures and her granddaughter's broken English.

"You're getting pretty good at that. You might want to reconsider your career choice," Nicholaus said to Suzanna with a smile. "If you and the granddaughter could please explain to her I'm going to place my hands on either side of her head. She might feel a little light headed for a while, but the pain will soon go away."

Suzanna was able to convey what to expect from Nicholaus with some help from the young teen,. The elderly woman nodded her head and sat in expectation. She grasped her hands tightly together, waiting for her treatment.

Nicholaus gingerly put his palms on either side of her temples and concentrated on the excessive pain messages being sent to her receptor sites. He led the abnormal cells causing the pain to subside and relinquish their hold. The message of healing from above came slow, but he was finally able to relieve the migraines she'd been experiencing.

He removed his hands and sat in front of her to determine if there were any side affects from the treatment. To his surprise her eyes flew open and she leapt out of her chair.

"Хвалите Бога!" she exclaimed in excitement. She patted her head and gestured the flight of something from her temples. "Более левый!"

"Grandma says the pain…" The young girl said pointing to her temples, "It flew away like the birds."

Suzanna jumped with almost as much excitement and gave the old woman a hug. She spoke to her as if the old woman could understand every word she said.

Nicholaus jotted down a few natural herbs for her to take to flush out the toxins in her system and handed it to the young girl.

"You can bring this to the health store on the corner of 4th and Stewart," he said pointing to the address on the top. "Tell them Dr. Brach sent you to get these things for your Grandma, all right?" he asked, making sure she understood.

"Yes sir, I will go right away. Thank you, kind sir. Thank you so much," she said, tears in her eyes.

"Have her take these herbs, as I've written here. Make sure she drinks a lot of water every day," he said gesturing the quantity with his hands. "She needs to sleep as much as she wants to. She will be sleepy for a while, as her body heals."

"Yes sir," she agreed enthusiastically.

Suzanna gave the woman a hug as they were about to leave. The old woman grasped her arm and pulled her back into the house, speaking to her granddaughter in Russian before she shooed her off to retrieve something from the pantry.

The young girl came back with two packages in her hands. The first smelled heavenly. She explained it was called 'Kulich', a sweet cake to be enjoyed with a rich dark coffee.

The other, the young girl blushed as she explained. "This is a gift for your joining. She says you're both to enjoy each other for a long life."

Nicholaus almost choked when he realized what the woman thought. Suzanna began to disagree with her assumption, but he placed his hand on her arm to keep her from going further. The woman was perceptive, but he wanted to be the first to say anything.

They stated their appreciation for the gifts and departed for their last appointment. Suzanna got in and thanked him for opening the car door for her. When Nicholaus came around to the driver's seat he could see Suzanna's stunned expression.

"She thinks we're getting married," she said, a deep blush flushing her cheeks.

"I know. It's better not to argue. I've had my experience with the older cultures. She wouldn't have taken no for an answer."

In the package, Suzanna pulled out a delicately handcrafted doily shaped with two hearts intertwined as one. The soft pastel pink and blue a definite message of what was expected.

"That's sweet." Nicholaus glanced at the gift. Then he saw Suzanna hurry to wipe away the trickle of tears running down her cheek. "Hey now, don't start breaking down on me yet. We've got one more stop to make."

Sniffling a bit, she looked out her window. Numb to any more emotion, he wondered what happened to make her cry.

What did I miss? He was too tired to try to figure it out. He had his own troubles at the moment.

"Why the sniffles?" he asked in innocence. As she turned back to face him she looked offended.

"No reason, nothing for you to worry about."

Oh, Lord. When a woman said that, there was plenty to worry about.

He knew there had to be more to it, but decided it would be better to ask later. For now he needed to get his head around their next stop.

Before he started the engine Suzanna placed her hand on his arm.

"Are you going to tell your father about your mother?" Suzanna asked pensively.

Nicholaus sat back and brushed a hand through his hair.

That's another thing I need to deal with. Why the hell does it all have to happen at once? He thought as he blew out the breath he held.

"I'm not sure. Should I believe all the stuff she told us? I mean, that's a little out there, don't you think?"

Suzanna placed her hand on his shoulder and began to massage the tension with her fingers. He moved closer to her, and stretched his neck, enjoying her touch.

"I can't say whether it's true or not, though I can tell you she truly feels sorry for what she's done. There's no question in my mind she's endured some very difficult hardships over the last few years. She's searching for some acceptance, and forgiveness, even though she doesn't expect it to happen."

Nicholas turned to hold onto the steering wheel. He stared straight ahead, trying to control the burst of emotion bubbling under the surface.

"You can't keep holding this in Nicholaus. I know how deeply she hurt you. You can't pretend it doesn't matter. You need to let go of the emotion." The soft touch of Suzanna's hand on his was all it took.

The tears burned again, as Nicholaus was suddenly overtaken by the pain of all these years living without a mother, of finding out he may now lose the father he loved, and the return of a mother he didn't know or trust. He dropped his head down on his arms and let the tears come.

Suzanna pulled him to her, easing the pain. He grabbed on tight and let the flow of tears ebb away.

* * * *

The little man, with graying hair and sunken cheeks, wasn't what one might expect after a good look at his offspring. He appeared to be a miniature version of his healthy, vibrant son. What once used to be a lush mane now lay in a graying mass of misshapen curls, oddly thinning on top. Stooped over, his limp sweater hung over his shoulders as he peered up through his bifocals to see who had come to his door.

He looked suspiciously at Nicholaus, then around and behind him.

"What on earth are you doing here?" he grumbled as he ushered them into the house. He stuck his head out to view the street then came back in and shut the door. With his back pressed up against the door, his hand stayed ready on the handle.

Nicholaus didn't answer his father's question, but was very aware of his actions. "Expecting someone else?" His dry sarcasm hit the mark.

The cough from his father's throat sounded very real. Nicholaus heard the depth of its origin, but realized it had also been used to cover up the discomfort of the situation. Roland Brach eyed his son at length then eased away from the door to move toward the front room.

"Of course not, just surprised you came to visit is all."

His father's curt response wasn't unexpected. Things hadn't been smooth between the two of them for some time. Nicholaus looked around the room in dismay. Papers piled everywhere left a slim path to get from one place to the next. Dirty dishes on the coffee table with half-eaten food had begun to smell. Disgusted, Nicholaus reminded himself of his father's condition. He turned to him, but not before he could change the repulsed expression from his face.

Roland's next remark sounded like a lion chewing on gristle. "I live how I like. Don't expect me to straighten up on the off chance you'll be here."

Nicholaus again felt unwanted. He responded back, "I'll end your surprise. Suzanna and I have come in response to your request of healing from the Gloves organization. There won't be anyone else coming to visit you today."

He watched his father's expression as it changed to one of disappointment and resignation.

"Why the hell did she have to send you?"

"Because I am a healer, and you apparently are in need of some help."

"You're nothing but a dog doctor. I won't have you giving me some canine medicine that's going to make me sicker than I am already," his father said in apparent contempt.

Nicholaus tried to keep his cool. *Lead with your heart,* Marianne had said, *don't allow the mind to rule in this situation.*

"You know very well I am licensed in the medical field as well. Healing takes all forms. The kind you need has nothing to do with what I do at the veterinary hospital. I'm fully capable of providing care in all forms."

Roland muttered to himself as he walked around the coffee table to brush the newspapers off the couch.

"Sit," he said forcefully. Nicholaus saw him catch sight of Suzanna. His father's expression changed when he realized she'd seen the whole thing. He regained his manners and gestured again toward the seat, ushering her forward. "Please, sit down."

Nicholaus sat on the arm of the couch next to Suzanna, trying not to show the emotion his father invoked. From the outside, he knew he remained impressively calm, yet on the inside he seethed over the comments his father made. Suzanna looked up at him, their eyes locked for the briefest of moments, but he knew she could sense the combat going on in his head.

Roland sat down in the recliner across from them, fidgeting with the frayed arms of the chair.

"She shouldn't have sent you."

"You'd have wanted someone else?" Nicholaus asked in defense. "If that's what you want, I can arrange it." He cursed himself for not being able to maintain control of his mouth.

The color rose into the old man's cheeks. "Fine, then. Why the hell did you come here in the first place? Why don't you go back to those damn dogs of yours where you belong?"

In fury, Roland began to rise from his seat, but the effort was too much for him. The short shallow breaths forced him to close his eyes and regain his strength.

Suzanna squeezed Nicholaus' arm and whispered to him, "He's not really mad. He's just scared."

Opening his eyes, Roland cast a scrutinizing glare her way. "I'm not deaf you know," he grumbled. "Damn right I'm scared. I'm dying here, and I can't do anything about it." With a wheeze, he gave another long look at his son.

It took an extreme effort for Nicholaus to put aside his anger for his father's reaction to him. Pushing through the emotional turmoil, he tried again.

"Marianne felt I would be the best one to connect for you to begin a healing."

He bowed his head to gather his composure. His father's failing health had progressed far quicker than he'd imagined. The last time he'd seen the elder man, perhaps a couple of months ago, he'd looked fairly healthy. Now, a shadow of his former self, it looked as if the life was being sucked from him. Nicholaus realized his father must have known then what he faced. He shook his head. If only his father had told him then. He feared now may be too late.

He looked back up and met his father's eyes. "Why didn't you tell me?"

Roland looked at the ceiling and Nicholaus saw his father's eyes mist with emotion.

"Damn thing hit me like a bomb. One day I'm fine, the next I can't seem to move. Now all I do is sit and stare at the wall wondering how much time I have left."

"You should have called me. I would have been here without question."

"You were best left alone. You don't need to be involved in all of this. You're better off with the dogs. You start healing people, the next thing I know you'll be taking off for God knows where, trying to heal the world."

So that's what this is all about.

"I'm not Carlotta," Nicholaus said referring to his mother. "I won't leave you. But you've pushed me away because of who I am most of my life. No matter how hard you push, I'm going to be what I'm destined to be."

His father made an indistinguishable sound and shook his head.

"Why did you call Gloves? All my life you've made me think you didn't believe in healing and everything I did was just a bunch of hocus pocus."

Roland's heavy sigh sounded like resignation. "I hoped if I didn't believe you wouldn't either. Lot of good that did," he paused for a breath then said something Nicholaus had waited years to hear. "It's not that I don't believe. God knows you and your mother have done some amazing things."

In his childhood Nicholaus had seen his mother perform some unheard of miracles. It softened his heart toward her a bit more to remember God had chosen her as well, for unknown reasons, to work as a vessel of His healing works. He thought again of the woman who had come to see him.

She seemed so sincere. Should I believe her?

"From what I remember she was a good woman. Maybe she just took some wrong turns in life." Nicholaus had thought hard about this since her first call. Marianne may have been right. Perhaps the wrong turns really had ended up with no way out.

"She had no right to do what she did. I don't know how you can talk about her being good. She left us for some made up picture of heaven. There is no heaven. There's no reality in that. We're all here just playing out some game God has for us until the life is sucked out from under us," yelled the elder man.

Nicholaus rubbed is hands together. Did he dare tell his father Carlotta had come back? He looked at his father's expression, scrunched into a frown covering his whole face. By the mention of her name the anger still poured from his father just as it had during his childhood. He then realized this was why he'd chosen his view of her. He'd learned it from his father.

This critical outlook on life hit Nicholaus square on the chin. Because he'd watched the man's depression over the years he'd chosen to never look at life in such an ugly way. What Marianne said about forgiveness was turning out to be true. His father was a perfect example of being chained to a trait which caused him constant anguish.

By forgiving his mother for her wrong doings, Nicholaus could free himself of the same misery his father suffered day in and day out. He needed to release the tendency to hold onto negativity and blame others. As his realization took hold, he felt the heavy burden lifting. The liberation was exhilarating.

Saddened to see the angry man his father had grown to be, he wanted to share this new discovery. But this was not the time to try to convince his father to change his outlook. It would take time, and unfortunately, might not be possible at all.

"So you called Marianne. I wish you'd come to me first Poppa."

The old man shrugged his shoulders, a look of exhaustion spread over his face. "You've been treating those dumb animals so long I figured you wouldn't know what to do with an old man like me. I've known Marianne for years now. She knows all about this kind of stuff. I figured if anyone would know what to do, she would."

"I went to veterinary medicine, because I felt I could help. Those animals need my help, the same as you do. Just because I choose to practice in a field you don't approve of, doesn't mean I'm incapable of helping people. The fact is I chose animals because they don't talk. I didn't want to fall into the same traps Carlotta might have."

Roland seemed to digest his words as he looked into his son's face. "I suppose that makes sense. You've had some tough decisions to make for yourself."

"I chose medicine because it's what I've been born to do. I realize now there is so much more I can do, for the good of all. I'm not a child anymore. There is nothing anyone can make me do I don't want to. Including you," Nicholaus said.

"I've known that for a very long time now," Roland acknowledged. They stared at each other for a long while. Finally, Nicholaus recognized this as the start to a long awaited understanding.

He needed to thank Marianne. She was right, lead with your heart and the Spirit. They will always bring you down the right path.

"So, are you ready to tell me what all of this is about, and let me see what I can do?" he asked, his faith lifted.

"Hell, anything would be better than this stuff they've been giving me at the hospital. Makes me puke my guts out, I can't keep a thing down for days. If the cancer don't kill me, the medicine will."

The next few minutes were spent discussing what the doctors had said about his condition. Between the little bits of information his father could remember, and Nicholaus' medical knowledge, he was able to come up with a fairly complete diagnosis.

"When did you see your doctor?" Nicholaus asked while listening to his father's vitals through his stethoscope.

"I don't know, maybe a couple of weeks ago," he replied with impatience. "I'm due to go back for another torture session on Friday."

"You said they thought it had spread?"

His father leaned back in his chair, nodding his head ever so slightly, eyes closed against the brightness of the overhead light.

"Suzanna, I need you to assist me. We need to find out where the malignancy has metastasized." Nicholaus motioned to her to come closer.

Opening his eyes, Roland studied his son. "It almost sounds like you actually know what you're doing."

Nicholaus was overjoyed to finally see a small sparkle of approval in his father's eyes.

Suzanna didn't move right away. At her hesitancy Nicholaus glanced up to see her blank look and remembered she had only a basic familiarity with medical terms. Without the knowledge she had no idea what he was talking about. Not missing a beat, he began to explain to his father what he would be doing, divulging just enough for her to pick up on what he needed from her.

"Suzanna can sense where the abnormal cells might be accumulating. It is probably in the areas where the most discomfort shows up, a tightness of sorts and pain at times. Sometimes you may not feel things until it's become worse than you realize."

Suzanna came around the back of the chair and politely placed her hands on the old man's chest. In a light touch she began to move her hands over his frail body. Her unwavering sympathy for those she helped continued to astonish Nicholaus. He watched her intently as she did everything she could to assist him.

Could there be anyone more perfect for him and his life goals in the practice of healing? Even more astounding, her perfection didn't stop at his work. She fit into every vision he had for his life.

He looked at her now with new appreciation. He'd never put all the reasons he loved her together. He just knew there was no question he loved the woman. As he watched her, he felt an incredible respect for her in ways he hadn't before.

Stopping in the areas she could feel the most damage, Suzanna would glance to Nicholaus, and he continued to watch her carefully. The look in her eyes at times told him his father's condition was worse than he thought. Now his only hope for a successful healing was his father's will to live.

The old man peered over his glasses at Suzanna and blinked several times. "You must be an angel sent to come take me away."

Suzanna's blush was priceless and Nicholaus fell in love that much harder.

"Nonsense," she replied. "You've plenty of life left in you."

"So you're telling me I'm going to live?" he asked her.

Suzanna patted the old man on the shoulder. "I'm not the doctor. You'll need to ask your son about that. I can only tell him what he needs to know to make his diagnosis."

"You're a regular x-ray machine, aren't you girl?"

She choked out a little laugh. "I guess you could say that, couldn't you?"

She confirmed what Nicholaus already picked up on by placing her hand on the two areas he suspected were the worst. The cancerous cells had spread to his father's chest and liver.

Frowning, Nicholaus pulled on every mental memory he could to remember what he'd learned about lymphatic cancer. It started in the lymph nodes and would quickly spread throughout the body, multiplying its abnormality at a rate much quicker than other cancers because of its ability to shut down the natural healing process of healthy lymph nodes. He'd need to deactivate the production of the abnormal cells, shrink them in size, and slow down their reproductive rate. At the same time, he needed to regenerate the healthy cells that hadn't yet been affected by the disease. He prayed, asking God to grant him this request.

"Dad, what I'm going to do you may or may not feel. I'll have to use the big guns on you this first time. After we are finished, you need to get as much sleep as you can. And I don't care what you think about water. You need to drink it, lots of it."

Seeing the crinkled look on his father's face, he knew his instructions would be especially hard for this individual to follow. His father had been a strict coffee drinker all of his life. Nicholaus couldn't remember a time he'd seen him without a coffee mug in his hand.

"Then we will be back for another couple of treatments in the next day or two. Hopefully, we can stop this thing before it can get the upper hand." Then with great care he added, "I can't promise this will work. But I'm going to do the best I can."

His father stared at him then reached out to take Nicholaus' hand.

"Then that's all a man can ask for," Roland said, blinking a tear from his eye. "Let's get to it then."

Chapter Twenty

Fatigued, Suzanna slid her arms into her jacket. The toll taken by the wakeful visions were unbearable. An effort to place her purse on the table seemed almost more than she felt capable of this morning. She was tired, very tired.

"Are you sure you don't want me to go? This being your first session with Marianne, you might need me there." Nicholaus inquired.

She wished he could. Suzanna shook her head. "No. You know your father needs you more than I do. I don't want to be the cause of you missing his treatment."

"You know I would come with you if you asked me."

"I know, but I can do this alone," she said, unsure whether she really meant it.

Nicholaus stood and wrapped his arms around her. "If you need anything, call me. I'll have my cell on me the whole time. When I'm finished I'll stop by to see if you're still in with Marianne."

She rested her cheek on his shoulder and took in a deep breath, his scent invoking a sense of safety and comfort.

"I'll be fine. Don't rush. You know he needs you." She rose to her tiptoes and kissed him on the nose, then turned to pick up her purse. "I do too, but I'll just have to wait," she said with a seductive wink.

He grasped her around the waist and pulled her against him. The kiss was excruciatingly sweet. Lately she'd begun to hope he might be changing how he felt about her. Her heart palpitated at the thought he could love her too.

"Anytime, anywhere…" He smiled with enthusiasm, and made her giggle as he wiggled his eyebrows up and down.

"We might have to explore that when I get back."

* * * *

Suzanna waited patiently outside of Marianne's office. Sarah, Marianne's assistant, took a few messages from what sounded like interested possible members and tucked them into a file on top of her desk. She turned toward Suzanna, head held low, eyes meeting hers once or twice.

She's scared. Why is she scared?

"Are you sure you wouldn't like some water or tea? I'd be glad to get some for you," she said in a voice so soft Suzanna could barely make out the words.

"No, but thank you, I'm fine." Suzanna had the oddest need to engage her in a conversation somehow. She felt as if they should know each other, for some reason. "How long have you worked with Marianne?"

The young woman blushed. "Not too long, maybe six months or so." She looked as if surprised Suzanna had wanted to talk.

"I bet this would be really interesting. I'd love to work in a place like this," Suzanna said looking across to the open areas of practice. "There must be all kinds of awesome things happening all the time."

Who was she kidding? She had a job like that.

"Oh, yes, it's never boring around here." Sarah brightened up a bit with the continued conversation.

Suzanna took a longer look with the continued prompt from somewhere to befriend the otherwise forgettable young woman. Her light mousy blonde hair was pulled up tight on top of her head in a knot looking almost painful to wear. She wore a simple white blouse tucked into a sensible gray skirt befitting a day in Catholic school.

Boy, she can't be comfortable.

"Do you live here in Seattle?" The girl didn't give much to talk about.

Suzanna sensed confusion from Sarah over the question. She shook her head. "No, I live in Renton, with my mother." She delivered the latter part of the sentence with the same lowered head at an almost whisper level. Sarah glanced back up. "Why?"

This isn't right. Suzanna started to become quite concerned for Sarah. Something is not right with her world.

"No reason, I just thought maybe…" Suzanna was about to ask if she'd like to get some coffee or lunch sometime when Marianne's door opened up.

To her surprise, Roberto stepped out, his head turned to acknowledge something Marianne was saying to him.

"Yes, I would like that, too."

Followed by Marianne, Roberto's first glance went to the young woman, whose first response was to climb back into her shell. Eyes averted she blushed, trying to pretend she hadn't been looking at the handsome dark Latino man. Suzanna felt this sudden surge of belonging between the two. Roberto's slight grin confirmed the fact he was attracted.

"Aren't I going to get a 'hello'?" Suzanna asked.

Roberto's head whipped around and the bright smile he melted hearts with came out. He came around and gave her a big hug.

"Suzanna. What a surprise. It's good to see you."

"I didn't know you'd be here today."

"I know, I pushed my meeting with Ms. Ross up a couple of weeks. My studies are progressing faster than we imagined. Looks like you are going to see more of me around."

Marianne came forward. "I've offered Roberto the opportunity to work with us during his internship. I look forward to seeing you again." Holding her hands out to take his between hers for a brief moment, she glanced back at Sarah. An odd connection between Roberto and Sarah floated by Suzanna before she even saw Marianne's grin. Now it was confirmed, though she wasn't sure what it meant.

Marianne knows something. Suzanna looked between the two of them and didn't believe there could be two more unlikely people to get together. But, who knows?

"Roberto, why don't you go ahead and make a tentative start date with Sarah. That way I will have you on my schedule." Marianne held out her hand and placed it on Suzanna's arm. "Suzanna, dear, would you mind giving me a moment. I need to prepare for our session."

Although, as tired as she was, Suzanna would have rather started right away, she understood Marianne's need to prepare. She said her goodbyes to Roberto and walked back into her office closing the door quietly behind her.

Marianne sat in her favorite chair, eyes closed, in the lotus position facing toward the windows of her office. In the background, the musical sounds of nature brought her into a place of oneness. Even though the day blustered around, darkened by clouds scurrying across the sky, the grandeur of the majestic universe still poured through the glass into the room. Connection to the Spirit came easily this way.

She heard her visitor come quietly into the room. Still open from her connection to the source, she received flashes of Suzanna's trip to the office. The poor girl was having a terrible time, her need to unlock the hidden secrets most prevalent.

"Should I come back later?" Suzanna whispered.

Marianne opened her eyes, her face aglow from her connection to the Almighty. She reached out to take Suzanna's hand in hers.

"Heaven's no. It just takes a moment to come back down out of the clouds."

Suzanna shook as she lowered herself to the couch. Marianne didn't need special powers to see the exhaustion on her face.

"How are you feeling?"

"I'm tired of this Marianne. I can't take anymore of these dreams. They are haunting me at night and during my waking hours now. You've got to help me."

The plea in Suzanna's eyes broke Marianne's heart. She sat next to Suzanna and reached up to touch the stones Nicholaus had placed around her neck.

"Doesn't surprise me, this is a very strong mixture of earthly properties. They would enhance your abilities, as well as super charge the progress on your own discoveries. Especially if you've been doing those exercises I showed you to open your chakras." She smiled. Nicholaus had listened to her suggestion. "So, are you ready to give this a try?"

Suzanna took a deep breath and looked around. "No weird spiraling pictures, or mood music, or anything?"

Marianne chuckled a little. The common perception of her field was so strange at times.

"No. But if you'd like you may lay your head back on the couch. It might be more comfortable."

Suzanna lay back on the surrounding cushions. "Let's do this."

"Close your eyes, and listen to the music of the Universe for a few minutes, this will prepare your reception to the sound of my voice." Marianne reached forward to brush Suzanna's temples with her fingertips in a rhythmic motion. "Relax and listen to my words. I want you to think of something you like to do, something that relaxes you. Find the place where you're the happiest. It could be a park, or a beach, maybe its home for you."

Marianne knew Suzanna couldn't help but be lulled into a place where she would drift between being alert, listening to the words and floating toward a sort of relaxed sleep. She could see Suzanna enter the final hypnotic state when her body slowly released its tension. Her hands instinctively formed the meditative state she'd learned.

"I want you to tell me about your youth. What can you tell me about your family and friends during the fifth grade?"

Marianne thought she would start the therapy with a time she'd heard Suzanna talk about. Fifth grade was the year after she'd started having the dreams, yet close enough she could ease the young woman into memories of that dark period. Suzanna began to tell snippets of stories about school and her fairly normal pre-teen years.

It went smooth at first. Suzanna was able to visualize herself at eight years old, when she, her sister and mother moved up from California. She remembered her teacher's names and events that made a big impression. Like the Christmas pageant when little tow headed Benjamin had glued his reindeer antlers to his head so they wouldn't fall off.

Going further back Marianne led her back to remember as far back as age four and five. Bit by bit they worked her back and forth until Marianne was able to identify large chunk of time missing from her childhood.

"You were having bad dreams then, weren't you Suzanna?"

In her sedated state Suzanna nodded her head slowly.

"What happened when you began to have these dreams? What was happening?"

Until that point, Suzanna had been talking softly and sweetly about her life. Now her face scrunched up like an angry child.

"I don't know. I don't want to talk about it."

"Why? Did it scare you?"

Marianne's words connected with the memory. Suzanna shook her head up and down and muttered, "Yes."

"What scared you Suzanna? What happened?"

"Mommy is crying. She keeps screaming at someone. She's scaring me." Suzanna's tears began to run down her face.

"Who else is there Suzanna? Who is in the room with you?" Marianne intended to lead her to the faceless person that needed to be revealed. What came next surprised her.

"Rachel is crying too, but she looks mad." Sniffling, Suzanna's youthful self showed through the layers of memory. "Mommy's mad too. She's so mad. I don't want her to be mad."

"Why do you think she's mad?"

"I…I…don't know," she said shaking her head more violently now.

"You were there Suzanna. Why is she so mad?"

Suzanna gasped for air and began to clutch the pillows around her. "I don't know. Go away. I don't know. I don't want to talk to you anymore. Go away."

Marianne could see Suzanna was still not ready to remember. The tension was too acute for her to go any further. If she pushed further Suzanna's memory might lock up, and refuse to reveal her secrets, ever. Marianne needed to bring her back out of the hypnotic state.

"Alright Suzanna, when I touch your left hand you will wake up. You will remember everything we talked about. Do you understand?"

Suzanna had already begun to return to a calm meditative state. Marianne placed her hand over Suzanna's now cold and clammy one. When she opened her eyes Marianne watched her intently.

"How are you feeling?"

"Why did you bring me out? Wasn't I getting close? Didn't you see I was getting close?" she asked in frustration.

"You were beginning to lock up. I couldn't risk pushing too far. If I did you'd end up where you started, and I don't think that's what you want."

"I remember," Suzanna got up and paced the floor. "I remember my mother was there. She was looking straight at me. She knew who that was. My sister, she knows too." Suddenly, it was all too much for her to handle, and she sunk back down on the couch. She looked into Marianne's eyes, the pain and suffering imprinted on her face. "Why haven't they told me, Marianne? Why have they let me go through this so long?"

Marianne was at a loss. She didn't know sometimes why people did what they did to each other. It broke her heart to see Suzanna's grief.

"I can't tell you why. But what I can say is there is always a reason for things to happen the way they do. Even though we may not understand it, everything happens for a reason, we just need to open ourselves up to receive the answers."

Suzanna breathed in deep and let it out slowly.

"You're right. I know. I'm just so tired. I can't do this much longer. Sometimes I feel like giving up," she said as she placed her head in her hands.

Marianne stood up. "You look a bit pale, dear. I'm going to go get you some tea. That might help you to rejuvenate. I think I know what will do the trick."

Suzanna shook her head. "I don't think anything will make a difference." She looked into the depths of Marianne's eyes. "You can't fix the helplessness I feel right now. The only answer is to find out who raped me and why my family hasn't told me."

* * * *

Nicholaus found Marianne going through paperwork when he stuck his head through the open door.

"Nicholaus, this is a pleasure. I didn't expect to see you this evening."

He walked in and looked around for Suzanna.

"If you are looking for Suzanna she left a short while ago."

"I told her I would try to meet her here. How did it go?" Marianne's expression concerned him. "What's wrong?"

"Nothing is wrong, really. She wasn't able to remember as much as we'd hoped. It might take some time for this to work, but I'm worried about her Nicholaus. She doesn't look well. I think she isn't physically strong enough to handle this right now. She needs rest."

She wasn't telling him anything he didn't already know. "True, but she can't rest when she wakes up screaming half the time. What's the next step? She can't keep going on like this."

"I told her to rest as much as she could and we would try again when she felt up to it. I think she should take a day or two and give her mind more time to work through it."

"Did she tell you she's been having these visions during the day too?"

"Yes. You know you put together a pretty strong concoction for her to carry around with her in that necklace. It's definitely speeding up the process."

"I wanted to do what I could to help. Do you think it will hurt her?"

"She's a very strong willed woman. I don't believe it will necessarily hurt her. She just needs to sort out what is current and what is the past. Then perhaps you two can begin working on the future." Marianne's expression told him all he needed to know. What he felt was true. There really was a future for them—a future together.

If only Suzanna could let go of the past.

* * * *

Suzanna tried in desperation to retrieve from her memory the experience causing her this life of turmoil. In her hypnotic state she'd felt the childlike fear surface. Fear of the unknown, mixed with having done something she shouldn't, and the trepidation of punishment.

The obvious blank spots never bothered her before. Now her inability to explain them frustrated her. She drove the car as if on autopilot. If asked what route she took home, she wouldn't be able answer.

She knew typical dreams represent themselves in symbolic manners. She'd thought this terror of being raped, reflected some other type of invasion she suffered, or perceived to have experienced. During hypnosis, she confirmed for herself, these distinct and repetitive nightmares were tied to a physical memory she knew in her heart had at one time happened.

If she was raped as a child, who could it be? And why hadn't anyone told her?

There were very few people she could remember around her during that time. Uncle Jose, her mother's brother, a softhearted man with children of his own. She'd always enjoyed his laughter and gentle ways. She couldn't imagine him doing something evil like that. Even now, theirs was a normal loving family relationship.

There were various others, teachers, principles and pastors, but none stuck out as someone she should consider. Could it be a stranger had broken into the house? Surely she would have heard stories of that nature. She didn't have memories of any police activity or emergency. You'd think something would trigger a memory, especially as traumatic as it would have been at such a young age.

The only other possibility was her father. Suzanna's stomach began to churn. Could the man she knew as a respected cornerstone of his community be a child rapist? She didn't remember much about him, but she had always attributed her lack of closeness to his departure so early in her youth. He left them a short time before her family moved up to Seattle. Her mother always told her there were circumstances beyond her control, and she and her father didn't love each other anymore. At no time had there been any mention of misconduct or impropriety.

He never remarried. That didn't mean anything, not everyone can find a mate so late in life. From Rachel's updates, she knew he dated off and on with no real commitment to any of the relationships. He continued to advance in the firm he partnered with and maintained the appearance of a model citizen. Other than that, she didn't know much more about him.

He had been a little too familiar the other night, but she passed that off to the quantity of liquor consumed and her sensitivity to the whole meal arrangement made by her sister.

She looked blankly at the road ahead and continued to go over every possibility. A gentle rub from the stones around her neck reminded her of Nicholaus. She reached to caress them in thought.

The repulsion hit so sudden, she needed to take a quick breath in and hold it to avoid becoming violently ill. The stench of gin, mixed with the acrid smoke from a foreign cigar, sickened her beyond reason. Grasping the steering wheel with both hands, all her effort was consumed by trying to keep the car headed in the right direction. The smell turned her stomach, and yet it was oddly familiar. She could feel the heat of someone or something as it pressed against her body. It stifled her every breath.

Her vision, now marred by images flashing feverishly through her head, clouded the reality around her. Some she saw over and over again in her dreams. Others were newly revealed memories she didn't yet understand. Her sister, revealed by the light from the hallway, watched in distaste as her nightmare progressed. She could sense her mother's tears and cries of hatred in the background. Then the sounds of labored grunts close to her ear brought her to the familiar agonizing pain that had become her reality.

As quick as the visions came, they left with her distraught and unaware of her surroundings. Her disorientation lasted only a second, but it was too late. The small puppy had scampered out into the street, ignorant of the unaware driver.

When the car's fender hit the dog's little body the sound was revolting. Suzanna slammed on her brakes. The dog's cry played over and over in her head like the jammed soundtrack of a scratched CD.

She almost fell out of the car as she scrambled to see if the puppy's injuries were as bad as she expected. The little lifeless body lay under the car, bloodied by the impact of its attacker. She didn't know what to do at first, her thoughts muddled by her distress.

Uncontrollable sobs poured out as she looked around to see if anyone could claim ownership of the animal. She reached under the fender carefully to pull out the maimed body and grasped it close to her chest. She could sense he still held onto life, though she questioned how long it would last.

She had to get help.

She realized Nicholaus was the only person who could save the poor animal.

Without hesitation, she clutched the dog to her chest and threw herself back behind the wheel. The car jerked when she slammed it into gear and she took off toward home.

When she reached the driveway, she scrambled out of the car, leaving the door open as she rushed toward the house.

Suzanna burst through the front into the clinic as she clung in desperation to the life in her hands, calling out for help. She bolted through the rooms in search of Nicholaus.

She wept with unrestrained emotion, the tears blurring her vision as she stumbled to the upstairs bedrooms in hopes he might be there.

He was nowhere to be found.

Nicholaus pulled into the driveway, acutely aware Suzanna's car door hung open. The incessant beeps of the alarm increased his anxiety level. He ran into the house, his heart beating thunderously in his chest. He could hear her voice, but couldn't tell from which direction it came.

"Suzanna. Where are you?" Without a response, he called out again. "Suzanna, I'm here."

She appeared at the top of the stairs. The paleness of her face frightened him. He could see the blood soaked deep into the cotton jacket she wore. His heart almost stopped when he saw her eyes roll back and her knees begin to buckle beneath her.

He swore as he bounded up the steps two at a time just in time to catch her as she wilted toward the floor.

* * * *

Straining to clear the fuzziness from her brain, Suzanna surfaced into consciousness and realized she lay on Nicholaus' couch in his office. As she sat up, her stomach clenched when she saw the amount of blood covering the front of her jacket.

She looked around, frantic to find the puppy she'd held in her arms. The last thing she remembered was Nicholaus at the bottom of the stairs. She jumped up and ran toward the exam rooms in search of the two.

Nicholaus stood in Exam Room Four, the one used for emergencies. His head bent over the injured puppy as he worked hard to stop the blood pooling around its little head. He glanced up and a frown covered his brow.

"Sit down," he said with a gesture toward the chair in the corner. "There's only so much I can do at one time. I can't deal with you passing out again."

Silent, Suzanna obeyed his order, more concerned with the puppy than her own well being.

"Is he going to be alright?"

"There is a small subdural hematoma clotting on the left side of his brain. I've been able to stop the hemorrhages along the anterior wall by a new healing technique Andrew showed me the other day. I don't think this would have worked as well without it."

He was in professional mode, as he focused solely on his patient, but to her it all sounded awful. She stood again and moved closer to feel the puppy's level of life energy. Her stomach curdled as she watched Nicholaus stitch its tongue.

Sucking in more air, she tried not to burst into tears again from the guilt of what she'd done. She reached out and stroked his blood soaked fur with a gentle hand.

She stuttered then managed to get out, "Is…is he…going to live?"

Nicholaus cut the remainder of suture off and replaced the instruments on the procedure tray.

"He should be fine. He's small enough only the bumper hit him. The impact is mainly to the top of the head. It didn't affect any of his internal organs. Trauma to the head is always a touchy thing. Looks like I caught the bleeding early enough to stop any massive cranial pressure."

The queasiness returned. Suzanna placed her hand on her stomach.

"He bit his tongue on impact. That's where all the blood is coming from."

Tears of relief sprang into her eyes and she gulped back the need to cry again.

"I'm going to finish up here. Then we'll talk about what happened. If you think you can make it, why don't you go home and get cleaned up. I'll meet you back there in a few minutes."

Overwhelmed, Suzanna could do nothing but what he asked. Her clothes were trashed. No amount of stain remover would take out the large amount of blood on her jacket to make it wearable again. Stuffing both the shirt and jacket into a trash bag, she thought she could save the jeans. She stood looking at the jeans in her hand.

What does it matter? She began to laugh hysterically. *My life is in shambles, and I'm worried about a pair of jeans.*

The laughter turned to tears as she sank to the edge of the bed. The shock of it all hit her square in the chest. She couldn't stop the utter destruction she felt, and her tears became an appeal for help. She sat, looking toward the heavens, her soul crying out for mercy.

* * * *

As she sat on the couch she took another grateful sip of tea. Nicholaus came in and sat down next to her. The tears had dried, but she was so tired. The dark circles of exhaustion showed ghoulishly under her eyes against her pale skin. She had tried to cover the worst with fresh makeup. Unfortunately, nothing would hide the effects of worry, sleeplessness, and recurrent trauma.

Silent, he took her hand in his. She sensed a tremendous amount of emotion boiling under the surface of his calm demeanor. Too tired to sort the feelings out, she attributed his extreme energy to the recent events.

"Want to tell me what happened?" he asked.

She sipped again from the cup, the effort to control her breaths and strengthen herself to explain the afternoon events almost too much to bear.

"I went to see Marianne today. We tried the hypnosis thing. It didn't work like we thought it would."

"I know. I stopped by Gloves on my way home and she told me."

"Then you know I saw more this time." Suzanna silently twisted the tissue she held in her lap. "Mamma was there. I saw her there in the room. Rachel was there too. They know something about this and haven't told me all of these years."

"I'm sure that must hurt."

"You have no idea," she said ripping the tissue in pieces. "How could they lie to me like that? Who are they covering for? Can't they see how this whole thing has affected me?"

"I'm sure your mother must have her reasons."

"There is no reason good enough to me to keep the truth from a child, let alone a grown woman."

"You're right of course. At some point they both should have told you."

"Whatever it is, I'm going to find out. Then we'll see what they have to say for themselves."

"Is that what caused you to have the accident?"

Suzanna shook her head. She brushed a hand through her hair falling into her face.

"No. On the way home I had another one of those attacks. It came much stronger this time. I could smell this horrible stench and I heard him this time. It freaked me out."

"Whoa, you were driving? That's not good."

She nodded and looked into his anxious eyes. "That's when the puppy jumped out in front of me. I didn't see him. He was just all of a sudden in front of the car." She remembered the horrible thud again and shuddered. "I could have killed him."

Nicholaus put his arms out to pull her close.

"Luckily you didn't, and I got there in time to stop any further damage."

He smoothed the hair away from her face to rest his cheek against hers.

"You scared me to death sweetie. I thought you were the one hurt." He pulled back far enough to look her in the eyes. "Do me a favor next time. Before you decide to faint, could you tell me you're alright first?"

"I must have looked horrible with all that blood all over me. I'm sorry."

Nicholaus sat back and took her chin in his fingers.

"I can't let something like this happen again. I'm not going to let you out of my sight until this is over. So you better get used to me being with you night and day." He kissed her lightly and again hugged her close.

"What if it never goes away?" she implored.

"I think you're on the brink of finding out what this is about. Don't give up hope yet."

He sat back to reach into his pocket, and pulled out the next business at hand. The little silver license tag glinted in the late evening sun coming through the front windows.

"What we need to do now is go tell Sammy's owners what happened. Then we need to get you something to eat."

Still queasy, the thought of food didn't sound good, though Suzanna knew she needed some type of nourishment. She scrunched her face in disgust. "I suppose I should eat something today. Must be why I'm feeling so weak."

"That's another thing. If I'm around you'll have to take better care of yourself. No wonder you passed out. This is all draining enough as it is. No food and not enough sleep won't help matters much." As he stood he drew her into his arms. "I care about you. I can't stand to see you this way." He nuzzled her neck with his nose and sighed softly. "I won't leave. I'll take care of you Suzanna."

She closed her eyes and enjoyed the warmth of his arms and the sound of his words. Her senses must have gone haywire. Whenever she was with him all she felt was an immense love bouncing back and forth between them. No difference in emotion separated them. As if no real segregation defined their individuality, the fluidity from one to the other indistinguishable. She couldn't make sense of it now so she blocked her empathic sense, hoping to be able to interpret the confusion later.

* * * *

Dinner was quiet, conversation left to the unimportant things of life. Suzanna tried to concentrate on the beautiful view of the water from their dinner table. The pinks and blues of the sky on the reflective surface of the water were resplendent. For Suzanna, its magnificence dulled with the exhaustion overwhelming her. Oddly quiet, Nicholaus watched her every move. She knew he must still be concerned for her. She couldn't think of any words to ease his mind.

Later that evening, she lay in comfort against his chest, the flash of light from the muted television played eerily against the walls. Earlier she'd found one of the few gifts her father had given her. The small meaningless trinket meant little to her, and probably even less to him.

She fingered it contemplatively as she watched the ridiculous antics of the characters on the screen, the laughter of the audience the only audible sound. Her intense connection with Nicholaus became so strong in her half sleep state she felt as if they were one being. An utter contentment settled over her. His steady heartbeat lulled her to sleep as her cheek rested over his heart, her hand on his chest. Her mind began to drift with a peaceful dream of love and happiness.

This time the pictures were vivid. Bright flashes of disgusting horrible sexual acts flitted through her mind like a reel-to-reel movie that had gone wrong. Nothing led up to any of it. They just appeared in plain view, in her secret dreams.

Suzanna screamed and bolted upright, sweat poured down her back, the flashes continued to play throughout her mind. She gasped in horror as the child before her was defiled by the larger more powerful figure, trapped in her own internal purgatorial hell.

"Jesus…Jesus…No!" she screamed in agony. Her hands tightened into fists, the memento she held dug deep into her palm. "Make it stop. Oh God, make it stop."

Nicholaus came alert as soon as she stirred. She felt him try to bring her into is arms. Unable to move her stiffened posture it forced him to push his leg up behind her back to rub her arms with his hands. The calm energies he tried to transfer were at war with the heightened effect of the visions racing through her head.

"It's going to be alright Suzanna. Come out of it. Come back to me. I'm here. Let it go."

She was aware him poured every ounce of power he had into the conductive energies he transmitted, but it just wasn't enough.

She continued to shake her head in denial, as Nicholaus whispered peaceful sentiments. Her whimpers and tears persisted as the visions flew through her head in succession. At times she screamed in anger. Then her body would contort in an effort to evade the physical pain that ripped through her torso. Suzanna reached out as if to grab the invisible invader, the item she grasped so hard dropped to the floor and rolled under the coffee table.

As if a wild runaway train had run out of fuel, the visions began to recede, leaving her limp and lifeless.

It took her longer she realized this time to become aware of her surroundings again. The first thing she perceived were the rigid muscles of Nicholaus' arms and chest, still ready to attack the silent intruder with whatever means necessary. She felt the gnawing sensation at the pit of her stomach as the uncontrolled horror was replaced with a knowing revulsion.

"Are you back with me, Honey?" Nicholaus asked anxiously as she felt him transmit another wave of calm forces meant to settle her down.

She nodded then turned into him to slam her whole body against his with such force they almost toppled over. Her immediate need for security so great, she felt as if she needed to draw every bit of positive energy she could latch onto. She was grateful he gave what she needed without question.

She wasn't sure how long they sat there, but the light had just begun to rise into sunrise when she breached the connection between them. Stiff, she saw Nicholaus lay awake, his blue eyes darkened by the intense concentration of energy. He stretched his neck, but didn't say a word as he got up to move into the kitchen.

He brought back a couple of mugs of tea, placed one in her hands, the other he set on the end table. Suzanna knew he waited to hear the explanation of what happened. When she spoke, what she said was more difficult than she imagined.

"It wasn't just me this time. I saw other children, Nicholaus." Appalled at what she needed to say next, she covered her face with her hands. "Oh God, Nicholaus, some of them were just babies."

Her stomach turned at the implication of her words.

"I could feel their confusion and the horrid invasion of their little bodies." She wanted to throw up, reminded by the intensity of the visions bombarding her psyche with unspeakable things.

"There are others then." Not a question, he spoke as a statement of fact. "Did you see his face?"

She shook her head negatively. Her whole world crumbled around her. Yet somehow she hung onto enough sanity to think things through. Her next thought was abhorrent.

"What if this isn't what has already happened, but what might happen in the future. Marianne said some clairvoyants can see into the future. What if that's what's happened? I might be able stop it from happening again if I knew who it was. I can't let this happen. This is going to kill me. I can't let it happen to someone else." Overcome by this newly revealed truth, hot tears poured from her eyes in a flash flood of emotion.

"I don't know honey. We will figure this out one way or another."

He sank down onto the couch to hold onto her. She could sense him battle with the same questions, the same emotions as she did. Suddenly they both became still when hit by a simultaneous realization.

"I think I know what might work," Nicholaus started.

"We're going about this whole thing the wrong way, aren't we?" Suzanna chimed.

"We've expected you to do all the work. We know you can't control where your mind goes once you get into the zone. Your abilities are not fine tuned enough for that."

Excited, Suzanna straightened to face him.

"What if you were there with me during hypnosis? You could calm my energies, and keep me from flying into total terror."

"We'll have to work it out with Marianne just right to keep it together. If we do this in your waking hours I think we might be able to pull it off."

Suzanna didn't know if she could love a person any more than she loved him right then. He never condemned her or tried to pacify her fears. He took what she said as truth and acted according to what he knew to be right. Empowered by the connection they shared, she grasped hold of him as if she would never let go.

"We need to call Marianne first thing this morning," he said while looking into her eyes. "It's early yet, but I don't think either one of us will be able to get anymore rest."

"I don't think I ever want to sleep again," Suzanna replied, dreading the possibility of a replay of the night before.

"We'll need something to sustain us through all of this. After last night, we'll both pass out if we don't eat soon."

"I know. I'm pretty weak right now." An unaccustomed fragility had begun to set in.

"What do you say we go get some good, hearty breakfast from the diner up the street?" Unsure if she'd be able to hold any type of food down, she gave him a soft smile, touched by his willingness to do whatever it took to make sure she would be alright.

"And before you ask, I won't leave you for one minute. So you'd better get yourself dressed," he said as he grinned and eyed the nightshirt and panties she still wore from the previous night. He shook his head and kissed her lips. "You know, it never seems to matter how tired I am, or what mood I'm in, you are still the sexiest woman alive."

Chapter Twenty-One

"I don't have time for your nonsense, Richard." Marianne retorted, impatient with his idle threats. "That's not true and you know it."

Movement from across the room drew her attention to her two guest's arrival. She motioned for both Suzanna and Nicholaus to come into the room, gesturing for them to have a seat.

"He didn't attack your flunky." She rolled her eyes at Nicholaus. "In any case I'm sure he deserved what he got."

Marianne tried to center herself, taking in a deep breath, expelled it with slow purpose. Richard Haughton could be such a pompous jerk at times.

"Yes, I know it's their choice, but they can't be forced into doing something they don't want to do." Closing her eyes, she waited for the man on the other end of the phone to finish his sentence. "Now see here, I won't allow my friends to be subjected to your lunacy. You won't be flaunting them around in some freak show, simply to feed your cash cow ego. Not if I have anything to do with it."

She stood and paced to the window and back. Anger did no one any good, of all the situations and people she'd experienced, Richard could instigate an argument in no time.

"Just try that. You and I both know I could have you and your stooges put away for a very long time. Goodbye Richard, you'll be hearing from my attorney." Marianne began to slam the phone down then held back. This was not the time or place to reveal her frustration any more than she had already.

Sitting back down, she saw Nicholaus and Suzanna look at each other with concern. "I'm sorry you had to hear that. Mr. Haughton has been a thorn in my side for a very long time now. He can be very unreasonable at times," she said, ashamed she'd lost her cool.

"I have a feeling that had to do with me." Nicholaus sat back, his eyes the color of steel. How quick he was to put up his guard.

Marianne knew she was running a fine line with him at the moment. Any trouble and he would be gone, never to come back. But, she could do nothing about his reaction to the situation. Relaying the truth was the only thing she could do. She simply hoped Nicholaus would trust his intuition.

"Richard is threatening to file charges against you for your confrontation with Starks. They claim you attacked him without cause." Marianne smoothed the crease in her pants. "And then proceeded to say they would drop the charges if you were to come join their little sideshow."

Nicholaus raised an eyebrow at her, but kept silent.

"No need to worry, dear. I'll have my attorney handle it for you." She smiled in confidence. This wasn't the first time she'd had to deal with Richard Haughton's stupidity.

"I'm not worried." Nicholaus returned a grim nod. "Just let me know if there is anything I can do to help put him away."

She gave a small silent prayer of gratitude to show how much she appreciated Nicholaus being led in the right direction.

"Thank you. I'll let you know if we need a statement from you in your defense." Now back to the matter at hand. She'd known they would be coming today. These two had a much bigger problem than she had at the moment. "So, tell me, what brings you here today?"

Marianne listened, intent on the details, as they revealed the previous evening's events. She stroked the silky smooth finish of her favorite silver encased pen.

Suzanna appeared to be drained. Marianne saw the fatigue clearly on her washed out face. Hearing their story, she understood why. Nicholaus looked tired as well, but she could tell his determination outweighed any exhaustion.

"So, you think by teaming up you will be able to beat this thing?" At their agreement she placed the pen back down on the desk and leaned forward. "You realize of course, the mind isn't always so easily fooled. I'm not so sure it's a good thing to push the boundaries so quick before you've had time to adjust. My gut tells me to wait to see what comes out by itself."

They looked at each other, obvious frustration spilled out from them both. Nicholaus reached out his arm to pull

Suzanna's shoulders closer to him in a hug. Tears filled her eyes, breaking Marianne's heart.

"I'm curious, what were you doing before this last episode of visions?" she asked Suzanna.

"We were lying on the couch with the TV on. I was fiddling with something in my hand, thinking about everything that has happened. I must have drifted off to sleep. Next thing I knew I was screaming at the top of my lungs watching my own personal horror flick."

Marianne's attention spiked at her words. "What were you playing with?"

"It was one of those fake coins you get at the fairs. I found it the other day. I think it was a prize for one of those ring-tossing games that suck up all your money. My Dad said he won it while he was dating Mamma. He used to keep it in his wallet."

Marianne made sure not to react. This was the clue they'd waited to find. Suzanna still seemed to be clueless though. Marianne shot a glance at Nicholaus and gave a gentle shake to her head for him to keep silent. She could see he'd recognized the trait and had opened his mouth to speak. He gave her a slow nod and closed his lips tight.

Psychometry was an unusual gift. The psychic's ability to get information or the events surrounding a person, simply by the touch or closeness of an object was no doubt very confusing at first. It appeared Suzanna had a variety of unique gifts to discover. Each could be beneficial yet frustrating at the same time, unless properly maintained.

Marianne remained silent, unable to reveal what she already suspected. She hoped Nicholaus would also realize it was up to Suzanna to find out for herself what her new experiences meant in this situation.

"I don't know what all this has to do with these freaky dreams I keep having," Suzanna moaned. "All I know is there is some perverted child rapist out there who may still be on the move. You can't let this happen to any more children Marianne. I can't let it happen."

Marianne couldn't ignore Suzanna's pleas. So distraught she'd been impaired by this new experience, unable to focus anywhere else. Marianne was also aware of the fine line existing between a push for discovery, and an unrecoverable interruption in the final stages to finally break through the impenetrable walls Suzanna had built around herself.

"I'll agree to another hypnotherapy session, on one condition. As you said, Nicholaus needs to pass every possible peaceful vibration he can while monitoring your physical state at all times. If at any point I feel you've gone beyond an acceptable level of stress, I'm going to bring you out of it. As you know, if you are pushed too hard you may experience negative results, and I won't do that. You know how fragile you are right now Suzanna."

"I know. But, if we don't do it now, I don't know how much longer I can hang onto my sanity."

Marianne caught Nicholaus' eyes with hers. He agreed by a simple nod.

"All right then, I'll need to prepare for the session. Give me about thirty minutes and we'll get started. Sarah will bring you back when I'm ready."

As they headed out the door Nicholaus turned and stepped back into Marianne's office.

"Do you have a minute for me?" he asked.

"Of course dear, what do you need?"

He looked down to the floor, then back up to meet her gaze. "You probably already know my mother came to pay me a visit. She wants me to spend some time with her, but I need to ask you a very important question."

Marianne had known he would come to her. "I'll do my best," she replied.

"Did she tell you her story?"

"Well, if you are talking about her experience at the religious compound, then yes. She knew you would ask me to confirm her story, so she had me do a complete analysis of her past experiences."

"Suzanna believes she's telling the truth. Do you?" Nicholaus asked, his eyes fixed on hers.

"In my analysis I found no major differences in what she told me," Marianne said. "And if you want to know my opinion, I believe she deserves the chance to make her peace with you. Don't you?"

Nicholaus changed the direction of his stare to the massive windows behind her. He slowly nodded his head.

"You're right."

* * * *

It must have been the longest thirty minutes Suzanna ever experienced. Exhaustion caught up with her. Though her body wanted to collapse, her mind was doing the nervous jitterbug. The breakfast she'd consumed had definite benefits, though now seemed to daunt her like a bomb ready to explode in her stomach.

She laid her head on Nicholaus' shoulder.

"Hang in there. It won't be much longer." Nicholaus comforted her by placing his hand on her knee and gave it a squeeze.

From the hallway, they heard voices. Sarah came into the room followed by a young woman about her age. Sarah sat down at her desk to quickly pull out a couple of folders from her drawer. As she took the few sheets out, she placed each one on the clipboard she handed to the woman.

"Here are the forms you need to fill out for the spiritual development class. Go ahead and have a seat and I'll make sure the instructor knows you will be attending this evening."

The woman turned and flashed Suzanna and Nicholaus the brightest smile Suzanna had ever seen.

"Hi, my name's Sunny," she said rushing forward to shake their hands. She seemed to hold onto Suzanna's hand a bit longer than expected, then reached out for Nicholaus' hand. A slow knowing grin replaced the smile. "It's nice to meet you both. Are you coming to the class tonight too?"

Bewildered by the bright glowing energy pouring from the woman, Suzanna shook her head and mumbled an uncertain, "No. I don't think so."

Nicholaus jumped in. "We are here for some one-on-one with Marianne today."

"Are you? Oh, she's the best. Don't you think so?"

Suzanna could only stare at the woman, her aura of many colors almost blinding her. So tired all of a sudden her words wouldn't form into sentences. She was glad to let Nicholaus take over the conversation.

In her fatigue, she watched Sarah busy herself at her desk, with an occasional glance at Nicholaus. Sarah dipped her head down, a slight blush coloring her cheeks when she caught Suzanna watching her.

There was a different aura surrounding her than the times they'd met before. Cloudier than before, dark holes were starting to form in places. On the outside, Sarah appeared shy, though Suzanna was again struck by the deep fear washing over her every time she looked at the young woman.

"Ms. Hawthorne, there are a couple of forms I need you to sign before you go back in for your session with Ms. Ross." Sarah set the forms on the edge of her desk.

The effort to rise to her feet took every ounce of energy she had. Suzanna glanced briefly at the waiver form, and looked around for another pen to use. Not finding one, she reached out to grasp the pen lying on the desk in front of Sarah.

"Can I use your pen?"

Sarah nodded, busying herself with another item as if not wanting to make eye contact with Suzanna.

The pen gave Suzanna a strange feeling when she signed the form. She all of a sudden wanted to shut herself off from everything around her, to go deep within where she would be safe. The intense image of someone yelling at her popped up, and an extreme urge to run away made her drop the pen and step backward.

That was weird.

"Thank you."

"No problem." Suzanna gave herself a little inward shake. Something didn't feel right.

She continued to feel the sticky gluey substance of anxiety surrounding her. As if her very presence would cause some type of discord.

Risking a sensory overload, Suzanna deepened her perception to figure out what was going on. As she looked around, she sensed the familiar strong masculine energy of Nicholaus, and the almost bunny like character of Sunny. When it came to Sarah, her energy was quiet and subdued, as if having withdrawn from life, leaving only her timorous and despondent actions. She appeared to Suzanna as scared as a bird in a cage full of cats.

Suzanna wondered how someone so guarded could have come to a group such as Gloves. The mix didn't seem cohesive, especially for the position of Assistant to someone like Marianne Ross. There must be a quality Marianne saw in Sarah nobody else could.

Maybe Sarah needed someone to talk to, like an older sister. Without knowing much about her, Suzanna's intuition told her she might be able to form a friendship with this woman. Perhaps she could honor that feeling once she addressed her own problems.

Sunny interrupted her thoughts as she got up from her seat and handed Sarah the clipboard. Flashing another smile at the two of them, she leaned in and said to Sarah, "It is so nice to see twin flames finally get back together after such a long time. I'm so glad it was decided you were ready to reunite." She moved over and took both of their hands in hers. "Don't lose sight of your purpose this time. Although, I'm sure coming back time after time to find each other has got to be the greatest gift." She gave them a wink and a little giggle, waved a goodbye to Sarah and almost hopped down the hallway to start a conversation with someone else.

Suzanna looked at Nicholaus, who had a slight grin on his face. "Do you know what she was talking about?"

"She was telling me she is able to see past lives. Maybe, she thinks we've been together before." He offered.

Suzanna turned to Sarah. "Do you know what she was talking about? What did she mean by twin flames?"

Sarah's cheeks turned a bright pink. "I think I've seen that phrase before. Let me look it up." She reached out to the bookcase beside her desk and pulled off a massive encyclopedic looking book. Flipping through the pages, she finally stopped at a page and placed her finger on a subject. She glanced up, then quickly back down to read, "The twin flame is a person's other half, or counterpart. First incarnated as two halves of polarity of a Devine Whole—one masculine and the other feminine. These beings have been created to fulfill a mission together and to grow spiritually together over their lifetimes."

This was a little too much for Suzanna to wrap her thoughts around at the moment. But it brought to mind the conversation she'd had with Marianne before. She looked over to Nicholaus who had gotten up to take the book from Sarah to read further.

Could it be, Nicholaus was her other half? If so, why did Sunny say they'd been separated for so long? How did that work? And, who was it that decided if they were to be together?

He came back and sat down next to Suzanna. It felt right. He felt right. He seemed to gaze back at her with a different perception. Or were those just her thoughts bouncing back?

He raised his eyebrows, and closed his eyes. "Brings a lot of questions to mind, doesn't it? That came from a section called 'Karma and Reincarnation'." When he opened them again, they were bright with new possibilities. "*Bunica* talked about this type of thing all the time. She said I would find the one. I never really thought about it much until now."

Pushing off the intense need to be enveloped in his arms, Suzanna tried to make light of a very serious subject, one she wasn't ready to delve into just yet. She shrugged, "I guess if you believed in that kind of stuff."

She wished she could have retracted the words as soon as they came out of her mouth. The flash of dejection in Nicholaus' eyes shot into her a deep feeling of remorse.

"I mean, I've never really looked into that before. I'll have to find out more about it before I can definitely agree with that frame of thought." This she really meant. She couldn't make a split second decision on something so profound and meaningful. This would take some time to digest.

Nicholaus squeezed her hand. "Of course, I understand. Reincarnation isn't the easiest thing to accept, especially if you've never studied it before."

Suzanna, felt a warmth flow through her. He was always so accepting. She leaned in and gave him a light kiss. His eyes warmed up as their lips met. If he truly was her twin flame, she needed to figure out how to keep him with her now and forever.

The buzzer on Sarah's phone sounded, and she picked it up. "Of course, I will send them in." She rose to her feet. "Marianne is ready for you now. You may go back in at your leisure."

The next few minutes were a blur for Suzanna. She didn't quite remember how, but she found herself comfortably positioned between Nicholaus' legs. Her back rested on his chest, his arms wrapped around her, one hand resting on her inner wrist. She could feel him using energy manipulation to slow down her heart rate and bring her to a serene state.

As before, Marianne sat on the opposite side facing her, the deep violet of her eyes set steady with concentration. As Nicholaus' therapy took hold, Suzanna heard the instruction to relax and almost laughed out loud.

What else can I do? Suzanna thought.

Marianne's gentle prompts to listen to her voice soon resulted in a slow relaxation of both her mind and body, and she began to drift...

Marianne began the session by leading Suzanna to the time they needed to illuminate.

"You told me a little about your childhood last time we were here. I want you to return there and tell me about the house you lived in when you were seven years old."

Suzanna's mind returned to her youth and she began to describe the big swing in the back yard where she and her sister used to play. Then she told the story of how the big teeter-totter had come down, and hit her on the head when her sister jumped off before she could climb on. The next few minutes of her memories painted a picture of a happy childhood, with no real worries.

Marianne's calm, fluid voice helped to move Suzanna to a much deeper place. She nodded at Nicholaus to maintain his sedative motivators.

"Your mother loves you very much, doesn't she?" Marianne continued.

Suzanna's childish grin was priceless. "Um-hmm," she nodded fervently. "And I love her very much too."

"You told me about a time when she got very, very mad." Marianne used simple words to connect Suzanna to her inner child. "Do you remember what made her so mad?"

Nicholaus glanced up and gave her the code they had developed to indicate a change. Marianne knew Suzanna's pulse rate had risen, so she signaled back to increase his level of conductive energy.

Suzanna nodded slowly in answer to the question.

Marianne continued, encouraged by the positive response. "Why was she so angry Suzanna?"

Suzanna hesitated before she replied shyly, "'Cuz Daddy was doing something really, really bad."

Pay dirt—their combined efforts were paying off.

Nicholaus and Marianne locked in an affirmative momentary glance. They'd both known Suzanna's father was involved, now it was fact.

"What did he do?"

Embarrassed, Suzanna giggled much like an eight year old would if she didn't know whether to tell a secret.

"He was touching me with his winkie," she whispered.

"Did he ever do this before?" Marianne asked, searching for the full picture.

"Um-hmm, lots of times," Suzanna responded.

Marianne saw this confession angered Nicholaus, and she motioned for him to keep his concentration level.

"Did Mamma know he was doing this?" Marianne prompted.

"No. Daddy said not to tell."

"So why did Mamma get so mad this time?"

She started to shake her head, refusing to tell. Her voice became frightened. "Daddy told me not to tell," she whispered again with a hitched breath. "He said he'd hurt me, real bad."

"Nobody can hurt you here Suzanna. You are safe here. You can tell me anything. Your secret is safe with me." Marianne said trying to lead the young frightened child to open up. Once more she questioned, "Why did Mamma get so mad this time?"

Suzanna's face scrunched up and it looked as if she were about to cry.

"This time it hurt. He told me to stop screaming, but I didn't like it."

"Tell me what happened."

Suzanna shook her head and began to back away. Then with Nicholaus' effort to keep her calm, she relaxed again. Something inside the hypnotized woman clicked, and she started to tell them everything about the night that haunted her, night after night in her nightmares.

In her little girl voice, Suzanna rapidly told them how he had come into her bedroom. "He smelled really icky, and he tore my favorite pink jammies," she said with a pout. "He said he wanted to give me something and I should 'preciate what I got."

She went on to tell them he'd told her he'd kill her if she made a noise. "So I was real quiet, 'cuz I do what my daddy tells me."

Suzanna got real still. "He…he tried to put his winkie in me. I didn't want to scream. But, it hurt real bad," she said in short bursts of fear. "It hurt real bad 'cuz's not what winkie's are for."

"What happened then?" Marianne prompted hoping to clear up the involvement of her mother.

"He yelled at me to stop screaming. That's when Mamma came in."

"What did Mamma do?"

"She yelled too. Then she kicked him. Daddy got real mad."

"What did your Daddy do then?"

"He hit Mamma and she fell down. I told him to stop, but he kept on hitting her."

"Then what happened?"

"Daddy left. He wasn't going to stick around a bitch and her kid won't keep their mouth shut," she said mimicking the voice of her father.

Suzanna became quiet, almost too quiet. Marianne then saw the tears begin to pour down the young woman's face.

"That's why Daddy had to leave. 'Cuz I screamed when he told me not to."

Marianne watched a sickened look pass over Nicholaus' face. She didn't need to push Suzanna any further. Enough had been revealed to allow the younger woman some clarity and closure.

"You're such a good girl to tell me all of this, Suzanna. Remember none of what happened with your father is your fault. When I touch your left knee, you're going to wake up, and you're going to remember everything you've told me today. Understand?"

Suzanna's nod was slow, but the response to the touch on her knee was instantaneous. Her eyes flashed open. Unable to move, she stared into Marianne's eyes as the cognizance of her hidden past rushed in with a fury.

The hold Nicholaus had on her continued to be constant and steady. Totally aware of every point in which his body touched hers, she felt his positive atoms continue to be pushed her way.

"Stop, you can stop now." She pulled away from him and sat at the far end of the couch. For some reason the connection became more irritating than useful.

Through the massive windows she stared out into the big blue sky, her anger building with every breath she took. Nicholaus placed both feet on the ground and his elbows on his knees, before sinking his head into his hands.

"I should have known it was him. Everything pointed to him in one way or another, didn't it?" Suzanna stated.

"Sometimes we can't see what is close to us. Your mind covered up your memories for so long you fought the truth even though it was right in front of you." Marianne's soft reasoning always made sense.

"I should have known. Especially at dinner, he was so overtly inappropriate. I just pushed it aside, like a child." Raw emotions tore at her with sharp claws. "I feel like a puppet, playing everyone else's game in life, not knowing where I belong."

She looked from Marianne to Nicholaus, her thoughts racing. "Everyone who matters to me knew what happened, but they didn't tell me. What gives them the right to play with my life that way? If someone had just told me, I wouldn't have had to live through this hell I've called life so far."

Marianne rose from her chair and reached out to place an arm around her shoulders. "Life isn't so simple, things happen for a reason. The higher being directs us through life, based on our choices and our knowledge. If you had known before now, your life may have taken a different path."

Motivated by anger, Suzanna pushed her away. "Don't patronize me. I'm angry and there is nothing you can say to make it right." She grabbed her purse, stopped and slowly turned around. "Those visions I had last night. They were real. Weren't they?"

Marianne nodded.

"These are things my father has done?"

"Or, one he might do in the future. We have yet to test your abilities, Suzanna. We don't know yet the range of sight you have developed."

"Oh, God," Suzanna covered her mouth with her hand. She began to shake her head violently and rushed out of the office without a backward look.

Nicholaus rose to follow, but Marianne stopped him at the door.

"Remember what I told you. Let her get past this in her own way. She's hurt right now, and I'm not sure in what ways it will come through. Don't push her buttons. If you treasure your relationship with her, all you can do is to be there for her. She'll come around in her own time."

Nicholaus breathed in deep. "She can have all the time she needs. Right now I have something I need to do to make this right for her."

"Be careful Nicholaus, you're on shaky ground. I've seen what you intend to do. Make sure you think it through. This could go either way."

Nicholaus stared into her wise and concerned eyes, then nodded his head and turned in search of Suzanna. Marianne's words followed him.

"Follow what the Spirit is telling you dear, it will always lead you where you need to be."

* * * *

Suzanna and Nicholaus came into the main house through the front door. Suzanna stood silent, a bewildered expression on her face. Nicholaus felt the waves of exhaustion, caused by the recent upheaval, must be overwhelming to both her mind and body. She needed rest, with no interruptions.

"Would you like me to get you anything?" Nicholaus offered.

She shook her head with obvious effort and grabbed her purse as it fell off her shoulder. "Would you mind if I went home for a while. You don't need to worry about me. I just need to be by myself."

The request was simple enough, yet he could hear the unsaid meaning. She needed time to sort through what she'd learned.

"Go ahead. I've got something I need to take care of. I'll check in on you when I get back." He kissed her cheek and watched as she headed toward the back. He'd allow her as much time as she needed.

As soon as the door closed, Nicholaus went to his office and pulled the phone book from the shelf. He turned the pages in haste to find the number. After dialing, he waited, impatient for an answer.

"Bellevue Hilton, how may I direct your call?" the hotel operator chirped.

"Yes. Would you please connect me to Franklin Hawthorne's room?"

"One moment please. Yes, I'll connect you to his room now."

"No thank you, I've changed my mind. I'll just buzz him when I get there."

He headed out the door, and prayed he wasn't making a mistake.

Chapter Twenty-Two

"Captain, you've got a visitor, someone by the name of Nicholaus Brach," the desk sergeant said into the phone receiver, a suspicious glare in his eyes. "Yes Sir, I'll bring him back."

Nicholaus followed the sergeant to the back of the precinct into an office along the outside wall. The man behind the desk was in his mid-fifties, and had his gray peppered hair combed to one side. His tie pulled open at the collar of his pressed white shirt, sleeves rolled up the forearm, indicating he'd been hard at work on the stack of papers spread across his desk.

His face lightened with a huge grin. "Nicholaus my boy, how have you been? How's business?" He set down his pen and leaned back in his chair, ready for a needed break.

"Hey John, I'm doing great. Business is good."

Nicholaus came into the room and looked around. The space appeared similar to the offices depicted on most cop shows. The sparse aged furniture, of a nondescript color, the stacks of files piled everywhere not a surprise. Captain Masterson, a lifelong self-proclaimed bachelor, had only the love of his job, and the devotion of his beloved Mastiff to keep him company.

"How's Rocko doing?" Nicholaus asked.

"Dumb bastard's still eating rocks. I had to replace all the rocks with beauty bark." It had been months since John had brought his dog into the clinic to have his stomach pumped. "So Nick, I don't figure this is a social call. What's going on?"

"I need help. Something I think you'd be interested in."

"Let's hear it."

"There's a jerk I know about, seems to like his girls young—real young." The Captain raised his eyebrows. Nicholaus continued to tell him as much as he knew, careful to omit the part about Suzanna's empathic skills. Not knowing the man's beliefs, Nicholaus didn't want to taint the Captain's perception of her.

"Well, you're right, if he was doing it back then there's a ninety nine point nine percent chance he's still doing it, if he hasn't been caught," the Captain said as he made notes on a yellow pad in front of him. "How old is Suzanna now?"

Nicholaus had to think back. He'd never thought about her age. What was the year on her employment application? Doing the math, he finally came up with her age. "Thirty-two, I believe."

"The problem is Suzanna's statement is way past the statute of limitations on both child molestation and rape. You said this happened in California?"

Nicholaus nodded, a sinking feeling setting in.

"They're a little more lenient in terms of rape, but child molestation is the same as Washington here. There's a 10-year limitation, and the case would have to be filed in the state where it happened. Even then, there would have to be some hard evidence and not just her testimony."

Damn! Well, there goes Plan A. Now it's time for Plan B.

"Without hard evidence we don't have a reasonable cause to search now. We need some current evidence. If we had enough probable cause we can get a search warrant and do a sweep of his residence. More than likely we'd be able to dig up something to tie him to his current activity."

"What if I said I could get you what you needed?" Nicholaus' plan B was ready to initiate.

"Really? Let's hear what you've got." The Captain raised his eyebrows.

"He's here at the Bellevue Hilton, hot on some big business deal. I won't have a problem getting you your probable cause. I have an idea I'd like to pass by you which is a little unorthodox, but I think it will work."

John listened as Nicholaus laid out what he planned to do. Agreeing the plan was a bit odd John admitted it might also have merit. Without much hesitance they worked out some of the minor details and agreed to give the plan a try.

"You're a good man Nicholaus. I hope Suzanna realizes what she's got in you."

Nicholaus ignored the compliment, more focused on making the plan work.

"How soon do you think you could get a search warrant?"

"Judge Whitman is an advocate for this type of case. She has no leniency for the scum who prey on children, and neither do I."

"Tell me what's next," Nicholaus said, attempting to hold in his building anger by focusing on the next steps.

"Why don't you go get yourself a coffee at Starbucks, then head on out to the Hilton? That should give me enough time. I'll meet you out there in an hour."

* * * *

As he walked into the hotel, Nicholaus set out in his mind the steps he would take to bring this scumbag to justice. Confident he knew what he would find when he got there, he hadn't supplied one piece of the plan to the Captain. It was something he needed to do, specifically for Suzanna. The legal ramifications of what he was about to do, hadn't crossed his mind, and frankly didn't matter to him in that moment.

He spotted John in the lobby and strode over to where he sat with another officer. John rose when Nicholaus approached.

"This is Detective Curt Mathews of the Special Victims Unit. He's here to verify the validity of recovered evidence, if there is any."

"So you think he's got something or someone there to show probable cause?" the Detective asked Nicholaus.

Nicholaus eyed the Detective, "In my gut, I have no doubt." Impatient, he took a deep breath to stay calm and gave the man a steady stare.

Detective Mathews paused, then reached into his pocket and pulled out the scribbled room number from the front desk. Giving a nod he said, "Let's get this done."

Nicholaus picked up the house phone and asked to be connected to Frank's room.

His first few attempts were met with voicemail. After a couple more tries, the man he assumed to be Frank answered. His breath sounded ragged.

"Is this Frank, Frank Hawthorne, of Hawthorne and Lowell Real Estate?"

The man's interest peaked, Frank's demeanor become more professional. "Why yes it is. How can I help you, sir?"

"My name is Nicholaus Brach. I was referred to you by your daughter, Suzanna."

"Yes, yes, of course. She works for you, doesn't she? You own the veterinary hospital out by the bay."

"Yes sir. I hope you don't mind me stopping by, but I needed to talk to you about a real estate deal I'm working on. Need a few pointers. Would you have a few minutes for me?"

Nicholaus knew the possibility of catching a new client would make the man more willing to see him.

"Of course, of course," Frank said stumbling over his words. "Give me a few minutes and I'll meet you down at the bar."

"Actually, I'm in a hurry, I'll come up to your room." Nicholaus hung up the phone without waiting for an answer.

The three men walked to the elevator.

"Remember Nicholaus, you go in, get him to talk and then you get out. Don't touch anything. If there is anything suspicious lying around, you need to leave it where it is."

"I understand," Nicholaus acknowledged.

"These guys are pretty closed mouthed. You have to make him believe you're just like him," Detective Mathews stated.

That was the part Nicholaus would have troubles following. He'd rather beat it out of him. He nodded.

"We'll be just outside the door, so if there's any trouble you know where we are," John said patting him on the shoulder. The two officers moved to the side where they wouldn't be seen.

When Nicholaus knocked on the door, he heard the rustle of papers and a closet door bang shut. The door opened to reveal a man in his early sixties, professional enough, although he appeared to be in a partial stage of undress. His shirt was stuffed sloppily into the waistband of his pants, which obviously had been fastened in haste. A conspicuous corner edge of the shirttail stuck out through the upper part of his zipper. He'd thrown on his jacket and attempted to tie a knot in his tie before Nicholaus knocked on the door.

Perfect, Nicholaus thought. He had hoped to catch him with his pants down, as it were.

"Frank Hawthorne?"

"That is me. And you must be Nicholaus. Nice to meet you, very nice to meet you," he said holding out his hand.

Nicholaus reached in and grasped the old man's hand and shook it aggressively, repressing the urge to wipe his own hand on his pants when they'd finished. He pushed into the room without an express invite and quickly scanned the room.

In various stages of upheaval, dirty towels were tossed across the chair in the corner, newspapers opened haphazardly on the table, and a half-empty bottle of gin sat open on the nightstand. The man's clothes were not in any better shape. The pant leg of a pair of suit pants hung through the door of the dresser, t-shirts and underwear sat in a pile next to the bed.

Frank tried to cover up his unclean ways by stuffing the pant leg back through the half open door.

"Sorry for the mess, I wasn't expecting company today. You didn't give me much time to prepare."

Under the pillow Nicholaus could see the corner of a pornographic picture peek out from its chosen hiding place. He turned and faced the man. He was rather large in stature. Not that it bothered Nicholaus. The profuse sweat on Frank's face caught his attention. It appeared the man had been physically exerting himself. His face had blotches of red, and sweat trickled down his forehead. It was definitely not the semblance of someone having a quiet afternoon in his room, not even for a man of his size.

"No problem," Nicholaus replied. "I hope I didn't catch you at a bad time."

"No, no, not at all," Frank's suspicious glances toward the television was another clue Nicholaus hoped to uncover.

"So what can I do for you? You said you had a big deal you were working on? I work mostly with commercial sites. Being you're a friend of my daughter's, I could work you into the schedule if it's a private deal large enough." The man's greed showed through his drink induced blood-shot eyes.

Nicholaus nodded. He noted the DVD still played, but the television had been turned off. A case lay open on top of the player, empty with a conspicuous 'XXX' mark on the front. He walked over and nudged the case causing it to flip down onto the dresser below. This caused the old man to take in a sharp breath.

"You like this stuff?" Nicholaus forced his eyes to twinkle with what the old man would hopefully interpret as interest, but it was actually the light of victory. He made his grin as perverted as he could to get the old man to trust him.

"Well of course. Doesn't every red blooded male on the face of this earth?"

This is where he had to take a risk. Using his knuckle he touched the 'on' button at the front of the television. The picture that came into view revolted him. He'd expected to find a porno flick in process, what he'd found was much more.

A healthy muscle bound man in his early thirties had a young woman pinned against a corner involved in an unspeakable sexual activity. The young woman however, was not a woman at all. She appeared to be a child, barely the age of fifteen. Nicholaus looked away. Too late, the image was already regrettably burned into his memory. He then realized his revulsion would blow his cover, so he grinned again at Frank and turned toward the screen, his inconspicuous stare pointed at the corner of the set.

"Like 'em young do ya?" Nicholaus asked, feigning appreciation. Frank had been caught in the act and couldn't deny the evidence on the screen, though he still seemed suspicious of Nicholaus as he gave him a distrustful intent stare. "It's hard to find guys like us. Most people get so offended," Nicholaus said trying to build the man's acceptance.

"The younger the better," his host replied, relief obvious when he began to grin. Nicholaus' acting as if their sexual likes were akin in nature had paid off.

"Ever had one, yourself?" Nicholaus asked, preparing for the next steps to his mission. The sting had turned out to be easier than he thought. The scum's eagerness to reveal his habits shot a blast of anger into Nicholaus.

"Plenty of times, it's about the only way I can get off these days," Frank boasted. Apparently excited by what seemed to be a soul sharing moment, he pushed to advance the frames on the DVD. "Here, let me show you. I found this company who will let you get in on the action yourself and burn it to disc too. For a hefty fee of course, but it's been well worth it, that's for sure."

The man punched in impatience at the button to advance the frames as quickly as he could. "Here. Here it is. Good quality snatch too, couldn't have asked for better."

Nicholaus watched in disgust as the obese man on the screen, undoubtedly the one beside him, defiled a young Cambodian child of about ten years old. The terrified look on the child's face told him she had no idea what was about to happen until it was too late.

"She was prime for the taking," Frank said, rubbing his stomach in appreciation. He watched eagerly as the scenes flashed forward. "Fresh too, never been laid, those are the best."

Now sick to his stomach, Nicholaus swallowed hard to keep the vomit from inching its way into his throat.

"Looks like a great source. I've been trying to find me one worth the money."

Frank grabbed the Hilton embossed tablet and jotted down some information. "Here, give Willy a call. Tell him I sent you. He'll take good care of you. They'll get you anything you want. Girls or boys, any age you want. I once paid a pretty penny for a young thing around six, just to see how my pecker liked it."

"Sounds like a gold mine. Hey, thanks. This is great." Pretending to be really thankful, he stuffed the paper in his pocket. "But what if you just want a quick fuck? I've had a hell of a time finding one. Where do you find them?"

The old man, more than willing to share his perversion, smiled deep. "Girlfriends who have kids, they're the easiest. But they're usually only good for a quick touch and tug. You get to know the kids, offer them something they want, and they'll do almost anything. Schoolyards are a good backup. You can't even imagine what a kid will do for some crack or a few bucks. But you have to get the older ones there. The younger ones end up telling Mommy." He thought for a minute. "There's a bar or two, usually down by the waterfront, where you can find some single mom meth-heads. Those tweakers will sell their own kid for a fix."

Repulsed by the response, Nicholaus pushed for more. "Ever get what's in your own backyard. You know, those two girls of yours are good lookers."

Frank's eyebrows rose up, as if surprised by the question then he puffed out his chest in perceived self-importance. "Noticed that did you? They are, aren't they? Taught the older one what it's like to have a real man. Got me the younger one a couple of times too, but her mother got in the way before she got to a prime age though. Too bad, she sure would have been a hell of a screw."

Frank chuckled over the conversation and continued to watch the horror playing on the TV screen.

His laughter didn't last long.

Nicholaus turned on him fast, his fist connecting square on Frank's nose. He heard the crack of bone against bone. Blood gushed out of the assuredly broken nose as Frank screamed in agony. He grasped Frank's collar with his other hand and slammed him up against the wall before bringing his face close enough to grab the old man's attention.

"You're lucky old man, I don't believe in killing. But if you ever come close to Suzanna again, I might just have to make an exception." He pushed Frank back down to the floor. "Suzanna remembers what you did to her, and I'm going to convince her to press charges against you." Knowing it wouldn't be true put a damper on the victory. It helped when he saw fear seep into the old man's eyes.

"You'll never prove a thing," Frank gurgled through the blood pouring down his face.

"You've got enough here to put you away. I'll bet you've got a shit load of this stuff back home." He grabbed the magazine from under the pillow and at first glance confirmed the black market publication meant to fit the need of a target audience. This wretched scum would pay for what he had done. "You're going down for this, you can bet on it."

Nicholaus came out of the room and stuck his hip in the door to keep it from closing. The scuffle had prompted John and Curt to wait close at the door. Nicholaus shoved the magazine into John's hand. From his pocket he pulled the name and address of the video producer. John stepped back and didn't take the piece of paper.

"I'll get that from the notepad in the room," John said, maintaining the integrity of the evidence. "Anything else of interest?" he asked.

"There's enough in there to put him away. Take a look at the treasure in the DVD player," Nicholaus replied.

Curt rushed in to assess the situation.

"Did you take care of what you needed to do?" John didn't need to ask any more.

"I did what I had to. Thanks."

"It's the least I could do."

Nicholaus watched John go in after Curt.

The old man ranted, "He broke my nose. Why are you arresting me? He came in here and attacked me."

Nicholaus smiled as he heard John's reply, "I didn't see anyone. Curt, did you see anyone?"

* * * *

When he entered the living room, Nicholaus found Suzanna curled up on the couch, her purse flung at her feet. Cali, stretched out by her stomach, lazily licked her paws. When he reached down to bring Suzanna into his arms, the cat trotted off to places unknown, offended by Nicholaus' inexcusable intrusion.

Suzanna barely stirred as he placed her on the bed, deep sleep enveloping her current existence. He tried to make her a little more comfortable by taking off her shoes and carefully undressing her, leaving her in her underwear. She opened her eyes for a brief moment to meet his then let them close again as she drifted back to sleep. He pulled the covers over her, and gave her a light kiss on her lips.

He would give her the time she needed. Hoping she would come back to him soon.

Hoping she would still love him.

Chapter Twenty-Three

When Suzanna first surfaced the next day, Nicholaus gave her a short account of what he'd done. Although she knew he had acted in her best interest, she was overwhelmed by the idea others continued to control the outcome of her life. She said nothing. As quiet as she'd appeared, she returned to the peaceful confines of her bedroom.

She floated awake a second time, and pulled the covers over her eyes, grumbling about the brightness of the sun shining through the window coverings she'd forgotten to close.

Later, in the middle of the night, she woke up and decided to slip on a nightshirt over her half-naked body. She found Nicholaus asleep on the couch. Cali peered at her from a position on his legs. The cat's glare indicated she was quite comfortable and didn't want to be disturbed. Suzanna assumed Nicholaus had thought best not to intrude on her self-imposed peace. She appreciated his consideration.

Her hero lay on his back, a brocade pillow tucked under his head, an arm slung over his eyes. She hadn't the heart to tell him to go home. Knowing he'd stayed with her comforted her, but she wasn't ready to talk, so she went back to bed. Sleep continued to invite her to shut down her mind, and ignore the inevitable.

The next time she awoke, Suzanna sat and groaned at the creakiness of her bones. The length of time she spent in a prone position, whether asleep or not, couldn't be very good for her body. She heard the front door open and close. She knew who entered and wished she'd gotten up earlier to shower. She grabbed the hair band on the nightstand and pulled back her unkempt hair. That would have to do.

"Good. You've decided to join the living," Nicholaus said as he peeked around the edge of the door. "I've brought you some lunch. Why don't you come out to the dining room and I'll serve you up some of my awesome Brach's Stew."

Your Martha Stewart attitude is sickening, Suzanna thought as she recognized the signs of depression settling over her countenance.

Though more than a little hungry, she grabbed her robe and followed him out. On the table sat a large stew pot, its contents still steamy, and two large soup bowls. Curious, Suzanna lifted the ladle to inspect the contents.

"It's an old family recipe *Bunica* taught me. She said someone needed to carry on the tradition." His smile was one of soft remembrance as he dished out the contents into their bowls. "*Bunica* was so insistent I study the family history. Nothing could be left out she claimed. Not even the stew."

"Smells wonderful, what's in it?"

"That's a secret. Only a Brach is entitled to know what the special ingredients are. I think I've been able to replicate the preparation fairly close to its authentic origin."

He watched as she lifted the spoon to her lips. She couldn't help the surprise spring to her face. The flavors were delicious.

"It's good. Isn't it?"

Good? It was the best stew she'd ever tasted. Then again, she hadn't eaten much except a slice of toast and some tea for quite some time.

"It's pretty awesome." She took another spoonful. "Thank you for taking care of me. You didn't have to. I could've fended for myself."

"No trouble. It's in my nature to take care of the wounded," Nicholaus said, brushing back a stray strand of hair on her forehead.

She chuckled. "I guess I've been one of your patients for some time now. I think I'm actually starting to understand what it's like to feel halfway normal."

"No nightmares?"

She shook her head. "I hope they're gone. Maybe now my mind won't keep trying to tell me something in the middle of the night."

"Marianne tells me there is a good chance you might never have the same dream again. However, depending on how you adjust, other issues might surface."

"Great. I didn't need to hear that," she muttered with a heavy sigh. She put down the spoon and wrapped her fingers around the water glass. "I've been remembering more every day."

Nicholaus reached out and took her other hand. "It can't be easy to remember something so horrible, especially when you've lived your life not knowing it existed."

Suzanna knew the time had come for her to open up. She'd needed some time to grasp what all of this meant, and longer still to figure out how she felt about it before sharing.

"He used to come to my room in the middle of the night. He told me not to tell anyone what we did in secret because they wouldn't understand. Sometimes he'd just touch me. Other times he'd make me touch him. I didn't want to, but he said if I didn't I was a very bad girl and he'd have to punish me." She heaved a sigh and looked away, as the sting of impending tears threatened to surface. "It got worse. The more he came to me the worse his actions. He started to play with himself as he touched me. Sometimes he'd get so rough I would want to scream. I was so scared. I didn't want to be punished."

"You never told anyone?"

"It confused me. The teachers talked at school about people touching you in the wrong way, but this was my father. Why would he touch me in the wrong way?"

"No wonder your sensitive mind shut everything out so tight. You told me before you had the ability early on. Being empathic, this must have been too much for your mind to handle."

Suzanna nodded. "I remember my mother telling me how special I was. I could always tell when she was sad or upset. She'd call me her little thermometer."

"You must have been confused by his actions and warped reasoning of right and wrong. You were too young to understand. You'd have felt he was convinced he was right, and that he had control over you. Your ability to assess what you felt hadn't developed yet."

Suzanna sat quiet. She'd needed to make a painful decision.

"I'm going to see him later today."

She saw Nicholaus raise his eyebrows in surprise. "Are you sure you need to?"

"I have to tell him how I feel."

She needed to finally stand up for herself and let her father know how his actions affected her life. She shared a contemplative gaze with Nicholaus. More pride than anger mixed with his emotions, and she sensed his torn response by her decision.

"Captain told me they have the search warrant for his residence. They'll probably find everything they need there to prosecute."

Suzanna gave a silent nod.

"Unfortunately, he also told me you wouldn't be able to press charges yourself because it happened so long ago. The laws state a limitation of ten years on any sexual crime where the victim is less than 18 years old. No matter how heinous. We hope they find current activity to incriminate him so they can put him away for a while."

"I pray they do. I can't stand the thought my visions might actually happen to other children. It would kill me." The depression lurking in the shadows of her thoughts made a jump toward taking over. In an effort to force the lethargy back, she stood up. "I've got to do whatever I can to make sure that doesn't happen."

"So does this mean you're not angry at me anymore?"

The concern over what he'd done wrapped around his words and touched her heart. She leaned forward and gave him a peck on the cheek.

"No, I'm not angry. I understand you did what you felt was best. Just happens this time I agree with what you did. He needed to be taken off the streets as soon as possible. I only regret not doing it myself."

Then a sudden burst of pensive emotion came from Nicholaus. She glanced at him as his brows knit together. "What?"

"There's something I didn't tell you before. Something you may not be too happy about."

She remained silent as he cleared his throat and looked into her eyes. She could sense he again worried about her reaction, but at this point her concern didn't include his feelings. He'd held back a piece of information she should have known. This angered her.

"When I was in the room with your father, he told me how proud he was of what he had done. So, before I turned him over to the cops…I broke his nose."

"You what?" she gasped.

"I couldn't hold back. When he started talking about you, I couldn't control my anger. So I punched him in the face."

So far Suzanna couldn't stir up any remorse for her father being taken to jail. His actions warranted worse. And again, somehow Nicholaus acted out what she herself may have done in the same situation. Her reflective pause seemed to increase his concern.

"He deserved it," she replied in sober reserve.

Now it was time to stand up and settle her own score with her father. She headed toward her room, stopping mid stride. Without looking back she felt Nicholaus watching her.

"Do me a favor. Don't ever hold information back, not when it concerns me. And next time, you feel you need to act on my behalf—don't. Not without letting me know first. I might have a different outcome planned for my life," she said, and closed the door behind her.

* * * *

Suzanna watched Frank's arrival through the glass as the officer ushered him to the seat directly across from her. He wore the required County Jail resident orange jump suit. His nose had burst into the vibrant color of an iris, bright purple with underlying yellows and blues. His excitement at seeing her dwindled when she told him she didn't intend to bail him out.

"I suppose that son-of-a-bitch told you what he did to me. What did you come for? Just to make sure he did it right?" The swelling made his voice almost unrecognizable as it resonated with an odd, raspy nasal sound.

"Yes he told me. But I came to see if you have anything to say for yourself?"

"What would I need to say? He's the one who should be in jail. I haven't done anything wrong."

Suzanna couldn't believe he could be so blind.

"Frank, they found evidence of what you've been doing to children, for God only knows how long. Have you no idea how wrong that is?"

"He's got me on some trumped up charges. Probably some fantasy coming from some of those outlandish stories you tell."

"What you did to me is not a story. That was wrong and you know it. I'm sorry I didn't remember before now."

Frank glanced over his shoulder at the guard posted at the door. He pushed closer to the glass separating them, and whispered feverishly into the mouthpiece, so no one else could hear.

"Oh get over it! You enjoyed every bit of my attention. Your boyfriend's jealous because he didn't get to you first. He should be happy I taught you what it's like to have a real man. If your Mamma hadn't gotten in the way you would have learned it real good. Just like Rachel did."

She stared at Frank in disbelief and almost missed his last words. His admission finally put the missing pieces together to the puzzle.

"You did this to Rachel, too?"

He glanced again over his shoulder and moved to where the guard couldn't see his face. "I'm not saying I did, and I'm not saying I didn't." His eyes twinkled at the true meaning to his statement.

Suzanna couldn't look at him any longer. Deep down, she sensed his absolute lack of remorse for his actions. It felt dirty and she cringed as his boastfulness surrounded her in his increased sexual arousal as he remembered his taking the innocence of his children in their youth. He sat back and grinned at her, proud of what he'd done.

Her anger began to boil.

"What you did to us scarred us for life. You can't imagine the pain it has caused me. You had no right."

"You've always been so over reactive. Neither you or Rachel are scarred," he blurted, before moving close again to whisper the next time bomb. "In fact she told me she misses what we used to do. Said that husband of hers doesn't match up to me."

At first she didn't comprehend what he said. Then she slowly began to digest the significance of his words. Was Rachel so emotionally scarred she actually believed what their father did to them was alright?

Now disgusted, she was almost too angry for words. She began to sputter her damning words. Suddenly a flow of serenity washed over her, and she felt the hand of mercy guiding her actions. She bowed her head to try and center her feelings. She knew the right thing to do, but it would not be easy.

Through gritted teeth she said, "I can't speak for Rachel, but what you did to me should never happen to a child." She took a deep breath before she could say her next words. "I can't hold judgment over you, only God can do that. It's going to take me a very long time to forgive you for what you've done."

"No skin off my nose. I have no interest in you any longer. You're a bit too old for my liking now, though you do have some nice curves on you. Rachel's daughter...now she has potential." Her father winked, his wrinkled eyes sparkling at the reference.

"You despicable human being," Suzanna said, repulsed by his attitude. He felt no guilt whatsoever. She stood and signaled to the guard. The door opened immediately for her. She started to walk away then went back to the glass mouthpiece. "I'm glad Nicholaus broke your nose. If it had been me, I'm not sure I would have stopped there."

As she walked away, she glanced back to see Frank's mischievous expression. "Tell your mother, Rodrigo says 'Hola'," he shouted.

* * * *

The meeting with her father had done nothing more than prove to her his guilt. Now she needed to confront her mother and sister. If she were to come to a full understanding it had to be done. She couldn't wait any longer. She needed to find out if what Frank said about Rachel was true. And if so, she needed to know exactly what Rachel thought.

"I'm not sure when I'll be back. Mamma said Rachel is supposed to come by around eight. I need them both to be there."

Suzanna picked up the dishes and placed them in the sink. Nicholaus had met her at the door with dinner in hand when she'd returned. Her appetite soured, she barely touched the selections.

"You want me to go with you?"

Touched by his offer, she went to him and gave him a hug.

"No, I think I need to do this on my own."

"I'm more than willing to be your backup."

She leaned forward and gave him a kiss. "Thank you, but I have to do this alone. I want to get it over with as quick as possible."

"Alright, I'll be here if you need me." He'd always been there for her. She needed to tell him how much she appreciated him, but not now.

She needed to find out the truth. Most of all, she wanted to let them know she was no longer the small, frightened child they believed her to be.

Chapter Twenty-Four

Rachel's car sat in the driveway when Suzanna arrived. Next to her confrontation with Frank, this would be the most difficult thing she'd ever have to do. How do you defy someone who put you down all of your life? And tougher yet, how do you attack the one person who loved you unconditionally—especially when it dealt with the same conflict? She didn't know how she'd handle it, yet she knew it had to be done.

Don't beat around the bush. Say what you came to say, and deal with the consequences later, she told herself.

She pulled herself together and stepped out of her car to walk slowly up the steps. She didn't bother to knock. She never had before. As she walked down the hallway she heard her sister and mother deep in conversation. Rachel's raised voice sounded as if she were irritated at her mother.

"Whatever she wants to say isn't important. I wouldn't worry about it mother. She's probably upset over some physical thing or another."

"What do we say if she remembers?" she heard her mother ask in distress.

Suzanna came around the corner and saw the surprised look on both of their faces. They hadn't heard her come in.

"Remember what?" she prodded with raised eyebrows.

The two looked back and forth, both at a loss for words. Suzanna came all the way into the room and slammed her purse down on the floor that caused Coco to jump out of Carmen's arms and scamper under her chair.

Disgusted by their inability to be truthful, she stood in front of them, hands on her hips.

"Let me help you answer that. What would you say if I discovered what you'd covered up all these years? Something so hellish, it caused so much grief and heartache I can't even put it into words. What would you say if I told you I know now what Daddy did to me?" She paused long enough to see the look, on both of their faces change visibly. "Something so horrible, I've had repressed memories and physical reactions all of my life. And you both knew about it!"

She saw tears well up in her mother's eyes, her face flushed with the revelation of their secret. Rachel's reaction looked somewhat bland.

"Don't be so over dramatic, Suzanna. It wasn't all that bad."

"Not all that bad?" she replied incredulously. "You call being raped by your father okay? Being molested night after night at the age of eight, was just something that happened? No big deal?"

"It's not like you didn't like the attention. You were always Daddy's favorite. He liked you best."

Suzanna shook her head. She still couldn't believe her sister's reaction. "I was a child. I couldn't protect myself. So were you. You can't tell me you felt right about what he did to you."

"*Ahi mio Dios…*" her mother whispered in horror. Suzanna glanced at her briefly. Carmen hadn't known about Rachel, that she was sure. The shock of finding out both daughters had been subjected to her husband's abuse was too much to take. Tears poured down her mother's face, her head held low, soft groans between muttered prayers followed.

"You're right. He did come to me, all the way up until you started to get all the attention. Then he left me for you." Rachel sounded like a forlorn lover who'd been left for a younger woman.

"And you think what he did to us was alright?" Suzanna narrowed her eyes while trying to get a sense of her sister's state of mind. The sound of her mother's soft cry in the background intensified. She now understood her mother's grief all these years. Coupled with guilt over this new discovery, Suzanna sensed Carmen's emotions overflow like a volcano. Her sister's incessant anger and irritation, however, continued without change except for a heightened level due to the conversation.

"Oh Rachel, *mia Niña*, you never say. Why you never tell me?" Carmen brought her hands to her face. The torrential tears ran free down her cheeks.

"There was nothing to tell. Daddy loved me. He just wanted to show me how much. Then baby sister Suzanna came and took him away from me. I don't know why you're both so upset."

Suzanna's jaw dropped and she made an indistinguishable sound.

Rachel looked bored, and brushed an invisible speck from her well-manicured fingers. When she looked up, her eyes were livid with hatred. "You made him go away. Because you spoiled things, he moved away, and we had to come to this God forbidden place."

"Rachel…enough, your sister she do no wrong. Your poppa he's a terrible, terrible man." Carmen shook her head grievously. "I should know these things. My eyes, they not see. My babies, my poor sweet babies," she agonized.

Suzanna sat on the edge of the couch. Her head hurt. She'd had enough pain and confusion to last a life time.

"Mother, he is not. He's a wonderful man and he didn't do anything wrong," Rachel refuted.

Suzanna stared at her sister in disbelief. Rachel's indignation and bent perspective baffled her.

"So you think he was right in what he did to me—to us?" Rachel's noncommittal stare made her even more confused than before. "What if it were Emily? What if Kevin raped your daughter night after night? How would that make you feel?" she asked.

A look of surprise crossed Rachel's face, as if she'd never thought of the idea. She shook her head in defense. "He would never do that to her. That wouldn't be right."

"Why not, think about it? Daddy did."

The pregnant silence filled the room as they stared at each other. Rachel's cell phone rang disrupting the silence. She hurried to retrieve the intrusive object from the bottom of her purse.

"This is Rachel," she listened intently. Her eyes began to blaze in anger. "She did what?" The voice on the other end could be heard speaking in rapid succession. "Yes, yes of course. I'll be there as soon as I can." She stood and shoved her phone back into her purse.

"Who was that?" her mother asked. "Are the babies alright? Are my babies hurt?" Carmen prompted, concerned for her grandchildren.

Rachel turned a wrathful stare at Suzanna. "That was Daddy's attorney. He's at Jackson's Bail Bonds. They have just arranged bail for Frank. He was picked up on child pornography and abuse charges. He said Suzanna put them up to it."

"You don't get it do you? He can't be allowed to do this anymore. There's been enough suffering," Suzanna yelled, devastated by her sister's inability to see the wrongful acts of their father. "He needs to be punished for what he did to us, and no doubt to other children."

She really hadn't wanted use her next disclosure, unless pushed to convince her sister of their father's wrong doing.

"Rachel, I know you don't believe I have a sixth sense, but I've found out I can see things that have happened and may happen in the future."

Rachel rolled her eyes at Suzanna.

"When I experienced the visions I saw something I couldn't dismiss. One of the children I saw was your Emily. It took me a while to recognize her—she was a bit older than she is now—but it was definitely her. Rachel, Frank had her pinned to the bed and he was doing those awful things, just like he did to me. If we don't put him away now, this horrible thing is going to continue to happen. Your baby might be his next victim."

The resulting look of disbelief told Suzanna her sister was not ready to understand. "I don't know where you get off saying something like that. Daddy would never do that to Emily. That's his grandchild." She denied even the remote possibility, the actions of the past buried so deep in the distorted viewpoint she'd created of her father. "Your visions, as you call them, are just some kind of paranoid schizophrenia. All of you freaks should be put away somewhere."

Ignoring her reference to a mental disorder, Suzanna tried one more time. "He has to be stopped. I can't let him get away with this. He has to pay for what he's done, if not for us then for the other children." She didn't know what else to say. It was obvious Rachel refused to admit the right from the wrong.

"Well, we will have to see about that. You have no proof." Rachel straightened her clothes and tossed her bag over her shoulder. "And if you think you're going to act out your little delusional fantasies because you have some perverted picture of who Daddy really is, then you've got another think coming. I'll get the best lawyer around to handle this. You won't have a chance."

Rachel didn't allow Suzanna or her mother to respond. She left them, mouths agape, at her inability to see the truth.

Perhaps convincing herself what happened was acceptable had become her method of survival. It was clear to Suzanna now. Rachel treated her so bad all these years because she blamed her for their father leaving them.

Suzanna stared blankly at the wall listening to the sobs of a shamed mother.

"Mamma, why didn't you tell me?"

Taking the hankie out of her pocket, Carmen dabbed her eyes and gave a ferocious blowing of her nose.

"*Novia*, telling it no good," she shook her head vehemently. "When I…how do you say…kick Frank out, your memory, it go. I think maybe it better not to say." She sniffled and dabbed at her nose again. "You grow so beautiful and healthy. Why tell you something so horrible?"

Suzanna was again reminded her mother really didn't understand the half of what she'd struggled with day after day. Because she'd never talked about her condition, her mother thought she functioned as a normal person. It was time to tell her what she'd withstood all of these years.

"I haven't been perfectly normal, Mamma. The lapse in memory is a deeper repression of that traumatic time in my life. Because of it I've suffered from night terrors, and more importantly, the sexual dysfunction I've had to deal with."

"You a little tense, you say it be alright. Many *Senoritas*, they have this, no?" Her mother tried to hold onto her belief the problem was inconsequential because Suzanna had presented it to her that way for so long.

"Mamma, it's worse than a little tension. I have something called Vaginismus. I've had a total inability to have sexual intercourse. The pain it causes is indescribable." Her mother's tears began to intensify, and Suzanna reached out to grasp her hand in comfort. "In this case it's caused by trauma. Let's hope it's not too late and can be reversed."

She released her hold, bringing her hands back to rest in her lap. The admission felt good.

"I've been so humiliated. Because of this I never kept a boyfriend for very long. They didn't understand and didn't want to have anything to do with me. I'd given up on all hopes of finding someone and having a family."

"*Oh, novia...Siento*, this causes me much pain. I not know."

"It's not your fault. I've been too ashamed to tell you. If I had, you might have taken this more seriously."

Coco came out from under the chair and peered around Carmen's legs to see if the cause for fear still existed. Suzanna stuck out her hand, and he ran to her, tail wagging, wet nose shoved into her hand ready to be petted.

"I can't say what this means. This is my fault. I'm no good, such a bad, bad mother."

"No. You're not. You've done nothing more than what you thought best at the time," Suzanna murmured.

Suzanna couldn't be mad at her mother. She'd meant no harm to her. Forgiveness was the only way to move forward. She couldn't afford to be stuck in the quagmire of hate and negativity surrounding so many people. It would tear her apart.

She scratched Coco's tummy and her thoughts moved to Rachel. "Mamma, you didn't know about Rachel?"

Carmen shook her head. "No, she never say this. Frank, he do this to her, too. My babies, they tell me nothing. You screamed for me. I come and push him out. Then he say what he did to you." Anger rose in her mother's flushed cheeks. "So damned proud he was. Said he treated you right. We all got it good and should appreciate his 'special' attentions."

"I don't understand. Why didn't you go to the authorities?"

Carmen dabbed the tears continuing to roll down her cheeks. "My Visa, it was to expire. Citizenship not come yet. Frank, he knows how to get his way. He say if I tell he have them send me back to Mexico. No. I not let that happen to my babies. If I go, they give you to that horrible man. He say if I hush up he not tell, and I keep you. So I keep quiet. All this time, I keep quiet." The sadness in her eyes was filled with the years of fatigue and resignation over the shame she'd kept to herself.

"Frank said something I didn't understand. He wanted me to tell you Rodrigo says, 'hi'."

The stricken look that came across Carmen's face surprised Suzanna. "*Ahi mio Dios!*" her mother whispered making the sign of the cross against her chest. "*Santa Maria.*"

"What?" Suzanna questioned. "Who is Rodrigo?"

"No, no." Carmen jumped up and rushed to the windows, pulling the draperies closed. She opened them a crack and peered out a moment, then pulled them shut again. Making the sign of the cross again, she began to pace back and forth.

"Mamma, why does this Rodrigo scare you? Who is he?"

Carmen shook her head, looking over her shoulder as if he would jump out of the woodwork at her. She ran into the kitchen and closed the curtains over the sink, scooping Coco into her arms as she came back. She sat down and buried her cheek in his fur rocking back and forth, muttering prayers of protection over them.

Suzanna started to feel a little scared too. "Mamma, this is ridiculous. You have to tell me what is going on."

"He is a bad, bad man from the past. You not need to know. We don't speak of him, ever," she claimed rising from her chair to pace back and forth again. "You hear me, we don't speak of him."

Confused, Suzanna was too tired to handle anymore turmoil. She would have to ask her mother more about this later.

She stood and wrapped her arms around the small woman, willing her to calm down. "Ok, we won't talk about this now."

But they would talk about it.

"*Gracias*," Carmen responded, and seemed to relax a bit.

Suzanna smiled on the inside. Maybe there was more of Nicholaus rubbing off on her than she knew. She led her mother back to the couch and sat down, encouraging her to sit down next to her.

"What are we going to do about Rachel? She needs help." Suzanna knew this would be the beginning to a very long ordeal with her sister. It would take time to work through in her own mind what she'd found out so far. No doubt, there would be more to come from Rachel.

For now though, she needed more rest.

"All her life, she be *negative*. Not like you, my novia. I not understand her. But now, I know why. I talk to her," Carmen said, shaking her head.

"She needs more than talk. She needs counseling."

"I know, but she is strong in the head. It will take time. Maybe she will hear me."

Suzanna patted the dog's stomach and looked thoughtfully at Coco's unconditional presentation of love.

"Maybe…I hope so," she said in doubt.

Chapter Twenty-Five

A few days passed, and Suzanna began to slowly realize her strength as a woman. It was time to take control of her life. For too long she'd allowed others to dictate her lack of self-worth, and inability to take care of herself.

The known injustices felt almost as bad as the previously unknown nightmares of her secretive past. However, the woman who unwittingly allowed others to decide the outcome to her life had changed into the butterfly God intended her to be. Now she would be the one to make her own decisions—to choose the life she intended to live.

She couldn't hold Nicholaus' actions against him. They were not meant as an affront to her. In fact he'd done exactly what she would have done if she'd been in his shoes.

Now she needed to show him she forgave him, and to express her love for him. If he was her twin flame, they needed to discover what that meant to them both, and this was the only way she could think to get started.

Suzanna looked in the mirror and dabbed her eyebrow to make it match the other one. The bottle of *Erotica* perfume fit seductively in her hand as she gave her neck a generous misting. She took another look in the mirror and approved. The final touches were completed with a pair of black sandals she'd found for the occasion.

Off she went in search of satisfaction. To prove what was stolen from her so long ago would no longer dominate her.

* * * *

Nicholaus heard the back door open and close. He could hear the soft tap of high heels on the surface of the hallway floor. Curious, he set his pen down on top of the computer keypad and waited for the visitor to enter. The most beautiful and surprising vision he had ever seen walked into the room.

Suzanna had left her dark hair loose and let the thick waves flow over her shoulders in a river of shine. Her long black satin nightgown was split high to the thigh on one side and showed off her curves with wanton abandon. The spaghetti straps and appliquéd black lace roses that ran in a flowing curve of seduction from breast to hip showed enough skin to tease the senses. Nicholaus could only stare in amazement at the transformation.

She sauntered into the room slow and confident to where he sat speechless, his gaze glued to her. She sat on the edge of his desk. The slit shimmered over her thigh and rose higher to coax the imagination with regions of sexual fantasy. Silently, she swung her leg between them in an intimate invitation.

"I wasn't expecting you." He couldn't believe he sounded as stupid as he felt.

"I missed you today," Suzanna replied, as she reached down to her bare knee and drew her fingers up her thigh in a zigzag manner.

"Oh," he said, stunned by the intensified effect she had on him. "Oh, I went to visit with my mother, like I promised."

"I see." She flipped one side of her hair behind her shoulder and revealed the neck he craved to taste. "I thought you might be lonely, so I came over to see if you'd like some company." She reached out to caress his cheek with her manicured red fingertips.

"Shouldn't you be resting?" Again, he sounded like a teenager. He could have kicked himself.

She placed her fingers on his lips and shook her head. The shock of energy running through her touch generated enough vigor to jumpstart the deadest of batteries. She stood again and took his hand to pull him from the chair. Their bodies touched and he could feel the echoing explosion of sexual energy he craved from her. She stood on her toes to offer her lips to him. When he reached out and grasped her around the waist, the smooth softness of the satin titillated his fingertips. She brought her hand to the back of his head and pulled his lips to hers, the kiss a mere precursor of things to come.

Nicholaus yanked her against him with unusual roughness. The need for her erased any thought of gentleness. If such thing as instant combustion existed, this moment would've been it. The flash of fire between them was enough to scramble what remained of his brains, as it made the blood rush in excited lashes down to his loins.

Suzanna stepped away from him to take his hand in hers. She gave him an indescribable look of mischief and intense determination sparkling with provocative invitation in the dark luster of her eyes.

"Come with me. I have something for you."

The soft glow from the lamp on the nightstand filled the darkness when Suzanna flipped the switch. Nicholaus stood in anticipation. She could feel the furious rush of blood through his veins, the same as hers.

"What...?" he started to ask. Again Suzanna held her finger to his lips and shook her head.

"Don't say a word. Just go with it. I need you to do what I ask. I've got to see something."

She took his hand and placed it on her breast, enjoying the warmth from his hand on the taut cool satin against her skin. She felt sparks of excitement ripple down her body as he began to knead the flesh he held in his palm. The bright blueness of his eyes glittered in the glow of the lamplight, their color changing to a deep slate as the knowledge of what she proposed came to light.

Close didn't seem close enough as she pressed herself against his hardened penis. She grasped the firm buttocks she'd dreamt about in her waking fantasies, pulling him closer still. The embrace produced a combined energy strong enough to generate a hazy illumination around their bodies, visible only by their highly attuned senses.

"Do you see that?" Nicholaus asked in awe.

Suzanna giggled. Nodding her head, she ran her fingers down the slope of her neck, inviting him to take what he wanted. More than willing he sought her neck with his lips to caress the area she knew held the haunting scent she wore. She moaned in submission as he clasped her nipple between his fingertips and the slippery satin. The intense pressure blended with the warmth of his tongue sent shock waves through her system.

It took a mere instant of these heated touches and fire laden kisses to bring her to her knees. Her desire for him reached an explosive level.

She needed to prove to herself she was a complete and desirable woman. Her feelings for him could not be expressed in words. She needed to show him how much she loved him.

Nicholaus' clothes ended up flung to the floor within seconds. She pushed him back on the bed and with seductive movements pulled her shimmering enticement over her head to toss it amongst his clothes.

Gone was the shy, hesitant woman of previous times. She felt like a siren, released from her entrapment, now ready to pounce and devour her prey. Her body burned with sexuality as she began to tempt him with her moves.

The lotion she'd used was intended to cast a tantalizing soft glow under the lamplight, enhancing the exotic color of her skin. As his hands traveled over her body she sensed he fought his instinct to take what he so desperately wanted.

For the first time in her life she made a movement she would never have done in the past. She hungered for control— to know what she wanted and to seize it without question. As she straddled him she leaned down to brush kisses across his face, her breasts lightly grazing his chest, causing a shot of desire to travel to her center.

No longer did she feel the need to guard her empathic senses. She let go of the force field she held around herself and experienced a wash of pure physical sensation come over her. It felt good.

Determined to feel every point of contact, and experience the sensation of skin against skin, need against need, she focused entirely on the sexual being blooming within her. With every touch she opened her empathic self up to the response within Nicholaus. Her own senses, heightened to an explosive point, mingled with his increased male need for immediate satisfaction. She envisioned no end to this exalted level of joy.

She desired more…she needed more.

Although incredible, the small amount she allowed herself to feel the first time they'd made love couldn't compare. She rejected all possibility of failure now ready to give her all to the man she loved.

She lightly touched her stomach to the tightened muscles of Nicholaus' groin, increasing her pressure as she moved against him. To her delight this incited a moan deep down within him. He continued to allow her to stroke and touch where she wished, his eyes closed. She could feel he too opened himself up to the experience of sensations she drew forth.

Then without hesitation, she slid down his shaft, her hot wet walls clasping down tight as she went. Past rejection hovered over her for only a moment. Then she forced it away, concentrating only on the present, and she began to relax and enjoy the sensation. This time differed from before. She acted not because of an expectation, but because she craved to feel his entire length against her innermost being.

He opened his eyes in surprise and Suzanna experienced the most intense feeling, as their eyes met the exhilaration was extraordinary. It felt as if they'd joined into oneness. No beginning and no end, just an enveloped love steeped in the act of expression.

She demanded more...she took more.

Greedily she tested the difference of entry and withdrawal, maneuvering with skillful intuitive movements, her intent to drive him crazy. No longer would the fear of rejection or embarrassment rule her actions. She couldn't believe this awesome feeling she'd avoided, until now. Never again would she allow herself to be controlled by the actions of her past.

Nicholaus grabbed hold of her hips and rose up to pull her down fully onto his pulsating erection. The action brought him to where she'd never been touched before. Through the tendrils of her hair, her eyes locked onto his, her focus on the sensations he evoked.

Radiating from Nicholaus' penetration, a jolt of electricity shot through her core and caused the fire from within to flare into a wildfire. He smiled and his eyes sparkled with the knowledge of what happened. She couldn't tell if he'd initiated more of his healing powers, or if their extreme connection had spurred this new sensation. As she came down over him, the tingling arrows of heat burst forth again, and he rose up to meet her rotating his hips to bring forth another sensation.

The need to increase the intensity of pressure was now so overwhelming she began to rock back and forth in rapid succession. Tension in her thighs and stomach built, progressing to an explosive point when he reached up to caress her nipples, pulling on them slightly and rubbing them between his fingertips. He rose to grasp one in between his lips and caress the full contours of her breast with his hand. The heat of his tongue and the rippled labor of his breaths on her skin sent her over the edge.

"Ooh…Nicholaus. Yes…yes…yes!" It was then her body began to buck back and forth. Her stomach clenched in the intensity of the orgasm ripping through her body.

"Lord, you make me want to let go. Not yet sweetheart. I've got something for you now."

She began to wilt down over him into an unknown abyss, but Nicholaus skillfully brought her down onto her back, his still hard erection begging to be released.

"Stay with me a little longer honey," he whispered in her ear as he entered her once again and slipped with ease into her silky wet folds.

Her heart pounded in thunderous beats as she felt him begin to move in and out, slow at first.

"Open yourself up to me honey. You're going to feel every possible sensation you've ever dreamed of having."

He didn't lie. She could feel flashes of intense heat, a tingling of every nerve and a deep blood coursing energy rush through her body. Each propelled stroke flowed with a force she could only describe as a full on encompassing fire. At every point of contact she could feel his energies invigorate a sensation so intense another massive orgasm began to develop, unmatched by any other.

His rhythm became quicker, deeper, and more intense as their bodies met time after time in search of final release. She moaned out as it became too much for her to hold back, and the orgasm once again took control, shaking her to her very soul. Fully open to feel his physical responses, she was delighted to sense his release as extreme as hers. The duration and power of his ejaculation so great she sensed his heart would burst with an elation matched to her own.

She couldn't be sure for how long she'd passed out, but she found herself curled up against the strength of Nicholaus' well formed body, her leg draped across his in a possessive manner. His breaths were shallow, eyes closed against the light from the lamp. She giggled lightly at the memory of what she'd experienced, enlightened by the knowledge of what two people could do physically to each other.

"What are you laughing at?" he chuckled, eyes still closed.

"Mmm…I was just thinking about how I'd like to do that all over again."

A grin came slow to his face. "You would, would you?"

"I can't imagine why I've waited so long. Is it me, or was that pretty damn amazing?" She knew what she felt from him, but needed to hear him say it.

He gathered her close to him and nuzzled the top of her head with his lips. "That was more than amazing. It was outright incredible. I'm so glad you came to pay me a visit tonight."

"Me too," she lay her head on his shoulder. "Is it possible?" she whispered.

"Is what possible?"

She began to move her hand over his chest and down his belly. "Is it possible to do it again?"

The movement of her hand was all it took. She giggled when she touched the responsive reaction in his manhood, already prepared for another round.

"I think, with you, anything is possible."

* * * *

The next few weeks became very hectic with interrogation procedures. Although she couldn't press charges personally, Suzanna's statements to the Special Victims Unit helped to build a case against her father. His guilt was unquestionable with the overwhelming evidence they retrieved. The authority's confiscation marked him as an active sexually abusive child molester, connected with the sale of drugs to minors. With some of Frank's admitted comments to Nicholaus, they obtained several credible witnesses, and started to gather a list of possible victims to prove his long-time abusive behaviors.

They were able to disband the company that produced the child pornographic video, and arrested all but one of the members involved on drug and human trafficking charges. Several children, between the ages of six and twelve were found on the premises. The officials took them to safe-houses where they received medical attention and the proper social services. Hopefully, with luck the children would find a gentle loving home where they could be raised without the fear of abuse and neglect.

Nicholaus' involvement in these interrogations was centered on the discovery of evidence. It was necessary to prove he'd acted on his own without a scheme set up by the police before the issuance of a search warrant. Frank tried to press charges against him for the assault, but based on the circumstances, the judge denied the claim without question of guilt.

Suzanna knew he also needed to prepare for his presentation at the veterinarian conference, so they didn't have much time to spend together.

She sat on the bed and watched him pack his things carefully into the suitcase, making sure he remembered his laptop and speech notes.

"Are you sure you don't want to go with me? It will be all right to close up the office for a couple of days. Mona said she would help out and Joseph will be back on Wednesday. He can open up for some of the more urgent needs."

Suzanna did want to go, but she didn't think she could. Still hesitant, he urged her again.

"I want you to come with me, Suzanna. It would be a good chance for us to spend some time together. Sit by the pool, eat some decadent food, and just relax. We need to enjoy some time away from all of this."

"I know. I really want to. I told you I'm not feeling well. I think I might have caught a bug. I better not chance passing it on to you." She'd felt nauseous for a day or two, her stomach pitching at any thought of food. "You go make a splash. Everyone will love you. You're going to be flooded with requests to speak. Once people find out you're a national speaker, the phones aren't going to stop ringing." She tried with her best attempt at motivational encouragement.

He zipped his bag and placed it on the floor before sitting next to her. "If you're sure," he inquired.

Time ran short. He needed to get on the road to make his three o'clock flight out of SeaTac, but he again urged her to go and told her he would take the extra minutes to help her pack.

"I'm sure." She wrapped her arms around his neck and held on. "I'm going to miss you," she whispered.

"I'm going to miss you too honey." After one last returned hug he stood to grab his coat and bag. "I'll call you every night. I'm back late Friday afternoon, so we'll have to grab some dinner. Then I plan on making love to you until you beg me to stop." His mischievous smile made her giggle.

As she sadly watched him drive off the nausea seemed to wane.

Maybe I should have gone with him?

Frustrated, she turned to go back into her house. All week she'd planned to go, only to find out she'd come down with a flu bug.

Of all the luck!

* * * *

Kimi sat on Suzanna's knees busily decorating the cupcakes they'd made for her contribution to the class Halloween Party. Orange frosting was everywhere. On her face, in her hair, and even a blotch ended up on the end of her nose when she claimed taste testing a part of her job. Sprinkles of black, silver and red shapes, equally abundant, rolled and gathered every which way on the counter.

"How are you doing with all this? Has anyone pressed charges yet against Frank?"

"They have two of the victims willing to talk. They're in the initial stages of investigation right now. It'll take a while to build the case against him. The hard part is getting the parents to allow the kids to go through any type of psychological tests. They don't want any kind of long term damage caused by police activity. It's bad enough finding out something like this might have happened." Suzanna had found the normal state of awareness of these parents to be the same as her mother— totally unaware.

"I heard only about thirty percent of these cases ever get tried. Over seventy percent of these lunatics are still out there on the streets doing the same thing over and over again. The victims are too young to know what to do, and the parents are too stupid to do what it takes to find out what's really happened." Lucy's disgust came out in the way she wiped up the frosting mess from a runaway cupcake.

"In my mom's case, she was threatened and couldn't do anything about it. A good portion of the cases are kids of an age who think they know what they want and are willing to do whatever it takes to get it. So they won't talk. It's a sick world, Lucy. Keep your eyes open and your ears alert. It's everywhere."

"This discussion is too deep for the moment." Lucy said, indicating her daughter's presence with a nod of her head. "We'll have to talk later."

In an expert motherhood move she changed the subject. "So you let Nick get away to Houston? Why didn't you go with him? Sounds like the perfect chance for some special time." Lucy raised her eyebrows up and down. Suzanna laughed. She knew little ears didn't need to understand her mother's specific reference.

"I haven't been feeling very well lately. I'm not sure what it is. It's been to long for some kind of flu, and it's never gotten any worse, so I think I can rule that out." The smell of the vanilla cupcakes made her queasy even then. "Maybe it's stress."

"What do you mean? What kind of symptoms do you have?"

"My stomach's been touchy. I can't seem to handle much of anything, keeps wanting to come back up. I guess I should go see a doctor."

Lucy's look was intense. "How long has this been happening?"

"I don't know, maybe a week or two."

"Sounds to me like you need to have him give you a pregnancy test," Lucy exclaimed.

Suzanna heard her, but couldn't seem to process the words. Then it dawned on her and she looked up to see Lucy's fixed gaze.

"You did use birth control didn't you?"

This thought hadn't even crossed her mind. She stared at Lucy, unsure of what to say.

"Mommy, this is the last one. Can we make some more?" Kimi held out the cupcake. Her artistic hand and the cupcake were covered top to bottom in frosting and a generous supply of sprinkles.

"Oh, Lord…" Lucy breathed. "Umm…Sweetie, why don't you go upstairs and get cleaned up. Change your shirt and wash your face. Then maybe we can talk Aunt Suzie into going to the park for ice cream."

The little girl, distracted by the thought of ice cream, happily jumped off Suzanna's lap and ran upstairs to do as her mother bid.

An unquestionable look passed between the two women. One full of consternation, the other draped in embarrassment.

"I didn't…I didn't think." The lame response surprised her. *Why hadn't she thought of the possibility of getting pregnant?* It should have been her first thought.

"Oh my God, I can't believe you didn't use contraception. What were you thinking?"

"I guess we weren't. It just kind of keeps happening."
She tried to convince herself against the ultimate truth and
shook her head in denial. "It couldn't happen that quick, it's
only been a couple of times."

"It only takes once." Lucy gave a knowing shake to her
head then jumped up excited. "Wait. Wait right here."

She returned with a small rectangular box in her hand.
"Here, go pee on this. I had an extra one from a month or so ago
when I thought I was pregnant again." She shoved it toward
Suzanna. Suzanna hesitated. Lucy gave her a little push. "Come
on. What are you waiting for? You have to want to know."

This could be the worst thing possible. She turned the
box over in her hands. She wasn't sure if she wanted to find out
or not. A baby was all she needed. She wanted children, and she
was pretty sure Nicholaus did too, but they hadn't ever talked
about it. But if she was pregnant, she'd better find out sooner
than later. With a sigh of resignation she took the box into the
bathroom to discover what life had in store for her next.

* * * *

Suzanna fixed a special Romanian dinner for Nicholaus.
The pot on the stove still warm as she'd completed the final
touches to the meal, and was waiting for him to arrive home.
She'd gone earlier to the little store located in the international
district off of Fourth and Jackson, near Pioneer Square, to pick
up the special ingredients she needed.

Now with nothing more to do, she walked from kitchen
into the hallway toward Nicholaus' office. She needed to feel
him close to her and thought his residual energy might help take
her mind away from assuming an outcome to what she needed
to tell him. He may not be as open as she was to the idea.

She sat down in his chair and immediately felt the
warmth of his energy coarse over her. There was nothing better
than to sense the energy of the one you loved. She imagined she
knew how he felt about her, although he'd never actually said it
in words to her. Every time he held her in his arms, she was
filled with a never ending love, that couldn't belong only to her.

Could it?

Though he'd never given her any reason to doubt their relationship, now would be the time to find out if it was real. She wished it was under different circumstances, but she needed to find out for sure tonight.

The glint of steel from the pen on his desk reminded her of his eyes when he was angered, and she started to wonder if he would be angry. She picked up the pen, running her fingers over the cold smooth surface.

Its shiny exterior seemed to lull her into a dazed state. She began seeing images in her minds eye, times when she and Nicholaus had been together, others when he seemed alone pondering something. She felt his intense concentration as he wrote with the pen in hand. Mona came floating into the picture and out again.

Then she saw the name of a hotel flash through her head, the sight of a big conference room, where many people stood in conversation with each other. Nicholaus appeared, with a drink in his hand, and he was talking and laughing with someone. He looked different somehow, but the flash of his face was quick to fade slowly as a woman appeared in plain view. She leaned in for a kiss. Suzanna felt the kiss. It was not a simple kiss of a friend. It had the heat of a lover. And she saw Nicholaus pull this woman closer, returning the kiss with ardor.

Then all of a sudden he was standing outside the little herbal shop in the International District he'd taken her to a few times before. The same sign she'd seen earlier that day, stating "All Green Teas 20% Off", was posted in the window. A bag from the store sat on the sidewalk beside him, his arms flung around a woman.

Suzanna jumped. It was that woman, that freakish spike haired bimbo who kept showing up in her life. Suzanna could feel the warmth of her body pressed up against his, her lips all but devouring a spot on his neck. Shivers ran down her spine when she realized his face was buried in Christina's neck as well.

She couldn't take anymore. The pen dropped out of her hand, making a clattering sound against the wood. She sat stunned. The images drifted away as if in a dream.

But this wasn't a dream. This was now and this was real.

Nicholaus was not the man she thought him to be. He was a womanizer.

Chapter Twenty-Six

Nicholaus flew in that afternoon. He called Suzanna from the airport to tell her he needed to stop by his father's house to check on the healing progress. His father had called him when he was still at the conference to tell him the medical doctors were amazed at the sudden recovery of such an advanced stage of cancer. It was a miracle they said. Never before had they witnessed the complete reversal of lymphatic abnormality and they laughed when Roland claimed his son cured him. He needed to pick up a few herbs for him before he headed out to check on him, so he stopped where he picked up all of his herbs.

This would be a quick stop. His father would have to understand. He had more important things to do.

"Nick. Nick…Wait up!" screeched the high pitched voice behind him.

Turning he saw the skimpily dressed woman as she scurried toward him, teetering precariously on the high-heeled wedges of her sandals.

The way the voluptuous blond flung herself at him demanded he drop his bag and wrap his arms around her to keep from ending up in the street along with the aggressive pile of curves. His face shoved into her neck as she all but climbed into his arms. Her lips landed dangerously close to his neck.

"Whoa. Easy." He placed her back on her feet. "Christina. Right?" he asked, testing his memory. He stepped away. With annoying perseverance she came closer yet.

"You remembered. I'm so glad." She smiled and placed a seductive hand on his chest. Feeling awkward, Nicholaus removed her hand and gave it back to her, and tried again to distance himself.

"How's Bruno doing?"

"He's as cute as ever. You healed him of that horrible skin thing he had. He's as good as new."

Nicholaus felt an uncomfortable awareness of being watched, though as he glanced around nobody seemed very interested in them. Although distracted by the incessant pawing of this woman, he couldn't shake the feeling.

"You should come out to visit him. And me too," she insisted with an obvious sexual invite.

"If you need him to be seen again, you'll need to bring him by the office."

She exaggerated a pout as she batted her blue eyes at him. "It would be so much more fun if you came to visit me."

That won't be happening, Nicholaus thought, appalled at the suggestion. Way too young and her obvious availability to any and all such encounters did not interest him in the least. Besides, he was taken now, no longer available for the nonchalant whims of a female.

Finally able to disengage himself from the conversation, he worked his way back to his car, his thoughts on the woman he loved.

When Nicholaus came through the front door of his place, the divine scent of a home cooked meal wafted through the air from the back. He walked into the kitchen and saw various pots and pans on the stovetop. Empty serving dishes littered the counter as if waiting to receive their intended contents. Burners turned off, the meal appeared complete. An empty grocery bag sat conspicuously on the counter.

Something seemed amiss. Where was the cook?

He listened for movement but heard nothing. Thinking she'd gone back to her house for something he went out the back door in search of Suzanna. Her door was unlocked, so he went on in.

"Suzanna, my love, where are you?" he called out.

There was no answer.

On a search through the house, he found the closet door open and conspicuously empty, a few items dropped to the floor in a trail toward the bed. Nicholaus became concerned.

She told him she would meet him.

Frantic, he began to go through the house again, that's when he saw it. On the kitchen table, an envelope marked with his name waited for discovery. A chill ran down his neck when he saw what lay next to it. As if in fondness of a memory once treasured, the necklace he gave her remained, where she did not.

Grasping the envelope, he ripped it open.

Dear Nicholaus,

> *It has come to my attention we have different priorities. I have come to care for you much more than you may realize. Please know I appreciate all you have done for me and hope you will achieve what you are looking for in life.*

> *I've decided to leave my employment with you and will move my things out of the house after I come back. Mona agreed to fill in for me at the office until you find someone to replace me.*

> *Take care, and give my love to your father.*

> *Suzanna*

Confusion quickly turned into anger. Her note made no sense at all.

What does she mean we're looking for different things? Doesn't she feel the same things I do? Doesn't she know how much I love her? Didn't she respond to me with the same love? How can she dismiss all we've been through as if its inconsequential?

He shoved the necklace into his pocket and went to the only person he knew could answer his questions.

* * * *

Marianne looked into Nicholaus' forlorn eyes. The desperation of his words stirred her soul.

"You've got to help me. What does she mean we are looking for different things? Doesn't she know how I feel about her?"

A soft smile came to her lips. Marianne pitied his innocence. "I believe we have discussed this before. Have you ever told her?"

She watched him turn thoughtful before answering. He shook his head. "No. She should know."

"Nicholaus, a woman needs to be told when she is loved, especially someone like Suzanna. She's never experienced this before. She doesn't know what to trust. She's confused by what she feels from herself and what she senses from you. Without you to confirm what she feels, she won't be able to sort it all out. Knowing in your heart you love someone is one thing. Backing it up with words and actions is another."

Nicholaus released a burdened, heavy sigh.

"You're right. I need to tell her I love her." He paused as he looked down at the floor then looked back up, his eyes filled with grief. "It's hard for me Marianne. I've never trusted myself to love anyone this much. Now that she's gone I know I can't live without her."

"Just like Suzanna, it's time for you to let go of the past, too."

He nodded. "I've been trying to figure out the best way. I planned to talk with her tonight, but how can I when I have no idea where she's gone?"

"She said in the note something came to her attention. What happened? Is there something you might have said to make her believe you weren't looking for the same things in life?"

"Nothing I can think of. I came back from the conference, and we were supposed to have dinner. In fact it's still sitting on the stove at the house right now."

"So she left in a hurry? That's very odd."

"Can't you look into the future or something to tell where she went? Or tell me what the hell's going on?"

"I can only tell what is going on with you. I'm unable to read someone who is not in my presence." She neglected to tell him she had talked to the one person who did know.

Frustration written over his face, Nicholaus sat back in his seat. "What am I going to do? She needs to know how I feel about her before she makes any decisions." He brought trembling hands up to give his face a vigorous rub. "Marianne, this is killing me. Can't you look into my future and tell me what happens?"

She again gave a soft smile. She already had and was quite pleased with the outcome.

"I will tell someone of their future only when I see their current path in life could be detrimental and result in a dangerous outcome. All I can tell you is you're on the right path. You need to follow your heart, and open your mind up to the universe. It will direct you where you need to go."

* * * *

He'd gone over every conversation in his head a million times. The note he read for the fiftieth time that day. He kept asking himself, where would she have gone?

Her mother was not much help either. Still frazzled over Suzanna's discovery of the secret and upset to find out her daughter might be missing, she only contributed to his frustration.

Sitting in his car, he held the note in his hands. He had no idea where to look next. The world became so much larger when you searched for someone you love. The words of the page seemed to blend together in front of his eyes, so he closed them and began to pray, asking for direction.

"I know I don't talk to you often enough on a personal level, but I need some help here. You've got to help me find her. If you really care as much as you say, tell me where to go," he prayed out loud.

The responding silence didn't solve anything. He opened his eyes again to look down at the note. All of a sudden his sight pinned straight to the one word he'd missed the whole time.

Mona.

She had talked to Mona. If anyone knew Suzanna, Mona did. She'd know where to find her. He started the car and drove straight to Mona's house, not caring whether she'd welcome him or not.

Mona sat outside in the garden pulling weeds from the pansies around the base of a concrete birdbath. Down on her knees, she looked up from under her floppy hat far enough to watch the determined steps of the young man coming toward her. She knew who they belonged to and didn't need to look up any further.

"Where is she? Where did she go?"

"Who dear?" she asked in feigned innocence.

"Don't play games with me Mona. I'm not in the mood."

"Seems to me if she wanted you to know where she was she'd have told you." She stood up from her position on the ground and stretched to relieve the tension of old age. "I don't know what you did to the poor girl, but she was in tears when she left here. She wouldn't tell me what it was all about. Perhaps you can?"

"I have no idea. One minute we were going to get together for dinner, the next she's done a disappearing act and she's nowhere to be found."

"She was obviously upset," she said with disapproval. "I told you not to play with her heart."

"Dammit Mona, I'm not playing with her. I don't know why she's so upset. I can't remember anything I said or did to make her take off like this." Mona looked at him in disbelief. "You've got to believe me. She doesn't know it yet, but I was going to ask her to marry me."

Now that put a different spin on the situation. Mona looked into the young man's face and saw his sincerity.

"You've got to tell me where she went. I know you know."

She considered thoughtfully, slowly taking the gloves off of her hands, reflecting on what she'd found out from Lucy that morning.

"All right, but you have to promise me you won't go feeling hurt and angry, saying things you don't mean. She may not be able to handle it."

"I just want to tell her how much I love her. She means the world to me, and I've been stupid enough not to tell her."

Mona felt his declaration might solve her god-daughter's problems, all of them. She motioned for him to follow where she led him into the house.

"I gave her the keys to the beach house in Anacortes. She wanted to get away to do some thinking on her own." On the counter she jotted the address on a slip of paper. "Be gentle with her Nicholaus. Her senses are all over the board right now."

Nicholaus, so thankful for her divulging Suzanna's hideaway, gave Mona the longest, hardest hug she could remember.

"You have no idea how much I appreciate this. There's one very important stop I need to make, then I'll be on my way there." He looked around as if to find something more. "Got a ferry schedule?"

* * * *

The crunch of rocks told Suzanna he approached. She didn't need to look to see who. She already knew.

She gazed far out to the water and wished she were anywhere but there right now. She wasn't ready to talk to him yet. Confusion of mistrust and betrayal rushed forth and flooded her mind with negativity.

Silent, she continued to watch the light of the sun begin to disappear at the far edge of the waterline as he stopped behind her.

"Mona told me where to find you."

"I wish she hadn't. I'm not ready to talk to you."

"Suzanna, what happened? What made you run off like that?" She chose to ignore the clear frustration in his voice.

She stared at the waves splashing against the rocks. Her thoughts returned to the horrible moment she'd seen him pull those women against him for a kiss the same way he'd kissed her.

It was obvious Nicholaus had eyes for more than one woman at a time. She'd had to deal with this same thing many times before. Though, this time hurt much worse. This time she truly loved the man with all her heart.

The ache in her chest was almost too much for her to handle.

"I saw you with…with those women."

A long silence loomed before he came around to face her. "What are you talking about?"

Irritated she would have to explain herself, Suzanna blurted out, "That woman at the conference. I know you were her lover."

Nicholaus shook his head, his brows gathered in bafflement. "I have no idea what you are talking about. There was no woman at the conference. I couldn't help but think about you the whole time."

"Yes there was. I saw you."

"You were in Houston?"

"No. Don't play innocent. You were all over her." Suzanna wrapped her arms more tightly around her.

He stared at her, his beautiful blue eyes becoming steely. "If you weren't in Houston, how did you see me and this supposed woman?"

She watched the waves as they rolled in, the roar no where close to the pounding in her ears.

"I saw you like I did those other times with my Dad's coin. Marianne and I have been practicing my abilities to see. I was in your office holding your pen, and I saw you, alright." Suzanna reached down and picked up a rock and threw it into the water. "You have a thing for blondes, don't you?"

Nicholaus stood, staring at her, all of a sudden the bafflement on his face turned to relief as he laughed and put his hands up in the air as if to stop the action.

"Ok, so you said you saw me. What did I look like?"

Suzanna didn't understand his question and shrugged her shoulders.

"Concentrate on what you saw. Was there anything different about me?"

Annoyed, Suzanna answered quickly, "No."

"Think about it. Did I have sideburns? And what might have looked like the start of a goatee?"

She stared at him a moment, the flash she'd seen before of him rising to her mind's eye. Of course, that's what was different about him. Nonetheless, it was still him. "Yes, but what does that matter?"

"Do you remember the name of the hotel?"

"I don't know…I think it said The Regal."

Nicholaus seemed to be having fun with this. He nodded his head and pulled out his cell phone. "I knew it."

After a few attempts, he handed the cell over to her. In big bold letters the header to an article he pulled up said, 'Fire Causes Irreparable Damage - Regal Hotel to Close Down.' The date reflected the year before.

"Think about it sweetheart. How could I have grown sideburns that quick?" Nicholaus placed his hands on her shoulders and looked into Suzanna's eyes. "I've been to more than one conference in my life. What you saw was something from my past. The blond happened to be someone I was involved with for a very short time. She came to the conference with me, and left when she found out a little more about my abilities."

A little uncomfortable, Suzanna started to question what she'd seen. Then she shook her head. Maybe she'd made an error judging that one. But there was no mistaking Christina. She was here. Now.

"What about what happened outside of the herbal store today? You can't brush that one off as past history." Suzanna glared at him.

"Wait, you saw that?"

"Does it matter? You were with her today." Suzanna became acutely angered by his nonchalant attitude.

"I should have known it was you I felt." Nicholaus laughed. "Actually, she was all over me. But that's not the point. I'm assuming you mean Christina, the woman with the Chihuahua?"

He obviously knew her. She nodded.

"And what did you see?" he asked with curiosity, a smile brimming on his lips. She frowned at his comical outlook. The underlying humor in his attitude irked her.

"You two are apparently intimate. You held onto her like a long lost lover. Your hands were all over her. You were kissing her like you needed to get a room," she exclaimed in disgust.

He started to laugh again, but Suzanna's expression must have stopped him short. "What you saw is a very young, sex crazed woman launch herself at me in the middle of the street. I had to hold onto her to keep from landing on my butt and getting us both run over in the street."

"You had your lips all over her. You were kissing her neck. Why did you do that if you didn't want to?" Suzanna began to play back the scene in her head.

Could it be he was defending himself?

"That's because she came at me from an angle and shoved my nose in her neck when she made contact. I couldn't stop it. If you waited long enough you would have seen my attempts to defend myself."

"The way you two talk, you looked like you've been involved."

"The only involvement I've had with her is the few times she's brought her dog into the clinic to be treated. First time was for his shots, another for a tooth cleaning, and this last time for mange. I think her name is Christina Moore. The dog's name is Bruno. Somehow she's deluded herself into thinking I'm interested in her."

Suzanna began to feel a little sheepish at the possibility he told her the truth. She could imagine this woman would do something like that.

The fact still remained she could no longer keep their non-committal relationship going. She feared her heart would break in two when the time came for them to part. He was only in it for the short term. He'd never told her he felt anything but attraction.

"I can't come back. I told you in the note I won't be able to stay. I appreciate what you've done, there's no way I can repay you for giving me back my life."

She'd thought it all through. He got involved because he felt sorry for her. He'd intimated the possibility of something more, maybe once or twice, when she'd been on the turning point of her recovery. But he'd never made any deeper feelings known to her.

They stared at each other. Nicholaus' eyes became steely, as they stood in silence. Suzanna told herself to be strong. What she thought came from him had to be her own emotions running high. She tore her gaze from his and sat down on the log, needing some support.

"Don't worry. I know you were doing a good deed. You've healed me, and we don't have to continue with the treatments anymore."

Nicholaus dropped his gaze, shaking his head. He came forward to grasp her hands. When he looked at her again, there was something different, something soft and comforting.

"Sweetheart, I only used the healing once. The very first time we made love when you couldn't go further. The rest of the time it was just you and me, nothing more." A twinkle came to his eyes. "Well…except maybe a little extra energy motivation, which we both enjoyed. What's important is what we feel when we come together. It's meant to be, not some forced therapy."

If their lovemaking was as he claimed, then she must be cured. His words made her heart shatter, knowing this must be the time to let him go.

"Thank you for telling me. It will help me put my life back together."

She could feel the tears pushing for release again, but swore she wouldn't let him see her cry. He couldn't understand how badly she yearned for a perfect union of two souls, such as Marianne had described. Up until a few days earlier, she'd been convinced he was the one. Even if he didn't see the endless possibilities between them, at least he'd given her a glimpse of what it could be.

"You really don't get it, do you?" Nicholaus pulled her to her feet. He placed her hand over his heart and looked deep into her eyes. "Tell me what you sense right now. Look into my heart, and tell me what I am feeling?"

Confused by the request, she tried to calm herself and do as he asked. Strength and determination poured out from him. A strong sensation of love surrounded him as well. So mixed up in her own feelings of the love and heartbreak, she thought she couldn't tell them apart.

"I don't know. I…I can't read you."

"Then let me tell you what I'm feeling." He wrapped his arms around her and pulled her hard against him, the instant flash occurring once again. "I am in love with you, Suzanna. I have loved you from the start. You can't tell me you haven't felt it from me. There's been no question in my mind as to where our relationship is headed. I can't believe you didn't know."

Suzanna drew in a quick breath and searched his emotions again.

Could he really mean this?

"I'm so sorry I've been so stupid and it took me so long to tell you. I guess I figured somehow you would already know. I'm crazy about you. I want us to be together. You are so special to me. We create this unique bond that can't be duplicated. I've never loved anyone like this before."

The tears began to roll down Suzanna's cheeks.

"We are perfect together. We do want the same things. We want to help people. We just need to discover where our gifts will take us in this life—individually and together as one. You see it, don't you?"

Suzanna nodded. The waves of negativity she'd held onto burst out and trickled away in the wind as she began to realize what he was saying.

"We have a mission together here on earth. I've seen it from the first time I set my eyes on you. We've belonged with each other from the very start. Twin-flames, remember?"

"Yes," she exclaimed.

"But you know, I don't think that's what we are."

Suzanna's heart dropped.

"I was reading about what that means. We aren't twin-flames. They are two souls created together and split, one male and the other female, to gather human experiences through their lifetimes. As they grow, they become more whole when they do reconnect. They sometimes come together in their incarnations, but not always in a loving connection." Nicholaus kissed her on the cheek, rubbing away some of the tears with his lips.

"Then what are we?" If not the twin-flames, then what were they? Surely the Universe had a plan for them together somehow.

"We are soul-mates. Our love for each other will never end. We share the same bond, the same frequency, the same need. Nothing is like the union of soul-mates. I want to explore every possible experience with you, and let you know every day for the rest of my life how much I love you. I didn't realize how much until I lost you." He drew her closer and kissed her softly on the forehead.

She held on tight, not wanting to let him go. The emotional turn was hard for her to comprehend and she couldn't form the words to tell him how she felt. He pulled away far enough to look into her face.

"Say something, sweetheart, please. If you love me, won't you give us a chance to see if all those things they say about love can be true?"

Swallowing hard, she nodded fervently. "Nicholaus, I love you so much." The true meaning of those words overwhelmed her. She grasped him as tight as she could and offered her lips to him. Suzanna's heart pumped harder than ever before with joy in the revelation of his love for her.

"I need to make up for not telling you how I felt before. I'm behind, so I'm going to start right now. I have something here for you."

Nicholaus stepped back and reached into his pocket, pulling out the necklace she'd left behind. She made a happy sound and as he placed it around her neck. She fondled the pendant lovingly with her fingers. It felt different. Looking down, she saw the shape had changed. Its swirling bar of gold had been artfully crafted into the shape of a fanciful heart, wrapped around the jade gemstone. The various other gems now hung in whimsical array around the gold heart.

"You've changed it. Oh, it's beautiful." She looked down again. "Did you know there are some stones gone though?"

Nicholaus reached into his other pocket and pulled out a box. When he opened the lid, a magnificent ring stood graceful against the red velvet. The small, beautifully colored missing gemstones were now interspersed around a new Princess cut diamond sparkling in the setting sun. It took her breath away.

"Remember before I told you the metaphysical properties of each gem?"

Suzanna nodded unable to say a word.

"What I didn't tell you is their traditional meaning." As he spoke with a reverence he pointed to each one. She loved the care he took to make sure she understood the true meaning of his gift. "Here, the emerald stands for my loyalty and faithfulness, the ruby, shows you my devotion. I've added the peridot to represent the love I have for you, sprinkled with the opals of happiness. This diamond symbolizes the strength of my love for you and manifests an abundance of the properties of all the other stones."

Still in shock, Suzanna watched as he bent down onto one knee before her in the sand. Looking up into her shining eyes, he said the words she longed to hear. "Suzanna, will you take this ring and become my wife?"

Her love for him flooded forth like a tsunami's crash against the shore. "Oh, Nicholaus…yes," she whispered and held out her hand so he could place the ring on her finger.

Rising to his feet he gave her a kiss. No doubt could exist now. He loved her as much as she loved him. Her budding elation made her a bit lightheaded.

They stood at the water's edge to watch the sun go down, his arms wrapped around her, the glorious colors in the sky a mere reflection of the splendor in their hearts.

"I need to tell you something," she whispered in his ear.

"Anything, my love, what is it?" He gave her a squeeze and looked down at the anticipation in her face. "Tell me."

"Remember how ill I was before you left?" He nodded slowly. "I found out why. There's a life growing inside of me. We've made a baby."

He appeared to be stunned into silence. His blank look scared her. Then a slow grin spread across his lips taming her fears. He sunk to his knees in the sand.

"Suzanna, I love you." There were tears in his eyes as he looked up into her face. He placed his cheek against her stomach and held her gently in his arms.

In that moment, Suzanna understood the true meaning of Marianne's description of love. The union between them, solidified by the formation of their child, brought the universe into her sights as a whole and harmonious place to be. The long awaited dream of love, life, and happiness, was truly Suzanna's delight.

The End

Upcoming books in the G.L.O.V.E.S Series

Ethereal Images - *The G.L.O.V.E.S Series: Book 2*

SARAH RAMSEY'S quiet and shy behavior causes her to be overlooked by most, but she begins to bloom under the careful attention of her new employer at G.LO.V.E.S, Inc. She doesn't want anyone looking too deeply into her personal life, as they may discover some things she wants to keep hidden away.

Unaware of how clueless he is to the reality of his life, ex-soldier ROBERTO GONZALES believes he is on the right track by going back to school to become a teacher. When his twin brother, an independent pilot, turns up missing from one of his scheduled flights, a slew of unexpected events involving Homeland Security, a crazed Mexican drug lord, and strange ghostly images begin to truly haunt Roberto's world.

When Sarah continues to bump into the handsome and sexy Roberto, her whole world gets turned upside down. The man is a mystery to her, and the spectral shadows following him don't help the situation. Her self-esteem shuns her from the possibility this man could be attracted to her. Yet she yearns to shed her inexperience in the ways of love to flourish in his arms as the passionate woman she longs to become.

Roberto has never needed anyone before, but now he is dependent on Sarah to make sense of his life. He begins to see she holds more than the answer to his questions. Soon, Sarah must decide whether to continue to ignore the ghostly figures she has seen all her life, or to listen to what they are trying to tell her. Unwillingly embroiled in his veiled past, what turns into a life or death chase against evil, forces her to reach for her inner strength and protect the man who has stolen her heart.

Made in the USA
Middletown, DE
07 July 2018